PICK YOUR POISON

A SHORT STORY ANTHOLOGY

Edited by Emma Nelson & Hannah Smith

OWL HOLLOW PRESS

Library of Congress Control Number: 2017956415
ISBN 978-1-945654-06-0 (paperback)
ISBN 978-1-945654-07-7 (e-book)

Cover Design by Les Solot

PICK YOUR POISON/ Nelson, Smith. 1st ed.

www.owlhollowpress.com

To the authors who have shared their amazing stories—may your work be widely enjoyed, and may we never be alone with you in a room where poison is available.

CONTENTS

Emma & Hannah

PICK YOUR POISON

In any given hospital, you'll find a plethora of deadly toxins…used to save lives. From chemotherapy to penicillin for curing diseases, to snake and spider venoms used to create antivenoms, to opiates that simultaneously relieve chronic pain and create the worst drug crisis in American history. The medical field is only one example of the paradox of poisons—the fine line between hurting and helping.

On the one hand are the harmful aspects of poisons: a toxic apple fed to Snow White out of envy. Hamlet's family rivalry escalating to poisonous drinks and blades. Socrates' punishment of death by Hemlock. Wartime experimentation with tainted food, bullets, and gasses. Cleopatra's collection of venomous animals and plants used to torment other humans. Albino body parts sold on the black market as potions for success. Whether reality-based or within fiction, man-made or naturally occurring, poisons will always be used for the darkest of purposes.

But the opposite is also true. Sherlock Holmes used cocaine to sharpen his mind, despite the harmful side effects. Australian citizens are paid to collect deadly funnel-web spiders, their venom used to create antidotes for bite victims. For centuries, midwives have used herbs, potions, amulets, toadstools, and charms for healing. King

Mithridates poisoned himself daily to build a resistance to poison-related assassination attempts. Poisons have their advantages, too.

Poisons come in all shapes and sizes, often resting in that murky, gray area between too much and too little, between right and wrong. Some poisons help; some poisons hurt. Some do both in the proper doses. But one thing is certain—whether good or evil, figurative or literal, fact or fiction—we can't escape its potent charm.

This collection of stories delves into the paradox of poisons: an anti-vaccine woman, plagued by ailments she'd thought to prevent, addiction to career, beauty, and power, but at what cost? People running from toxic parents and home situations, a family reunion turned deadly, oceanic chemical spills, venomous flowers, assassination attempts, insecticide-riddled cats, a deadly math equation, a family history of spiders, tainted recipes galore, snakebites that tell the future, and so much more.

Throughout this anthology, poison takes many different forms, both literal and metaphorical, in a wide variety of genres and styles. And they're all yours to enjoy, so go ahead. Pick your poison.

SNAKEBITE

A coral snake bit Arthur Boykin in the hand, giving him the power to find lost things. The poison was killing him too, surging through his blood, swelling his hands, his feet, and his face into pale yellow balloons. He lay in the Medical University ICU sweating, dying and hallucinating. His pores wept, he stared blankly at the ceiling, and a ventilator connected to a hole in his neck breathed for him. He could not speak, but he silently mouthed words. His wife could read his lips and said he made mostly no sense. But when asked about something lost, Arthur's heart raced as he mouthed a precise location with intense clarity. He proved to be correct seven out of seven times.

His wife and daughter had been at his bedside when his wife discovered the interesting and potentially lucrative side effect of the venom. Simply feeling nostalgic for better days, she asked her unresponsive husband, "Artie, do you remember our wedding album that we put together while on our honeymoon?"

Arthur's heart monitor beeped faster as he croaked each syllable carefully: "In the attic behind the box of Clara's high school annuals."

"I think you're right, Artie!" she gasped. "I'd thought we'd lost it. How in the world?"

Surprised and curious, Clara asked: "Daddy, do you know what happened to Granmama's diamond pendant and earrings?"

Again, Arthur's heart beat faster and he silently mouthed the words. Watching his lips with reverence, his wife repeated his answer: "Jerry Dean sold them to Money Man Pawn for five hundred dollars."

Clara stood up in a rage. "Five hundred dollars! He stole Granmama's diamonds from me and then sold them for a measly five hundred dollars? Combined they're over two carats! That evil, hillbilly rat!"

Her mother shook her head. "I've always told you Jerry Dean cares about only one person, and that's Jerry Dean."

"I'm going to Money Man to get those diamonds back right now. Damn that rat!"

Clara left in a red-hot fury, Arthur slipped back into restless sleep, and his wife determined that the snakebite would not be entirely unfortunate.

She scanned Craigslist for opportunities. A woman in Goose Creek had lost her gold wedding band while staying at the hotel on Folly Beach. She was willing to pay two thousand dollars to anyone that found it. When she asked Arthur about it, his heart raced as he silently, slowly mouthed the answer: "The ring fell down the drain of the second sink in the women's bathroom in the hotel restaurant." She called the hotel, claimed she had lost the band herself, and the hotel's maintenance man did indeed find it an hour later. The woman in Goose Creek was grateful and paid two thousand as promised.

A Charleston man had lost his standard poodle's engraved leather dog collar. The engraving on the collar read "Winston." For some reason, the man was willing to pay twelve hundred dollars for its retrieval. Arthur said the collar hung in the bushes directly east of the fountain in Waterfront Park. His wife fetched the collar and, for some odd reason, the man nearly came to tears when he paid. "Fools and their money," she muttered as she returned to Arthur's bedside.

Another woman paid a thousand for her missing laptop (she had left it at a shoe store downtown), and a couple who lived south of Broad Street in a very fancy house paid four thousand dollars for the return of a baseball signed by Bill Murray and all the members of the Charleston Riverdogs baseball team. The ball happened to be in their own yard in their azalea bushes, most likely deposited there by their cocker spaniel. They couldn't understand how she could have possibly known. But still, they paid.

In just a week's time, while Arthur's blood pressure and life expectancy continued to drop, she had collected eighty-two hundred dollars. She couldn't help but brag of her husband's profitable psychic abilities to the night shift nurse, Ashley, who diligently charted Arthur's poor vital signs through the night. She told Ashley that that vicious snake might be the death of poor old Arthur, but at least the bite had made him ten times the provider he used to be.

Ashley had heard patients and families say, believe, and insist on many ridiculous things during her twelve years as an ICU nurse, and she would have certainly ignored this woman's story under normal circumstances. But, her fifteen-year-old daughter had not come home for dinner yesterday without a call or even a text. Ashley had needed to leave for work before even knowing where she was. It was two in the morning, and while taking care of Arthur, she had been texting everyone she knew and all of her daughter's friends, trying to find out where she might be. So when her patient's wife went to the bathroom, Ashley only hesitated a moment before whispering into her patient's pale ear:

"Mr. Boykin, if you can, tell me where my daughter–Melody Washington–is right now. *I beg you.*"

Arthur's eyes opened again, his heart rate jumped critically high, and as he thrashed against the bed restraints, he tried desperately to sit up and shout. But his words weren't even a whisper. Twelve years of nursing had made Ashley a fair lip-reader, and she got the answer she needed: "Melody Washington passed out after drinking too much. Her friends left her on the bench outside the ER."

Ashley cried out as his wife returned.

"What are you doing?" his wife screamed at her. "Are you taking advantage of my husband? No one asks my husband questions but me!"

Ignoring her, Ashley gripped his arm and cried, "Which ER? Which one?"

The ER downstairs," he mouthed, staring bug-eyed, straining so hard to speak that he was able to wheeze out audible words: "Her. Heart. Is. Almost. Stopped."

Ashley fled while Arthur's wife complained to the other nurses outside the room. She ran down seven flights of stairs, praying as she went. She flew through the ER toward the glass ambulance entrance doors.

And there was Melody, just as Arthur had said—slumped on the bench outside, wet from rain. Her heart *had* almost stopped. But Ashley scooped her up and carried her inside to an empty bed, yelling for help as she went. In no time, a team of her coworkers surrounded her and the dying girl, and very quickly, like robotic angels in green scrubs, they gave Melody back the life that she had almost let slip quietly away.

Lauren woke to a text from Ashley: "My patient can find your son."

Not even knowing what the message meant really, Lauren burst into tears. It had been over a year since she had seen Joseph. She was already driving to the hospital when she finally got Ashley on the phone who was just finishing her shift.

Ashley was crying, too.

"I can't explain it. This could be God or black magic, Lauren, but Melody nearly died last night, and this total stranger *knew* where she was. I don't know if the snake venom activated some psychic part of his brain, or maybe he's so close to dead he's a guardian angel now, but I think he will find Joseph for you."

Lauren thought Ashley must have been delirious from near tragedy and lack of sleep. If anyone knew that feeling, she did. But still, she drove faster.

"What are you saying, Ashley? Tell me what you're saying."

Her friend on the other end of the phone spilled out the night's events, saying that spirits of mercy did exist and lost children could be found. Already, Lauren wanted to believe.

"Sweetheart," Ashley said softly, "My patient will find your Joseph. Hurry, because this blessed old man is gonna die any minute."

She believed, easy as that. She had to, because now, after a year of looking, Lauren had nothing left to get her from morning to night. She had been let down by police detectives, private detectives, remote relatives, and distant friends. She had spent everything she had on useless trips to Denver and Salt Lake City and Missoula, chasing rumors. He was washing dishes at a café. No, he was selling firewood off the back of a truck. No, he was hitchhiking to find himself and maybe write a novel. No, he said quite clearly that he didn't want to talk to her.

As Lauren drove faster, she pounded on the steering wheel, frustrated that if this man died before she could get to his bed, she knew she'd be done. She was a woman without money, abandoned by a gambling fool. She was a mother without a child, abandoned by an angry son. Really, she'd been dead for months. Ashley's call had shocked her back to life, at least for today.

She parked and charged up the stairs. She pressed the ICU buzzer and asked for Ashley, who had been waiting for her inside.

"It might be too late, Lauren. I'm sorry."

Still, Ashley took her to Arthur Boykin's room, which had filled with people—nurses and doctors and Mrs. Boykin. Arthur was trying to die.

A nurse shouted for dopamine. Another shouted for a pulse check. Another told everyone to just be quiet please. As he pulled her out of the room, a doctor asked Mrs. Boykin to wait outside and be assured that everything that could be done was being done.

"But that's my husband in there!"

"I know, Mrs. Boykin."

Lauren gripped Ashley's shoulder. "Tell her about my son," she said, feeling her last chance quickly fading away. But Ashley didn't think Mrs. Boykin would react very kindly to such a question right now. Still, for Lauren, she tried.

"Mrs. Boykin—" Ashley started.

The tired old woman turned and concern for her husband transformed into rage.

"Oh no! Not you! Nurse! Somebody! Get this *girl* away from me."

Lauren stepped forward. "Ma'am, if you please. I beg for your mercy. I know your husband is really suffering right now, and I shouldn't ask—"

"THEN DON'T."

Lauren pressed her back against the nursing station counter. As they all watched the numbers on Arthur's monitor drop down and blink alarmingly red, Ashley took Mrs. Boykin by the arm and squeezed before she could protest.

"*Mrs. Boykin, listen.* The snake venom in your husband's body is killing him, and his heart is about to stop. But I also know that same poison—for some reason—jump starts his heart when he's asked about anything lost. I saw it on the monitor—every time you asked him a question, his heart beat faster. He needs a jumpstart right now. And my friend is desperate. *She needs to find her son.* You can save two lives with just a question. *Please.*"

Mrs. Boykin looked at Lauren for the first time. Lauren's eyes had sunk and gone dark, except for this one small, glimmering hope.

"I don't do nothing for free."

Lauren shook her head. She had nothing to offer. Well, almost nothing.

"You can have my car. It's a 2002 Honda Accord. It's got 140,000 miles on it. It's all I got, but you can have it."

Mrs. Boykin sighed. "All right. Maybe I can get a couple thousand for it on Craigslist. Come with me."

Mrs. Boykin took Lauren by the hand and pushed by the nurses in green scrubs. When the doctor tried to push her back, she said, "That's MY husband dying in there, Stringbean!" She pulled Lauren up to Arthur's head where the respiratory therapist was squeezing each and every breath into his old swollen body. "Go ahead," Mrs. Boykin said. "Ask him."

All the nurses turned to watch her, and the room fell silent except for the fading beep ... ... beep ... ... beep of the heart monitor. Lauren considered her question carefully, as if a clever, bloated genie lay before her, and proper wording meant everything. Finally she asked: "Mr. Boykin, where is my son, Joseph Grayson Perdue, at this very moment?"

Arthur's eyes flung open, he sat straight up in bed, his heart beat beepbeepbeepbeepbeepbeepbeep, and the nurses jumped back from the table with a collective "Oh!"

Then Arthur Boykin fell back on the table and died.

Lauren walked with Mrs. Boykin to the parking lot to hand over her Honda Accord. When she gave it to her, she really would have nothing, and it was a long walk back to her apartment. When they approached the car, Lauren said, "There it is."

Mrs. Boykin put out her hand. She wasn't crying—her face showed nothing for her dead husband. If she had seen some trace of emotion, Lauren might not have felt justified in voicing what she felt.

"This wasn't a fair transaction."

Now Mrs. Boykin's lip curled. "You offered a car to ask your question. That dumb friend of yours said asking it would save my husband's life. You asked, my husband died, and now you have the gall to say this wasn't a fair transaction. Give me the keys and don't say one more word about *fair*."

Lauren held the keys in her fist and raised them above her head, high enough so Mrs. Boykin would have to jump for them.

"You're being childish," she said. "And you're not honoring a promise you made to a woman who's just been made a widow."

"You can have the keys," Lauren replied firmly, "If you bring me to the snake that bit your husband's hand."

Mrs. Boykin stared at her for a long time. "What?"

Lauren couldn't believe she had said the words herself.

"Maybe the venom will work twice."

Mrs. Boykin clicked her tongue. "You got no reason to think it will."

"I won't be able to live with myself if I don't try."

"You won't be able to live *period*!"

"If my son is in trouble, I'll know, and I'll have a chance to help him before I die."

She grunted and laughed and looked away. "Young lady, are you even sure your son *wants* to be found?"

Lauren let her hand drop from the air and go limp as she pressed the keys into Mrs. Boykin's hand. "Whether he wants to be found or not isn't the point. I need to know where he is, and if I can, give him what he needs. I have to do this for me just as much as him. I can't live another day not knowing—*not now*—now that I know a snakebite can give me the answer."

Mrs. Boykin took the car keys and nodded to the passenger seat. "Get in," she said. "If you want to commit suicide-by-snake, I reckon that's your prerogative."

They drove for miles through the salt marsh. They turned left and right and left again, and Lauren very soon had no idea where they were. She supposed it didn't matter. When the snake bit her, she would need an ambulance to take her away. She told Mrs. Boykin she'd have to be the one to call an ambulance after the bite. In fact, on second thought, maybe she ought to call the ambulance twenty minutes *before* she got bit to give them time to come all the way out here.

Mrs. Boykin shook her head. "You said you got nothing but this car, which means you got nothing to pay for an ambulance ride. I'll take you to the ER and leave you there, but don't you dare give them my name, or I'll come back and kill you myself."

"All right," Lauren agreed, watching the water and the weeds go by, and Mrs. Boykin could see this crazy woman was re-solved.

"You don't have to do this."

Lauren didn't answer. She was praying, preparing herself for the spirit her body was about to receive.

Mrs. Boykin turned the Honda down a long gravel driveway that led to their tiny house that sat in the sand above a tidal creek. They got out and Lauren was shaking.

"You want to eat before you start rummaging around for the snake? It might take you the rest of the day to find it. I don't know exactly where it might be."

Lauren shook her head. She didn't expect she'd ever eat again. "Just show me," she said.

Mrs. Boykin led her to their dock. The tide was out, so there was no water beneath it, just mud, periwinkles, damp leaves, and a coral snake—somewhere.

"There," Mrs. Boykin said, pointing beneath the dock. "That's where the snake bit him. Arthur was banging around with a hammer, talking nonsense about installing a floating dock for a kayak. The man never been kayaking in his life. Guess he never will."

Lauren was already moving to the spot, as if in a dream, her feet slipping out of her shoes as if she was already being pulled up and away from this earth. But when she stepped beneath the dock, her feet sunk in, and as she searched through the leaves, she felt herself sinking further, until she was up to her knees in the wet, gray-green mud.

Then she saw its face. The snake curled around the base of one of the dock posts, most of it buried in mud to keep cool. As it lifted its head, she saw its bright red and brilliant yellow bands, and she knew that this was the very same snake. She took one step further, holding on to a dock post for balance. The snake raised its head up higher, arching back, readying to strike. Lauren put out her palm, whispering a prayer for forgiveness if this snake came from the devil, but also for guidance if this snake was holy and blessed.

She didn't even see it move when it sunk its teeth in. It retracted, and the two holes in her palm were already swelling into red, angry wounds. She backed up out of the mud as fast as she could. The world dipped and swayed around her, and she felt her stomach twist. She hadn't expected the symptoms to come on so fast. She couldn't even walk back to the car. She crawled on all fours.

"I think I made a mistake," Lauren gasped, her throat already closing.

"Damn right you made a mistake!" Mrs. Boykin yelled, pulling her by the shoulders through the sand to put her on the back seat of the Honda. "Don't you vomit until we get there! This car is mine now, and I can't sell it if it smells like throw up. And remember, don't you dare give them my name."

She drove them out of the salt marsh as fast as she dared. If a traffic cop pulled her over, there would be far too many difficult questions for her to answer.

Lauren knew that she lay dying in an ICU bed, but whether it was day or night, she could not say, and when the blurry figures in green drew close to her, they either brought sharp pain or soft sleep, and as they came and went, she dreamed.

Her dream came into focus far more clearly than the hospital room. She never wanted this vision to end, because she could see Joseph as if he stood only inches away. *And he was happy*, his hair longer than she had ever seen it, his beautiful brown eyes bright, and he was laughing at a girl's joke.

He served her coffee while she continued with her story, and he shook his head in disbelief. He told her that his shift ended in three hours, and he could meet her this evening at eight—if she wanted to. She said, "I'll see you then." He nodded to himself in victory, smiling all afternoon as he made drinks, scrubbed dishes, and mopped the floors.

Lauren was as excited for the date as he was, and it was almost as if she could see through his eyes. When he stepped outside, she saw license plates on customers' cars that read *California*, and the sky was full and gray. Through Joseph's eyes she saw a carved wooden sign—"Eureka's Best Coffee." *My son is in Eureka, and he's happy*. He walked to his apartment, which was small but warm, and even though the Pacific was thousands of miles from her ICU bed, she swore she could smell the ocean herself.

She tried to speak. "Joseph, I'm so sorry that Roger gambled away your college fund. I was lonely and too trusting. I should have known that you were the man in my life, not him." Lauren yelled as loud as she could, knowing she wasn't making a sound, because a machine breathed for her through a hole in her neck. But she hoped, somehow, Joseph would hear her apology. She felt like the venom coursing through her blood really could let her tell him everything she needed to, and that he would hear every word.

"MY NAME IS MARTHA SHELLNUT, AND I NEED TO KNOW WHERE TO FIND THE KEYS TO MY 2017 MAZDA MIATA."

Lauren felt herself flying away from Joseph and Eureka, pulled across the miles by a giant invisible hand around her neck. What was happening? She landed in the parking lot of a liquor store on James Island, and the keys to the Miata glowed in the grass nearby. She just wanted to go back to Joseph! She told Martha Shellnut where to find the keys to make her go away.

As soon as she did, she flew back to Joseph's apartment like a dove on the wind. He was ironing a shirt and humming along with a Chet Baker record playing on an old-fashioned turntable. He flipped the record when it was over to play it again. His cell phone vibrated on the glass coffee table to let him know that there was a text from her confirming their date tonight. Lauren could almost sense his joy, and she never—

"EXCUSE ME, MAAM, I'M WITH THE CHARLESTON POLICE DEPARTMENT, AND WE'RE LOOKING FOR A FUGITIVE NAMED CHARLES AMERY GOODLETT. IF YOU COULD HELP US, WE WOULD BE FOREVER GRATEFUL."

The giant invisible hand yanked her across the country again to a shack outside of Georgetown, South Carolina, where Charles Goodlett and his friend smoked cigarettes, arguing about where to go and how to get there. Lauren didn't care. She told the officer the address of the shack so he would go away and she could return to the vision of her son.

As soon as she mouthed the address, she flew back to California in a blur, and Joseph was riding a bicycle along the beach highway because he didn't have a car. She could almost feel the ocean breeze on his face herself—

"WHERE IS THE COMBINATION TO MY HUSBAND'S SAFE? I KNOW HE WROTE IT DOWN SOMEWHERE. HIS NAME IS MICHAEL LEE CARLSON."

Please, Lauren begged, please. Go away, go away. If I tell you the combination is 12-34-3, will you all just go away and let me be?

But the line outside her ICU bed grew every day, and when a local reporter called her The Miracle of Charleston, the number of desperate believers only increased. This woman who had been bitten in the hand by a coral snake and lay sweating and bloated in an ICU bed, seemingly only a few heartbeats away from death, held on to dear life to give so many pilgrims the hope to find the things they had lost and could not live without.

Colleen Quinn

BEAUTIFUL SHADOWS

Val had spent most of her adult life pretending to be jolly. She had been an ordinary girl, thin as a stick and running everywhere, but when she hit puberty, her body exploded. She went from looking like a child to looking like a mother of three, with hardly a day in between. Breasts, hips, thighs— suddenly everything jiggled, and running wasn't fun anymore. No one else in her family was like this. She remembered looking in a three-way mirror in some shopping mall department store and catching the expression on her mother's face as teenage Val struggled to fasten the button on a pair of jeans. Her eyebrows could not have risen any higher, and her mouth was pursed in dismay.

Keeping her expectations low was essential in her adult life. Just because a man asked for her phone number, it didn't mean he would actually call. Just because some celebrity lost weight on one bizarre regimen or another, it didn't mean it would work for Val. Nothing worked for Val, not wheatgrass or grapefruit or cinnamon supplements, at least not for very long. Her weight fluctuated; she might lose ten pounds, then be up fifteen a few months later. Currently, she weighed almost a hundred pounds more than she had in high school and knew that her weight would only get worse as she got older and losing it got even harder. The flabby ghosts of diabetes and heart disease lurked around the corner, approaching on swollen ankles; she could hear their mouth-breathing as they got closer.

She was an office manager at an enormous legal firm and knew far more than her employers imagined about virtually everything. There were laws to protect the obese from job discrimination, but nothing saves you from other people's judgments. If it hurt when even the most aggressively flirtatious junior partner fell silent when she walked by, if she resented being the first person asked for birthday cake recommendations, she smiled. She was not crushingly lonely.

Every other email Val received was a diet tip, or an ad for workout clothes, or gentle reminders from Weight Watchers about attending meetings and weigh-ins. She deleted them without opening them. Somehow, despite the absence of personal photos on her page, even Facebook knew she was fat and peppered her feed with ads for bariatric surgery and generously sized clothing lines.

When she received the invitation to try Zaftyme, the envelope was dropped in the inbox on her desk. The paper was heavy and smooth, like a wedding invitation; there was no postmark.

You have been selected.

Val hated it when they tried to make her feel special. And when she realized it was just more weight loss snake oil, she called out, "Who put this here?"

No response from her posse of interns and clerks. Really, she could take being teased or overlooked, but this bordered on harassment. She threw it in the recycling bin and tried to put it out of her mind, but when she ate lunch—a salad at her desk, of course; she had eaten more lettuce than most rabbits—her eye fell on it again, and she fished it out. She had forgotten to bring a book with her and preferred to read something while she ate.

Transform your life.

Interestingly, the brochure was not written in what Val thought of as "big sister" language, full of advice and tips and nagging suggestions on how to achieve some impossible state of perfection. It didn't pretend to be fun.

It's very simple. If you take Zaftyme, you will reach your ideal weight in one month.

That was not possible. How could they claim that she would reach her ideal weight when they didn't know the weight she was starting from? Val knew that if she kept to a diet barely above starvation level and exercised every day, she might lose two or three pounds in a week. It would take her most of an extremely well-behaved year to lose all the weight she wanted.

Zaftyme worked by ramping up the power of digestive enzymes. "We weaponized them," the president of the pharmaceutical company claimed in a video on the company web site. He had big white teeth and showed all of them when he grinned, as if he was joking. The enzymes developed a voracious appetite for human fat, the brochure claimed, and simply did what they were designed to do.

On the back of the brochure was a list of possible side effects, but Val wasn't terribly interested in science. Pancreatitis? Ketoacidosis? She had never heard of them. There was a footnote in type just barely big enough to read that cautioned that Zaftyme had not been officially approved yet, and the proffered invitation was on a trial basis only. All responsibility was shirked; try at your own risk.

Tick the box for your free sample.

Val ticked. What the hell, right? She had tried everything else.

Her sample arrived by the end of the week. The packaging was impressive, blue gel capsules in a clear plastic case with no words on it at all. It looked expensive. How do they decide what color pills should be? Or do they just come out that way? A thin sheet of paper included just one instruction: take one a day at bedtime.

The first night, she dreamed of water, rapidly swirling down a drain, and the next day she found—for the first time since she moved to the city—that she could fit in a single seat on the subway. On the second night, she dreamed of whittling, not something she had ever done in real life. A knife flashed in her hands as she carved, and the wooden curls fell away to nothing. She was left with a small likeness of a woman, her arms raised in triumph. In the morning, she needed a safety pin to keep up the waistband of her pantsuit.

By day three, she had visible cheekbones.

"Val, is everything all right?"

Mary Jane, stationed in the billing department, was a woman Val was friendly with at work, which was somehow different from being a friend.

"Of course," she smiled.

Mary Jane frowned. "It's just that I've never seen anyone lose so much weight so fast without some horrible disease involved. Like cancer."

Jealous. Val should have known. Mary Jane worried and complained about her weight all the time, unaware of how irritating this was in a woman whose weight was exactly average.

"I don't have cancer." Val couldn't seem to stop smiling.

"Well, good." Mary Jane did not sound convinced.

It was a little scary to lose so much weight so fast. How did she know it would stop when she reached her ideal weight? What would happen then?

But, like a gymnast who performs a spectacular display of flips, twists, and tumbles, and sticks the landing exactly where she was supposed to, Val's weight loss levelled off when she hit a perfect size 8.

"Wow," said Mary Jane.

"Thank you."

Bob, the ridiculously flirtatious junior partner, stopped by her desk. "Hey Val—"

He stopped dead in his tracks and stared at her. "You look..."

Val smiled and waited for her compliment. Great? Amazing? Fantastic?

"Different." In a rare departure for him, he looked at her face, not her body, and he seemed troubled.

Val saw it for herself over the weekend. She needed to replace her entire wardrobe, so she went to a large department store, delighted for once to preen in public. She looked much younger and trim, as if she had been swimming and playing tennis all her life. She could wear anything—pants without elastic waists, blouses that didn't gape between buttons—and she practically skipped between departments.

She was trying on black satin pants and high heels with a gorgeous turquoise blouse—coincidentally the same color as Zaftyme capsules—when she noticed that she looked a little pale. She had always been fair-skinned; her skin had been her best feature before Zaftyme, but this was something else. If she looked close, she could see the blue veins in her face, and they seemed to get darker and lighter, as if she could actually see the blood coursing around her body. She blamed the lighting; everyone knew department stores made people look green. She kept her spirits up and maxed out a credit card in one afternoon.

Later that night, she looked down as she worked a crossword puzzle and realized she could see the veins in her hands as well. They were very clear, like lines on a roadmap, and underneath them, she could see how her muscles cleaved to her bones. She thought it was rather beautiful.

The child sitting across from her on the subway car as she went in to work on Monday did not see it that way. She was a small child, three or four at most, but she had a big voice. When she saw Val, she started screaming and didn't stop until her mother dragged her off the train, both their eyes wide with terror. This could be a problem.

Val's condition had advanced over the past few days, and she was now translucent. If you looked her in the eye, you saw her eyeball, ensconced in muscle, the optic nerve stretching back into her skull. If she ate something, you could see her chew and swallow and then watch until the lump of food disappeared past the neckline of her stylish new clothes. She had accepted that she would never take off her underwear in the presence of another person for the rest of her life. But she still had to go to work, didn't she?

She kept her pace measured and professional, easy to do when people fell over themselves to get away from her. The elevator car was empty, and Val enjoyed the ding-free quiet as she ascended to her floor. She had only been at her desk for a few minutes when she was summoned to the office of the general director.

"Val, what in the world is going on with you?" Mrs. Harris, the general director, was a tall, skinny woman with enormous eyeglasses that gave her an insect-like appearance. Val had always liked her but knew she would never understand.

Val filled her in about Zaftyme and its miraculous results.

"My God, Val, you have to stop taking this drug. You look grotesque. Please bring me everything you've signed, every scrap of paper. I'd be happy to help you take legal action against these people."

"I'm not going to stop, and I'm not going to sue them."

"But Val, let's say those enzymes went from eating fat to eating skin pigment. What do you suppose they will eat next?"

"I feel fine."

"You are not fine, and we have a real problem. I can't have you on the office floor. People don't like looking at you."

"They never did."

"What will our clients think?"

"Mrs. Harris, you're a lawyer. I'm sure you realize how risky it is to fire people for their looks."

"Oh God, Val, just go home while I figure out how to handle this."

Val rose from her chair.

"And don't smile! That makes it even worse."

But Val did smile. She left the office with only her handbag, although she knew she was never coming back.

Out on the street, a hand gently grazed her arm and she looked up into a face as strange as her own. She ought to have known there were others—who knows how many?—and that they would find each other somehow. The woman smiled in greeting, and it was every bit as horrible as Mrs. Harris had claimed. Val could see every muscle straining and twisting, like the ropes that work a sailboat.

"Beautiful, no?" The stranger gestured to their twin shadows, slender women laid out on the sidewalk in front of them.

A SHORT ON ROB'S LIFE

*P*an-Seared Sea Bass with Lemon
Served with: Wild Rice and Endive Salad with Caper
Dressing
Paired with: Escherbach Estate Sauvignon Blanc 2013

My earnings graph was a big turd shot into the ground.

Lean against the desk, I thought. Take a few deep breaths. Then take a few more. Take so many deep breaths that you actually start to feel the calm that you think deep breaths are supposed to deliver. That other people tell you deep breaths deliver. Take those deep breaths and don't skip even one. That way you won't be tempted to find Rob and bash his head in with a meat tenderizer.

I thought of my wife's warning.

"Rob destroyed any remnants of hope our family once had of being a family," she'd reminded me before her last birthday. This was not abnormal. Grace would remind me over and over again, as to the reason that we had not once invited Rob to any family function or holiday.

"I didn't ask you to invite him," I said.

"Yes, but you were thinking it," Grace said.

Honestly, I don't know if I was thinking it that time or not. I do tend to think that and other things quite a bit. I think when I run the kitchen, I think when I'm ordering guys to soufflé, I think when I'm chopping, I think when I'm stewing, I think while I'm cleaning shit out of my ears with the end of an egg beater. So who knows, maybe I almost did ask her about inviting Rob.

All I really knew at that point was that my brother-in-law was a man possessed of the market. He was high king of the tiny isles of fledgling startups. I'd seen him drive his team of penny stock oxen through the wintry bastion of a bear market more than once. Sure, my wife hated his guts and believed with every fiber of her being that he'd single-handedly killed their father and torn apart their family. But what was the harm in taking a few tips from him, I remember thinking. What was the harm in putting some money into his new ETF fund? I guess those kinds of questions are rhetorical, or hindsight-determinate, or just plain ones you shouldn't fucking ask.

"Hey, boss," my sous chef, Ramon, yelled over the sounds of sizzling. "Your brother is here." I looked away from the monitor on my desk in the back office, where all graphically rendered indications pointed to the fact that I was totally fucked.

"My brother?" I stared at my chef's hat. I tried to remind myself that stocks are a long-term game. A thinking man's game. But Rob was not a long-term man, nor did he do much thinking. The guy was a drunk. A coke-head. Into something called krokodile with a "k" that ate your face and was made by Russians, who can't afford real drugs. And Rob could afford whatever he wanted. "My brother lives in Cincinnati, Ramon."

My sous chef shrugged, a blank look on his face. "A man who says he is your brother is here."

I started to follow Ramon out to the front but suddenly caught a glimpse of the pile of bitter almonds I'd left on the counter. Bitter almonds, unlike sweet almonds, needed their own special cordoned off space beside the rear door, because raw bitter almonds contain a compound that breaks down into hydrogen cyanide. Every morning I'd collect them from the tree on the banks of the Susquehanna below, just as Grace's dad had done before me, then cover them with a red tin on the counter so that no one could mistake them for another ingredient and absentmindedly murder every patron in the restaurant on a given day. I thought about what would happen if I chucked a handful of them into my mouth right then and there. "That's all it would take," Henry used to say.

I was shaken from my suicidal woolgathering upon turning the corner to find Rob's ugly grimace deflating the air in the room like an exploding Nazi zeppelin. I shook my head at Ramon, who I'd introduced to Rob on several occasions. Ramon had never been keen on details, or verbal nuance, or even the job requirements of a sous chef, and if I had not just tanked all of my savings by purchasing bullshit stocks, the thought of firing him might have crossed my mind for the umpteenth time.

Rob hadn't bothered to sit down and impatiently checked his ten-thousand-dollar Swiss whatnot. He was a lot like my biological brother, come to think of it. Both of them were dog shit. Then he sniffed at something as if it didn't just smell bad but actually pissed him off. One of the things I am is not confrontational, so I let it go.

"Hey, kid," Rob said from across the foyer. "Kid" was something he called me, despite us being only three years apart in age. Because of my aforementioned lack of confrontationality, I'd been letting that go for years. "It's reeeaaallly nice to see you." He stretched out words sometimes, as if to demonstrate exactly how much slime could fall from his forked tongue as he spoke.

I stared into the lobster tank along with Grace's dad, Henry, who peered into the rustling water from the comfortable vantage of multiple picture frames mounted on the wall. "What do you want, Rob?"

"How's that any way to treat a customer?" he said. "Hey, look at me."

I blinked back sudden tears and looked him in the eye. Suddenly, every adrenaline-filled bone in my body melted into unsculpted clay. Confrontation-averse, I've even heard it called.

I hated that I was like this.

"Come on, we took a beating, but it's not like you had all your money in the ETF fund." He knew very well that I did. "You're kidding," he said. I couldn't tell if he was feigning surprise because it was the polite thing to do or if he was deliberately rubbing it in. Anyway, I said nothing. I tried, but my open mouth stood frozen in place as Henry's gaze fell silent on the water in the tank. In that moment, he looked more disappointed than I'd ever known him to be in life.

I ultra hated that I was like this.

Rob took a twenty from his pocket and said, "Hey, where's my takeout?"

I turned back to look at Ramon like, "Why didn't you fucking tell me he ordered anything?"

Fried Yam Salad with Raw Salmon and Sadness
Served with: Crushed Walnuts
Paired with: Ice Water

When Ashley was born, I'd acquiesced to Grace's dad's offer to make me managing partner at the restaurant. I was young, just out of grad school, and basically had no idea that the rest of my life was something I was going to have to figure out. And Henry had been genuinely humane about that fact. Before then, on my own, it had sort of felt like the sky had opened up and swallowed part of my brain, spitting it back out into my skull with the agreement that I pay interest on it for the rest of my life. Unbeknownst to me at the time, running a restaurant was sort of like that too, like having your brain replaced and indebted to the sky. Nothing in life was really any easier than anything else.

We did a lot together, Grace's dad and me. Henry was kinder to me than the actual old man. The actual old man was the kind of guy who'd work hard selling insurance for six months out of the year just so he could take off hunting for the next six months. He broke all kinds of records and made enough money to hide away at least two and a half million dollars after the split, or so my mother swore until her dying day.

Grace's dad liked to fish, and we did that aplenty. Right up until the time I accidentally killed him and blamed her brother Rob.

Braised Honey Pork Tenderloin with Red Cabbage
Served with: Your Choice of Potato
Paired with: Non-Alcoholic Bud's Carbonated Grape Juice

"No, I haven't talked to Rob," I lied to my brother Julian over the phone.

"Grace's dad's food is delicious," Julian said. "Those little burgundy dumplings, Christ. Even so, if you think for one fucking second I'm going to let you get away with this, you have another thing coming."

I did not remind him that in addition to now owning the restaurant, I'd designed the menu for the last eight years. "Nobody asked you to invest in Rob's ETF."

"Nobody asked me?" Julian yelled. "You practically begged me to underwrite your investment! And then he took my money and wiped his ass with it! Your money too, for God's sake!" He whistled in a sharp intake of breath. "I'm just looking at these losses here, and Grace is going to drop you so hard."

I hung up the phone just as Ramon knocked at the door of the back office. When it swung open, flames leapt from the stove closest to the front.

"You have a men here. Two of them," Ramon said.

"What kind of men, Ramon?"

"The kind of men in suits," he said.

I closed my laptop, the path of a drunken dart withering sadly toward the ground; the impotent dick of lost profits, disappearing into the nether.

I walked into the kitchen, taking the scenic route through my meager inheritance, memories kicking and screaming against the glass walls of my eyes, and watched myself shake hands with two limp zombies in the reflection from the stainless steel freezer.

They could have been anyone—Secret Service agents, math professors, men responsible for covering up the evidence of downed spacecraft from distant galaxies—or just two guys looking for some Mediterranean fusion. Instead, they were lawyers.

"We're lawyers," they said.

"Is there a place we can talk?"

Swordfish Panini with Avocado and Olives
Served with: Cafeteria-Style Grill-Fired Hashbrowns
Paired with: Orchardmaster Chassagne Montrachet 2014

My wife is obsessed with two things: musicals and *The Lord of the Rings*. It just logically follows that Christopher Lee's 2010 rock opera album about Emperor Charlemagne was at the intersection of those interests and the unintentional background music to the end of her father's life.

In the one song, intermingled with the execution of thousands of Saxon prisoners and the subjugation of Western Europe, Christopher Lee opines the fate of the beleaguered ruler, who, having spent his entire life immersed in various conflicts to secure or expand his domain, faced constant and emerging threats until the day he died. The man closed his eyes to the world at the onset of the Viking invasion of Europe.

It's like, why do we even try?

So that's what I'd been singing about, or humming, maybe, lower than Grace's dad could hear, when I noticed that we'd drifted pretty far from Pearle's Dock. It was Henry and I in the boat, while Rob wandered along the riverbank alone. I pictured him pacing up and down the water's edge, mulling over some innovative new way to fuck over a mark.

Henry's skiff, like everything else he possessed, was modest. Just a rowboat that he'd built himself in the eighties. It was more than an actual wonder that it still floated, let alone that it floated while two people and their fishing gear fought side-by-side with the physical laws of the universe to plunge the thing into the riverbed.

"I got a bite!" Henry yelled. I stopped humming mid-note. I felt my phone buzz angrily in the waterproof bag hanging at my side. Something tugged on my own line before I could free the device. I hesitated a second or two before it tugged again and I jerked my rod upward, sticking the hook into the fish's gills. I wrestled with the river monster while Henry fought his own grindylow, and we melded into nature like two boys bonding over ghost stories at sundown. We each bared our teeth to the river, slaves to the timeless code of men outdoors, inscribed in a rulebook by the scraggly branches of ancient trees on the long-frozen first layers of the earth.

My phone buzzed again, tearing me from my reverie. I noticed for the first time how fast we were moving. I looked back at Pearle's Dock. It had disappeared around a bend in the Susquehanna.

I dropped the rod and called out to Henry. The riverside houses jogged by, their peg legs holding them propped high above the increasingly manic waters. The angry red flashes from the phone screen screeched and lurched into my eyes and ears.

Flash Flood Warning.

I dropped to the stern and grabbed the oars. The boat rocked and Henry tripped. I rowed like a fiend, and by the time I noticed Henry's off-kilter flailing, it was too late. He held his rod over the side in one white-knuckled hand as the rushing waters battered the oars into submission and swiveled the bow into the rocks.

*Roasted Mushroom and Shallot Risotto with a Parmesan Crust
Served with: A Hefty Loss of Eighty-Nine Percent and the Awful
Shrieking of a Woman who had Once Declared her Undying
Love
Paired with: Brooks Sparkling Zinfandel*

In fairness, I didn't blame her brother so much as nod when Grace automatically assumed that Rob was responsible. The fact that I'd never mentioned the truth—that I was practically the only party accountable to her dad's death—is something that I guess you might say I've never lived down.

Which is why it's been so hard to talk to her for the last seven years or so, give or take eternity.

"A couple of lawyers came by today," I said without looking up. "Two guys claiming to be with the bank's legal team showed up to talk about *the transition*."

"What are you talking about?"

I leaned over the sink, emptying the Tupperware container with the remnants of my uneaten lunch into the garbage disposal. I pictured Henry thrown against the bow, just moments after leaning in to plop a bobber over the side where he'd have enough leverage to pull a leviathan straight from the frothing depths.

"They say the bank has a controlling interest in the restaurant." I could feel a tremolo run through my voice, injected out of fear or, more likely, a simple lack of courage.

"Well did you ask to see their identification?" Grace asked.

"Their...what? No. I wasn't being frisked." I paused to collect myself. Why was this so hard? "Grace," I finally said.

She might have been looking me in the eyes had I possessed the courage to find out. "What are you not telling me?" she asked.

I absently wiped my hands on the dish towel. The zombie-like motions of my body surprised even myself. I wanted to look at the face of my wife, but I couldn't. How could I possibly tell her what I'd done?

"I've done something terrible," I said.

"Honey, you can tell me," she said, saddling up beside me. She took the dishtowel from where it hung from the cupboard and finished drying my hands. A static discharge shook my wrists.

"No," I said. The word came out more forcefully than I'd thought words could possibly sound.

Grace took a step back, surprised. She took another step back. Our daughter Ashley's laughter rang out upstairs.

"I've done something," I said again. Grace didn't try to argue.

"What did the lawyers say?" she asked.

I sighed and buried my courage with the memory of Henry lying limp and helpless in the waves.

A Fondue Pot for One
Served with: A Hand-Picked Selection of Finger Foods
Paired with: A Milkshake with One Straw

"They said that control reverts to them if the owner's assets aren't consistent within a reasonable range of cash-flow equity," I said in machine-gun parlance.

Rob stood on the threshold of his McMansion, the domain of his exuberance spread out behind him like the wings of the golden eagle of Rome.

"Yeah, well, just why wouldn't the owner's assets be stable?"

I sighed and pushed my glasses back up the bridge of my nose. I didn't want to do this with him, not now. But I had nowhere else to go.

Rob looked down at my suitcase. "What's that?" he said, pointing like an idiot.

"My suitcase," I said, lifting it up like an idiot.

"Oh man…" he said, holding up his hands. "Listen, me and the lifestyle—"

"Let me in, Rob."

I followed him through the two-story foyer and into the house. It was less like a house and more like someone's mom's basement every time I saw it. I almost said something about the

1950s chandelier with fake Halloween cobwebs still clinging as it leaned against the kitchen island.

But then I saw my wife's face in the cobwebs, in that Rorschach way kids see dragons in the clouds. It was frozen in a combination of agony, betrayal, and outright validation.

"They said this was contractual," I heard myself saying. The echoes of my voice were snatched up by curtains that might have spent a previous life or two as mainsails on a Gothic prison barge.

"Like, in the will?" said Rob. "Why would Dad do that?"

"Maybe. Who knows what I signed back then. My mind was...elsewhere." We walked past a painting of the Battle of the Nile that might have been scribbled by a lemur on Ritalin. I shuddered and kept moving. "Whatever it was, the bank must have snuck it in somehow."

"Must have," said Rob absently.

"Grace was...upset," I mumbled over my shoulder to Napoleon. I wondered how upset she would have been if I'd also had the courage to tell her about how I'd killed her father. My knee buckled at the thought, and I almost careened headlong into a vase that looked like a distended colon.

Rob came to a halt next to a pair of big French doors that led into a sitting room adjacent to the three-car garage. "Just stay in here," he said. "Sleep when you want." He pointed to a thing that looked like a couch but didn't have a back or arms. I hoped the cheap plastic wheels on my suitcase were scuffing up his hardwood floors. Rob closed the doors with a look on his face that said he was only doing this because I had just literally made him.

I unzipped the suitcase and pulled out my chef's hat, stood it upright on the nightstand and stretched out on the dismembered couch. My eyes caught the fuzzy borders of what looked like an antlered rabbit sticking out from behind the far side of the fireplace.

"I'm not planning to stay long," I said, patting the chef's hat.

Snack Food Sampler
Served with: Assorted Protein Bars
Paired with: The Jumbo Sprite, Because it's Just a Quarter More

I sat on the smooth linoleum floor, chef's hat between my legs. Legal papers spread to the four corners of the garage, intermixing with the scattered remnants of Rob's life. He hadn't been exaggerating; the lifestyle extended all the way through the vast square footage of the house in the form of the inflexible tones of electronica music that assaulted my senses even here.

I pored over page 955f, paragraph eleven, section three double B, with towels stuffed around my ears and eyes so bloodshot they might have been two shards plucked from a ruby. What was it with finance guys and uppers?

The third time I almost nodded off, I stood up and put on the chef's hat. I paced around the garage, the cavernous space a gymnasium of auto parts, coaxing the blood back into my brain. Halfway through the second lap, page 955f slipped out of my hand. I bent to retrieve it from beneath a matte gray GT C Roadster Edition 50, and felt my phone fall out of my pocket and clatter to the floor. It was ringing, and probably had been for who knows how long, a picture of my brother Julian peering upward with a stern smile, looking ever like the overbearing asshole he'd been since we were boys.

In my sleep-deprived, stress-induced delirium, I checked my reflection in the chrome rims of the Roadster and saw the worry-ravaged face of a man I didn't know. I took a deep breath, peeled the towels from my head and yanked balled-up cotton balls from my ears, and answered the phone.

"Hey, buddy," said Julian. "I know I was hard on you the other day, but…but…Hey, what's all that racket?"

"House music," I said. I pressed my palm to my left ear so I could make out Julian's voice.

"Jesus. I know Grace kicking you out must have been hard, but I don't think this is the way to get past it."

"No," I said, slinking deeper into a corner of the garage, looking for a way to retreat from the noise.

"What?"

I knelt on the ground, tucking my head below the floating tool cabinets. From here, I could see a puddle of something liquid spreading from beneath the Roadster. There was a twig in it that reminded me of the almond tree, out alone on the banks of the Susquehanna below the restaurant.

"I'm at Rob's," I said into the phone, my hands cupped around the receiver. "He was actually kind of cool about putting me up after the bank came by and Grace kicked me out."

There was silence on Julian's end for so long I wondered whether or not he'd heard me. I pulled the phone away from my face for the split second it took to check if he'd hung up.

"You're at Rob's?" he said a second later.

"It's not like I could come stay with you," I said. "I have a restaurant to run."

I heard Julian hiss into the phone. "Who do you think actually owns that restaurant now?" he said, a strong memory of him at fifteen and me at eleven flooding back.

"What do you mean?" Again, I couldn't tell whether or not he'd heard me.

"Think about it moron," he said. "Grace's dad has owned that restaurant for fifty years. And banks don't just take restaurants that are paid for. Not without a special contingency that a prospective inheritor would have to cosign."

"But that would have to be…" My eyes darted to the garage door. I picked my head up to take in the assaulting sounds of robotic cacophony and slammed my head into the bottom of the floating cabinets.

"I'll give you one fucking guess who that would be."

I heard him even through the music, even though I'd dropped the phone on the floor, the black and white checkered pattern dancing before my eyes as my vision blurred and stars shot through my line of sight. I rubbed my head and looked around at Rob's life and saw the prison I'd been living in for years.

My eyes wandered almost involuntarily to the twig in the puddle. The almond tree. Bitter almonds. The red tin on the counter.

Rob's Impending Fucking Death
Served with: Chef's Choice
Paired with: Caparzo Sangiovese 2004

"Thanks for agreeing to meet," said the lawyer.

We sat around the oblong table in the center of the floor—Rob, one of the two lawyers from the bank, and me. Ramon brought the soup and shrimp tempura, and we started in.

"Sorry that Grace still hasn't taken you back," said Rob. "Obviously sorry." He looked up from the soup, and his eyes were almost panicky in their sap-ridden need to be convincing. I had been shockingly pleasant to Rob, even through my planning. Fortunately, I'd moved out not long after Julian alerted me to the truth, otherwise I never would have had the gumption to see this through.

My entire life, I had suffered the shit-flinging of people like these men. I stroked the chef's hat in my lap. *Just pretend it's me and you, alone in the garage, like we practiced.*

"I'd let you stay with me longer, but…" said Rob. "I mean I'd obviously offer, but with you and Grace on the outs, I have to remain a neutral party." He held up his hand in a boy scout salute. "Geneva Convention," he said with a laugh.

Just me and you.

"I'll keep using the air mattress in the back office," I said.

"Mmmph!" The lawyer dribbled coffee from his mouth in a mad rush to set down the mug. "You haven't heard from the bank?"

I gave him a questioning look. "You are the bank," I said.

"I know we said you could keep working here. And we want you to feel like this is still your restaurant. In a sense. But we're going to need that office to keep records in."

"Records of what?"

"Records of records," he said with a wave of his hand.

"Listen," said Rob, "I know that we've had our differences," he began.

I squeezed the chef's hat. I caught a glimpse of the lobster tank in the foyer and thought of how the water had launched up the rocks to lick at Henry's blood.

"I know what you've done," I told Rob.

"Pardon?"

"This place…" I said, taking it all in with a wistful sigh.

"That's what we're here to talk about," the lawyer said with a smug smile.

Julian's voice came back to me through the haze of electronic house music. I pictured the roots of the almond tree sinking into the river to drink in what was left of Henry.

"You're behind this," I said. "I know that you get the restaurant after I sign these papers. Don't you?"

Rob shifted in his chair. "Now listen—"

"I called Grace to confirm this contingency agreement," I said. "She wouldn't let me talk to Ashley, but she did look up Henry's will. We found something nobody thought to mention the first time."

Rob scratched his chin and adjusted the collar of his button-down, peeling it away from the skin of his neck and clearing his throat.

The lawyer appeared concerned. "We need this to go through," he said.

"Rob needs it to go through," I said.

"You think this was my idea?" Rob said.

"I don't care whose idea it was," I said. "I just want to make sure that Grace gets the restaurant."

Rob pulled the fork out of his mouth and paused with his hand mid-air. "Grace would only get the restaurant if both of us were gone," he said. "If she was the only one left, somehow."

He considered a moment before his face deflated and he looked down at his plate. The lawyer picked up his dish and switched it with mine, his face expressionless. I grabbed a piece of his shrimp and bit into it.

I saw Rob's jaw twitch.

I swallowed a huge gulp of air and put on the chef's hat just as Ramon came out with the entrée—a broiled salmon dish with citrus and honey marinade, couscous, and a banana pâté. Then I leaned back in my chair and put my feet up on the corner of the table.

Rob looked from me to the salmon, pink flakes cragging like river rocks, waiting for the next asshole to drift by. "What have you done?" he said.

"Oh, don't worry," I told him. "It's not in the fish."

There was an awkward pause, my eyes pressing against his. Then the lawyer started to laugh. I let him keep at it for a few seconds before I joined in.

"What's not?" the lawyer asked.

"Bitter almonds," I said, yawning. "A whole six cups in the soup."

We both looked to Rob's empty bowl.

"Six cups!" Rob shot to his feet. "Dad said it would only take a handful to kill someone!"

"That's right," I said calmly. "If that."

The lawyer pulled a packet of papers from his briefcase and began to shuffle them like the world would end if they didn't make a particular sound. He splayed them out and collapsed them, then set the whole thing down in front of him as if we hadn't just careened past the prospect of business as usual.

"God, I'm getting tired," I said, reaching out to steady myself. The plate of food slid beneath my weight and smashed against the table's edge before dumping its contents in a jagged mess on the floor. I managed to grab hold of the table and plant my feet on the floor before I fell backward over my chair. "Woozy," I said, fanning myself with my hands.

Rob waved down a couple of encroaching onlookers. "Christ, you're making a scene. Do you want me to talk to Grace for you, is that what you—" He stopped mid-sentence and made a deep sound like *oomph* and held his stomach. He glanced at me with absent eyes, the light starting to fade. Then he tried on a new look, as if for the first time in his life he was aware of the feeling of hesitation.

He looked incredulous. "Give me the antidote," he said.

"That's ridiculous," I said. "You know that's not how this works."

More people were starting to gather, but I just exhaled slowly and put my head down. I heard Ramon's voice. *Yeah, it's fine, you can keep working for Grace*, I thought. *As long as somebody else has to put up with you. As long as Grace and Ashley have whatever they need.*

"Do you have any idea what you've done?" Rob said, his words coming tortuously slow.

I raised my hand in a thumbs up without looking up.

"This wasn't my idea," Rob hissed. "It was Dad's."

I rolled onto my temple like a bowling ball skittering into the gutter and peered up at him with one eye half-shut.

"Yeah, that's right. We all knew you were a fuckup, but no one actually expected you to prove it."

I decided that I needed to see him die.

I picked up my neck slowly, like a brontosaurus waking from a long nap, and wiped at my eyes. I didn't know why they wouldn't clear. What was this in my face? It was thick, like river muck. I swallowed more of it than runs through all the tributaries of the Earth. Its weight collapsed my insides and sent me helplessly to the bottom. I felt my body sink into the mud, the slithery kelp wrapping around my arms and holding me firm. I had the distinct and clear understanding that I would never leave the river. I pressed my hands into the table, forearms like columns, coaxing myself into a forward lean.

My vision unfurled and I saw Rob's head sinking into his bowl. The lawyer's mouth was open but no sound was coming out. I saw Ramon more than felt him slapping my face. Then I realized I couldn't hear. Then I couldn't see. Then there was nothing.

The Chilled Gazpacho of the Soul
Paired with: The Ethereal Nectar of Memory

I could hear a voice calling from somewhere distant. I felt like letting go. It was nice where I was, warm. I felt like a tadpole. A kangaroo baby. This must be what the womb felt like.

Something tugged at my hair. I tried to bat it away but it yanked harder. Fingers ripped follicles from their roots. Suddenly I was breathing again. I coughed and sputtered, the light blinding my eyes.

"You alright?"

I recognized the voice. I missed the water.

"I'm not going to kiss you or anything, so you better be alright."

Loud and offensive laughter shocked my system. I rubbed my eyes and calmed my sputtering lungs. Deep breaths.

Hands groped my shoulders and I sat up. I opened my eyes and saw Rob's face silhouetted against the midday sun. Leaning over, a smug, obnoxious smile plastered to his mouth like garbage to a wet shoe. Birds chirped. The river rushed. There was a desperate smell in the air, like all the world had been on fire. I was still clutching an oar.

"Where's Dad?" he asked.

We both looked toward the river and the big rock that ran with red.

Frank Oreto

GOD, BINGO, AND PIEROGI

Janice opened the ornately carved doors of St. Barnabus and slipped inside the cool quiet sanctuary. She glanced up at the enormous face of Jesus staring down at her from over the pulpit but didn't stop to pray. She was not here to worship. She was here because of her grandmother. Or baba if you'd grown up in Pittsburgh's South Side like Janice had. This church had been part of Baba's trinity—God, Bingo, and Pierogi.

God and bingo Janice had come along for. The call and response of the liturgy always calmed her. Made Janice believe for a moment there was a plan for the world, and her life was a part of it. And bingo could actually be fun. Not so much the game itself, but the stories Baba and the others told over cigarettes and ham barbecue. Stories they would never repeat in the house of God. The pierogi making, Janice had stayed away from.

Baba had chided her, especially when things turned bad with Rob. She firmly believed good cooking made a good marriage. "Come make pierogi with us," she would say, reading the worried look on Janice's face. "You feed your man, show him respect, and if that don't work so well, you feed him again."

But the pierogi ladies scared Janice. They gathered every Wednesday, making hundreds of the potato and cheese filled dumplings to sell for the church. As a child, she would peek in the large basement kitchen, watching them at their work. They'd seemed too much like the crones from her fairy tales. Speaking words Janice didn't understand and cackling with laughter. They seemed even more crone-like now—all wrinkles and sagging flesh as Janice entered the Church kitchen.

Condolences in both English and Polish washed over her as the women approached. "We loved your baba so much. She will be missed." They didn't ask why Janice hadn't been at the funeral. Quick glances at her closed right eye and swollen lip advertised the answer.

"Baba said Zofia should teach me to make pierogi," Janet said after the initial wave of conversation died away. "For my husband."

The women said nothing for a long moment. Only exchanged thoughtful glances as if years of cooking together made speech unnecessary. Finally, Ava, a round-faced woman as wide as she was tall, nodded and took Janice's hands in her own.

"Of course. Your baba knew best."

The crones led her to a long, steel table at the rear of the room. Zofia, the oldest of them, stood alone, eyes white with cataracts, pressing dough into paper-thin circles. The women left Janice there and went back to their own mixing and shaping.

Janice stood in silence, watching Zofia's rapid, dexterous movements. The woman's skin didn't sag like the others. Instead, it wrapped around her thin bones mummy tight. Fine wrinkles lined that skin like spidery letters in a language Janice couldn't decipher. Pregnant seconds ticked by. *Was the old woman deaf as she was blind?* Janice wondered. *Does she even know I'm here?*

Without warning, Zofia's flour-dusted hands rose. Her long, thin fingers probed Janice. Somehow locating each spot where Rob had hit her. With each touch, the old woman's face grew darker. Zofia spoke in Polish. Janice only understood bits and pieces of the words. However, she knew what was required. Watch. Listen. Do what I do.

So, Zofia taught Janice to make pierogi. Shaping dough, mixing the potato, onion, and cheese. Much of it Janice was familiar with. She'd watched Baba perform the same steps a thousand times in her tiny kitchen on Pious Street.

But there were differences. A way of holding your left hand, three fingers splayed, two curled, as your right hand drew symbols in the scattered flour. And the words. Harsh and jagged, completely unlike the Polish Janice had grown up hearing. Words that made Janice's mouth tingle as if she'd eaten hot peppers and, once spoken, fled her mind completely.

Janice felt dizzy. The dough burned her hands and odd colors flowed over the filling. She saw Rob's face. His anger. She remembered the love she'd felt for him. Once so huge and all consuming. How his rage transformed those feelings to fear and despair as miraculously as God's love transformed communion wine into blood. "He's going to kill me one day, Baba," Janice had said. So, Baba had told her what she had to do.

Janice wept, mourning the loss of her Baba, of her marriage. The hot tears flowed down her cheeks, adding themselves to the flour, eggs, and oil. Janice blinked away the tears to find Zofia's blind eyes upon her.

Rough hands found hers, stopping their motion. Janice blinked again. Her mind tingled like a sleeping limb regaining circulation. A plate stacked with half-moon shaped pierogi lay on the table before her.

Zofia spoke for the first time in English. "Not for you."

As Janice walked from the church, the special pierogi covered with a napkin, she heard her Baba as clearly as if the dead woman walked beside her: "You feed your man; show him respect. And if it work out not so well, you feed him again."

A week later, there was another funeral. This one Janice did attend.

Clair Watson

THE QUIET ONES

The thin sheet of skin Rune sliced off her arm sizzled when it hit the top of the bubbling gray liquid. Sacrifice was easy to pay and worth the horrendous scar along her arm. She coated the bleeding flesh in a purple salve then wrapped it snugly in gauze. Rune grinned at the frothing concoction. Soon her plans would be put into motion. Soon.

"Glorious," she whispered as her room filled with the pungent odor of week-old gym socks and decayed corpse. Her nose wrinkled at the stench and she held back her gag reflex, but her smile never wavered.

Her eyes darted to her bedside clock. Just past four a.m. was a good enough hour to go to bed when she had to get up in three. It was going to be a great day, even if she yawned through it. She stood up and stretched to the ceiling. Already in her pajamas, she took one more glance to the miniature caldron. It was above a three-wick, enchanted candle and was still boiling nicely. Her bedroom door was closed and her window was opened to help against the noxious odor.

A flashing light from her cell phone indicated a message or update of some kind. She picked it up from its resting place on the nightstand: a calendar reminder for the family dinner. To-morrow—she paused as she stared at the digital clock—was going to be fun.

Even before her alarm went off, Rune's eyes were open. She was making imaginary constellations in the stucco paint on her ceiling. Sitting up, she gazed over at her caldron. The candle was sending up faint smoke signals, but the potion was still bubbling as it should be. Her room smelled gloriously like a dumpster behind a fast food franchise. She drew in a deep breath of the rot and the fine smell of moldy fruit. She could even taste it on her tongue; she licked her lips.

The floor was cold against her soles as she pattered over to her potion.

A bubble popped, releasing more unpleasant gas into her lungs. A repugnant gray with streaks of a blood red that swirled with each bubble burst: perfection. She snickered. Now, all she had left to do was bake: the easy part. Grab the boxed cake mix, add a few eggs, some vegetable oil, and water, mix in her own special ingredient and some lemon juice for flair, and her cup-cakes would be irresistible, especially after the charm she'd placed on the buttercream frosting on top. The charm would en-sure the treats looked their proper color. She picked up the vial and topper she had set next to the cauldron. The liquid was cold even as another bubble burst against her skin.

She tucked the vial into her pajama pocket before heading downstairs to start gathering the normal ingredients for her des-sert. It wasn't until the cupcakes were cooling on the island that her parents joined her in the kitchen.

"Hey, morning." Rune said from where she sat munching on her cereal. "Anything else besides dessert that we need to bring?"

Her mother rubbed at her eyes as she set the kettle on the stove. Her father was attempting to make coffee at the one-cup coffee thing, but he quickly had to place a mug under the spout as the coffee began to run.

Her mother stared at the twenty-four cupcakes on the cooling racks. "Sure you want to go through with this, Rune?"

"They're lemon. I even put in zest and lavender in the frosting. It will be delightful and pleasant." Rune beamed. Milk dripped from her lips, and she held her spoon like a weapon. "Until it's, you know, not."

"Go for it." Her dad plopped down in a seat next to her. Coffee was drying on his hands, and his mug was barely half-full. "Never did care for those people."

"Oh, I am." Rune took up another big spoonful of her breakfast. Milk splashed around her bowl. "No worries on that."

"If it goes badly, I knew nothing." Her mother sighed as she joined them with her cup of tea.

"No worries," Rune repeated. "Neither of you knew."

"Course not. I can't condone this." Her father huffed into his coffee mug.

Her mother shook her head, and Rune stood up to place her dish in the sink. Rune had an outfit to plan. Normally, she just threw on the first few items that she found, but today, she would pull off the conventional look. First, jeans. She had never understood their appeal, but it was part of what normal society wore and that was the look she wanted to rock as she watched her cousins crumble.

The jeans she had bought for the occasion were dark blue with a floral pattern creeping up one of the flared legs. Next, a simple blouse of red with black roses and a gray cardigan to go over it. Although unconventional, she could not go without her pentagram pendant. Rune even went so far as to brush her unruly, shoulder-length hair. It glistened as she clipped in a simple black bow to contrast her blonde hair. She smiled at herself in the mirror. There had been a minor debate in her head over make-up but that was too much effort, though she did use nail polish. She painted her nails crimson before spattering on black dots.

Rune went back downstairs to pipe on the frosting, finishing off with lemon zest sprinkled on top among the purple crystal sprinkles. With care, she placed each cupcake into the container. When the lid popped into place, she couldn't hold back a grin.

A gentle hand fell onto her shoulder. She squared her expression and turned to see her father. Her dad had the face of a father from the old black-and-white television shows, the kind right before they give a speech to give the moral of the thirty-minute plot. The outcome the audience should take. He drew in a breath as he turned his gaze away from the container and put it onto her. His mouth thinned and a corner of his lips turned down before he spoke: "Positive you want to do this?"

"Certain."

He gave a tight nod. "Just making sure. You can't go back from this."

"It's worth it." She fisted her hand. "I know it is."

Her dad shrugged. "For something like this, it's best to keep questioning yourself. We're all for it, too."

"Thanks. But I'm more than sure." Rune patted the top of the container. "It will be a night of memories."

"Added to the Mythos of the Williamses." Her dad laughed.

Her mother was coming down the stairs, dressed for the day. Her short hair reminded Rune of flappers from the Roaring Twenties. However, the emerald sundress did not match the era of her hair: it looked too modern, as did her tennis shoes. Her mother stopped at the bottom of the staircase, giving her husband a harsh glare before saying, "Go get ready. I don't want to be late."

"They're always late," he muttered under his breath before going up the stairs to get ready for the day.

"You got everything?" her mother asked as she turned her attention to Rune. Her eyes fell briefly to the cupcakes before rising back to Rune's face. "It's going to be a long car ride."

"I've got some true crime books. I'll grab one before we get in the car." Rune answered the unvoiced question after the silence lasted too long: "Yes, I'm sure, Mom. I'm positive. I won't change my mind. And I know there is still time to think it over."

"You can still back out." The way her mother said the phrase told Rune they were filler words. Just something to fill the silence to show understanding, but the dead monotone told Rune what she already knew: her mother didn't quite approve.

"It will be fine, Mom." She gave a smile that she hoped looked reassuring. There was too much malicious glee that had built up in her as she devised and thought up the revenge plan. She would feel like a Poe character if she had a torch and catacombs instead of a well-lit park in late afternoon and cupcakes. But it was a maniacal happiness built from the schadenfreude she would feel once everyone ate the dessert she brought. There was no doubt her aunt, uncle, her cousins, and whoever their current mystery guest was would all partake in dessert.

Her mother scowled but then said: "You can make your own decisions."

"Do you have everything?" Rune asked, ignoring the tone that hovered in her mother's words. That tone said she wasn't ready to make drastic decisions, that she was still too young. Rune knew that by societal standards, she still had a year to go before the government allowed her to be an adult. But even then, she would be looked down upon until she reached a certain age or look that truly told the other adults that she was one of them. She was labeled as too childish for her tastes in shows and books, and even the fact she read avidly made her more of a blemish in her cousins' eyes. She wasn't fine with them spreading their hatred and trying to pass it off as logical and kind, as if they were the epitome of humanity.

"Of course," her mother huffed. "Hey, that's my line."

Her dad came down the stairs, tucking a flask into one of his pants pockets as he made a joke about how dealing with family was worse without liquor.

Five minutes later, they piled into the car, Rune's cupcakes on the backseat beside her. They were silent. Her mother scanned her smartphone's screen, her lips tense, and her father kept fiddling with the radio. The drive was long and an hour-and-a-half away from home, traffic built to a standstill on the highway. Rune watched the passengers around her, suspended in trips just like hers. From the way they looked, she doubted any of them were off to do nefarious deeds, but she knew of costumes. Being in a costume herself, she suspected others too were no doubt behind a façade of their own.

The drive was three hours total yet they beat the others who lived right near the park. Rune snatched her cupcakes from the car and placed them on a picnic table. Rune and her dad began to push and pull the picnic tables into a line, creating a long buffet and other places to actually sit and eat. She placed her cupcakes at the end of the buffet, where the desserts always waited. She huffed and gazed over at the nearby pond scattered with quacking ducks, who looked hopeful, as if someone would be throwing them breadcrumbs. They, too, would be getting quite the meal soon, Rune mused.

Not too long later, a motorcycle followed by a van pulled in. Rune surveyed as her cousins, uncle, and aunt, and their obligatory random unpacked themselves from the motor vehicles.

"Hey!" Came her uncle's obnoxious voice as he went up to them, his helmet held under an arm. Her parents both verbally greeted him as Rune merely raised her hand in acknowledgement. "As talkative as ever, Rune. You'll have to calm down some day."

Rune stared back at him with a flat expression. She had heard that joke so often it was a permanent echo in her ears, and it had only ever garnered his own gruff laughs. Her aunt was the next to notice her. Her aunt had a big dopey grin and too much make up, giving the resemblance of a poorly painted doll in shapeless dress. Her hands went to the sides of Rune's face as she took in her niece. Her hands were too sweaty and stank of over-used, vanilla lotion. "Oh goodness, Rune, you've dressed like a normal person."

Rune's mouth was forced into a stilted smile as her aunt fawned over her outfit, marveling how she looked beautiful now, and if she kept it up Rune could get a boyfriend in no time. Her cousins came next, asking about food and grumbling over the choices. The food was laid out, and her uncle started up one of the barbeques the park provided: the weird square-ish kinds that always were crusted in rust and stuffed with trash.

Dinner took too long. Everyone's stomach growled before the feast had been finished. Once the burgers were complete, she sat surrounded by her cousins. They each munched on their burgers, chips, and their macaroni salad. A good portion of them talked through their munching about asinine things, mostly about sports and their dogs, and the latest boneheaded things the others had done. Rune was certain they each tried to out-dumb the others as some sort of rite to be the stupidest of the bunch. Rune made a comment now and again, whenever she accidently reread a sentence of her book more than thrice.

"What's with the trying to be normal?" one of them asked. Rune didn't bother looking up from her book to figure out which one it was.

"Normal is relative. It just means that more people do it than don't, and that if you don't, you're just more of an individual rebel," Rune grumbled. "So to me, you guys are sheep."

"What?" It was a rumbled statement from several of them at once.

Rune shut her book with a satisfying thud, then set the thick hardback down on the picnic table beside her. The obligatory random had asked to be her friend and offered the seat next to her. Rune was still unsure of this girl's affiliation with her cousins, and none of them had introduced her. Judging by the conversation there were plenty of shared memories that Rune was not a part of: it was something about movies and concerts and mustard. Rune didn't care enough to figure out the connecting factors to the stories.

Rune changed the subject. "I made cupcakes. Lemon with lavender frosting."

"Gross. Won't they taste like bath products?" one of the female cousins asked. Her tongue stuck out and her eyes squinted. Her shoulders already had a red tinge from the sun and her lack of sunscreen.

"Only if you put soap on it."

"You're so dry."

"You're so pediculous."

Her cousins just gave her weird looks, but even if they didn't have lice they probably had fleas. Just as bad. Even the nameless nobody next to her looked put off.

"Sorry to befuddle you all." Rune shrugged, picking her book up. They'd be facing much worse than verbal forays soon. She tuned out their conversation as she waited for the call that dessert could be claimed.

Her cousins chatted away. They pushed around insults: back and forth, some word version of hot potato. It bounced from each of them. Even the newcomer joined in. Rune was beginning to suspect the girl might be one of their numerous neighbors. Rune knew they were hypocrites. One moment they were all talking about the dangers of motorcycles and how idiotic their father was for riding them. Then they switched to the "but we want one too" argument. Or how Jehovah's Witnesses were obnoxious to push their agendas onto them, whilst pushing theirs on to her. She rolled her eyes at the memories. Snapped her book shut with another thud.

"I think it's time for dessert." She stated it clearly in a volume louder than usual and in a firm tone. She stood and brushed off her jeans, not trusting the public picnic tables to not taint her with unseen particles of dust or for the badly-drawn graffiti to soak into the fabric.

Her aunt had brought store-bought cupcakes, and Rune grabbed one of the toxically colored treats. She grabbed a bright orange one with red sprinkles before promptly flipping the whole tray off the table. She feigned shock and hid a grin behind her hand. "Oh, I'm so sorry." She played up the crack in her voice and shrank back as others collected her mess.

"You're so clumsy. Damn, Rune." It was her oldest male cousin. She didn't even bother putting names to them anymore. He wore a football jersey with some player's name she didn't recognize, but she knew enough to recognize it as the local Oregon team. "We wanted those."

"There's still the ones I made. I put blood, sweat, and tears into them." Rune shot back, as she rubbed her hand against the gauze on her arm. She had put so much more personal effort into them then her cousins, who had stopped by a grocery store.

"Yuck; as if being made of bath products weren't disgusting enough, weirdo." The youngest female pinched one up. Her nose crinkled in disgust but her tongue swiped out at the frosting. She made several faces, as if she were a wine connoisseur trying to find the nutty tones. "Oh, it's fine," she said.

Rune observed her parents at a different table. They both had scrunched-up expressions as they watched Cousin Number 2 reach for, then bite into, a cupcake. The rest followed suit. The youngest cousin brought some to their parents after a demand from their father.

"Maybe you ain't useless." Her uncle cheered as he bit into the mini cake. It looked even smaller in his big, dirt encrusted hands. His moustache got coated in lavender frosting and sprinkles that glistened in the sun. She heard the others munching on theirs. For once it wasn't an infuriating sound.

"Did you want to try one?" Her aunt offered an extra cupcake to her parents. "You must be so proud of her."

Her father just raised an eyebrow and shook his head. Her mother looked half like she wanted to whack it to the dirt or scream, but she declined in a stiff voice that was only half polite.

"Thanks, Rune," the obligatory newcomer said, as everyone licked frosting from their fingers.

Rune shook her head and offered a smile. "You're welcome, collateral damage."

"Huh?" was the inelegant grunt back.

It made no difference. Rune could hear the rumblings, as their stomachs grumbled, growled, and roiled with nausea. They were cursing up a storm, calling her all the names that were allowed in PG-13 all the way up to R-rated movies and some, much to her amusement, were even creative. She had never been called a "bakery trickster" before. It had a nice ring, even over the sounds of retching.

Her cousins had fled to the two garbage cans. They shared. They could no longer talk. There were more shrieks, and Rune grinned from her perch atop a table, knowing she had done her research well. This park was isolated and it rarely had visitors. It was hidden away, and no one lived close enough to hear the ruckus. The first cousin shrieked and began to cry as she curled herself up. Slime oozed from her pores and the smell of bile and burgers overwhelmed the pavilion. It smelled even better than the potion. Rune calmly ate her chips.

"We'll wait in the car," her parents said, as they rushed past. She wondered if they would leave her there to suffer consequences, but if there were no bodies there was no crime. And soon there wouldn't be any bodies. Her aunt and uncle, and cousins, and the person who knew her name despite having no formal introduction all began to shrink, limb by limb, as more goo discharged from their skin coating their tiny bodies. Antennae sprouted from them as their skins changed to yellow. Some gained the black spots, but they were all banana slugs by the end.

Rune hopped from her spectator's seat with glee and twirled over to the tongs by the hamburger plate.

She lifted up the tongs and laughed as she watched her relatives and that one random victim try to slime away, but that was the beauty of slugs. They were slow. She picked up the aluminum throwaway pan and skipped around the pavilion and lifting each slug into the pan with the tongs. She even ripped apart a couple of buns and scattered it over the banana slugs: all nine of them.

She walked to the pond. The ducks slowly drifted toward her, quacking in a questioning matter, looking for handouts. "Did you know," she said to the contents of the pans, "that ducks eat slugs?"

Rune imagined what a slug screaming in terror would sound like. A gurgling kind of shriek full of gargles, pebbles, and the disgusting noise of putty slapping against a hard surface. She grinned. She set the aluminum tray down in the grass and pushed it over to the edge of the water with a grin. "I'm sure you'll learn."

Rebecca Snow

CRY ME A RIVER

Stephen teetered as the hermetic doors hissed, allowing him entry into the sterile hallway. His shoes shuffled across the floor like whispers. The rubber tip of his cane squeaked as the overhead air filtration system ruffled wisps of his white hair. He tossed a strained smirk at the woman who held his arm for balance. An errant sob edged into the corridor. The old man's smile faded as his head lolled toward the noise.

"Martha, did you hear that?" His voice cracked like broken glass.

"Yes, sir," Martha said, patting his wrinkled hand. "But you can recognize the sound of someone crying, can't you?"

Stephen scowled and poked her in the ribs with a crooked finger. "Fiddlesticks, of course I can." A pinched grin spread across his face when she flinched. "The point is I'm not *supposed* to hear the crying. Millicent will be unhappy."

Martha drew her thin lips into a decided frown as her head leaned like an Italian bell tower. Again, the cry slid into her ears. Her low heels clicked on the polished tile as she skittered past the long row of flat metal doors. At each ingress, the tapping slowed as Martha checked the latches. She skidded to a halt at door seventeen and turned back to wave at Stephen before reaching out a hand of gnawed fingernails and pulling shut the offending door. Silence enveloped the hallway.

Drawing up beside Stephen, Martha held out her arm. He wrapped his gnarled knuckles around her wrist, and they continued.

"How many rooms are filled today?" Stephen asked. He fumbled a sideways step.

Martha wrapped her arm around him before he toppled to the wall. With her free hand, she retrieved an electronic device from her lab coat and pressed a few buttons with her thumb. A spot of gelled blood oozed from a ripped hangnail.

"It seems we have forty-two subjects today. Five rooms need to be disinfected after the last procedure. Three electrodes failed. The electrician should be in this afternoon." Martha slid the handheld back into her pocket as the two turned a corner and stopped in front of a glass panel.

"How much product have we collected?" he asked, reaching his thumb toward a recessed biometric scanner. A buzzer sounded as the door slid to accommodate their single-file entry.

Martha left Stephen standing in front of a partition of one-way glass and swiveled to read an instrument on the wall. The needle hovered near the top of the cylindrical gauge.

"We're at four point eight liters." She returned to his elbow. "We should be ready for the first trial by this afternoon."

The old man stared through the glass, murmuring words of contentment. In the adjoining room, a young woman sat in a reclining chair, her head strapped with electrodes. A stuffed elephant rested in her hands. She watched a wall-mounted monitor. A montage of faded photos flicked across the screen. A birthday party, a pony ride, a lost tooth, and a mangled car wreck all featured a single child. The woman's mouth twisted, and she released a silent cry as tears streamed down her face and into a trough at her chin.

"Good," Stephen whispered. "Good. Millicent will be pleased."

He hobbled past two dark spaces before stopping in front of a room identical to the first. A uniformed man slumped in his chair. Images of explosions and torn limbs filled the screen in front of him. He shouted unheard words as saline tunneled through creases in his skin and dripped into the receptacle. Stephen's gaze followed the track of the tubing until it disappeared into a hole in the wall. Imagining each drop splashing into the collector and pooling with the others, a serene smile masked his face.

In a third room, a woman in a dark, tailored suit shrieked at the display as it flashed images of spiders creeping across human flesh. She cowered, pressing herself into the soft leather of the seatback, but the conduit attached beneath her chin collected her weeping terror.

"Excuse me, sir," Martha said. She tapped his shoulder. "We may have a problem in room twelve."

Stephen turned and waited for her to continue, drumming his fingers on his dragon-headed walking stick.

"Most of his emotional levels remain steady." Martha scrolled down a short list on her touchpad. "However, his pleasure center has a heightened response."

Tottering toward number twelve's readout panel, Stephen fidgeted with the ragged hem of his suit coat. He punched at the screen and perched his glasses on the end of his nose. With his head back, he read the information.

"It says here, he's come to us from an asylum outpatient program." He pressed his spectacles to his eyes and glared at Martha. "Did we *not* have a discussion about proper subject selection?"

Martha scurried to the board and fluttered her hands on the flat surface. She scrolled to the end of the list and backed away from the old man. She wagged a finger at the bottom name.

"Marcus admitted him," she said, her eyes wide and frightened.

Stephen slammed the tip of his cane into the floor. A distinct crack sounded in the wooden shaft.

"What's that boy trying to do, ruin me?" Stephen's nostrils flared, and a shock of hair swiped his forehead.

Stephen peered through the glass and stared at the seated man. The man leaned toward the monitor with a toothy grin plastered to his face. Scenes of carnage and mayhem reflected in his eyes while he rested his elbows on his knees.

Stephen tapped on the window with his cane. A hidden door slid into the wall. He stepped through into the cave-like confines of the small room and flipped a switch. The seated man flinched and squinted as the brightness of the overhead light flickered to life.

"What the..." The man's voice trailed as his eyes adjusted to the sudden illumination.

"Your services are no longer needed, sir," Stephen said, standing as straight as his bent spine would allow.

A duo of technicians scuttled through the opposite doorway and approached the seated subject.

The man glanced at his watch. "I've only been here for twenty minutes." His eyes searched the ceiling while his fingers made a quick calculation. "That won't even buy me lunch."

The two men in lab coats peeled off electrodes and unstrapped headgear as the man attempted to swat away their hands.

"Sir, it is a waste of your time and ours if we allow you to stay." Drawing a deep breath through his nose, Stephen continued. "And you won't help Millicent."

The man stood, tore the smock from around his neck, and hurled it onto the tiles. The fabric slid into a far corner, covering a wad of feathery lint.

"The hospital sent me here for some sort of test they said I'd get paid for." His arms windmilled, and spit flew from his lips. "I get all glued in and start to enjoy the movie, and now I gotta go?"

"Yes, sir." Stephen tilted his head toward the exit. "Your check will be waiting at reception."

"Fine." Stomping to the opening, the man stopped. One hand rested on the door jamb. "Can I ask one question?"

Stephen twitched his head in a quick nod.

"Why?" he asked.

"Because you can't cry." Stephen's mouth drew into a sneer at his final word.

The two techs hustled the man into the hallway and shut the door behind them. Stephen extinguished the lights and returned to the back hall and Martha.

"Please make a note of this in Marcus' file."

Stephen turned to survey the next room as Martha's fingers flew across her handheld device. Through the one-way glass, the dim interior flashed with pictures of four fluffy Saint Bernards. The ancient woman seated in the recliner clutched a lace hand-kerchief in both hands as, one by one, the dogs met their ends in front of her.

A wan smile seeped onto Stephen's lips. Millicent had loved dogs of all kinds, but she had been allergic and unable to have one of her own. When she'd given birth to a son and then a daughter, her desire for having a pet of her own vanished. She had seemed content.

The next window was dark, so Stephen lowered himself to one of the cushioned benches that lined the wall opposite the windows. Reaching into his pocket, he removed a small sterling pill case, popped a dose, and swallowed it without the benefit of water. He rested his head on the wall and felt the nitroglycerin tablet slide down his throat.

"Is there anything I can get for you, sir?" Martha asked, her back toward him as she scanned subject fourteen's wall board.

"No thank you, dear." Stephen heaved himself to his feet and retrieved his cane from the bench. "My old bones can't move like they used to."

Martha nodded without turning and continued to check the vital signs listed on the screens. For the next few rooms, the pair leap-frogged the observation windows. Stephen scrutinized the people while Martha focused on the statistics.

A man with ropey biceps sniffed over a sinking ship. He could have been upset at the bodies bobbing in the surf, but Stephen couldn't be sure. A young face belied by creased eyes wept at pages of scrolling text. Stephen squinted in an attempt to read the type, but his eyesight failed to grasp more than the words *I'm sorry*. Graying permed curls quaked as a woman stared at a single picture of a broken vase. Stephen knew there was a reason the machines had pulled this memory for number twenty-six, but he wasn't interested in her thoughts, only her tears. On closer inspection, he knew they poured from her ducts and that Millicent would be pleased.

The old man passed the next few windows with no more than a quick glimpse to determine the collection progressed as planned. Arriving at the glass etched with the number forty, the scrolling images grabbed a memory in Stephen's mind. A woman smiled in the sun, her golden hair captured by a checkered kerchief. Sunglasses sheltered eyes he knew to be the color of forget-me-nots. He gasped and fell to the wall for support as a red stain blossomed across the woman's chest. Her face tilted as if she'd heard an odd noise. When she looked down, her mouth gaped as her fingertips dipped into the spreading blemish and came away crimson. The scene repeated.

"Sir," Martha called from where she'd been examining room twenty-eight's digital panel. "Are you all right?"

Stephen's forehead rested on the glass that separated him from the violence. Martha's shoes tapped a rapid cadence. When she reached him, Martha bent her knees to level herself to the old man's height. Stephen's glazed eyes stared, and his jaw sagged.

"Sir!" Martha snapped her fingers.

Stephen flinched and blinked. His gaze slid over the monitor, and he straightened to block Martha's line of vision.

"What is it?" he asked, his voice huffing like a riled panther.

"I was concerned," she said, breaking for silence. "You sounded startled."

"A pinched nerve," Stephen said. He ran a hand along his bony hip.

His lips pulled into a tight line. He gripped her upper arm with his free hand in an attempt to steer her from the pane. Catching a glimpse of the repeating scene, Martha shook herself free and stared.

"Isn't that Mother?" she asked. Her voice squeaked like a trapped rodent on the last word.

"No, dear." Stephen replaced his hand on her shoulder. "Just someone who bears a striking resemblance."

Jerking from his grip once more, Martha returned to gawp at the sequence.

"She used to wear those exact shades," Martha whispered as her fingertips hesitated at the glass.

She shrieked when the red stain appeared.

"Martha, you were only four when Millicent died." Stephen dragged his mouth into a deepening frown. "You can't recall her in detail as I can." He pointed at the flickering face. "And I can tell you that the woman in forty's memory is not your mother."

"How can you be sure?" Martha's crumpled face wrenched toward him.

Stephen regarded his daughter's eyes, eyes identical to those of the woman in question if she were to remove the obstructive sunshades, and lied.

"I know because she was my wife." He shifted his weight onto his better hip. "I still dream about her face. Every night." He drew his head an inch closer to Martha's. "Her memory haunts me."

Martha pulled her sleeve across her eyes and swallowed. "You're sure it isn't her?" she asked.

"Positive." Stephen patted her wrist. "I think you should take a break and get some air."

Nodding back a sob, Martha spun and scampered to the end of the hall. She disappeared around the corner. Stephen held his breath as he waited for the sliding door to echo through the corridor before he turned back to the window.

Millicent's eruption played out twice more before he turned his attention to the reclining chair. A withered man sat motionless. Tears dripped, making rivulets around the stubble on his chin before finding their ultimate destination in the receptacle around his neck. He made no sound as his eyes drained. A battered fedora rested on the floor.

The hair on Stephen's neck rose. Blotches of red spotted his sallow complexion. His fist clenched around his cane, and he rapped on the window making the sliding door rattle as it moved. The panel stuck when Stephen entered the room.

"Who told you to come here?" Stephen asked. His eyes narrowed to slits.

The other man craned his neck and stared at Stephen. No sign of recognition cracked his expression.

"Excuse me?" the man asked, his lips sticky with sadness.

"Why are you here?" Stephen asked.

"They recruited at Shady Pines, and I needed money to buy Christmas presents for the grandkids." Beads of sweat oozed from the man's hairline.

"That memory." Stephen flung an arm toward the blackened screen. "Do you remember what you did to make that happen?"

"I…I…I don't know what you mean." The man's eyes grew wide. A line of fluid blue surrounded his irises.

"Who was that woman to you?" Stephen spat the question as if he'd swallowed a spider.

"Her name was Millie. I courted her. We were on a picnic." The man gasped. "On the beach."

The monitor in the hall chirped as a red light blinked. Stephen shuffled forward and tore a Velcro cuff from the man's arm. The alarm quieted.

"She was hit by a stray arrow from the bluffs. Some kids playing cowboys and Indians, I suppose." His panting grew more pronounced. "By the time the police arrived, the upper lot was empty." The man gripped his left arm. "I need my jacket." He gulped. "My pills are in the pocket."

Stephen pressed the tip of his cane into the man's chest and held him to the recliner.

How long were you with her?" Stephen asked. His mouth pulled into a snarl.

"Please," the man wheezed. "My pills."

"Answer my question." Stephen watched the man's lips tinge blue.

Five years," the man panted. "We were together, on and off, for most of five years."

Stephen watched the man strain for air and writhe in the seat. As his struggle lessened, the man's face resembled a slab of boiled flounder. Stephen leaned toward his ear.

"She had children. She had a husband." He choked back a wail. "She had me."

The man's body fell limp, and Stephen attached the strap to its lifeless arm. The buzzer in the hall resumed its din. He backed out and yanked shut the crippled door.

Stephen plodded to the window of forty-three not seeing what was behind the glass. Martha sprinted past him and skidded to a stop as she forced her way past the blaring whir of noise. When Stephen reached the entryway, she had the old man on the floor, pressing on his chest. Her lips moved, but her counting made no sound.

"What happened?" Stephen asked as he leaned on his stick.

Martha breathed into the old man's mouth before cycling through the motions a second time.

"Didn't you hear the alarm?" She continued her rhythm. "His heart stopped."

Stephen tottered to where the man's coat hung from a hook on the wall. Fumbling through the pockets, he retrieved a worn, leatherette billfold and a bottle of pills.

"Nitrobid." He shook the container, the sound reminiscent of a game of Yahtzee.

The wallet fell open in is hand. A photo ID stared up at him from behind a plastic barrier. Stephen tilted his head to read.

"It says here, his name was Paul Evans." Stephen flipped through the thin compartments as Martha continued to pound on the dead man's chest. "He was a resident at Shady Pines."

Stephen tossed his findings into the chair. Martha leaned back on her heels and drained her lungs of breath.

"That's the second one this week." She checked the time on her portable unit and pressed on the pad to log it into the man's file.

"He did sign the wavier," Stephen said. He wiped a stray piece of lint from his coat. "And he was very old."

Martha glanced up at her father with half-opened eyes. Something about that look gave him pause. The cut of her jaw and the bridge of her nose were an exact match, under younger skin, to the man lying on the floor. Stephen scowled and shook his head, dismissing his thoughts.

"I suppose you're right."

Martha pressed her palms into her thighs and rose. Her knees popped in complaint. Exiting the small enclosure, she tapped instructions on the wall screen. Before Stephen had made the hallway, the mortician was collecting his quarry.

A piercing buzz filled the corridor. Martha's face twisted at the racket.

"It seems that the collector is full. Millicent will be pleased." Stephen held out his elbow for Martha. "Shall we proceed?"

Martha rested her hand in the crook of his arm and nodded. The two snaked their way through a maze of walkways and up two floors in a hesitant elevator.

The silver doors slid open to a darkened room that smelled of disinfectant and lavender. Thick blue velvet curtains covered the curved walls. A waist-high basin stood in the center of the floor. Its black porcelain shone in the light from a pair of shaded lamps. Martha entered an alcove and returned with a large beaker of liquid and an eyedropper. Eyeballing the measurement of tears, she poured the contents into the vessel and watched it settle. A door opened and an oafish man stumbled into the room. He steadied a wobbling archery trophy and backed away as if watching it would keep it stable.

"Did I miss anything?" he asked. His gaze flicked from face to face once it left the gold-toned bow.

"No, Marcus," Stephen said. "We have yet to begin."

A gap-toothed grin spread across Marcus' features. His hooded eyes disappeared into jovial creases. He dragged a tall wooden stool to the bowl and sat, elbows resting on the edge.

Martha passed the eyedropper to Stephen and strode to a bank of switches. She dimmed the lights and lit several black pillar candles. Stephen poised the eyedropper above the static solution.

"What's in the dropper, Pops?" Marcus asked, pointing a meaty finger.

"Hush." Stephen paused. His eyes rose to meet his son's. "It's a tincture of palladium to activate the tears."

Marcus nodded and rested his cheeks in his hands, his focus intent on absorbing the ritual.

Stephen squeezed five drops around the perimeter of the dish. The shadows crept to the edge of the rippling pool of tears.

"Martha." Stephen kept his gaze on the small pool. "The bracelet."

Martha reached to her wrist and removed a silver band filled with dangling charms. A small dog snagged a loose thread on her sleeve. As she jerked the chain, the polyester fiber gave way. Martha hovered the bauble above the dish before releasing it. The shiny metal glittered as it settled at the bottom of the bowl.

"As you once were, so shall you be, as if what has passed had never been." Stephen stared at his reflection. His eyes drifted past it to the delicate silver bow and arrow linked to the wristlet. His image fused with the trinket, and the thousands of tears began to steam.

"I see her," Marcus said, a giggle in his throat.

Martha peered into the clearing mist. Her pursed lips creased at the edges.

"I can't see anything. It's just a big puddle." She rubbed her eyes with the tips of her fingers.

"Look beyond your own reflection," Stephen said, euphoria evident in his tone. "Your mother is with us."

Millicent's face, wrinkled as though she'd lived longer than her thirty-two years, wavered at the surface. A scowl marred her evident beauty. Her lips formed a single word that echoed in Stephen's mind.

"Children." His voice snapped like a broken rubber band. "Leave us."

Marcus toppled from his seat and scooted from the room. The stool spun across the floor and came to rest against a curtained wall. Martha's lip thrust out in a pout as she stalked from the chamber. She slammed the door behind her.

Stephen heard his wife's word repeat in his head.

"Why?" she asked.

"I had to see you again." Stephen gripped the side of the basin. "I needed to know what we would have been, what we could have been."

Millicent shook her head.

"Why did you pull the bowstring?"

The words shot through his consciousness.

"Your betrayal destroyed me. It was the only way I could survive, the only way we could always be together."

A fleck of spit flew from his mouth. Tiny splashes disfigured the image before it settled back into stillness.

"You never cared for me." Millicent's lips fluttered. "I was only a possession to you. And it seems that I still am." She scanned her watery surroundings. Her hands pressed the barrier between them, and the meniscus reversed. "You never saw me through your research."

"I loved you," Stephen whimpered. "Look what I've done for you."

A drop of sweat plunged from his temple and into the bowl.

"You brought me back for you, not for me."

Millicent pressed her finger at the center of the circling ripples. The surface stretched around the tip. Another droplet of perspiration fell to the basin, and Millicent punched her small fist through the shell of tears. She stretched her liquid hands and reached for her husband.

"You took my love. You took my life. You trapped my future."

Her fluid fingers grasped Stephen's brittle neck and pulled him to her. His withered hands found no purchase on her slippery veneer as he scrambled to free himself. Stephen's breath came in short bursts as he inhaled his subject's secreted brine. His eyes bulged, and his throat stung as she held him under the surface.

"Consider us even."

His mind absorbed her words as his body fell lifeless to the damp carpet.

A knock punctuated the silence like a shot in a ghost town.

"Sir?" Martha called.

She swung open the door and peeked into the flickering light. Marcus bound past her, throwing her off balance. He stepped to his father and toed the man's shoulder.

"I think he's dead," Marcus said, his arched eyebrows accentuating his slack jaw.

A deep sigh wracked Martha's frame. A wry grin blossomed.

"Well, he did sign the waiver." Martha shrugged. "And he was very old."

Leigh Statham

JOSIE

Josie walked into the park, humidity wrapped around her like a wet rag. The tree branches hung low, even their leaves bowing with the morning heat and atmospheric sweat. She pulled out her last cigarette, threw the package at a trashcan and flicked her lighter on. She sucked in smoke and heat, savoring every second of the nicotine, and started working out how she would get money for a new pack that day.

She was fifteen years old. She had a short, black fro—natural was in; natural was cheap. She had ripped jeans and a lace headband she found at the women's shelter two days ago. Her t-shirt was from a church service group she'd never heard of, but it was blue, just like her eyes, and it was tight, so she felt almost sexy in it.

She'd left home at eight pm on a Tuesday. They had a presentation in school about empowerment and advocating for yourself, so she went home and tried it. It didn't go so well. She was lucky to get out without a beating.

She spotted Spinx sitting on a bench not far away. He waved Josie over and patted the seat next to him.

"What's going on, baby girl?" Spinx grinned at her. "You're up early."

"Rough night on Martin. Couldn't get a bed at the shelter."
She sat on the ground at his feet, crossed her legs and leaned
back, taking another deep inhale of her cigarette, lingering on it,
holding it carefully between two fingers—breakfast in a cloud.

She liked Spinx. They met at the Salvation Army a couple
of weeks before. He'd steered her to the line with the lady who
gave the biggest portions at dinner, and they talked a bit after.
He was nineteen, always in a good mood when she ran into him,
and had twice hooked her up with what she was craving. Never
made her feel like she owed him.

"You shoulda come and found me. I've got a place for
you."

She rocked back and forth a couple of times, feeling the
earth solid beneath her jeans. "I'm sure you do, but I'm not
hanging around here anymore. You got any smokes in that
bag?"

He was overweight. His clothes were dirtier than hers. His
black hair was curly, but hung in limp waves. She couldn't tell if
it was greasy or wet with sweat. He was wearing a Pokémon
shirt with short sleeves that left his arms naked, the track marks
blazing. She guessed he was Hispanic, maybe black too, and
something else. They never talked about where they came from.
It didn't matter. He always carried a huge green backpack with
him. Sometimes it had food in it, sometimes drugs. Last week he
had a whole case of Hostess cupcakes. This morning he pulled
out a soda and handed it to her.

"Sorry, this is all I got, but it's yours," Spinx said. "Where
you headed? Why aren't you hanging around?"

She took the bottle and sipped the bubble brown drink. It
was warm.

She had the sudden desire to flick her ashes into the small
plastic opening before handing it back to him, but a crack under
his smile exposed something dark. He wasn't himself today. A
snake better left untouched. She hesitated before she answered.
She considered lying, but in the end told him the truth.

"I've got an aunt in Charlotte. I've almost got enough for a
bus ticket down there. Was thinking about calling her." She

handed the drink back, then flicked her ashes on the ground behind her.

"That's not smart. How long you been out? You made it to the milk carton yet?"

"I don't drink milk, Spinx."

"They'll haul your ass off to juvie and foster care."

"Better than my house," she muttered.

"You got something lined up for tonight?" he asked.

"Not yet."

"You know I got room."

"Where are you stayin' that you got so much room?"

He took a long drink of the soda and put the cap back on. "Down off Blount. Found a room with a guy I know from back in school."

"And he's just letting you crash there?"

Spinx stood up and shouldered his bag. He took another drink of his soda, then handed it to her. "You come down to Blount tonight, and I'll make sure there's room for you—415, east side with a big gray truck out front. I'll have smokes, too."

"What'll it cost me?"

"Nothin', baby girl. You know I love you." She saw the smile, but the crack was still underneath it.

"You all right, Spinx?" she asked.

He held his hands up and smiled as he walked off. "Better than ever." His words fell flat on the grass at her feet.

The day was as long and hot as the morning. Josie flagged for a while and picked up twenty dollars in change. She bought lunch and a new pack of cigarettes, then stuffed the rest in the top of her left black converse.

She thought briefly about the day her mom bought them for her. It was one of few happy memories she had left, but she shoved the memory aside anyway. She only kept the shoes because they were easy to stash stuff in. The lady with the peach stand at the farmer's market let her help load the truck at the end of the day and gave her another twenty.

"You look like my sister," the peach lady said.

Josie nodded. She looked like everyone's sister/daughter/cousin.

She was walking down Wilmington just before seven when she spotted a man across the street, head down, thumbing at his cell phone. His jeans were new, clean. His shirt was a blue-striped button up, and he had on bright red shoes. She shuddered a bit and turned on the first cross street she came to, heading east. She put her back to the brick wall and breathed. For a beat, she thought it was her dad. He had red shoes and a shirt like that. He liked that bar on the corner. She normally avoided it. How did she forget to avoid it tonight? She stepped off the wall and looked back at the man. He was gone.

Even if it was him, she knew he would never come looking for her. He'd come downtown for a drink, but not for her.

"Get your ass to school on time today—no more excuses. I don't want your mother to have to deal with that counselor one more time."

That was the last thing he said to her. So she did. She went to school on time that day. She went to class instead of smoking out back with Mason and Amy. The health teacher's words still bounced around her head like a rubber mallet slowly crushing her brain.

"Abuse isn't something that any of you should have to deal with. No one of any age should feel they are less than anyone else. But it's up to you to call out the wrong doers. It's up to you to take control of your life."

The memory followed her around like a specter, the ghost of bad choices past. She stood up for herself, and now she was locked in a corner, sleeping on concrete, begging for nicotine.

There was Blount Street. She paused a minute. Looking up and down the sidewalk. Spinx's new place was to the right. Benny's corner was to the left, and she knew she had enough money now for a solid hit. He might even do her a favor and throw in enough for Spinx.

She found him in front of the Cut and Chop barber shop, his blue hoody and long goatee hanging around his neck like a noose. He smiled at her and tipped his head as she made her way toward him.

Benny didn't disappoint.

"Tell Spinx I said 'Hey.' Tell him to drag his ass down here once in a while instead of sending you to do his errands."

"I'm not running his errands. We're just hanging out to-night."

"Whatever. You his girl?"

"I'm nobody's girl."

"Pimp's gonna snap you up. You got a fine body and all your teeth."

"Shut up, Benny. You got a phone?"

She handed him the cash, and he gave her the little bags.

"Yeah. Who you gotta call?"

"I need to look up a number," she said.

"That cost extra."

"Why? Lemme borrow it for a minute."

"Data. Rates double at night. It's this suckass program my mom got us on. Come back in the morning."

"A'ight. Thanks."

"Spinx is gonna end up doin' time if he get caught with you."

"Spinx is just a friend." She meant it. Spinx was soft. He was smart, but not mean. He was a good person. He never looked at her the way her dad looked at her—hatred and owner-ship all over his face—like a preacher, like the guys at school, like the cop at Oakwood and Tenth, like they knew what was best for her. But they didn't know her, and none of them knew her story.

"Whatever." Benny threw his hands up and turned his back to her as he walked away. "Someday you'll pass by, and I won't know you. Your fine ass and teeth'll be gone, and you'll pay me double for half a hit."

But she was already walking away. She stuffed the bags in her pocket and stopped at the burger place on the way to Spinx's. Why sleep on the street when he had a room and a bed and she knew he'd keep his hands to himself? She had twenty dollars left. She shoved fifteen back in her converse, mentally labeling it bus fare. She got a burger and a chocolate shake and ate them as she walked to Spinx's.

415 Blount was crumbling between two houses obviously owned by hipsters. They had new stone porches and flower beds. The siding was painted in sky blue on the house to the right, mint green on the left. One had a plastic swing for a baby, while the other had a BMW in the driveway. 415, on the other hand, was dirty gray, the same color as the crumbled sidewalk. Weeds grew around its sagging veranda, and a man was on the roof spreading a blue tarp across the peak, cigarette hanging carelessly off his lips. She stared up at him, and he nodded at her.

"You Spinx's girl?"

"No."

He ignored her reply.

"He's in his room," he said and went back to securing the tarp with a brick.

Inside was as gray as the outside, and just as hot. The weight of the night air followed her as she stepped over the threshold and looked around. The place was a shrine to a lost family. Green carpet on the floor was stained and pocked with burn marks. The walls were gray but had the faint hint of one time being blue, or maybe even lilac.

There were square outlines of dirt and dust on top of the faded paint, ghosts of pictures long since gone. She wondered for a moment whose faces were trapped in those frames and what happened to them. The whole place felt wet, and the smell of mildew mugged her nose. But they had a couch that looked new, and a TV, and a kitchen, so it was already better than the women's shelter.

She walked to the sink and turned the faucet. Water ran cool and clear over her hands. There was no soap, but she scrubbed at the black streaks of dirt from the market and the sugar from the dripping shake. A cloudy glass sat on the countertop next to an ashtray overflowing with butts. Grease smears in the shape of a mouth scalloped the edges of the cup. She bent forward and used her hand to get a drink instead, washing down the milkshake and burger. Then she wiped her hands on her shirt and continued deeper into the little house.

She found Spinx sitting on a bare mattress on the floor, reading a Thor comic book. A window air conditioner filled the room with cool, breathable air. It made her shiver, and she sucked it in through her nose and held it while the sweat on her skin turned to ice drops.

"What's up?" she asked.

"You came!" He sounded like a kid. He rocked his massive body up to standing and spread his arms. "How do you like my place?"

"It's freezing cold."

"I know. Isn't it awesome? Have a seat. You like Thor?"

"Not really."

She reached in her pocket and pulled out the two baggies and held them up between two fingers. "I brought some rent."

"Baby girl! Now you're talking." Spinx pulled a fifth of Turkey out of his green bag.

After they were sufficiently high and sufficiently drunk, Josie lay wrapped in a quilt, curled up in Spinx's arms on the mattress, dozing. She sensed a complete feeling of security for just a sparkle at a time. She didn't have to worry, then she'd check herself. You always have to worry. She wasn't hungry. You will be tomorrow. She didn't have to be afraid. Fear keeps you safe.

"Spinx?" she asked.

"What?"

"How come you never try to get on me?"

Spinx laughed a little in the dark. "'Cause you're just a kid."

"That doesn't stop other guys."

"Yeah, but they're assholes. You're like the little homeless sister I never had."

"Who you get high with?"

"That's different. We all need a little vacation from the shit hole now and then."

They lay in the dark listening to the hum of downtown Raleigh for a few minutes. Then Spinx said, "Baby girl, I want you to come with me."

"Where?" She asked.

"Back to my house."

"You're so stupid, Spinx. This is your house." She giggled at him and pulled the quilt tighter over her shoulder.

"No, I mean, I saw my mom the other day. She's in town. She tracked me down. I guess my dad left, and she wants me to come back."

Josie wasn't sure if she was hearing him right. She sat up, letting the quilt fall around her waist. "Back up, Spinx. Is this why you were all weird this morning? You got people who want you around?"

"My dad never did. He threw me out a few years back."

"But you got a mom who came to find you?"

"Yeah. She's always been great. It's my dad who's an asshat. We never got along. He found out I was playing for both sides and—"

"I don't need to know your sob story, Spinx. You lost me at great mom."

"What are you talking about?"

"Spinx, everyone has a story out here, right? Everyone has some sad sap reason they are living on the street and drowning themselves in whatever they can get their hands on. But one thing none of us have is a great mom."

"Don't say it like that. She really is great. I think I'm going to go back with her tomorrow."

Josie laughed. "You've got to be kidding me."

"What? Don't make fun of my mom. You'd like her. You should come meet her."

"Did you just ask me to meet your mom?"

"I'm serious. Why wouldn't you want to get out of here?"

"I'm serious, too. I do want to get out of here. But where does she live? Chapel Hill? Carrboro? Please, don't say Cary."

"She lives in Richmond, smart ass."

"Well, that's better than Cary. What do you guys have, like a perfect three bedroom house on a cul-de-sac lot with a dog?"

"No. Why are you being such a bitch, Josie? I'm offering to help you."

Josie knew she was out of line. She knew it was the chemicals talking. They always dug up everything mean in her and pushed it out her mouth. She knew she should be happy for this big messed up kid, that someone actually cared about where he was. She owed it to him to be straight.

"Because I don't have an awesome mom. No one has come looking for me, and they never will." It twisted her gut to say the words out loud. But there they were, hanging in the air between them.

Spinx put his head in his hands and took a deep breath before he spoke.

"Listen, you said it yourself, everyone has a stupid sob story. I don't want to hear yours either. But that doesn't mean we have to keep living them. We can head up there together, get decent jobs, get our feet underneath us. My mom even offered to pay for me to finish my GED. I bet she'd help you, too."

"What the hell? You got a rich ass great mom?" It was like he didn't hear her at all. Jealousy and hurt pulsed through her like a tidal wave. She knew it wasn't rational; these feelings were pushing her down a road she did not want to travel.

"She's got plenty of money, Josie. But that doesn't matter. You know you aren't making it on the street, and you can't call your aunt."

"It matters a lot, Spinx. And how do you know anything about my aunt?" She got up from the bed and fumbled around in the dark looking for her shoes. It was getting hard to breathe in the cold room, but only because she knew there was plenty of money back home, too. There was plenty for posters, for commercials, for a milk carton. But none of that crap was being made. None of that money was being spent to find her.

"Because, I know this shit, Josie. They turn you in. They all do. When you're under age, that's what they have to do, and you end up in foster care, or back where you started, or some juvie hell hole where you are sardined in with a whole pack of losers worse than us."

"I bet your real name is Edmund or some fancy shit like that."

"It's Emanuel."

"Nice. Figures." She double checked her cash and laced up her shoes.

"Where are you going?"

"It doesn't matter. I'm getting out of here. It's too damned cold anyway."

She opened the door, and a burst of warmth and humidity pushed back Spinx's AC, soothing the goosebumps that had sprung to life on her arms.

"Josie…"

"Have fun with your mom.'"

She slammed the door and made her way through the damp night. The stains in the carpet and the squares on the walls hid in shadows as she passed. She felt herself walking in the footsteps of ghosts as she made her way to the front door. I'm never coming back here, she thought. Just like they never came back here. The warmth of the night air felt good on her shoulders and arms, but her face was too hot from the argument. Her eyes were stinging.

She would have given anything to have her mother, great or not, believe her and come look for her—in the dark of the night, back when she was still crying, at seven, at twelve, at fourteen, even tomorrow. The thought of Spinx having that chance made her want to vomit. Why wasn't she happy for him? Why couldn't she go with him?

The only answer she could surmise in her mental haze was that she must be as evil as her parents. She must be as bad as them. She might even be worse. Genetics couldn't be refuted.

She shook her head and took a deep breath. She needed to think or Benny's prediction would be right. She had nowhere to go, but she knew she'd figure something out. She would get her bag from the bus stop, count her money again, and buy a ticket to Charlotte.

The gray sidewalk beneath her seemed to crumble under each step. She wrapped her arms around her waist and trudged forward, her head down, watching for cracks and stomping solidly on each one.

Break her back, break her back, she chanted in her head. Break it. Break it, every crack.

But the way before her blurred red in the lamplight. She stopped short. She had walked to the bar again. Her dad's favorite bar. A body was blocking her way, two red shoes on the ground in front of her.

"Josie?"

The cool voice was one she knew well, one she avoided at all costs, one she'd heard raised in anger and murmuring in her ear, hot breath carrying evil words. It was smooth like butter and twice as greasy. The ache of jealousy and her buzz from moments before washed away at the same time, broken glass on a beach.

"Dad."

He had her by the arms before she could react. His face was a mixture of shock and fury.

"I have no words for you right now. No words. If you understood an ounce of the misery you've heaped on your mother…"

Josie felt her insides start to melt back into a little girl under the pressure of his hands and his voice. Her eyes watered and spilled freely now. Her nose instantly ran, and her whole body began to shake—with terror, and even worse, with an equal amount of relief. He had come looking for her. Revulsion took its turn spreading through her body as she realized what she was letting herself feel.

Of course he came to find her. Of course he did.

"Dave, who is this?"

Josie was so caught up in the shock of her father standing in front of her, holding her in place, that she didn't notice the woman.

She blinked at the tall, thin woman with a long weave and big boobs. Realization settled slowly. This wasn't her mother. He hadn't been looking for her.

"Don't look at her, look at me." Her dad shook her back to meet his gaze. "I'm taking you home right now. We're going to work this out. We'll go to counseling, you'll get meds, we'll work this out. You're a sick girl, but we can fix it."

She felt him steering her, his fingers a steel cuff on her right arm.

"What about tonight? You swore you weren't going to bail on me again," the woman said.

"Get lost, Dina. I'll call you later," he growled.

"You decided just like that you want a younger one?"

"Don't be sick; this is my daughter," he said.

Josie turned tight, throwing her arm down, yanking it from his stronghold.

"Yeah, he likes them young," she said. Tears running down her face, her breath heaving one gulp at a time. "He likes them young and stupid and scared. But I'm not scared of him." She took three big steps backward.

He lunged for her. "You are coming home with me." It was a statement, a matter of fact, not a threat, not a wish.

"What the hell is she talking about, Dave? You put your hands on this little girl?" The tall woman had her hands on her waist and jutted one hip out.

"He did a lot more than that. And I am never going anywhere with you again."

Josie turned to run down the sidewalk of pebbles and gaps, praying she wouldn't slip or stumble. Her head was achy and throbbing. She knew she couldn't go to Spinx now, even if she apologized, because her dad would see the house and that was more information than she ever wanted him to have on her. But as she moved from a pillar of light to a cloud of shadow, someone else had her by the shoulders. Large, soft hands, pressing, not hurting her.

"Josie, I got this."

Spinx had his backpack and was unzipping it. Josie stepped behind him as he pulled out a gun.

Her dad stepped into the light in front of them and stopped. Josie could see the woman walking away into the shadows on the next block.

"Go back to your hooker," Spinx said.

Josie's dad put his hands up and took a step back. "Whoa. I don't think we need that."

"I didn't ask you what you thought. I said get lost."

"Fine." He took another step backward. "But Josie needs to know what she's done to her mother. She's not eating; she's been crying uncontrollably. I'm probably going to have to take her to the psych hospital."

Josie's tongue went numb, and her hand flexed and then flexed harder. She couldn't speak.

"Yeah, I'm sure. Everyone's got a sob story." Spinx elbowed Josie, "Right? But we don't want to hear it. Just get lost."

Her dad took another step backward. "I know where you're at now. You owe your mother an explanation."

Josie mumbled a reply, something that was bubbling up from deep in her shoes, popping in her mouth.

"What's that, baby girl? You say you want me to shoot him?"

Josie's dad froze, his hands still up, his foot mid step.

"No," she said. "She told me I was sick. And jealous of her. That I needed therapy. She said I was just jealous of her. That's why I said those things. She screamed at me. She accused me..." the last words wouldn't come. She choked on them. They had their hands wrapped around her neck, a phantom squeezing.

She reached for the gun, and Spinx gave it to her.

"Hang on," her dad said, his hands shaking, his face twisted as if he actually hurt, too. "I think we all need to get a little outside help. Don't you, Josie? Don't you think we should all get help together? I'm sure you didn't mean the things you told her, and I'm sure she misunderstood."

"What about you?" Josie didn't wait for him to answer. She had never held a gun before. It felt heavier than she expected, but also solid. It matched how she was feeling inside, heavy, dangerous. She pulled the trigger, a resounding crack tore the night open, and the bullet ricocheted off the sidewalk at her dad's feet.

"Shit, girl!" Spinx grabbed the gun. "I didn't think you'd really shoot him."

Josie got off one more shot before Spinx pushed her away. It was lost to the night just like the first, but her father was running away from them now.

"We gotta get out of here. Cops going to be looking us up. Come on."

Spinx shoved the gun back in his bag and steered her down an alley between houses.

"She thought it was my idea, Spinx. She thought I..."

"Yeah, I know. But I don't need to hear it. Remember? You don't need mine either. We're both screwed up. That's all. And neither of us want to be in jail tomorrow morning."

Josie wiped her face on her shoulder and nodded, even though she knew he couldn't see her.

After a few blocks, Spinx turned into the alcove of a large, brick building. A concrete platform lay in front of them, spread out under an eve, waiting to receive trucks the next day. Spinx hopped on top of it and reached down to give Josie a hand up. She sat next to him, her hands cradling her face, elbows on knees.

The hot night settled in around them as their breathing slowed and their hearts slipped into stable rhythms.

"Spinx," Josie said.

"Yeah?" He whispered back.

"Can we call your mom tomorrow?"

"Yep. That's the plan."

"Spinx?" she asked.

"Yeah?"

"If I told you my story, would you believe me?"

"I already do."

Josie pulled the gun back out of Spinx's bag and wiped it off on her t-shirt, then she hopped back off the platform and dropped it into the open sewer grate at her feet. Her hand, now empty, was shaking.

Aaron Max Jensen

UNPARDONABLE SIN

The snake's rattle shook violently beneath Joyce's porch. Her hand tightened around the handle of the heavy picnic basket as she said a prayer to the God of her father. She asked the Holy Ghost to protect and keep her, to safeguard and bless this best of all days. When her skin began to feel warm, Joyce knew she'd be safe from the serpent below. The Holy Ghost would remove all threats and obstructions to her plans. He'd said as much in one of her dreams, but only when she pressed Him.

She was having lunch at the pond today with Helen Waters, an affair she'd planned for weeks, with an eye to cement her position as Helen's best friend before school started end of summer. Last year she was saddled with stuttering Eleanor Hembree as her desk-mate. The other girls paired off into crooked combinations first thing, leaving Joyce to an entire year of hiccupping through the reader. She didn't know what she might have to do to poor Eleanor if forced to endure it again.

Helen's speech was like pouring heavy cream, and Joyce wanted badly to hear silk instead of old Eleanor. When Helen's family moved to Liberty Falls in June, Joyce made a point of laying her claim, cultivating her harvest. She'd done a good job, too, 'cause they were swell friends now. Today's picnic was the spit to seal the deal.

Joyce scrimped and hustled all summer to pay for the picnic. She found pennies in the gutters on Walter Bozeman Boulevard and the lot behind Gillman's bar where the men fought on Fridays. A nickel pressed in clay under the rust-eaten head cap of an ancient still off Sweetwater Creek. But most of the fare was funded by hard labor: doing odd jobs and yard chores, minding children for the rich families near town. The fruits of calculation hung heavy on her arm. The white woven wicker held ham and cheese sandwiches, with sliced yellow apples, a battered box of Goobers, an arm of deer jerky, and peaches from the trees skirting the Hembree property.

Joyce stepped toward the porch stairs, which led down to the clotheslines where Papa's overalls hung limp and still. The clatter of the serpent's warning became louder. She stepped back. Typically snakes steered clear of the area around the ailing clapboard house. Joyce came across them on the County Road mostly, warming their scaly bodies on the gravel in the mornings. She'd killed her share, but never a shaker.

She set the basket near the door to the kitchen and followed the porch around front to cross into the yard. She could no longer hear the rattle, but the vibrant thrum still reverberated in her bones. Like being filled up with the Holy Ghost.

Papa had been filled with the Holy Ghost when he decided to do something about little Ronnie—who was afraid to go on the porch after their dog, Harry Truman, was killed by a rattler—tormenting the boy with a tin can and dry beans: shaking and shaking.

Her papa brought the Holy Ghost back home with him after the Fascists exploded a fair portion of his leg, and the spirit still burned from him even now, years after the fevers of war subsided. It was his duty as their patriarch to exorcise the demons of

cowardice possessing the child. Joyce would've been happy to
see him express his fatherhood in simpler ways—earning a
wage, perhaps—but Papa felt folks' souls were in greater need
of tending than sinful mortal bodies.

Joyce approached the line of fat, towering pines at the far
edge of the clearing, where the blackberry bushes were thick and
tempting. It reeked of honeysuckle and yesterday's rain. The
comfort of the woods pushed the threat of snakes away from her
thoughts, and the single-minded determination to have a successful picnic crept back in.

The creek was narrow and lazy. Near the edge, four red-
capped glass bottlenecks jutted from the cool water. Joyce
plucked the soda bottles from the creek and shook the wet away.
She could have kept the Coca-Colas in the icebox but had worried Papa might take holy umbrage with the extravagance of
Joyce and Helen enjoying two soda pops each.

The bottles tinkled as she hurried back to the house. She
hoped to arrive at the pond before Helen to set up. As the kitch-
en door on the side of the house came into view, Joyce stopped
in her tracks.

The picnic basket was gone.

Joyce knew Papa took the basket. Her mother and brother
would be gone till evening, off at Mrs. Marlowe's—there was
no one else who could have. She rushed into the house and
through the kitchen.

Sweet, heavy pipe smoke hit her hard as she pushed through
the screen door onto the back porch. Papa kept an old Eagle
peach crate next to the creaky wooden chair where he spent his
days and nights. The crate was turned up on its side to form a
makeshift table, where Papa could keep a tin cup of chicory and
his tobacco box within reach. Her picnic basket sat atop the
crate, lid turned toward the hot blue sky. Papa sat upon his splin-

tered throne, holding a ham sandwich in his tobacco-stained hand.

"Don't you eat that," she cried out.

Papa stared at her with a look that might have been confusion, and Joyce felt a sliver of hope slide into her panic. Perhaps it was a simple misunderstanding after all. Then his eyes shifted and slithered the way they always did when the Holy Ghost came upon him fierce.

"Vile, unclean child. Hold your tongue, lest ye choke upon the vomit of your shameful dishonor." Each word hit Joyce with the crushing impact of a timber truck set upon saving her soul in a collision of gore and grace.

She cast her eyes to the deck boards and kept her mouth shut. There was no going against Papa. His eyes were like pale forest moss. "Confess yourself."

"Forgive me, Father, for sinning against you."

"I said *confess.*"

The acid in his voice made her shiver. "Forgive me, Father, for dishonoring you and hollering at you."

Papa leaned forward, elbows across his knees. "Very good then. Two lashes at supper, and the Lord be with you." He raised the sandwich to his lips and stopped short, teasing.

"Now," he said, gesturing to her basket, "Tell me about the thievery you've done here."

"But I didn't steal nothing, Papa. I bought it all myself, and the man with the mustache at the market will say so if you ask him. It's for my picnic."

Papa stood suddenly, as if thrust up and forward by some invisible hand. There was none of the shaky weakness she was accustomed to seeing in his posture.

He leaned down to grasp his cane, sliding a hand down the shaft, wielding it like a whipping switch. He strode forward in a fire of spirit: the risen Lord wearing Papa like a suit to church.

He stepped behind her; the sensation of his menace prickled the back of her neck.

"Papa," she said. "Please. I ain't done nothing bad."

Joyce cried out as the sting of the blow snaked across her shoulder blades. She fell forward onto one knee. A soda slipped from her grip, thumping on the deck boards and rolling away.

"Lying lips are an abomination to the Lord, but those who deal truly are His delight."

She set the bottles on the floor beside the screen door and pushed herself up to face him. "I ain't lying, Papa." Her face was flushed, wet with tears and sticky sweat.

"Am I the blind man? That you think I cannot see?"

"I earned that money," she told him, "And what I didn't get from working, I found fair and square."

"*Thievery*," he said. "It's not for you to seek silver in the streets. It is for you to overcome temptation. But you *take*." He threw her ham sandwich to the floor of the porch.

"But Papa—"

Papa swung the cane down smart, slamming its crooked head into the sandwich many times over, obliterating it in explosions of swine and rye.

Joyce blubbered like a baby would. He kicked the debris of her sandwich to the dust, bad leg working so well one might wonder why Papa couldn't channel the Holy Ghost long enough to get through a shift at the mill. He held the cane at his side, tensed to strike. "Now give me them Co' Colas, you lazy little thief."

She moved to comply, but the sting of his accusation stirred a fury of injustice in her heart. She took a Coke bottle in her hand, held it upside down by the cold dripping neck.

"You're calling me lazy? All *you've* ever done is sit on the durn porch. You say you can't work, on account of your dumb leg, but it works just fine when—"

He charged toward her. If she'd had time to think of what to do, Joyce might have reacted differently—but it was too fast, and when things happen fast, sometimes you just do a thing. She drew her arm back and threw the bottle square into Papa's pale face. It struck him above his bloodshot left eye.

Her father stumbled to the side, dropping the cane, and pressed his hands to his head. "*Demon*," he said.

Joyce darted past her papa and ran for it. The soles of her shoes beat like hammers upon the weathered deck boards. She cut the corner and followed the porch around the side of the house, heading for the yard.

As she approached the steps, Joyce remembered the snake lurking beneath, and leapt over the stairs. She hid behind the drying laundry, peering at the porch between the legs of Papa's dangling britches.

He turned the corner of the house a moment later, fevered animal tracking quarry, both imaginary and corporeal, in a delirium of rage. There was a dark knot raising his brow. Papa ran toward the stairs.

A cry of warning rose in Joyce's throat and then died. She might have done something to draw him away from the danger coiled in the dark. But the truth of the Holy Ghost, and her dealings with Him in times past, assured her this was nonsense: Papa was singularly focused in his ungodly wrath, and the Holy Ghost was never keen on listening so much. He wouldn't have stopped. He'd have simply known where she was.

Papa was moving fast when he reached the steps. He missed the top stair in the frenzy; his right foot hit the second at an odd ugly angle, and the shrapnel-ridden leg finally gave way. His impact traveled the heavy humid air to shiver Joyce's core, a thunderclap of flesh and bone.

Papa writhed and groaned. She couldn't see the first bite, but the way he shrieked and jerked told the tale. Papa struck out at the snake with his cane, hitting the serpent solidly, and it attacked again. A second rattler emerged and entered the fray.

Papa swung the cane in storm of panicked cries, and the diamondbacks bit his arms and legs over and over. Joyce watched in wonder and horror. After taking far too many bites, Papa stopped trying to fight them off and began to crawl away. His eyes met hers, yellowed with weakness and truly revealed.

"Help me," Papa said. "Gotta get help."

He wheezed with every breath, limbs swelling and bruising. Tiny punctures covered him: a pox of snakebites weeping blood and pus and venom into the dust.

Joyce knew snakebites, even from the Eastern Diamondback, wouldn't usually kill a grown man, so long as he got treated fast enough and didn't get an infection. Papa would survive if she acted fast.

"Please," he begged, quieter now.

It wouldn't be a fast death. Mama and Ronnie wouldn't be home from Mrs. Marlowe's till after dark. Given how bad Papa looked, Joyce didn't think he had more than a few hours at best. Mama and the undertaker would want to know why she didn't try to help him, if he were to die. Surely saving her father was what God wanted; what the Holy Ghost wanted.

The snakes retreated victorious.

Papa was unconscious: a battered revenant, restless and defeated beneath lye-tinged banners of underwear and table linen. Joyce knelt and prayed. If God loved her, then let Him fill her with the spirit. Let Him show her the way. God wouldn't say nothing at first, so she pressed Him harder.

Somewhere amidst the fear and guilt, the Holy Ghost found her heart and carried it through the veil. Her skin felt warm, and knew she would be safe.

She went to her father's dying shell and kissed his blackened cheek.

"I forgive you, Papa," she said. "And by the merciful power of the Holy Ghost, absolve you of all worldly trespass, that you might know the glory of heaven."

She waited for something to happen and heard some birds whistling off in the woods. The Holy Ghost urging her forward, Joyce fetched her basket and Coca-Colas from the back porch and headed down the twisting gravel road toward the pond.

Charlie Hughes

IT HIDES

For Dillon McCafferty, it started with a piece of paper. An innocent note tucked into an envelope by a local GP and sent to him, first class, on Monday 22 October, 2017. The envelope lay unopened on his doormat for three days.

This omission was not the result of overwork or ill health or a family emergency, but a more welcome distraction. Dillon had met Gina.

Aged thirty-nine, he'd started to think he had some fatal flaw, something rotten, which precluded the content, long-term relationships which came so easily to his friends. He might even have confronted it on a clinical level had the prospect of self-referral not filled him with a cold dread.

He kept going, until he met Gina.

She arrived late to the party. The stupid, annoying party which he'd done everything to avoid because he knew it would be filled with Tom's friends from work: over-serious bores working in third sector "developmental aid." Gina had walked into the room, took him by the arm and led him away from a tedious conversation about fishery policy in West Africa.

"Tom told me to rescue you from the conscience police," she

said and smiled.

He slept at Gina's that night and didn't leave for three days. Cancelling all his appointments, ignoring his phone, Dillon lost himself in her. When he finally left for home on Wednesday morning, he floated across South London in an adolescent daze, recalling her mischievous smile and the weight of her slender arm resting on his chest.

Arriving home, he took the unopened mail upstairs to his office.

The mechanics of work snapped him back to reality. A bill, a letter from his father, a credit card offer and an envelope with his name and address scribbled in blue biro.

Inside were the printed details of a patient, nine years old. It included a hastily handwritten note from Dr. Oliver Hinckley.

Strange one this, Dillon. The boy is obsessed with numbers. Can't talk about anything else and becomes angry when his parents (or I) try to move on to other matters. Speak to his mother, will you? Tell them you'll see him.

The friendly, personal tone of the doctor's note felt askew. Hinckley was usually such a cold fish.

Via email, he booked an appointment with the parents. He liked to put space between this initial session and seeing the child for the first time.

The parents arrived the following day. Stephen Willow, hair unkempt, wore a jacket over blue jeans. His thick beard did not suit his face. Alison Willow gave Dillon a strained smile when they met at the door. She hustled her husband up the stairs when he paused in the hallway.

They sat on the couch, space between them, and waited in silence as Dillon collected his notepad and settled opposite.

"So, how can I help?" he said.

The husband let out a sigh. "Our son needs help, not us."

Alison Willow reached across her husband, tilting her head in silent apology.

"Stephen is struggling to process this. It's put us under a lot of strain."

"Not a problem. In your own time, just give me some background."

"Ben. Our boy." She shifted in her seat. "He's always been such a sprightly thing. Happy and clever and funny. Nothing fazed him. But in the last two weeks he's become so, so morose."

"Morose? Disengaged?"

"Kind of. He goes to school, he plays, a bit. But he seems so unhappy. His teacher says he's stopped contributing to classes. When I speak to him, I get one word answers."

"Has there been anything that might've upset him?"

The husband answered, a little too quickly. "No. Everything is just the same."

Alison Willow spoke softly, soothingly. "I don't think it's anything like that. We moved house a year ago, but not far, and he likes the new place."

Dillon shifted into more sensitive territory. "And your relationship? Any major arguments or problems?"

Mr. Willow rocked back in his seat, pursed his lips and looked up at the ceiling. Dillon scribbled in his notepad.

Mrs. Willow answered. "Nothing. Nothing new." She was flustered. "Nothing that would explain this."

He could have pushed further, but Dillon felt sorry for Alison Willow. Interrogating would only confirm his first impression: The relationship was on the edge, and they didn't know what to do. They'd probably muddled along for years, without ever really being tested. Now here they were, worried sick about their little boy and turning on each other.

Dillon let the silence linger, curious to see how they would fill it.

The father blurted out. "He won't stop counting. Sometimes aloud, sometimes under his breath. He counts all the time. It's weird."

Dillon nodded. "Kids often count. Predictable structures can be comforting."

"He's not comforting himself. If you heard it, you'd know what I mean."

"Really?"

Stephen Willow replied. "It's difficult to explain. I can play it to you if you like."

Alison Willow screwed up her face and turned to her husband. "What?"

The father looked at Dillon, not her. "I recorded it. Last week when I sat outside his room, waiting for him to go to sleep."

"You recorded our son, having a...an episode?" She shook her head.

"It wasn't an episode. I just wanted to capture it. For the doc."

Dillon interjected. "Okay. Play it."

Mr. Willow took his phone out of his pocket, touched the screen, then placed it on the coffee table.

There was a rustling sound, a muffled cough, then the sound of a child's voice. It was lilting, painfully innocent. The sound of an infant relaxing into sleep.

"Four, five, six, seven." He stopped. "Eight, nine...Not there. Not tonight." Behind the tired voice, a note of distress had been introduced. He kept on. "Eleven, twelve, thirteen. Hmmmm. I don't think it's there."

Then Stephen Willow's voice. "Ben, buddy, time for sleep now, mate."

"Fourteen, fifteen, sixteen, seventeen, eighteen, nineteen, twenty. I'm only checking, Dad. Sometimes I need to check."

"Go to sleep now, buddy."

"Twenty one, twenty two." Silence.

In Dillon's office, Mr. Willow raised his finger, indicating more to come.

A full minute passed with nothing but empty background noise. Then the child's voice came back, high pitched, shrieking. "Go away. I don't want it." The boy started to cry. Softly at first, then with an intensity Dillon would not have believed possible from a nine year old.

On the recording, Mr. Willow said, "Hey mate, what happened?" There was more rustling. The recording ended.

Things moved quickly. A week after they'd first met, Gina moved in with Dillon. He carried her boxes from the van and placed them in various rooms at her direction.

Dillon astounded himself. Ordinarily, he'd have balked at anyone tampering with his carefully ordered home and workplace. He hardly ever had guests, aside from his patients. Yet here he was, inviting Gina in to tip the whole thing upside down.

He watched her place an ornament above the fireplace, a weighty rendering of a moggy cat, sleeping on a cushion. He should have hated it, the thing itself and the fact someone else placed it in his living room, but he didn't. These things were hers. They made her happy and now they made him happy.

"It's beautiful," he said, his eyebrow raised, a smile at the corner of his lips.

She grimaced in mock fury. "You'll learn to love it."

Gina moved closer, taking his hips in her hands. She pulled him close and laughed, avoiding his attempt at a kiss.

"Uh, uh. Say you love Boris the Cat, or there'll be none of that for you."

"I luuurve it!"

They kissed until she pushed him onto the sofa. She walked over to the bay windows. It was 2 PM with bright sunshine pouring in. Gina closed the curtains and turned back to Dillon.

"Show me," she said.

Dillon met Ben Willow in his own home. It was a tactic he'd used previously to ensure clients were relaxed and comfortable.

His mother led him into the living room, where toys and games littered the floor. Superman models, a full sized Millennium Falcon, a huge box of Lego. Dillon sat down on the sofa, taking in the high ceilings, sturdy fitted bookshelves and family photographs.

In one, he saw a smiling boy with red hair, no older than seven, sticking out his tongue at the camera.

"Ben. Come down. Dr. McCafferty is here to see you."

The child walked into the room with his shoulders slumped and his eyes on the floor. He was pale and thin.

"Hello, Ben."

The boy looked up, made eye contact and looked down again. Dillon noticed his mouth moving, his head nodding to a rhythm. Counting.

Dillon stood and walked over to a coffee table in the corner of the room. Resting on it was a small pile of paper. On top was a picture, drawn in crayon, of a superhero battling it out with flying monsters. The hero, in red, had a yellow ball in the centre of his chest and rockets firing from his arms.

He held it up to the boy. "Does Spider-Man win?"

Ben looked again and stopped the counting. "It's Iron Man, not Spider-Man."

"Iron Man? Iron Man?" He pulled a comical, bemused face. "The one who goes 'round ironing everyone flat? Yeah, I know him. Very neat shirts." Dillon smiled.

Despite himself, the boy smiled back. "You're silly."

"A little. Do you know who I am?"

"Mum said you were going to find out why I'm sad."

"Maybe." He approached the boy with mock formality and offered his hand. "Dillon McCafferty. At your service."

The boy held out his small hand and shook Dillon's middle two fingers.

They sat together on the sofa, their feet almost touching.

"So, I hear all this started a couple of months ago. One minute you were fine, the next you weren't."

The kid looked at him and shrugged.

"You know, I speak to lots of boys and girls who have problems. They're all different, so many things to be worried about, I suppose." He held out his palms. "But there's one thing that's always the same. Do you know what that is, Ben?"

Ben shook his head, eyes wide with expectation.

"The boy or girl never wants to tell me what is wrong. But as soon as they do, things start to get better."

Ben said, "Always?"

"Always." Dillon said it, then realised it was true. "So, let's keep this simple, shall we? Why are you sad?"

"I shouldn't tell. I don't want to."

"If something made me sad, I'd want to talk about it."

The boy paused to consider this. "But what if telling could hurt people? Would you want to tell then?"

"I'd still want to tell someone. Maybe someone who couldn't be hurt."

"That doesn't work." The boy's demeanour changed in an instant, as if a terrible thought had just crossed his mind. The silent, rhythmic movements of his lips started up again.

"Hey. Why doesn't it work?"

"I can't tell someone it doesn't hurt."

"Why?"

"Because this will hurt everybody."

Dillon sat back, involuntarily moving away from the child.

There was no hint of insincerity in the boy's face.

Dillon changed tack. "You've had a fright, haven't you?" The kid's eyes moved to the top left. Memory retrieval.

"What about the counting? Does counting the numbers make you feel better?"

"Sort of. I'm just checking them."

"Checking what?"

Ben pursed his lips but said nothing.

"Has someone done something, which you didn't like? Done something to you?"

The boy shook his head.

"Have you done something you feel bad about? An accident, maybe."

"No. I've been good."

"Sure. I know you have. So what is it?"

"I can tell you a bit, I suppose. But if I do, will you promise not to say anything to Mum and Dad? They might be angry."

Dillon should not have made any such promise, but he needed to break through this, and he had only one way of doing it.

"I promise," he said.

"I found a way up, and I wasn't supposed to go up there."

"Up where?"

"To the attic."

"What's wrong?" Gina said. She lay beside him on the bed, her hand on his shoulder.

"Wrong?"

"You've gone quiet. You're normally such a talker, afterwards."

"I hadn't realised," he said, turning over to face her. He smiled. "I guess. Work issue. I don't want to bore you."

"You won't bore me."

"I'm not supposed to, y'know. Confidentiality."

Surprising him, she moved her hand down his body and grabbed. "Tell me, or I'll take them off." Her smile was wicked.

"Oh my god. Glenn Close, already?"

She gave a yelp of offence, but moved herself on top of him, their noses almost touching.

"Tell me. I want to know."

He couldn't refuse. "This kid who was referred to me. Nine years old, smart as a button, skittish parents, but nothing out of the ordinary. A few weeks ago, he goes into a depression. I met him for the first time today. Nice kid. Needs help, but he won't talk to me, won't open up."

"You can't get inside, hey?"

Dillon was silent for a moment. "There's this other thing. He counts. It's the strangest..."

She considered this. "Have you seen this before?"

"Not like this. I can hear him doing it under his breath, nodding his head to a rhythm. Whatever reason he has for doing it, the strain is telling. Poor thing doesn't know how to stop."

"He didn't explain?"

"He said one thing that didn't make much sense. He said he'd found something in the attic, and I wasn't to tell his parents about it."

"Have you told them?"

"Not yet. I want more time with him before I report back."

"So, what did he find?"

"He won't tell me. Says I have to see it for myself."

"And when will you do that?"

"I wasn't planning to. I don't usually sneak around my clients' homes."

"Not even if they ask you to?"

Dillon was about to say Ben's parents hadn't asked him to, then he stopped himself.

Arranging to be in the house, alone with Ben, did not prove difficult. Alison Willow understood her son might open up more if they were given some time alone.

She had her coat in hand when they met at the door. She kissed her son on the head and left them to it. As the door shut, Ben shuffled into the living room. Dillon followed.

"We had a deal, didn't we? I haven't said a word about the attic. So, shall we take a look?"

Ben looked up and smirked. There was something different in his expression that Dillon did not like. The boy held himself upright, more confidently. Ordinarily this kind of change would be welcome, but Dillon was suspicious of the speed this was happening.

"You really want to?"

Dillon nodded.

Ben smirked, as if Dillon had cracked a joke. The expression was all wrong for a child's face. As quickly as it appeared, it was gone.

"Sure. You can see it."

He followed the boy up three flights of stairs. When they reached the final landing, to the right, was a closed door. Ben opened it and stood against the wall, letting Dillon go ahead.

Inside, he found a room containing a cheap desk, some box files resting on top and a stack of plastic chairs. The room smelled musty, neglected. Old, yellowed net curtains hung over the window. A room untouched by the Willows' renovations.

"It's in there. At the top." Ben pointed to a door at the back of the room.

Dillon went over to the walk-in cupboard. It was dark inside, with an empty clothes rail at the back. Curiously, the walls were unplastered, exposing the naked brickwork. He looked up for an attic entrance and saw only a plain white ceiling.

He turned back to the boy. "Ben, this is just an empty cupboard. There's no ladder, no entrance."

"You have to use the blocks to climb up, then push the ceiling with your hand."

When Dillon turned back he spotted five thin blocks of wood nailed into the brick, forming a rudimentary step-ladder. He looked again at the ceiling and frowned.

He shifted up onto the first step, steadying himself by holding the door frame.

Once balanced, Dillon shifted upwards. When he was within touching distance of the ceiling, he reached out, and to his surprise, it gave. He pushed again and the panel moved, revealing a large black hole above him.

He hooked his hand onto the ridge and pulled himself up. As he rose into the cold air of the attic, a new smell hit home. An acrid mix of decay and ammonia. Years before, Dillon had visited care homes, looking for a place for his father. In the worst of them, this scent had lingered in the background. Here, it was front and centre.

He clambered into the attic, covering his nose and mouth with a hand.

It was dark, almost pitch black. The only light came from the edges of a boarded window at the far end of the attic. Dillon took his phone out of his pocket and turned on the light.

Large white sheets of paper covered the walls. Each one nailed down against the wooden studs. The top third slanted with the pitch of the roof. He stepped closer. They were covered with tiny, uniform handwriting. Not words, but equations—numbers and symbols crammed together in lines half-a-centimetre tall.

Dillon began to count the lines. He reached fifty when he stopped, no more than a tenth of the way down this first page. Five hundred lines of equations per page. Swinging the light around the room, he counted sheets. Fifteen in all.

The tiny black writing was impeccably neat. Not a single mark out of place, not a single correction made. He stood in the corner, in front of what, he supposed, was the first page of this work. Dillon moved to the right and inspected the next page: the same, more equations.

He walked down the line of sheets, scanning them for anything other than numbers and mathematical symbols. Occasionally there would be a word: "Therefore," "Phase two," "If false."

Nearing the final sheet, he noticed a small desk underneath the boarded window. A wooden chair resting beside it, toppled on its side.

Next to the desk were two buckets, surely the source of the smell. Somebody had been up here for long periods. Pissing and shitting had not been allowed to interrupt their work.

On the desk was a book, bound in rough brown leather, with a locking mechanism on the cover. The lock had been forced, clumsily, the catch ripped from the binding and hanging by a thread. Dillon picked up the chair and sat at the desk. Still holding one hand over his mouth, he opened the book. Inside he found the same uniform handwriting. Page after page of calculation.

When Dillon's fingers brushed the edge of the final page, he noticed something different. It was thicker, heavier than the rest. Opening the book out flat on the table, he saw the tiny writing had abruptly ended on the second to last page with the words "is TRUE."

On the page opposite, the last in the book, a piece of thick card had been attached, taped down the length of its left edge. It was a page on a page. The kind of covering flap you might find in a children's book. In the centre of the card, written in the same hand, were two words, in block capitals:

THE UNIVERSAL

Dillon placed his hand on the card and began to pull it back. As his hand touched the card, a curious nausea gripped him, and his hands started to shake.

He went back to the book and sat, looking at the card. He could easily have just reached out his hand and revealed what was behind it. But he did not.

He closed the book and gathered it under his arm. He scrambled down the opening, not wanting to spend another moment in the attic. Still in the cupboard, he shoved the book down the back of his trousers.

When he left the box room, he found Ben sitting on the landing, waiting. He passed the boy.

"Did you see it?" Ben asked, eyes wide, manic.

Before Dillon could answer, they were interrupted.

"Hello?" Alison Willow stood on the stairs, watching them. "What are you two doing?"

Dillon, flustered, gave the only excuse he could muster.

"Ben, err, Ben just wanted to show me some of the house. Didn't you, Ben?"

The child nodded.

She seemed unconvinced. "Okay. Shall we have a cup of tea? In the kitchen?"

Dillon rallied. By the time he'd made promises of a full assessment soon and reassured Mrs. Willow, he'd spent another half an hour in the house. All the while, acutely aware of the book hidden behind his back.

Eventually, he shifted the conversation away from Ben. "Your house is spectacular. I'm very jealous."

"Thank you." She seemed pleased.

"You own it?"

"Oh no. We couldn't afford it on our wages. I'm a librarian, and Stephen is an academic. He gets the house with his job. Even the improvements are paid for by the University."

"University?"

"UCL."

"So, before you lived here, there was someone else? Another academic?"

"That's right." She seemed confused. "Why do you ask?"

"No reason. Just curious."

He escaped the house and hurried to his car, tossing the book onto the back seat.

He drove away. Involuntarily and unaware, he began to count under his breath.

Professor George Seaton Weyl.

Dillon's friend, Tom, had found the name for him on an old electoral roll.

With some assistance from Google, he researched the rest for himself. An American mathematician who'd graduated from his West Virginia high school three years ahead of schedule, he'd breezed through MIT before he was nineteen. A Ph.D. at Cambridge brought him to the UK. His theses on Euclidean Geometry generated considerable academic acclaim. By the time he arrived at UCL, Weyl was being touted as the next big thing in mathematics. Then he disappeared off the map. No more journals pieces, no more blogs and no more posts on social media.

Three years later, he killed himself.

The only news story served up by Google came from the *South London Press*. The brief article identified Weyl as a mathematician who'd died in a suspected suicide. It added that his wife and children had moved back to America some months before. No note had been left. A passing neighbour spotted the body. Professor Weyl had not closed the living room curtains before placing the noose around his neck.

It took several phone calls before Dillon eventually tracked down a former colleague of Weyl's, a Ph.D. student named Selma Martinez. The next day he met her in a coffee shop on the Strand.

"So, tell me again. Why are you so interested in George?"

"I'm doing research for a psychology journal. Looking for links between obsessive behaviour and suicide."

She sat back, arms crossed. Dillon continued, "Look, if you're not comfortable doing this…?"

Martinez shrugged. "I'm sorry. I shouldn't be suspicious. It's not like any of this can hurt poor George now."

"You knew him well?"

"As well as anybody. He was a difficult guy to get close to. But everybody wanted to, at first. He was brilliant. His work blew us all away. George could have been famous."

"What do you think drove him to suicide?"

"Work. Some people said it was his wife and kids going back to the States. That was bull. They left because he'd stopped caring about them. For the six months before he died, George was a total mess. Didn't turn up for his lectures, stopped eating properly, stopped washing. He was like the crazy guy around campus. In the last two weeks, he just holed up in his house."

"Was he working on something?"

"Supposedly, although he wouldn't tell anybody about it. He'd let himself go so much by then. He would come into the office, use the library, retreat into his office and lock the door. He wouldn't speak to anyone after a while, not even me."

"What about 'The universal'? Does that mean anything to you?"

Martinez put her coffee down and leant forward in her seat. "How do you know about that?"

"I've spoken to some of his other associates." He took a chance. "They said he kept talking about it. That he was obsessed."

She nodded. "I assumed that might be part of it. Some of the others, in the faculty, they laughed about it behind his back. He'd written a couple of pieces. Not in the usual journals, you understand. Thought pieces on his blog. A theory. No calculations, no hard maths."

"So, what was the theory?"

"An odd idea. No offence, but it's a little difficult to explain."

"Could you try?"

Selma frowned and drew in her breath. Dillon knew she was on the verge of packing it all in, getting up and leaving.

"Please," he said. "From one researcher to another. It would really help me with my work."

Martinez held up her hands "Okay. Okay." A deep breath. "Where to start? Quantum Theory. Quantum Mechanics. You've heard of that?"

Dillon knew the phrase. "Something about atoms, maybe?" He nodded.

She laughed. "Matter and energy on the atomic and subatomic level. How they behave and the laws of physics which govern them."

Martinez stirred her coffee and continued, "About a hundred years ago, the scientific community discovered that, at that level, particles were not playing by the rules. Neutrons, electrons. The principles of classical physics break down. The more precisely you measure one property of a particle, the more flawed the measurement of another property becomes."

"I don't get it."

"Simultaneous measurement of two values, say, the position and momentum of a subatomic particle. It becomes impossible. Unlike larger matter, measuring these values at the same time will always, always, be wrong. Totally counter intuitive, I know. But that's what happens."

"So, for this very, very small matter, we can't know anything?"

"Kind of. The maths doesn't work at that level, so theory fills the gap. Heisenberg came up with the 'uncertainty principle,' which says 'we simply cannot measure these things and get an answer. The act of measurement itself dissolves knowledge of an objective reality.' Pretty bleak, hey?"

Before Dillon could respond, she continued.

"Then you have the many worlds theory, the one Hawking prefers. Every event occurs in a separate, alternate reality. Infinite realities to accommodate every outcome of every event."

"Mind-bending."

"True. But if you'd told someone in 1850 about general relativity, they'd have said the same thing."

"So Weyl came up with his own theory?"

"At first, but then it became…more. After a while he believed he could solve it. Not just theory. The whole thing."

Dillon shook his head. "How?"

"By making the maths work. Making it work in a way nobody had ever considered before."

"Like a new formula?"

"A new number."

Dillon considered this for a moment. "A number? Like pi? To make it all add up?

"No. More radical. That's why he got laughed out of town. A new number. A number that moves. A number that hides."

It was coming together, and Dillon didn't like it.

He decided to lay it all on the line for the parents, to tell them everything he knew.

When Selma Martinez left him in the coffee shop, he picked up his mobile phone and called their home.

He was about to hang up, when the phone was answered.

"Hello, Mrs. Willow?"

Nothing.

"Mr. Willow?"

Then he heard it. The low hum of a child counting under his breath.

"Hello." It was the boy, but his voice sounded older, tired. "You stole the book." There was a strange mixture of confusion and menace.

"Ben, you okay? You don't sound okay."

"You stole the book." Louder now, more aggressive.

"Ben. Can I speak to your mum or dad?"

"Shut up!" Ben screamed. Dillon held his breath for a moment, shocked by the child's ferocity.

"Tell me. You stole the book, didn't you?"

"I didn't steal it, Ben. I took it away because I thought it might, somehow, be hurting you."

The child's voice was so adult, so furious. "You know what it is, don't you?"

"There's something odd happening Ben…something wrong. I don't want anyone to get hurt."

"I need the book. Holding it, touching it. It made things okay. It's special. It's mine."

"Ben, neither you or I can explain this." Dillon could hear the note of panic in his own voice. "It's time to speak to your parents about this."

"Are you going to give it back?"

"I didn't look at the last page, you know. I just touched it with my hand. But you did, didn't you? You saw it."

The boy sniffed. "Some. It still wants me though. In my head, all the time, I can see the number." With that, the boy seemed to break a little.

"Look. It's okay. I can help. Put your mum on the phone."

"I can't." Ben laughed, the menace returned. A dirty, high-pitched cackle.

"Why not?"

"Daddy said I needed to stop. He got angry and said I was a bad boy."

Cold dread crept into Dillon's gut.

"Mummy was crying and Daddy was shouting. I had to stop them."

"What did you do, Ben?"

"They aren't shouting anymore."

"My God. What have you done?"

The boy took his time, counting to himself again. When he got down from twenty-seven to twelve, he spoke again. "I made the shape. On paper. I made the number, and I showed it to them."

"And what happened? What happened, Ben?"

"Now they're counting."

Dillon knew the boy was smiling. Ben hung up the phone.

Running to his car, Dillon called for an ambulance on his mobile and sent it to the Willow's address.

He tried not to drive too fast, but it was hard. The boy had done something terrible, and Dillon knew it was his own fault. He should have told the parents. Instead, he'd played detective, and now people were getting hurt, maybe worse.

When he got to the Willow's road, he slung the car onto the pavement, jumped out and ran towards the house.

As soon as he saw the leg, he slowed his pace.

A green-trousered leg with a black shoe protruded from the gateway of the Willow's home. It was twitching. Beyond, parked a little farther down the road, was an ambulance.

Getting closer, he saw the leg belonged to a woman, a paramedic. She sat on the concrete path, her back against the open gate, whispering to herself, a vacant look in her eyes. When she noticed Dillon standing over her, a queer smile crossed her lips, and she began to giggle like a child.

"It's in there," she said. "On the walls. We both saw it." She laughed to herself again, then pointed to the ambulance. "Geoff's done a funny thing."

Dillon said, "What the hell?" He walked away from the paramedic, towards the ambulance. Approaching, he could see the back doors were open.

He looked inside, stopped, bent over and began to puke, retching up acrid bile. When he was finished, he looked again.

Inside the ambulance, another paramedic sat on a trolley bed, slumped against the inside of the vehicle. His green uniform turned black from the blood. Red pools covered the floor of the vehicle. Both his wrists and his throat were cut with deep gouges. The man's eyes were still open, staring directly at Dillon.

When he turned away from the dead man's gaze, Dillon saw part of it, written in blood on the inside wall of the ambulance, a strange concave line at the base of a numeral.

It was in that instant that it came to Dillon, all of it. A realisation with almost physical weight.

He was the only one who knew not to look. The only one who knew that to do so would mean insanity and death.

He closed his eyes. For a second he feared he might have seen too much. The nausea he'd experienced in the attic, days before, washed over him again.

When he opened his eyes, he was scrambling along the floor, towards the house. He got to his feet and sprinted down the path, slamming the open door against the wall, smashing the glass. He reached the doorway to the living room and stopped.

In the same room George Weyl had hung himself in the year before, two more bodies swung gently above the ground. Mr. and Mrs. Willow had used belts for their nooses.

Behind them, on the wall, the same symbol was written over and over again.

Dillon turned away and ran.

When he got to his car, his mobile rang.

Without a greeting, a child's voice came on the line. "Where are you?"

"Ben. What have you done?"

"Are you at your house?" the boy asked.

"No. Ben, I just found your parents."

"They're not counting anymore, are they? They couldn't take

it." The child's disregard for his mother and father was chilling.

"Where are you, Ben?"

"I'm standing outside *your* house."

"No." Dillon experienced a thudding sensation in his gut.

"I can see your lady friend, inside. She might be lonely."

"Leave her alone. Do not go anywhere near her."

"Tell me where the book is, or I'll show her the number, too."

"It's in the drawer, under the stairs. I have a key. I'm bringing it with me."

"You need to hurry." The line went dead.

Ben drove with abandon, cars blaring their horns at him as he ran red lights, pedestrians screaming abuse as they dodged him. Afraid for his own sanity, Dillon counted. Up to one hundred, then back again.

As he drove, he called Gina's mobile, over and over. On the fifth attempt it was finally answered, but it wasn't her on the other end of the line.

"Leave us alone. We're having a chat." It was Ben. The line went dead.

Dillon screamed into the phone. "Leave her alone! Please, leave her…"

It was rush hour. No matter how recklessly he drove, it was taking too long.

In Camberwell, he got stuck at the traffic lights, checking on his phone every ten seconds. Panic had taken over. He ranted abuse at the cars blocking him.

That was when he noticed the man, out of the corner of his eye, on the green flanking the Walworth Road. The man, dressed in designer jeans and smart jacket, was walking a dog. He was no older than thirty-five and dressed like all the other upwardly-mobile professionals in the area. Smart, yet casual. Relaxed, prospering. But there was something wrong with him.

He meandered back and forth across the pathway, letting the dog lead him. A mother and son had to step onto the grass as he zigzagged in front of them. He paid no notice as the woman swore at him.

After a few more steps, he stopped and released the lead, then started towards the road.

He walked directly in front of Dillon's stationary car, looking down, deliberately placing one foot in front of the other.

When he reached the white line in the middle of the road, the man lifted his hand and looked at the screen of a mobile phone. It had been there the whole time, clutched in his left hand. He chuckled to himself and dropped it at his feet. There was a gravelly crack as it hit the road.

The oncoming traffic thinned, the lights about to change. The last vehicle through was a double decker.

The man stepped out in front of the bus, his arms stretched outwards, in repose. It hit him, hard, face on.

The driver had no chance to swerve or brake. There was a sickening thud on impact, propelling the man into the air, his neck snapping backwards, his arms and legs flailing.

As he landed on the side of the road, a woman screamed. People ran to him, trying to help. Dillon knew they were running towards a corpse.

The bus driver sat stock upright in his seat, eyes wide.

Dillon's gaze was drawn to the phone next to his car.

His breathing quickened, and he lost control, hyperventilating. He stretched over his steering wheel and tried to breathe.

Dillon could think only of the laptop, open on his living room table. A laptop with an Internet connection. A laptop Ben would be more than capable of using.

The number had been shared.

Dillon tried to focus on the road as he drove, but the city had begun to fall apart.

Cars and buses careered into the pavement. Inside some, the windscreens were painted red, heads and bodies smashed against them. From one office building, they were jumping, one by one, in a steady rhythm. Every couple of seconds, another hit the ground.

The terror of those who had not yet seen it, the ones who hadn't checked their phones, was worse than among those who had. He saw one woman, dressed in bright green jogging gear, kneeling on a street corner, her arms covering her head.

But he kept on driving. Amidst the pain and chaos and suffering, he had to get home.

Turning into his street, Dillon saw two houses burning, smoke billowing from the windows. Three doors down, a car had piled through the wall of a front garden. A woman he knew, a teacher at a local school, cowered in the middle of the road, crying. She had a piece of chalk in her hand, writing on the tarmac.

Dillon ran to his house and rushed into the living room. Gina was there, eyes dazed, slumped on the couch.

Ben was nowhere to be seen.

Pinned to the open door was a note:

"I've got the book. I showed it to your lady." Underneath, he'd drawn a hideous smiling face.

Gina would die soon, Dillon knew it.

The trauma of seeing it, this evil thing, was too much.

The burning, the screaming, the destruction in the streets around the house was intensifying, but he could not bring himself to care.

The most perfect thing that had ever come into his life had been destroyed.

He went up to his office, opened the secure box which sat atop the shelf and took out the pills. Sedatives and painkillers supposed to be used for extreme trauma cases. He took them all.

Downstairs, in the kitchen, he emptied the capsules, one by one, into two glasses.

Gina was still on the sofa when he returned to her.

He lifted up her cold, sweating body and kissed her. She gave no response; she was not there anymore.

He put the glass to her lips and poured it slowly into her. He whispered, "It will make the pain stop."

When it was gone, he laid her back down.

Dillon took the second glass, paused for a moment, then drank it down.

He nestled into Gina and let the peace overwhelm him.

The impact varied from person to person. Their age, mental health and intelligence were all factors. Some would descend into catatonia and suicide instantly; others could function for a significant period, before succumbing. It could snap a mind in an instant or eat away for months, but the end was always the same.

What united them all was the desire to render the image, to reveal what they had seen, so others might know their afflicted mind. They daubed it on walls, they carved it into their skin, they wrote it in blood on the bodies of their loved ones. More terrible than any of this, they networked it. They reproduced its image digitally.

On phones, on laptops, on tablets, they all saw it in the end. The curve at the base which Dillon witnessed, the upwards flick of the cross stroke and the dots stemming from its head. How many dots? Nobody was ever able to say.

In another age, in a time when our thoughts could not be shared instantly with thousands, millions of people at the touch of a screen, some may have survived. Our species could have endured. But not now.

Facebook, Twitter, Instagram, Snapchat: perky brands with kooky names became the agents of our destruction.

A mind fixated on the number steamrollered the oldest instincts of human survival, the hard-wired behaviours which had perpetuated the species. Mothers slew their children, friends killed their friends, with a share, with a like, with a retweet.

Devon Widmer

THE ORDER OF THE BLACK PILL

Gripping the gnarled tree branch between her knees for support, Retta unfurled the slip of parchment to check the encoded directive one last time. "Iwfltsgwjfym Nss, Wttr Ymnwyjjs." *Dragonbreath Inn, Room Thirteen.* Her eyes darted to the dark window at the end of the tree branch. Though the chill night air stung her cheeks and neck, the scar running down her left bicep burned. She rolled the parchment and tucked it into her shirt.

This was it. Her last second chance.

Nary a floorboard creaked as Retta crept to the bedside, her dagger poised to strike. It did no good to wonder about the person curled under those covers. Their fate was sealed. As was Retta's.

The slightest draft of air tickled the nape of Retta's neck. She ducked just in time—*swish!*—the arcing sword slit only a few stray hairs instead of her throat. Retta ripped the covers from the bed, revealing deceptively arranged feather pillows, and whipped them up at her attacker. Under cover of a rain of goose feathers, she darted behind her attacker and nuzzled the tip of her dagger between their shoulder blades.

The attacker froze and then, slowly, craned their head to the side. Pale moonlight illuminated distinctive features.

Retta gasped—those stony grey eyes, that long, crooked nose, the jagged purple scar streaking from cheek to lips— *Grand Master Avelyn*. Instinctively, Retta lowered her weapon.

Thunk!

The corner of the bedside table jutted into Retta's back while Avelyn's sword rested against her jugular.

Avelyn's cold, harsh face pressed close. "So this is what it's come to."

The blade pushed forward, nicking Retta's neck, before withdrawing. Avelyn turned, head bent and shoulders slouched, to sit on the bed.

"My crime, my fall from favor, is known to all. But *you*. What have you done this time, little one? What have you done to offend the order?"

Retta rubbed the scratch on her neck, smearing a faint streak of blood across her throat. Her eyes blurred as she re-membered the chase, the clandestine battle that raged on for days. And of course, the girl with the soulful eyes and sunburnt cheeks. The girl who, despite her naivety, was very much Ret-ta's equal. The girl she had spared the assassin's curse: the sting of a poison tipped blade that forever bound you to the order's bidding.

"I failed an initiation."

Avelyn shook her head, muttering, "And for that they would send you after a disgraced Grand Master."

"If I had known it was you, I would never have…"

"Would never have what? Accepted the order?" Avelyn scoffed. "Don't kid yourself, girl. Even if you'd known, you'd have come just the same. Only already steeled for the task. You wouldn't have hesitated, and you'd have killed me. I know it as well as you." She paused, taut lips relaxing into a tired frown, to rub her temples. "But you have nothing to fear. They know all too well that I could never harm you. Not my own initiate, my protégé. No, they have use of you yet, little one. But I?" She sighed. "My only two options are death. My only real choice: the means."

She slipped a hand into her dark robe and pulled out a locket, an identical sister to the silver coiled snake latch that nested between Retta's own bosoms.

"Here." Avelyn dropped the locket onto the bedside table. "Take it. I was saving it for when the pain began to truly drive me mad." She rubbed a finger gingerly along her facial scar. "Now I realize it will only prolong my suffering. But it might ease yours. Go on, take it!"

Slowly, Retta reached out. She entwined her fingers around the locket and pulled it to her heart.

"There's a good girl." Avelyn swung her legs onto the bed and tilted her head back against the headboard. "It wasn't all bad, this life," she said softly. "I've had some good times—none more so than when training you, little one." She closed her eyes. "I'd like to think that if I could do it all again, I'd have spared you this doomed fate, like you spared your initiate. I'd like to think so. But I know myself too well." Avelyn raised her left palm, her sword clutched tightly in her right hand. "Even if I had a second chance, I wouldn't do a damn thing differently." With one smooth stroke, Avelyn sliced the sword across her wrist.

Retta bowed her head but uttered no protest. Though she loved this woman deeply, she knew first hand that the other choice of death, death by the poison that coursed through both of their veins, was by far the worse option. Her own scar throbbed nearly unbearably, a pain that drove her to kill without question. Anything for the temporary relief only the order could provide. She could only imagine the pain Avelyn must be suffering after so many months of exile.

Dejectedly, Retta knelt by the bedside. She cupped her mentor's bleeding hand, allowing the blood to bubble over the locket and ooze out between her clenched fingers. And so she remained as Avelyn's breaths slowed, becoming ragged, and the sheets stained dark crimson.

When the moon descended and the sun threatened to light the sky, Retta at last untangled her warm fingers from Avelyn's chill ones. She dipped her hands into the basin of washing water on the bedside table and watched the blood swirl lazily to the bottom of the bowl.

With steady hands, she pried open the locket and shook its contents into her palm. She toyed with the treasure, a compact black pill. Such a mundane, innocent appearance. Yet this was the object she killed for, suffered for. For without this antidote, taken monthly, the poison would eat away at her body until the pain became too overpowering and she, like her mentor, succumbed to her own blade. Such was the life of an assassin. Serve the order, give them your heart, your soul, your very breath, and receive the gift of temporary relief from the pain.

Retta placed the pill on her tongue but found her mouth too dry to swallow. Was it all worth it? Was relief worth becoming an instrument of death to those she loved?

An angry pulse of pain shot from Retta's scar, through her arm and straight to her heart. Her chest constricted. It had been forty-seven days since her last dose of antidote. She breathed deeply. This life wasn't worth the pain and suffering, but she would live it all the same. Without flinching, she raised the basin of water to her lips, forcing the bitter antidote down with a metallic swig of bloody water.

Nichole Celauro

ANTI-HEXXER

Under normal, ordinary, untainted by evil circumstances, a garden so lush should not have been able to thrive in such sandy soil.

The overgrown jungle of weeds and herbs encompassed the yard of a cedar-shingled cottage, apart from the crushed shell driveway off to one side. Half-rotted, a driftwood split-rail fence was all that guarded the neighboring yards from the enthusiastic overgrowth. Yet, somehow, despite the darkest fears of the homeowner's association, the split rail kept the plants perfectly at bay.

The HOA even thought the decorative glyphs carved into the wood were, to quote, 'quaint.'

How all those plants actually managed to flourish on a glorified sandbar of an island that was in danger of sinking off the coast of New Jersey with every high tide was beyond them.

It was, in every way, a witch's garden.

Patience, the witch who tended it, ripped a stem of mint from the lavender plot, chastising it for trespassing, when a black cat scurried over her toes, not even pausing for an ear scratch.

Oh dear. An omen.

She rose, brushing sand from her knees, and turned to find a woman at her gate.

"*You're* saltwitch1716?" the woman moaned.

Recognizing her Twitter handle, Patience wrinkled her nose and lied: "No."

Hell's hug on her soul tightened just a smidgen.

"I recognize your photo!"

Unlikely. Patience had been careful that the thumbnail did not reveal her face, but was instead a trendy *aesthetic* shot of a wide brimmed hat pulled down over her eyes, waist length, white-blond hair billowing around her. The comment was some kind of trap to provoke her into confessing, and any witch worth her salt knew better than to confess. Anything. Ever.

"You're wearing the same hat," the woman continued. "And you can see that lighthouse in your cover photo from the bridge. I can't believe I found you! It's a miracle!"

Patience winced.

"I'm Felicity. *Feliz*—with a *Z*—*CityXO* on Twitter. You put a hex on me!"

Felicity tried opening the rickety gate, but, lacking an invitation inside, no doubt found the wood inexplicably strong. Upon realizing her attempts were futile, she gave climbing over the waist-high split rail a shot. So strange how she couldn't manage to find solid footing. Once it became clear that she was no match for the fence, Felicity moved around it, jogging up the neighbor's yard till she was parallel with the witch.

The branches of the willow shifted back onto their side of the fence, and Felicity squinted against the sudden assault of sunlight.

At distance, *FelizCityXO* was a mess. Up close, she was a shipwreck. Puffy cheeks, eyes red and swollen, makeup smudged across her lids. A breeze whipped her third, maybe fourth, day hair from its sloppy bun. Her hands shook as she ripped through her purse, chewing on her lip all the while. And she sagged. Felicity could have been no older than thirty, probably closer to twenty-five, but her body held the poise of an eighty-year-old crone with sciatica.

The witch did not recall hexing this woman specifically, but, knowing herself, she figured she must have had a good reason at the time. "I hex a lot of people."

"Through Twitter?" Felicity choked.

She tore a handful of papers—medical records, Web MD articles, homeopathic propaganda, all mixed in with what appeared to be printouts of runes, Tolkien's Elvish, Twitter screenshots, and a credit card offer—from her oversized purse. Felicity riffled through her wrinkled documents in no particular order, all the while babbling.

"I didn't believe it at first, but it's been months! Doctors can't find anything wrong with me. Nothing! I haven't gotten my period. I'm not ovulating. I'm not *pregnant*. And, no, I am not going through early menopause!"

Patience felt the distinct absence of a venomous '*mother*' at the end of that sentence.

"All I want is a baby and now, because of you, I can't! Why? What did I ever do to you?"

Felicity shoved her documents at the witch. Patience took them—but only because the earthworms would bitch about her littering for days—and studied a screenshot of an old Tweet.

P the Witch @saltwitch1716 Tweeted • Mar 2
@FelizCityXO this is nonsense your womb is barren now

Patience looked at the printout and chuckled. The spaghetti looking sigil was meaningless clip art. What really would have made Felicity barren was a bundle of dandelion, red clover, and raspberry leaves tied—with a witch's hair—to a photo of *Feliz-CityXO* burned to ash over a saucer of raw milk (unpasteurized).

In fact, Patience vaguely recalled performing such a ritual not too long ago.

"You need to undo it," Felicity stomped her sandaled foot. "My marriage is suffering. I'm suffering. You took away the most sacred, most meaningful thing…if I can't be a mother, then, what good…what's the point!" She swatted at a bee. "You're young. You'll get it in a few years. It'll hit you."

Immortality and a natural babyface had its obvious drawbacks.

The witch replied to the comment with a glare that froze the sweat as it leaked from Felicity's pores. Watching her shiver and peel her crunchy blouse out of her armpit made Patience feel better.

But still, she couldn't dig out of her brain why she'd have cursed the woman in the first place.

Focusing back on the paper, Patience channeled a bit of Hellfire up through the soles of her feet, felt it race through her bloodstream, and used the energy to zap the page to life. For a moment the inked images flickered, buffering till they could snag a decent WiFi signal. Once balanced—and Patience remembered the WiFi password—she scrolled through her temporary window into Felicity's Twitter feed.

Felicity @FelizCityXO Tweeted • Mar 2
anybody kno of any herbs/foods 2 boost fertility?? looking 4 ALL NATURAL only plz xo

Felicity @FelizCityXO Tweeted • Feb 18

this is the all natural remedy doctors don't want you to see

Felicity @FelizCityXO Tweeted • Feb 5
Jenny McCarthy: "We're Not An Anti-Vaccine Movement…We're Pro-Safe Vaccine"

Ah, well, that would be it.

"I remember you," Patience sighed (eh, well, still not specifically, but whatever).

"Oh, thank God!" A flock of crows—no wait—seagulls cawed and took flight. "You'll undo it!"

"No." Patience crumpled the paper stack and tossed it into a composting bin. "Drive home safe."

If Felicity had been a witch, smoke would have risen from her reddened ears. "But, why?"

"You should get going; traffic is bad at this hour."

"No! I demand an explanation! I. Want. My. Baby!"

"And to resurrect the big nasties."

"What?"

"Your womanhood," Patience rolled her eyes, "isn't worth a plague. Or stalking me. So, no," she cupped a bee that Felicity had been swatting and guided it onto the petal of a very pollinated sunflower. Hell's grip softened. "Well, yes. But on a condition. Don't be selfish. Vaccinate the kid."

For a moment the Earth stilled. No cawing gulls or buzzing bees. Only the gentle sound of distant, lapping waves. Patience drew a breath. She loved these moments, but they never lasted long e—

"How dare you!" Felicity kicked the fence, knocking the sunflower, causing the bee to tumbled off its petals and then become trapped beneath her sandal in her second kick. "I'm selfish? You cursed me, an *innocent woman*, you spooky cow!

Why? Because you're so…you're misinformed, and you call me selfish! I'm the one who's trying to protect—

The, the links to autism, they, it's fact! Abstaining from vaccinating works! My sister's children are the healthiest, and they've never seen a doctor! Holistic works! The science—"

Patience scraped the bee from the fence and spread its squashed remains into a stone bowl. Poor dear. He'd been a good worker, loyal to his queen, how tragic an end to befall him. "It's not science."

"Says the *witch*."

"Magic doesn't negate science, it just sort of…" Patience made an odd twirly gesture, as if that would clarify her meaning. It didn't.

Felicity snorted. "God, I am such an idiot. You're not a witch. You're an evil hag, but no witch. Witches don't exist. If you really had magic, you'd fix me to prove it. But you're just some lonely, dirty hippy that's got nothing better to do than troll already stressed-out people online."

Oh. So that's how Felicity really felt about the not exactly sacred practice of witchcraft. Well.

Patience plucked a cluster of blueberries off a bush, a sprig of rosemary, sunflower petals, pollen, pine nettles, oh, the trespassing mint, for flavor, sure, why not, and added them all into the stone bowl. And then, hmm, something old as—ah, yes, dirt. Patience restrained her grin and slit her finger on a garden knife, slathering the blade in a mix of blood and soil. She closed her eyes, humming. Her blood—laced with hellfire and brimstone and the darkness that had settled into her aura when her soul moved out—warmed the knife.

She murmured—something in Latin that she could never remember the English translation of—and thought of dysentery. Yellow fever. Smallpox.

Smallpox ravaged the original colony of the island. Clearly, the disease was the result of witchcraft. How else could it be explained? God would never allow such a tragedy to befall the pious village, and therefore, obviously, it was the Devil's dark forces tormenting them. Dark forces in the form of the local evil hag who danced naked in the moonlight and bedded goats (allegedly).

So they prayed and stuck themselves with leeches and died in droves and with their final breaths warned their dying children to stay away from the witch's cottage. It was her black magic that had cursed the village. She did it to lure away the children, make them suffer as she harvested their souls for her demonic keeper. Do not eat a speck of anything she gives you.

Honestly, Patience was only trying to protect the children with those potions. Little innocent souls. Even Hell had rules about taking innocent souls. It wasn't the babes' fault their parents were righteous pricks that assumed any woman shunning the idea of motherhood must be possessed by the Devil himself.

Well, they weren't exactly *wrong* about the origins of the village plague. Just the motivation.

In her mind's eye, Patience saw Reverend Janssen, writhing in his deathbed. She frowned, suddenly and vividly recalling what an ungodly bastard he'd been to his wife. His face was speckled with oozing sores. She reached out and popped one with the tip of her knife. Pus gathered on the blade. Reverend Janssen moaned.

And then Patience opened her eyes, back in her bright and sunny garden.

"What just happened?" Felicity was white and shaking. "You were, like, in some kind of trance. The...your bowl."

The sigils carved into the inner walls of the bowl glowed when the bloody knife scraped against them. Once the leafy contents had been ground and stirred to a fine, odorous mush, Patience poured the potion into a mason jar.

"I added some mint, but it won't taste pleasant. You might want to mix that with some baked goods."

Felicity choked, nearly falling to her knees as she snatched the jar. "Ohmigawd. Ohmigawd. Thank you, thank you so much! You've no idea! I can't express...thank you!"

"You're welcome."

Two-faced bitch.

Summoning demons was bad. It's a bad, bad, very nasty thing. They were cunning and cruel and clever. And was it difficult. Well, the actual summoning bit was no more difficult than making an interoffice phone call; all you needed was your party's extension and a ritual blood sacrifice. But—as most women felt about relations with coworkers—protection was necessary.

In a seaside witch's cottage, the pentagram was set, salt circled, sacrificial animal bones artfully arranged. Patience ignited a bouquet of roses over a votive, the flames black. She closed her eyes, inhaling the scent of the burning flowers. On a thorn she pricked her thumb. Blood dribbled onto the pentagram, sizzling where it landed. She spoke aloud the name of the demon that granted her these unholy powers.

It was date night.

The pentagram glowed red.

Black smoke rose, thickening, solidifying into its favorite form—dark hair, dark eyes, just the right amount of stubble—in the pentagram's center. The Demon smirked. "Did I feel you cast a time displacement spell the other day?"

Patience shrugged. When it was clear no wandering spirits had hitchhiked along, with a toe, she tipped the black candle into a pile of salt, extinguishing the flame, breaking the circle with audible snap, and canceling out all the protective enchantments that went with it.

He pounced on her.

There were sparks. Literally. The Demon tore his mouth away from Patience's to blow out a smoldering strand of her hair.

"Will she be joining us tonight?"

"Who?"

"You don't sense that? Have I taught you nothing about expanding your aura? There's a woman at your gate."

"Oh. No." Patience slid her hands up his neatly pressed shirt. Honestly, why he even bothered to manifest with clothes on was beyond her. "Must be just passing by."

"Will Chuck from your yoga class be joining us again?"

"No. He found Cristo."

"Ew."

The Demon raked his sharpened nails over her thighs hard enough to leave swollen, pink trails in their wake.

"Not what you think. That's his new boyfriend."

"Eh. They could both—" the Demon tensed, set her feet back on the floor and sighed. "She's not just passing, Pay. And she's pissed. What did you do to her?"

A pustule on Felicity's cheek popped against a decorative sofa pillow. Sweat soaked and shivering, she hugged the matching woolen blanket tighter around her shoulders. She hissed when the wool scratched the sensitive pox covering every visible inch of her skin. And the not visible bits too, undoubtedly.

Patience made a mental note to burn the pillow and blanket, then scatter their ashes at sea later. Shame.

"This thime," Felicity croaked around her swollen tongue, "My thoctor, thix thoctors, say Hi have a hisease that's thupposed to be hextinct. Hat Hi hood have been head haze ago. My hister had who thuggle me out the thospital—who's he?"

The Demon plopped down beside Felicity, draping an arm over her. Another blister burst, staining his shirt. He rolled up his sleeve.

"Kay, girl, proud of you. But this little *project* is a bit," he grimaced, "overdone, don't you think?"

Nope, Patience did not think it was overdone. Sickness spells were a classic. Like red lipstick and lace underwear, they never went out of style.

Felicity shot the Demon the most indignant look she could muster for someone whose facial expressions were obscured by a plague, before snapping her attention back to Patience.

"Hew did this to me!"

Lounging across the love seat opposite the diseased woman, Patience absently twirled her lock of singed hair.

"Did I?" Judging from the color of her popcorned face, Felicity's fever spiked. "Huh. Well, I hex a lot of people."

"Hunt!"

The Demon laughed, shoulders shaking, heels kicking frantically at the wood floors. He dug his nails into the arms of the sofa. Patience heard the rips and glared at him. That was a new sofa. But he didn't notice.

"Sorry," he said, "But not really. You sound so stupid. I love it. Really, un-ironically, I love this. It's—"

"Cat, the sofa."

Silence.

Glowering, the Demon deepened his nails into the plush cushions. Patience felt his power surge; the hair on her arms rose, sulfur attacked her nostrils, and her muscles twitched at the sudden rise in temperature. His name. She'd given away a bit of his name. For that, she'd be punished later. Fine. She had a few *punishment* ideas of her own she'd been meaning to run by him.

"Yes, dear," he said.

Felicity's eyes flicked between them. "Har you a witch too?"

He turned to her, chin in hand, eyes glowing just long enough to reveal snake like slits for pupils.

"No, sweetie, we've got more of a..." the Demon made the same gesture Patience had given Felicity days ago, as if it would clarify his presence. It didn't. "You know, relationship."

"Wha—"

"I own her soul."

Again, Felicity glanced between them. Patience could see the flood of questions forming behind her eyes. She opened her chapped mouth...and vomited. Her whole body, pox and all, gushed with the force of her heaving.

"Oh, honey, ew." The Demon lifted his shoes.

Patience ground her teeth as she watched Felicity stain her rug. It had matched the pillow and blanket. Pale blue with soothing, wave-like swirls. All part of a set (witches had a weakness for *Better Homes & Gardens*). Vomit-soaked was repulsive, not soothing.

Puke dripping from her lips, Felicity panted. "Hey-ham hi gonna hi?"

Patience shrugged, eyes never leaving the yellowing spot on her rug. "What's the point of a curse if it eases your suffering?"

She swore she heard Felicity whimper before her voice was drowned in a barrage of coughs. The witch very nearly threw another curse, perhaps one to sew her mouth shut, to keep Felicity from puking, or worse, popping all over the floor again. But the Demon had beaten her to it.

He slapped Felicity on the back like a mother patted her child choking on chocolate milk. Except the Demon smacked her with enough force to nearly knock her off the sofa and land face first into her own bile pile. Patience wished he'd strike just a *teeny* bit harder.

Black smoke puffed out Felicity's mouth. The Demon plucked a bit of ash from the cloud and flicked it onto the carpet. The vomit puddle ignited. It reeked while it burned, though it only lasted a few seconds. Patience dragged a lock of hair across her nose, inhaled the scent of coconut and wondered when was the last time she had washed it.

The flames cleared. Her rug was ruined.

"There," said the Demon. "Feel better?"

Jaw quivering, eyes wide, Felicity nodded. She ran her tongue over her teeth. "Did you," she cleared her throat, "Did you fix me?"

He looked at Patience, eyebrow raised. She shook her head.

"Sorry, dearest," he pinched the sick woman's poxed cheeks, "but she sounded stupid. I wouldn't be able to listen to her *thpit* again without laughing. Now, honey," he squished a sore between his fingers and Felicity recoiled, "I can't just *fix* you. I can do lots of things. For you. If you ask me oh so—"

Felicity swatted him—like that bee—and jabbed her finger at Patience. "She did this! She needs to undo it! Please! I can't live like this! Really, please, *please*, help me."

Eyes rolling, the Demon stood, and Felicity flopped against the cushions without his arm supporting her. He brushed her pus off his shirt. "You people just don't know a good deal when you're offered one. I'm bored. Darling, do what you must with her. Who am I to stifle your creativity? I'll be poking sinners till you need me," he waggled his brows and blew a kiss at Patience as he bound up the stairs.

She watched him ascend and admired the way a force of evil could fill out the behind of his skinny jeans.

"*My* husband won't come near me." Felicity reached a hand toward Patience, but apparently thought better of it, and retreated. "He's afraid of getting sick, too. I, I won't get him sick, too?"

Patience narrowed her eyes, suddenly, vividly, and for the second time in not nearly enough time, remembered what an ungodly bastard Reverend Janssen had been to his wife. "I'm not married."

"Oh," Felicity nodded, coughed, wiped spittle from the corner of her blistered mouth, "I didn't mean to. I'm sorry. I'm just afraid for—"

"Afraid of making the people you love ill?"

She swallowed.

Good. Fear was the whole point of the curse. Over the years, Patience had taught plenty of unsuspecting townsfolk lessons through the very effective tactics of fear and magic.

She giggled. It was just for effect, really, but a good witch knew when to dish out a good, unsettling giggle. "Anybody who's been vaccinated should be just fine."

"He doesn't understand what's happening though," Felicity scratched at her sores. "Neither does my sister. She's helping all she can, but—"

"How's your tongue? Fixed enough to call me a spooky *hunt* again?"

The sick woman flushed.

"Oh. No. Listen, I'm sorry I said that. I was so pissed; I didn't mean to come off so…but you cursed me. I didn't do anything to you and you just butted into my business without warning, you had no right, and you—"

"Well, it sounds fixed enough for you to tell him I gave you a condition."

Honestly, Patience thought she preferred the swollen tongue. In a few more days, Felicity would be back again. They always came back, groveling and pleading: *oh powerful witch, I swear I've seen the error of my ways and promise to behave*

from now until my last breath precisely as you'd instructed!
Naturally, the great and wise sorceress that she was, Patience
would exercise pity and release the poor, simple townsfolk from
their hexes. And although she *had* been content to let Felicity go
the rest of her life without the ability to reproduce (Mother Earth
needed a *little* bit of break), she only expected another week out
of the woman before sickness convinced her to surrender to the
witch's demand.

Patience let the door hit Felicity on the ass on her way out.

Demons were horned, winged, monstrous creatures with fiery
red eyes and pointed tails that fed on the fear and sin in your
soul, but not before they tortured you, broke your spirit and
bones, till you begged for death a thousand times over.

Or that's what Felicity had read online.

Her body was weak. And hot. And cold. And sweaty, itchy,
disgusting, oozing. Yet, she managed to scrape a pentagram in
chalk on her cellar floor. She surrounded it with Morton's ko-
sher salt. Tea lights would have to do in place of black flamed
candles molded from the wax of loyal bees, whatever that
meant. Her husband, although he didn't understand why, had
been supportive enough to take her word for it and swung by the
butcher for a very necessary pint of pig's blood.

Felicity gagged on the rotten scent of it—or that could have
been her own odor at this point. It was truly hard to tell.

It took a few tries to get the pronunciation right, but when
the pentagram glowed red, she knew she'd managed to summon
a demon from Hell into her half-finished basement, pinched
right between the dusty futon and the wash machine. She collapsed into a beanbag chair, a relic from her husband's fraternity
life. Lately every task—from changing the toilet paper roll to

dodging quarantine tape to practicing witchcraft—seemed to require more energy than she ever had.

In the pentagram, the creature that appeared both surprised her and *didn't*.

"Well," said the man from *saltwitch1716*'s cottage, "this is unexpected."

Felicity sank lower into her beanbag, and the sores on the soles of her feet itched. Always on her feet. Her puffed up and bleeding feet. Was that part of this stupid curse, too? Itchy feet? Had that creepy, stuck up, air-headed witch intentionally written that into her curse?

God, she hadn't expected that whole Namaste, 'I'm superior because I don't eat anything that casts a shadow,' Coachella crop top wearing vibe from a *witch*. Green skin and warts and Hot Topic corsets. That's what Felicity had pictured; a crone cackling into the glow of her smart phone. Although she had to admit, *saltwitch1716*'s soft, airy voice was a thousand times more unsettling than Margaret Hamilton's hoarse shouting.

"You're..." Felicity heaved, repressing the sudden nausea rolling through her stomach. "You're really a demon?"

"You're really perceptive." He clicked his tongue. "Couldn't even pull a chair into this circle for me? That's rude. You know, it's not like a basement makes the trip from Hell any shorter. And it smells like mildew. Why don't we move this some place more comfortable? If you just blow that candle out—"

"No!" Felicity flattened her beanbag reaching for the candle. She cupped the flame in her palms to protect it.

The Demon narrowed his eyes. "And you've done your homework. How did you get this spell?"

"The internet."

He groaned. "Did Patience post it?"

"I...I don't think she meant to. But then, in her house the other night, she called you a cat, and you said you were poking sinners, and I read Dante in junior high. The translation is, I don't know, I don't speak Italian, but I put it together. She also does free tarot readings if you Tweet at her. What is it?"

The Demon was staring. After a moment of doing only that, he cleared his throat, and wiped his jaw off the floor. "You're smart."

"I, thank you?"

Felicity wasn't sure if he meant it as a compliment, or if she should even be accepting compliments from strange monsters in her partially finished basement, morally or magically speaking, but at this point, whatever. She felt like Pestilence, Rider of the Apocalypse, had touched her himself. She didn't give a damn about proper conversation etiquette with the minions of Satan at the moment.

"It just surprises me, with all your, you know, 'medical expertise.'"

"She had no right—" Felicity bit her tongue. On a blister. It popped, tasting like sour milk and iron.

If her fever hadn't been running at over a hundred every second of her life for the last week, she probably would have felt her cheeks turn red from anger. Felicity didn't deserve this. She hadn't personally done a thing to antagonize that witch. And now, because she shared a few (perhaps unverified) articles on Twitter, she was doomed? Cursed to live her life as a leper. Alone. Wondering what would kill her first, the infection or starvation (she hadn't kept anything down in days), or would it be the CDC breaking down her door in search of patient zero?

And what about her family? They didn't need to suffer.

"I want to make a deal with you."

The Demon raised a brow; Felicity thought it made him look like a Telenovela star.

"Make me a witch too," she continued. "Just a little bit a witch. Just enough so that I can undo the curse."

"Standard exchange for undone curses is your first born child. Kidding, no! You should see the look on your face! Thanks, but no, honey."

"Why!" Felicity kicked the washer (feebly) the side was dented and she was breathing far too heavily. It felt good. "Why won't anybody tell! me! why!"

"I tried making you an offer once, remember? You refused."

Shit. On the witch's sofa? That had been an offer, and she'd spurned it? "I take it back. Please. I need this! I—"

"Aunt Liss?"

A tiny cough. Felicity spun. Heart squeezed into an iron maiden, which had then been squeezed into her throat, she whispered, "Aiden! Go back to bed, sweetie, you need your rest."

Her nephew stood on the stair, head resting against the railing. His face only held a fraction of the same, putrid pox that polluted her own. But still, one of his blisters squished and smeared against the wood.

Felicity looked back at the Demon. "I told my sister I could fix him."

The Demon groaned, "Goddamnit, Pay."

He held Patience by the shoulders and shook her.

"You know the rules. You can't do this again! Again, Pay! You snuff out another innocent soul and, as your damn familiar, I'm the one who gets skinned for this. Darling, one more strike against me, and I'm back to poking thieves in the ass with a pitchfork!" The Demon swept a strand of hair behind her ears, pressing his forehead against hers, sighing with the whole weight of his borrowed body. "No more casual visits. No more freedom. Your power reduced to a boardwalk palm reader and we're restricted to bimonthly, chaperoned visits. You don't want that for me, do you? For us, darling?"

Patience was fairly certain he was exaggerating, but still. Gently, she pried his fingers off her, his nails leaving little crescent moon dents in her skin.

"I don't want to kill a kid," she confessed.

His jaw clenched. It was the truth; she knew he knew it. But it was also a perfect dodge at what may have been his attempt to define their relationship. Honestly, this was supposed to be a casual fling between colleagues. A fun way to pass the time until Judgment Day. Patience had no interest in being (metaphorically) tied down. Couldn't two servants of the Devil hook up for a few hundred years without things getting so—

"So you'll fix him?"

Felicity adjusted the boy—shivering, poxed, and unconscious—on her lap and kissed his forehead. Hell's grip on Patience's soul felt like a stranglehold.

"Fine."

She pushed her Demon aside and reached for the bundles of dried herbs above the kitchen sink. He retreated, taking up a post against the fridge. His call (which for demons and witches was less a ring and more of the sound of your own voice screaming in agony as the blood boiled in your veins) had woken her just past three in the morning. Felicity and the boy hitched a ride with him between summoning circles.

The child stirred on his aunt's lap. She held his hands to keep him from scratching at the few sores that had already sprouted on him. Felicity seemed good with children, clearly possessing the instinct Patience notably lacked, and had no desire to gain. The boy groaned and squirmed, and Felicity hummed a lullaby to soothe him. Or, wait, was that 'No Scrubs?'

Unconsciously, Patience hummed along, matching the grinding of her mortar and pestle to the rhythm.

Felicity stopped. "Thank you," she said to the witch, before turning to her nephew and whispering. "I'm sorry."

"Cat, the milk." Patience snapped her fingers at him. "I need the raw stuff."

He obeyed, wordlessly setting the milk beside the growing heap of dried plants, berries, and charmed oils.

"At twenty one," Patience spoke low over the sound of her mortar and pestle grinding, "I hadn't given my husband any children. That was a big deal at the time. When he discovered I had *ways*—" she smeared a droplet of her blood on a sunflower seed and flicked into the mortar, sparks rose, Felicity jumped "—of keeping his seeds from taking root, he knew his sweet maiden must have become mistress to the Devil himself.

"Well, not the Devil." Her eyes snapped up to the Demon as he chuckled and rearranged the alphabet magnets into profanity on the fridge. "But marriage was a property deed back then. I wasn't really feeling it. At the time. Anytime." Patience chopped a bustle of dandelions into fine confetti and added them to a jar of milk. "Anyhow, the plague came. Smallpox. And nobody trusts the witch to whip up a simple inoculation. It's barely even magic, really."

Felicity stiffened. But she kept watching Patience's hands mix ingredients; the powder gathering under her nails, the stems caught in all her jangling bracelets, the way she ripped a hair from her own head and swiftly followed it by snagging one of Felicity's. The latter halted Patience from touching the boy, and instead softly picked a hair from him herself, handing it carefully over to the witch.

Patience nodded in thanks.

"Self-righteous pricks preferred to let the whole village die out, kids and all, than let the witch give them one teeny weeny potion," she sighed. "Selling my soul didn't harm anyone but myself, unlike…" She blew out a candle in Felicity's face; the sick woman's eyes watered. "You know."

"I'm sorry. I will tell my sister to get him vaccinated. I'll do the same, I promise," Felicity's voice was weak as she cried. "Please don't let him suffer—I, I'm an idiot. I get it now. I promise. Don't let him die. He's too young; he doesn't deserve to go to Hell."

A worm of guilt wriggled in Patience's gut.

"It doesn't work like that. His soul's not in any danger. They're so mad about it." She stomped her foot like Hell was just the noisy downstairs neighbor. "'Cause I've wasted re-sources for no profit."

She sealed and shook a pair of mason jars. For a moment, the liquid inside glowed, before the thickening potion settled.

"Besides. He's not going to die. This one's for pox." Pa-tience tapped one of the jars. "Half a jar for you, and only a few spoonfuls for him. Don't mix it with anything, even if he says it tastes bad. It doesn't react well to sweets—"

But Felicity wasn't listening, already twisting off the lid and guzzling the contents. She gagged, a bit of bubbling potion drib-bled down her chin, her eyes watering. Patience slid her a spoon, which she snatched with enough force to shake the table. Simul-taneously, Felicity nudged the boy awake and dunked the spoon into the jar. With it halfway to his lips, she paused, gasping at the sight of the swollen blisters on her hands already beginning to recede.

"Aunt Liss?" mumbled the boy. "Where are—"

"Hush." Felicity slipped the spoon into the boy's mouth. "Take your medicine." He coughed, and made a face, but even as groggy as he was, eyelids half open, the child was surprisingly better at keeping the potion in his mouth than his aunt had been.

She kissed the disappearing pox on his cheeks.

The witch cleared her throat. "And this one is to un-barren your uterus. Drive safe."

Felicity hugged the boy so tight Patience thought he might die of asphyxiation the moment he was cured.

"Thank you. Thank you so much. I'll make sure they all, him, his," she sniffled, "his future cousins, they'll all get their vaccines. On time. I promise, I—"

"I called you a cab," the Demon said, pocketing a cell phone.

"Oh. I live in Connecticut though."

Grinning, the Demon withdrew a shiny credit card from his jacket. He nuzzled it into the pocket of Felicity's sweatpants.

"On me," he winked.

"Right. Okay. I, I don't know…"

Felicity rose, one arm around the child balanced on her hip—who burped and promptly laid his head back on her shoulder—and extended her free hand in the universal gesture of 'truce.' Patience didn't take it. Wiping her hands on her harem pants, she felt, irrationally, like touching Felicity would only infect her all over again.

"Of course, right," Felicity said (though probably not understanding the meaning behind Patience's snub), "I, uh, I won't bother you again. Thank you."

The Demon packed the spell jars into a mud-crusted tote bag.

And then, more quietly than Patience was expecting, Felicity was gone. The witch felt the tightness in her chest ease. She hadn't meant to, but it escaped her in a loud sigh. Her stomach hurt. Acid and guilt. She never wanted to actually harm a kid. *Again.* How could she have been so careless? Felicity had even warned her, in a way. *Abstaining from vaccinating works! My sister's children are the healthiest, and they've never seen a doctor!*

Patience felt the Demon run his fingers through her hair, playfully tugging at split ends. "Cute. The way you turned your little massacre into a sob story." He kissed her ear. "It was sadder than those feed the children commercials. You're a fabulous actress." Another kiss. "That's why you're my favorite."

"Not tonight, Kitty. I'm tired."

At first she tugged herself out of his grip—he didn't attempt to restrain her—but changed her mind, missing his warmth the moment it was gone. So Patience slumped against his chest, and folded his arm around her like a blanket. She didn't cry. She didn't know why her eyes felt all prickly and wet all of a sudden, but she certainly wasn't crying over a kid she narrowly avoided murdering. This time.

The Demon's hug around her waist tightened just a smidgen.

Benjamin Thomas

PAINTED MEMORIES

He was being fired. Vadim Altov walked to his supervisor's office, a glass-walled room overlooking the Institute for Artistic Living's atrium and reception desk, utterly certain that he was being let go. But, as he sat across the room from Elaine Mohan, the all-business, mahogany-haired executive who had asked him to hang tight while she finished an email, Vadim's unease began to dissipate.

Elaine's fingers danced across the surface of her desk, pressing letters on an LED keyboard projected from her monitor while Vadim shifted in one of two leather chairs angled toward the executive. If he was being fired, shouldn't there have been at least one person from human resources present? Maybe that's who Elaine was emailing.

"Okay," Elaine said turning her attention to Vadim. "Have you had the opportunity to think over the institute's proposal?"

Vadim swallowed hard, saliva like a rock. He had been avoiding this. "I'm sorry, Elaine, but I can't go along with it."

The executive exhaled. Inched back and forth in her chair.

"You run the risk of being terminated," Elaine said. "I won't push for that, but we're talking about a donation of over seven million dollars; it's unheard of. You would be the sole person responsible for turning that down."

"And if I said yes, then I'd be killing him."

Elaine picked a stylus off her desk and held it at each end. "Not legally. He's agreed to sign a waiver. Make any statement required in order to prevent bad publicity. It's a win-win. Think of the research you could do with even a fraction of that money."

It was true. Even with the resurgence of arts and humanities after the dark decade that left them unfunded and nearly nonexistent, donations were still just trickling in.

Vadim said, "Speeches aside, euthanasia—which this technically would be—is still illegal in this state, and the press would eat us alive. Besides, can the board really terminate me for saying no to this? I hold the patents for the machine, and being the sole operator was part of my contract."

"Vadim." There was a pained expression on Elaine's face. As if her words were spiked and cutting the inside of her mouth as she spoke. "I am only telling you this because we're close. They'll reverse engineer the tech, they will build another one, and they will do it regardless of whatever contract you signed when you started here. Don't ruin your life over this. It's not like it used to be. Things are so cutthroat now. Scrapping over what little funding there is. They won't just fire you. They'll blackball you. You're going to want a family someday. Apply for a populi permit or maybe adopt. And you know as well as I do that you won't be able to do either of those things if you can't validate your income."

Vadim opened his mouth, but Elaine held up her hand. "And don't say that you'll fight them because the best lawyer in the world won't win. It's almost funny...You're one of the only steady sources of income for this institute, and now it's biting you in the ass."

"Yeah," Vadim said. "Real funny."

Vadim's office was located below ground, on the institute's bottom floor. It was a rectangular room with a large observation window cut into one wall. Vadim's desk was positioned beneath it, allowing him to see both of the dual monitors at his workstation as well as the room beyond. Through the glass was almost complete darkness. Dim purple running lights lined the circular exterior and, for the moment, provided the only source of light.

Vadim tossed his plastic ID badge on his desk and slapped the spacebar on his keyboard. How could he put a living man inside the machine? Who would even think of it? With what it did to a cadaver, how could anyone want to suffer through that while still alive?

Diagnostics scrolled across the right screen; no readings appeared abnormal. Beyond the observation window, ceiling lights hummed on and illuminated a yurt-sized dome made of frosted glass. Four metal support beams curled upward, clasped around the dome like fingers holding tight. As the roster was loading, Vadim couldn't help but chuckle at the absurdity of the idea. *Fine, put him in. Idiots.*

A list of names appeared on the left monitor. **In Queue: 748**.

"Jesus Christ."

Thirty-seven new names had been added since he left less than twelve hours ago. Despite Vadim's unwillingness, his curdling objection, they would need a second machine. The institute in Paris—an offshoot funded by The Louvre—had already approached them to purchase construction rights. Vadim, much to the dismay of Elaine and the board, had declined with no further comment. He couldn't bring himself to allow it. If he wasn't able to monitor it as closely as he monitored the original, then how could exploitation be prevented?

Regardless of his reasons, Vadim's decision had placed him on thin ice. Regret had started to poke at him. Mostly at night. Mostly when he was trying to sleep. Tossing and turning in his studio flat with the broken air conditioner hanging idly in the window.

He didn't regret declining the offer, only building the machine in the first place. And he loathed them for making him feel that way. The machine was his pride and joy.

Vadim clicked on the first name and entered the execution code. A whirring sound came from beyond the glass partition. Two mechanical arms descended from the ceiling above the dome like hands with wire and cable veins. They reached into a slot in the room's wall and withdrew a silver gurney topped with a cadaver inside of a biodegradable body bag. A portion of the frosted glass slid into itself, exposing a square hole in the side of the dome. The arms slid the tray inside, body and all.

Vadim's monitors went black and then flashed white. The machine hummed, processing the body that had been deposited inside. On the left display, streaks of black swirled against a gray background, while the monitor on the right showed a spinning array of music notes. Rests, quarter notes, sixteenths all twirled outward from the center of the screen. Vadim tried to focus, his eyesight bouncing between each monitor while shadows danced inside the dome.

Minutes passed. Spots of blue and purple color twirled amongst the black. G-Clefs and eighth notes spun faster and faster while the shadows inside the dome spastically danced until—

The dome shut down. Sounds and lights completely off until the purple running lights flickered on, buzzing as they warmed up. The right monitor went black, taking with it the only hint of music. Vadim nodded at the other display. An image was frozen on the screen. An abstract piece of various colors. Artwork transposed from the body of…he looked at the roster…Anita Rivent. A philanthropist.

Two floors above him, canvas was being stretched across a wooden frame in preparation. It would take an hour for the image to be transferred and then the call would be placed, security would follow the family member home, and the second half of their payment would be sent to the institution.

Vadim had hoped to hear a song. Songs were rare. Very rare. At some point he would hear another song. Unless they forced him out. Well, if they did that—Vadim tapped his fingers on the desk—no one would hear anyone sing.

Shay put down her Long Island Iced Tea and pushed curls of acorn-colored hair from her face. "I'm sorry; he wants you to do what? Who is this guy?"

Vadim shrugged. Picked at the label on his beer. "An anonymous donor. That's all Mohan would tell me. Oh, and that I'm pretty much fired if I don't."

"You mean if you don't murder this fucker?"

A waitress looked at them as she passed. Shay nodded at the woman. A polite *mind your own business and move on.*

"I don't know," Vadim said. "Maybe it's not the worst thing in the world."

"Wait—what? You aren't actually considering this, are you?"

Vadim stammered. Why did he always lose his confidence around this woman? What was it about her? Except that he knew the answer: everything. Her intellect. Her attitude. Every bit of Shay Carter was perfect. "I—I don't know. Maybe."

"I'll never talk to you again," Shay said.

That's harsh. I mean, Shay, you do have to admit, it's a little interesting to think about what would actually happen."

"No, it's not. It's inadvertent murder. I mean you're sure he would die, right?"

Vadim took a sip of his beer. "Well, the machine breaks down human organs and tissue, analyzes the synapses and nodes of the brain, and abstracts its findings into a form of art. Nothing comes out of it aside from a painting or a song. So, yes; yeah, it would kill him."

Shay snagged the waitress as the woman passed back around. "Can I have another?"

"Of course. Would you like another beer, too?"

Vadim shook his head. "No, thanks."

The woman nodded and weaved through a group of grad students to reach the bar.

"Vadim, if you do this and he dies—like you're saying he *one hundred percent* will—then you will be a murderer. Can you live with that? Because I don't think you can."

"Yeah." Vadim bit his lower lip and sucked, releasing it with a pop. Elaine's threat of blackballing him weighed heavy in his chest. "But would I really? I mean, he's signing a waiver, and he wants to do it, so in actuality—"

"Fuck off." Shay glared. "You'd be killing him. You don't think you'd have any regrets about that? I'd hate to see you wind up like the Manhattan boys. You know, people say they regretted what they did after we dropped the bombs."

Vadim rolled his eyes and scoffed. "I think there's a slight difference between 200,000 innocent people and a single individual who understands the consequences, thank you."

"Art's not meant to kill, Vadim," Shay said.

But that wasn't necessarily true. Actually, it wasn't true at all. Entertainment news was constantly filled with singers and actors who lived inside a golden spotlight yet existed utterly alone. Suicides. Appendages hacked off for the sake of art inspired love. The best of the best performances and pieces came from tortured souls. Vadim's machine was nothing more than a fitting final resting place.

"Vadim, you need to listen to me on this. Please."

He gave the best smile he could fake and took another swig of his drink.

In Queue: 803

Vadim stared at the screen until the number became fuzzy and pixelated. This was reaching a level of insanity. The problem was the cool-down period. While the conversion process took under five minutes—ten at the most and even that he had only witnessed once—the reset was variable. Hours or days. He never knew until the conversion was complete.

There was a knock on his office door. Vadim spun in his chair to find Elaine in the doorway. He started to stand but the executive motioned for him to remain seated.

After a few seconds of tense silence she said, "Vadim, I need an answer."

In his head Vadim saw Shay. Her disappointment. The same look she had given him when he made a drunken move and, instead of getting her lips, had pecked her cheek. Crashing on her couch that same night led to an awkward morning. Until Shay's son Jay wanted breakfast and Vadim made him blueberry pancakes.

Vadim bit his lower lip, careful not to drop eye contact with Elaine. "I am considering it."

Elaine pursed her lips. Checked her phone and flashed a brief smile. "That's good. The board's looking for an answer by the end of the day."

"Elaine, it's Friday. I'll give it heavy thought over the weekend and come in on Monday with an answer for them."

She was nodding, but Vadim sensed she wasn't really listening.

"Here." She pushed off of the wall. "Come with me."

Vadim followed his supervisor to the elevator. Elaine pressed the button marked 2F and stood with her hands behind her back.

"Do you read the news, Vadim?"

Aside from science podcasts and the journals put out by MIT, he did not. There wasn't a bit of him that cared about the current political turmoil. The droughts and water wars of the West Coast. The dust storms and lack of jobs in the former Rust Belt. Farms and famine. Arctic changes. ISIS. Domestic shots fired. The general population's closed mindedness and fixation on tragedy was nauseating.

The elevator lurched to a stop. Vadim stifled a rising bubble in his throat. They walked down a long corridor with an angled glass ceiling. Overhead, the Boston sun shone down, passing through branches of both natural and artificial trees. They passed doors and windows of classroom-style rooms occupied by artists, writers, and composers.

The hallway opened to a shared area with couches, chairs, and a juice bar. When Vadim had toured the institute years before, after they had funded his project—then only an idea—this area had still been under construction. Hard hats required.

At the other side of the common space, Elaine swiped her access badge and led Vadim through a door marked **Administrative Access Only**. Vadim followed his supervisor into a vacant boardroom and took a seat at her direction while she walked to a computer at the front of the room.

"We have two major projects for the upcoming fiscal year," she said. "Both of which will thrust the institute further into the future then we ever thought possible. It will also allow our influential touch to reach thousands, if not tens of thousands, more lives than we already are."

"Elaine," Vadim said too quietly.

His supervisor continued as a hologram appeared at the end of the conference table. It was a blue-tinged image of an architectural project; a sprawling campus with several buildings that looked like dormitories, two central pavilions, and several other structures.

"This is our design—our hope—for a West Coast campus. It would allow an additional eight thousand students and researchers of the arts to study, work, and even live if they wanted to. It is a pivotal step in the fight to keep the arts alive." She turned to him. "We are still clawing out of the ashes, Vadim. And this...if we can fund this...it would give us the opportunity to save thousands of people. Prevent them from working jobs they hate when they would rather be creating. Can you imagine what that's like? To hate your job? Your life? We can cut through the veil of depression, Vadim. But we need funding to do it. We need this deal to go through."

Vadim sympathized. While the last few weeks had been increasingly stressful, and the added pressure from the board didn't help, Vadim had accomplished his dream. He had built the machine.

But he knew someone who hated their life. *Used to know.* And the thought of his brother made him want to crumble into a thousand pieces on the boardroom floor.

"And the grant funding isn't enough?" Vadim asked.

"Unfortunately, it's dried up," Elaine said. "Building a massive wall may not have cost much, but who knew the maintenance behind it would be exponential."

Vadim chuckled. "You mean, who knew people from both sides would continually throw hand grenades and homemade bombs at it?"

She nodded.

"I can't believe that there is no revenue from donors that we can use. There are over 800 in the queue right now. It's going to take a year to clear them all."

"Right," Mohan said. "And that's part of the problem. Because it takes so long for the machine to cool down, we need a place to store these bodies. Our costs have increased with the demand for a larger warehouse and more refrigeration units. It's a rolling expenditure. Not to mention, the donations are received in two parts: half to be put on the list, half upon rendering of services."

Vadim bit his tongue and kept his gaze on the hologram.

"I'm going to level with you, Vadim. With declining to allow the Paris institute to build a second machine and turning down this most recent offer, you have effectively cost us over thirty million dollars. That is beyond a substantial amount of money. Far beyond. The board has already contacted legal. They're meeting this afternoon to begin analyzing your contract and the patents. I am asking you, not just as your boss but as your friend: please accept this offer. If you don't, they will fire you and accept it anyway. Do not do this to yourself."

Vadim shook his head. "The patents are mine and mine alone."

Elaine sighed. Ran a hand over the top of her head. "I don't think you'll win this, Vadim. Like I told you yesterday, they will drain you and then they'll ruin you. The art world is so small. If you burn one, you burn them all."

They sat in silence for several minutes. Inactivity caused the computer to go to standby, and the hologram disappeared from the conference table. Vadim looked up and met his supervisor's eyes.

"I need you to give me the weekend. Please."

Mohan nodded. "Whatever you need, I'll try to get."

Shay had called him twice. The first was to make plans. The second was to cancel those plans.

"Jay is throwing up. I guess he hasn't felt good all day, but his teachers never told me anything."

"No worries," Vadim said into his phone. "Give him some soup and tell him I hope he feels better."

In truth, Vadim was relieved; he needed to think. And if he were around Shay when he tried to figure this out, then his feelings for her would sway his decision.

Vadim stayed on the T until it reached the end of the green line. Shuffling off, he weaved amongst the throng of commuters: businessmen and women, salespeople and construction workers who, despite hours spent performing demanding physical labor, couldn't afford to live in the city proper.

Checking his phone, he saw that his Uber was waiting for him on the far side of the parking lot.

"Where to?" The driver said.

He was an older guy with half-a-head of gray hair and a mustache. A picture of what Vadim guessed to be his granddaughter was wedged into the man's dashboard.

"Luna Cemetery."

The man shifted into drive without saying another word. Vadim watched the trees pass. Breaks in the foliage gave way to excavated building sites with projects in various stages of development.

He rolled the window down and warm air pushed against his face. The brakes squealed slightly as the driver stopped in front of a red light.

"Do you live in the city?" The man asked.

Vadim caught his eyes in the rearview and nodded.

"Busy place."

Remaining silent, Vadim continued to nod. The light turned green and the car picked up. A mile down the road, Vadim spoke, the sound of his own voice surprising him.

"Do you do this for a living?"

"Uber? No, I'm retired. This is just for a little spending money and, honestly, to cure the boredom. You know, you never think that you're going to miss work, but once there's no place to go every day—"

"What did you do?" Vadim interrupted. "For work?"

The driver flipped his blinker and turned down a side road. The distance between building lots increased as they drove.

"I was an engineer. Worked at Hailey General, one of the last non-profit hospitals in the country. Of course now it's privately owned. I think the only one left that isn't straddles the Canadian border some place in northern Maine, but I doubt even that one is still on its own."

"Did you like it?" Vadim asked.

The driver rocked his head from side-to-side. "For the most part yeah...I suppose."

"You don't sound like it."

"Well, I mean, no one *likes* to work. It's whether or not you can tolerate it. I mean, there are so many things: management, the job itself, downtime, budget, raises, strikes, the people you work with. Did you know that if you work a normal forty-hour work week—and come on, let's be honest, nobody works forty hours anymore. All this bullshit that went down when the unions left meant people worked until they couldn't tolerate it, you know? Anyway, what was I saying? Oh yeah, if you work just a normal work week, you spend more time with your coworkers than you do with your family. How fucking sad is that? Sorry, I didn't mean to swear, but it pisses me off, you know?"

Vadim was nodding. He didn't want to, tried to will himself not to, but he asked anyway. "If you could have done something different, not been an engineer, what would you have done? What would have been your dream job?"

The driver didn't answer for several minutes. He eased the car to the side of the road just outside the cemetery's main gate. The engine clicked and idled quietly. Vadim leaned over, ready to repeat the question, when the man said, "I think I would have been an actor. Not like Hollywood, silver-screen-type actor but on Broadway. Or off Broadway, when that used to be a thing. I had taken a couple community college theater classes and loved it. You connected with the audience, you know? It was like everyone was on stage with you in some way."

"Why didn't you do it?" Vadim asked.

"Money, I guess. Unless you were lucky enough to make it big, you starved, and I had got my first girlfriend pregnant and couldn't feed her with promises of food. So I worked two jobs and put myself through school at night."

Vadim nodded. "Thanks for the ride."

Clouds had begun to form over the western side of the sky. Gray, summer evening clouds that threatened heat lightning. Vadim walked along the paved pathway, a route he hadn't traversed in nearly a decade but remembered like he had walked it everyday for the entirety of his life.

A rabbit looked up from the grass, its mouth moving in closed circles as it chewed its dinner. It froze as Vadim approached, waiting as long as it dared until finally bounding toward a pair of thick bushes.

Vadim turned from the path and weaved between head-
stones and grave markers until he came to one void of any
flowers or flags. It was a small headstone, curved at the top in a
rounded wave. The engraving read: *Cole Altov, Son & Brother.*

It was four miles from Luna Cemetery to the Green Line station.
Vadim walked with his hands in his pocket and his head down.
The air had become hot and humid; thunderheads blotted the sky
in shades of gray.

He was a mile away from the train station when it started
raining. Little pats of cool water on his shoulders and his head.
Lightning flashed across the sky followed by thunder that rolled
for what seemed like eons.

He swiped his CharlieCard and rode the T until he reached
Shay's stop. The rain shower had been brief, leaving Boston's
streets to steam the way they do following a heavy summer
shower. The smell of wet concrete and discarded cigarette butts
hit his nose like acrid smoke. Cars whooshed past, splashing water on the sidewalks. Vadim hit the buzzer and waited until the
lock finally clicked and he hiked up to her apartment, the door
swinging open to Shay greeting him with disappointment on her
face.

"I thought you were the delivery guy."

"Sorry."

Shay paused for a moment and took in the sight of him. "Jesus Christ, you're soaked."

"Yeah." He hooked his thumb in the air. "Got caught in the
rain."

"Well come on in."

She shuffled back to the sink, Vadim following her inside.
Her apartment was a two bedroom that must have cost a fortune.
But that explained why the desk and laptop were set up on the

kitchen table along with the fact that her workday never really ended.

Shay looked up from scrubbing dirty dishes. "What is it? What did you do?"

"Nothing," he said.

"You agreed, didn't you?"

"No."

His eyes met hers. She squinted, one hand poised above an empty pan. "Where were you?"

It took him a second, but when the words came, they came smoother than he thought they would.

"Luna Cemetery."

Her face shifted. The muscles holding her lips and eyes relaxed. "Oh."

"Yeah."

"Vadim…"

"Don't." He shook his head. "Just."

"Okay."

He heard coughing from the other room quickly followed by the door buzzer. Shay dropped the pot with a clang and wiped her hands on the back of her sweatpants. A second volley of coughs came from Jay's bedroom.

"That's the delivery guy. Can you check on Jay, please?"

"Aren't you cleaning up from dinner?" He asked.

Exasperated, Shay replied, "Yeah, but lucky for me, Jay threw up dinner. So, I ordered some takeout."

Jay's room was illuminated by a spaceship-shaped nightlight. Glow in the dark stars clung to his ceiling in odd little clusters. His walls were plastered with animated movie characters and cartoon heroes. A Superman emblem hung from the chair of his little desk, the sight of it making Vadim smile. The medallion had been a gift two years ago for the tyke's seventh birthday.

Jay seemed to be sleeping fine, but as Vadim moved to leave, the boy coughed again. He stepped back into the room, easing his weight on the apartment's hardwood floor, but the creak was inevitable. It didn't seem to wake him though. Jay only stirred, rolling under his blanket and weakly coughing into his pillow.

Vadim quietly stepped toward the boy's desk. He flipped through the kid's school books: math, Spanish, Chinese, and biology. His notebooks were scribbled with equations and vocabulary words. The amount of information they shoved at children was ridiculous.

He held the notebook open to one of the last few pages. It was a drawing of a landscape. A sun, trees, and shadows cast on a hill of blue and purple grass. Vadim looked over his shoulder at Shay's sleeping child. One he would have willingly read to before bed each night. He flipped to the next page and found himself looking at a sketch of ocean waves. Half of a lighthouse was on the edge of the page, diagonal stripes of red and blue curling up its side.

"Uncle V?"

Vadim dropped the pages shut and quickly took a seat on the edge of his bed.

"What's up, little man?" he whispered. "How you feeling?"

"OK." Jay rubbed sleep from his eyes. "Where's mom?"

"She just went to get some food. I saw your drawings."

In the glow of the nightlight, Vadim saw the boy's eyes widen.

"I'm sorry. I finished my homework first, I promise. Mom wasn't home, and I was bored, and if you want to throw them out—"

"Whoa, whoa. Shhh." Vadim rubbed the top of Jay's head. The boy coughed. "Why would I throw them out?"

"Because I should be studying. That's what mom and Ms. Vasquez say."

Vadim clenched his jaw. Ground his teeth together. He formed a fist and playfully bumped the boy's shoulder.

"You gotta do what makes you happy, little guy. Trust me."

Jay nodded and yawned. Two teeth were missing, their voids forming little black squares in his smile.

Vadim pulled the comforter up to the boy's neck and co-cooned him inside. Back in the kitchen, Shay was pulling several containers of Chinese takeout from plastic bags.

"Damn guy forgot the lo mein," she muttered. "How is he?"

"Jay? He's fine, just coughing. Feels like his fever's finally breaking."

Shay nodded. She stood with her hands on her hips, staring at the food with eyes that refused to blink. He walked over to her and put his hands on both her arms. His heart was racing. She looked up at him, and his chest tingled. His stomach fluttered. His lips parted slightly and, to his complete shock, Shay leaned forward and kissed him.

They separated, and she laughed, raising her hand to her lips. Vadim's voice caught in his throat. His head was a rush of jumbled thoughts. Words formed and split away before he had a chance to say them aloud.

"Sorry." Shay moved to the sink and washed her hands. "My head is just—I'm just exhausted and hungry."

"No," Vadim nearly shouted.

Shay looked at him in shock; his cheeks burned. He was ruining it. This was his chance, and he was ruining it. He took a deep breath and regained conscious control of his vocal cords.

"Sorry. I don't want you to think that was a mistake."

Shay pressed her lips into a straight line. "Vadim, there's just too much—"

"Mom!" Jay called from his bedroom.

The boy's voice was scratchy and tired. He called a second time, and Shay forced a smile. "Set up some plates; I'll be back in a second."

But Vadim knew from the flash of regret in her eyes when they parted that there was no going back. She would tend to Jay, and then deliver a talk that would crush him, like it did the last time she said it. He couldn't hear the words again.

"I should get going. Let you and Jay rest."

He met her eyes and Vadim knew that she understood. "Okay. Stay dry."

At the door, as he was shoving his feet into his shoes, he asked. "How's he doing in school?"

"Good." She paused in the hallway as Jay called a third time. "On track for advance placement in mid-grade math."

Vadim pursed his lips. "That's good."

"Damn right," she said with more relief than pride. "He keeps it up, he'll be set. Maybe get a job in finance or accounting. Who knows, maybe an engineer or something."

"Think he'll like that?"

She shrugged. "Probably. But even if he doesn't, long as it pays well, who cares."

"Right," Vadim said quiet enough to be a whisper. "Happy or secure. Whatever's more important."

Vadim stared at the monitors on his desk as the machine went through its boot-up sequence. The purple running lights pulsed around the base of the dome like a thready heartbeat. The lights faded, trading their glow for the illumination of those in the ceiling.

"Okay," Vadim said quietly. "We're set."

Behind him, Elaine nodded. "You're making the right choice."

It was different than he had expected. There were no cameras, no reporters. The donor had wanted the utmost secrecy. He had signed his waiver and disclosed who the final piece (assuming there would be a final piece) was supposed to be delivered to. Vadim had never even learned the man's name. According to his roster, John Doe was waiting, relaxed and ready on the other side of the wall.

Elaine's hand rested on his shoulder. "With the money he's donated, we'll be able to reach thousands more lives."

Vadim wouldn't be able to lie to Shay. He could put off telling her, avoiding the subject until she asked him directly. But when that inevitable encounter came, sitting at the bar, walking, or maybe even watching a movie…

"Just," Vadim said, his voice heavy. "Just keep your word."

Elaine's fingers squeezed his shoulder. "It's in the agreement. As soon as he turns sixteen, he's guaranteed a spot. Don't worry."

Vadim entered in the commands and watched as the mechanical arms descended from the ceiling and reached into the room's outer wall. They retrieved the metal tray with the body on top. His heart fluttered. He leaned forward, but Elaine held a firm grip. Vadim watched the rhythmic rise and fall of the body's chest. This was wrong. He bit his lip. He could cancel it, punch in the terminate command, and be done with it.

The body's chest moved faster, and so did Vadim's. He reached forward, felt the painful pressure of his supervisor's white-knuckle hold on his shoulder.

"Think of Jay," she said.

And he did. As the arms slid the tray inside of the machine, he thought of little Jay living a life he actually enjoyed. Sponsored by the institution, so he could continue to study and create art without being chained to a desk and miserable. The dome slid shut, and he saw the sketches in Jay's notebook. The ocean, the lighthouse.

Vadim's monitors flashed and spiraled music notes and streaks of vibrant colors. They both marveled at the full spectrum of the color wheel as it twirled toward them in vivid, blending swirls.

"That," Vadim's voice was raspy. "That's never happened. I've never seen those colors before. Ever."

"Never?"

Vadim remained transfixed by the display. Captivated and trancelike, as if he were hallucinating. His eyes refused to blink.

Shadows danced inside the dome. An arm raised, a leg kicked. The man was dying. John Doe was taking his last breath and—

The sound of a voice, humming, came from the speakers embedded in the right monitor; all the while, colors rotated, slowing until they formed a piece of magnificent art splattered on the screen.

Soft at first, the voice formed words, growing from a melodic hum to a powerful song. It gave Vadim chills. A vocal harmony. A baritone and a tenor melted together in a crescendo of emotions.

"Wow," Elaine breathed. "How 'bout that?"

"Yeah," Vadim said, unable to blink. "How about that?"

Tom Howard

WHEN THE BOUGH BREAKS

Xex was an unusual Xex.
Although she looked like the others, tiny and slender with wasp wings, they preferred reclining on branches and wrapping themselves in dreamtime cocoons during the winter. She asked a lofty spruce if she could rest on one of its upper branches for a while and waited as it slowly rumbled a reply. Fortunately, the young spruce's answer would come before sunset. Xex didn't mind. Some Xex didn't bother to ask permission; they rested their slender brown bodies and transparent wings on any branch. Xex, however, tried to be more respectful of her forest friends.

She spotted a two-legged creature walking upright through the forest and left her branch for a closer look. She avoided the open spaces and kept herself concealed in the shade. Although tiny and fast, her dark brown body could be seen against the occasional snowdrift.

A human walked through the ferns and brush, making enough noise for a dozen two-legs. He wore layers of unnatural material in bright colors and walked as if the path belonged to him. Atop his shoulder rested an ax. He stopped to mark an elderly cedar by chopping a large X in its living flesh. Xex winced.

The pain of the ax was replaced by fear as she spotted the smoking stick in the man's mouth. Fire spelt death to those in the forest. The melting snow extinguished the spark of fire, and she moved upwind to avoid the noxious fumes.

Under the forest canopy, the snow wasn't as deep. She flew behind a rhododendron bush as the man climbed the corpse of a giant cedar felled, not by two-legs such as himself, but by age and tree rot a century earlier. Xex recalled the ground shaking and the wumf when it fell.

The man stood atop the majestic mountain of rich red wood and took a deep breath. He smiled as if he looked over his kingdom. His thick coat partially covered a red shirt and his pants had the bottom hem cut off. Xex had seen this before. "Loggers" did that to their pants to prevent being caught by broken limbs if they had to move out of danger quickly. If there were loggers this deep in the woods…

Xex flew closer. Humans stank and made too much noise, and this one was no exception. She'd watch him and his ax until he left. No one stayed in the deep woods very long.

In the crisp air, she smelled an approaching Pridii. The large, shaggy creatures walked on their hind legs and had enormous feet. They were simple-minded and guileless, staunch protectors of animals within their territories. The gentle giants feared humans and hid themselves deeper in the woods every year. Xex wondered what would happen to the Pridii, and to all the forest creatures, if humans such as the two-legs below took over.

She had no time for those dark thoughts. The Pridii drew closer, unaware of the human ahead of him. Perhaps the early snowfall had confused the giant, and it thought night approached. She flew up so she could look down at a larger area with her sharp eyes. The large cedar deadfall probably served as a boundary marker, a landmark indicating the edge of the Pridii's usual patrol.

Even in the gloom, the giant Pridii couldn't help being seen by the human. How could she ensure the man didn't spot the approaching beast? He might run and bring more two-legs to chase and hunt the Pridii.

Xex flew toward the human, and without thinking, she pushed the ax handle off the man's shoulder. Fast as lightning and strong for her size, she darted away, hoping not to be seen. The man exclaimed and jumped out of the way of the ax head as it fell. He avoided it but stumbled and slipped from the log. He hit the tree on his backside and slid onto the snowy ground below. Fortunately for him, the ax fell away, and he landed on a cassock of moss.

The smell of the approaching Pridii increased—they always smelled of fallen leaves and pinecones—and she flew to warn it of the human's proximity on the other side of the log. She waved her arms and flew around its head until it stopped and focused on her. The language of the Pridii consisted of a few grunts. Xex gave the universal sign for danger, arms crossed and uncrossed over her chest, until finally the Pridii repeated the gesture and looked around. Pointing toward the fallen cedar, she gave him the sign for human: hands over her eyes. It was a relatively new sign, but the Pridii recognized it and moved back the way it had come.

When she returned to the log, the human on the ground had not moved. The man lay against the tree as if asleep, his eyes closed and his expression blank. Had he hit his head against a burl on his way down? Was he breathing?

Diving to the man's shoulder, she peered anxiously at his face. If he wasn't breathing, perhaps she could convince the Pridii to return and place the human's body under a windfall's root bundle. Xex, distracted by her plan to prevent the body from being found by more humans, didn't realize he'd opened his eyes and was staring at her until it was too late.

"Aha!" he exclaimed and grabbed her before she could fly off. He held her tight in his grasp—too tight. Without thinking, Xex acted defensively. Her body, a sleek shape looking like a piece of darkened wood, had spurs at wrists and heels. Short and rarely used, these barbs contained a toxin created from the ingested resin of hemlocks. Suited more for hungry spiders and myopic birds, the venom made short work of attackers. Those that survived did not prey on Xex again.

Her wrist barbs pierced the skin of his fingers and pumped dark liquid into him. The man jerked and released her. He gasped once before his chin dropped to his chest. This time Xex could see him breathing but couldn't decide whether to be grateful or disappointed. She fluttered her wings to ensure they weren't damaged and pondered what to do next.

She'd never injected a creature so large but doubted she'd killed him, only knocked him unconscious. She approached the man and placed her palms against his temple. Images flashed into her head, and she jerked her hands away. Xex entered other Xexs' dreams but never a human's. She'd never encountered such stark images with one of her own kin.

Although frightened by what she'd seen, she didn't fly away. She forced herself to touch him again, sharing the man's dreamscape. She told herself she was making the attempt to make sure he was all right, but the truth was she was curious.

She walked down a dark tunnel into the light. Instead of her chocolate brown body, she looked down to find herself one of the two-legged humans. A female. They were in a room and a small boy sat on the ceiling, not floating or flying, just sitting. He was using a pair of pruning shears to decapitate a struggling rat. When it squealed, he released the pressure until it stopped and then applied it again.

"You can't hide in here forever," Xex told him, accepting the boy's role for her as his mother. Languages, gravity, and reality didn't matter in dreamscape. "Your favorite program is on."

The boy screamed at her, slicing the rat in half with his fury. In a flash, he jumped at her.

She pulled her hand away from his temple, shaking and sick from the dream. He slept fitfully, fighting the toxin, while she calmed herself.

Not many Xex could influence another's dreams. Xex could. The Xex relived fond memories or picturesque places. Occasionally, they invited friends to accompany them, but those visitors were merely spectators in someone else's dreams. Xex's friends stopped inviting her when she changed their dreams.

Could she do the same with a human?

She touched the skin of the man's temple. Back in the room, she watched the boy scissoring away at the screaming rat. When he bellowed angrily at her, she found herself back in the real world again. Angered by her inability to remain in the dream, she forced her way back in. Again and again, the boy mutilated the rat and banished her back to the real world. Her head throbbing, she couldn't let the human's violent dreams defeat her.

The man moaned, and Xex realized she didn't have much time to affect his dream. This time when she entered the tunnel, she pictured a doorway at the end. It was just a small change, but she saw it and felt satisfaction at being able to control some aspect of the dream. What else could she influence?

Opening the door, she saw the boy and the rat, but this time, she imagined the rat in the position of power. A giant rat sat on the ceiling cutting into the neck of a tiny boy who screamed and screamed while the rat laughed. Xex gained more control of the dream and lowered the rat to the floor. It stared at her with yellow eyes. The boy looked at her for help, and she banished the blood pouring from his neck. Next, she removed the rat.

"So," she said, replacing the woman's body with her more familiar one. "Humans dream. What shall we do with you now?"

The man called out into the forest as he awoke, and Xex fled to a nearby bush. Staggering to his feet and shaking his head, he retrieved his ax and made his way back the way he'd come.

Xex flew into the canopy and wondered what to do with her newfound information. Perhaps someone wiser could tell her what to do about the unwelcome visitor and her discovery that she could enter—and control—their dreams. With a few thrusts of her wings, she gained altitude in the crisp air and glided around the mountain to a clump of ancient trees. Xex passed many sacks of webbing. Never had she seen so many of her people dreaming before.

She approached a stone mountain situated in the middle of the wood. Two bull elk moved away through the underbrush as she drew near. Xex nodded to them as she passed and dusted the snow from her usual rock before sitting. Behind the tranquil pond, and causing it to be there, a small but enthusiastic waterfall spilled from an opening in the stony mountain. Above, small bears had dug holes in the side of the mountain, giving it a rudimentary face.

"Hello, Xex," said the gently rumbling waterfall. "It is good to see you again."

"Thank you, Ancient One," said Xex. "Am I interrupting? I saw the elk."

The hole in the stone made a sighing sound. "More territorial disputes between our animal friends, Strange Xex." In the forests lived many Xex, Pridii, bears, elk, wolves, Sinistri, and smaller creatures, but only one Ancient One existed. He somehow combined the wisdom of the stones with the alertness of the water.

She smiled. "How do you know which Xex I am?"

The waterfall laughed. "You have been here many times, little Xex, and are a memorable...individual. My name for you is Dreamless."

"I dream," said Xex. "I am Xex, the powerful but infrequent dreamer."

"Ah. And what has brought about this change, Infrequent? Are you nearing podtime?"

"No!" Xex insisted, fluttering her wings indignantly. "I'm not ready to leave behind a new me. I'm here because I am disturbed by the number of two-legs coming into the forest and the damage they might do."

"Yes," said the bubbles in the pond. "They are becoming more plentiful."

"I just prevented a logger from encountering a wandering Pridii."

"Oh, yes," the old voice said. "I have heard of the men who harvest the trees."

Xex said, "They are a sickness. They do more harm than an entire band of beavers."

The Ancient One laughed. "Do not concern yourself with mankind. They will soon pass away. The forest is infinite."

"It is not infinite if they destroy it!" Xex exclaimed. "We must do something."

The Ancient One sighed again. "Child, you have existed since this forest sprouted from the ground, but even then I was ancient. The humans may damage us, but soon their time shall pass. They reek of transience."

"What if they destroy the forests before they leave?" she asked.

"As long as one seed survives, you and I will live again. Someday, even I will wear away to nothing. You will eventually age and create a seedling from your passing."

"In the meantime, we watch them chop down our friends?"

"You still dream, don't you?" consoled the Ancient One. "Find yourself a comfortable spot to slumber and weave yourself some dreams from the times before the two-legs appeared. When you wake, they will be a memory, their bones buried deep in the dirt."

Xex couldn't wait that long. "They dream."

"Who?"

"The two-legs," said Xex. "I have seen it. I have entered one's dreamtime and made it my own."

The waterfall remained silent for a time. "Interesting. Exercise patience, little Xex."

Xex tried not to show her disappointment at being told to wait. "I will speak to you again."

"This I know," said the Ancient One and spoke no more.

Xex flew across the pond and into the forest. The Ancient One had helped her reach a decision, but it was not the one he suggested. She was determined not to hide while her forest was destroyed. Her dream experience with the man had proved she and the forest were not defenseless.

This was war. From now on, any human who entered the woods would be her target. When they slept, she would get to them. Once in dreamtime, she might even be able to keep them there forever or give them nightmares. She'd convince her fellow Xex to assist her. Soon humans would fear the forest as much as she loved it. It was unprecedented for a Xex to think so aggressively.

Then again, Xex was a very unusual Xex.

Katie Sherman

THE THIRD GENDER

When she traveled, Nadia's first picture was always from the plane. In the states, she looked for the symmetrical angles of Little League fields—white plates, red clay, pure green grass. In London, she focused on the bridges. Fishbone scales of ecru against the murky tan water. In Egypt, Nadia noticed the buildings—tall skyscrapers that looked like they were sculpted from the sand itself. She scratched her left hand, focused the lens, and slowly applied pressure to the shutter. The plane bounced three quick times and rolled to a stop.

Nadia had been arguing over her place as a war correspondent since she graduated from Medill nine years ago. There was still something taboo about women in combat zones. But now that she was five months pregnant, the stares and warnings were so redundant she regularly ignored them. Her mother sent pleading emails of genuine concern guilting her. Jonathan, the baby's father, wanted her to take local assignments exclusively. After he suggested this one too many times, their relationship unspooled like yarn dropped to the floor.

Post bitter break-up and determined to make a feminist statement, Nadia finagled a job with *The Associated Press* as a stringer. She was penetrating the Libyan insurgence, risking her life and that of her unborn son for a nominal wage. During previous assignments, she had seen car bombs and grenades, chemical weapons and famine. She saw babies with bloated, distended bellies and visible rib cages. She'd heard cries so raw they were terrestrial as they imprinted themselves permanently in her mind. She'd been shot at. She'd been injured. But none of that could keep Nadia from the field. Work was an escape. Her job placed her in situations where she witnessed first-hand the cruelty and benevolence of humanity. Nadia had a partiality for Arabic countries, a preference past down from a mentor who revealed that female journalists had an advantage there.

"In a lot of places, but mostly Arabic speaking countries, we're the third gender," she had said over cocktails in a crowded, low rent bar when they were imbedded in Afghanistan. "Unlike men we can speak to Islamic women, but the men view us as more male than female. It's the one advantage we get."

They'd toasted one another then, their lukewarm beer skunked and reeking of yeast.

This trip, Nadia traveled light with two small leather bags worn around the edges and consistently dusted with sand. Her heaviest was her camera case, a graduation present from her parents that had seen nearly forty countries. It held her two favorite DSLR bodies, three lenses, an independent strobe flash, a modifier, ten flash cards, a stack of erotic letters that helped with checkpoints, Leo's sonogram, and a smudged and wrinkled photocopied picture of Martha Gellhorn. Part of her felt guilty that she stared at the image of her idol more than the ultrasound of the fuzzy jellybean that was her son.

She stepped directly from the airport's entrance to the asphalt surrounding it, searching for her escort. The weather was balmy and tropical with humidity that hung around Nadia's shoulders. She knew only two things. Her escort would be a man and he would be young. Guides were almost always English-speaking students. Muhammad stood beside a beat-up black SUV. In a sea of hijabs and aging men, he wore a New York Yankees hat with a black insignia and camo background. It was pulled low over deep-set brown eyes. He was the type of man who shouldn't have a beard, but he did. His was filled with a handful of bald patches. The peninsulas of hair were black and wiry. He wore a blue shirt buttoned to his neck, and it looked like his Adams apple was erupting over it. He stepped forward, extending his hands to accept the bags. A musk that was pleasant but overwhelming rose from him.

"Here," he said eagerly. "I'll get that."

Nadia readjusted the camera bag on her shoulder, allowing the weight to cut into the pale skin beneath her tunic. She handed Muhammad the smaller duffle that carried her maternity pants, body armor, pajamas, and a few packs of Nutter Butters to ward off nausea. Muhammad fumbled with the single bag and aggressively opened the rear door. Nadia clambered into the front instead.

Muhammad kicked the tires and clumps of red clay poured down. "Most journalist ride in the rear," he said.

Nadia pulled at the edge of a red Nutter Butter packet, biting into the cookie and allowing the creamy peanut butter to coat her tongue. "I'd prefer the company." She held out the bag. "Want one?" Muhammad snaked a hand through the opening in the cellophane, took one, and began to chew loudly. The air conditioning blasted air as Nadia wiggled in the seat to get comfortable. Muhammad walked around the tail of the vehicle before flopping into the driver's seat. He adjusted the angles of the vents and navigated the car onto a narrow side street adjacent to the airport.

"You're from Egypt?" Nadia asked Muhammad as he shifted gears, careful to ensure their forearms didn't graze.

"Ajdabiya," he said. He stared directly ahead as he steered the car onto a two-lane road surrounded by a residential neighborhood.

"Your family's there?" Nadia asked, referring to the coastal town in Libya now infamous for protecting a mob that attacked four European journalists. Muhammad nodded. The wind rattled the windshield as they drove through a neighborhood with tall stucco apartment buildings, laundry hanging on stretched lines across the roof.

"Most of them are still there. There were eleven of us," he said. "Eight girls, me, my parents."

"Are you close?" Nadia chewed slowly, careful to ensure she wasn't loud. Jonathan once claimed her chewing sounded like grinding bolts.

"I was close to my oldest sister," he said, allowing the word *was* to dominate.

"And now?"

"She was a refugee in Tunisia," he said, the words coming slowly. "There was a garbage fire in the camp. She tried to help a few children who were watching the flames. She couldn't."

Nadia closed her eyes. She instinctively rubbed her stomach, and her son savagely kicked her hand. She stared out the window. During the next three hours, most of the villages that skirted Nadia's peripheral vision looked similar: grungy white walls and arched windows coated with iron bars. In the seaside village of Marsa Matruh, black graffiti covered the houses' lower halves but it wasn't the foul language of New York vandals. There were a number of mocking portraits of Gaddafi, meticulously drawn, with oversized ears and wide, cartoonish eyes. Nadia snapped a quick picture of one.

"Why are you here?" Muhammad asked after they passed Marina El Alamein and had been on the road thirteen hours. He flexed his fist. Nadia watched the veins bulge. She hadn't expected the question. Even more puzzling was his tone, a tone that was neither aggressive nor friendly. It teetered somewhere arbitrarily in between.

"I don't know. Maybe, I have something to prove." Nadia gnawed on the outer edge of her tongue. The raised taste buds were metallic, like pennies. "Are you angry I am?"

"You'll have a family soon. Why put yourself in the middle of this chaos?"

"It's my job," Nadia answered, annoyed but also aware that it wasn't the whole truth. Her answer was far too simple. She paused but no dramatic effect was created. "My dad calls me Shark because sharks never stop moving. They're perpetual motion. I just, I don't know who I am without a camera."

"What happens when the baby comes?" The question surprised her, and the intrusion felt like a nagging needle in her spine. She tried her best to ignore it, knowing she was guilty of peppering Muhammad with questions as well.

Nadia rested her head against the cool glass and allowed awkwardness to fill the car. They bounced over a rut, and Nadia's camera slipped from her lap. She needed a moment to erase the question so she retrieved the camera, raised it to her right eye, and took an errant picture of the coast. The camera felt heavy in her hands. Leaden. Waves peaked and broke in a foamy froth. *What happens when the baby comes?* Nadia pictured Jonathan's murky gray eyes. The way he squinted when he read in their dimly-lit living room, his fingers prying at the frayed edge of the sofa. When Nadia imagined her son, he was a carbon copy of his father.

In the border town of Salloum, Muhammad stopped at an open-
air fish market. It smelled of dust and salt and the blood from
mackerels. The fish were packed tightly, balancing on back fins.
Their eyes were unnerving—staring up at Nadia as she passed.
The scarf tied tightly under her chin absorbed her sweat. She
tucked it behind her ears before readjusting it so her hair
wouldn't show. Broad men in green aprons stood and sliced thin
slivers of the fish's fleshy underbelly. They would extend
bloody knives to the people, offering a taste of fresh sashimi.
Nadia snapped a photo, but only one, to relieve some of her dis-
comfort.

Muhammad ducked into a restaurant and Nadia followed a
few paces behind. Wooden stools sat underneath rickety tables
with iron legs. They ordered a fish skillet. Two gray plates were
slathered with yellow rice, peas, and oversized prawns the size
of a millionaire's engagement ring. Momentarily forgetting
where she was, Nadia slipped off her shoes. Her compression
socks had left deep red indentions on her ankles and heels. She
began to peel them off.

"Confining?" Muhammad asked, blushing slightly presumably at the sight of a woman's bare ankle. Nadia nodded, rubbed
the indention, and put the socks back on.

Muhammad crushed a lemon in his fist over the food. He
ate quickly.

"How are we going to get through the border?" she asked.
She was becoming unnerved by the lack of a plan. A thin bead
of sweat formed at the base of Nadia's neck. During the drive,
she hadn't slept much and Muhammad hadn't slept at all. It was
too intimate, the thought of closing her eyes, drooling, snoring,
sighing next to this man she barely knew. Muhammad preferred
to drive straight through. When he stopped for gas, Nadia
stretched and walked. Muhammad ordered tea in oversized paper containers. The heat turned his palms a deeper shade of red.

"Anything?" she asked again. Muhammad continued to chew loudly.

"I have these letters," she began, knowing that Muhammad wouldn't like them. This was Jonathan's idea, something he'd heard other female journalists used. A stack of erotic letters strategically aged with tea, to distract young guards. Often the boys stood drooling with quickened pulses over references to pink clitorises and rosy nipples. *The color of femininity was a blush, blooming pink,* Nadia thought, knowing she owned nothing that color.

"They're sexual," she said. "Distracting."

Muhammad worked to continue eating but blood filled his neck and jawline. The exposed skin throughout his beard was pink.

"Unsavory," he mumbled. "Disgraceful."

"They work. The letters will get us through."

"No. You don't have credentials?" His mouth was still filled with food.

"I'm here to report on the rebels," she said and wondered how much Muhammad knew about her assignment. Did he support Gaddafi? "If you have no plan, the letters will have to do."

"What do they say in your country?" Muhammad asked. "It's your rodeo." There was a catch in his voice. A pucker that made Nadia think he was aiming for nonchalance. "We obviously can't take weapons in, but you'll wear your body armor."

Nadia bulked at the suggestion, a vein in her neck throbbing like a recently stubbed toe. Jonathan would have asked her to take such a precaution. He would have massaged the muscles in her shoulder blades as he told her how necessary it was. Goose pimples spread like a rash over Nadia's forearms. She didn't want to miss him.

At the car, Muhammad crumpled trash in his fist, tightly squeezing the Nutter Butter packages like a stress ball. He tossed the overnight bag onto the gravel parking lot.

"The armor will protect you," he said.

"It might keep me from getting across the border." An Iraqi Army sergeant once told her body armor was a red flag in unstable political climates. It meant she needed protection from both inanimate objects and from his people. He hovered near her, so close she could smell the Skoal on his breath. So close she could hear his jaw click as he spat.

"Not if your letters are all you say they are," Muhammad said, bringing her back. He kicked at the clumps of dirt and small rocks.

Nadia pulled the gauzy charcoal tunic over her head. Underneath, she wore a stretchy flesh-colored tank top and jeans. Muhammad stared intently at his palms, wiping them on his jeans.

"There a restroom inside," he said gruffly. "Doing that here is just foolish." His jaw was a tense line. "Remember where you are."

Nadia positioned the mesh harness across her chest, pulling the shoulders taunt. The bulky vest constricted her back and torso, causing Nadia to instantly sweat and pant. The vest would've come just under her belly button had she not been pregnant. But now, she stretched the Velcros sheaths as far as they would go and lightly folded them over. Barely an inch or two to spare. Her headscarf sat six inches from her forehead. Thin wisps of hair were plastered to the corner of her eyes. Glued to her cheeks. Her eyes watered, and she wondered if they were tears from the disagreements and the sudden homesickness and the embarrassment of her rookie mistake or if it was just the result from the elements.

"I'll humor you now," she said. "But in the field, I can't get around with both the baby's weight and the weight of the vest."

Muhammad rolled his eyes, still staring off into the distance. He crossed his arms begrudgingly as Nadia spoke.

The border was crowded with long lines of cars. Many were piled high with rolled rugs and filled laundry bags. The air smelled like sand and sweat, like a feral animal. As Muhammad steered through the traffic, Nadia snapped a picture of three little girls. There was dew in their hair, evidence of the cool nights. The sparkling balls looked like hundreds of mirrors reflecting the refugees who were coursing an escape route through Libya.

If it weren't for the odd background—the piles of clothes and the mass of people—the scene would feel pedestrian. A man leaned arrogantly in front of a wall of garbage bags selling bottles of water, flashlights, batteries. His long black beard was freckled with white hairs. Muhammad spoke to him, and he began flailing his arms wildly.

"Who was that?" Nadia asked after they drove away. Muhammad accelerated too quickly and a fume of smoke engulfed the man.

"Kadar. A friend I see when I cross," Muhammad said. "There's a guy in the far lane. Kadar says that guy will let us through, papers or not, when Kadar gives him a hand signal."

Nadia rummaged through her camera case for the erotic letters but they weren't there. There were ten total but the one on the bottom was the only letter that was real. It was pristinely white and crisp. It was from Jonathan and unlike the others, it outlined life rather then sex. Nadia had always loved his slanted script as he spelled out things like procreation and legacy and son. The words beat against her like pellets in a hail storm. It had been Jonathan's idea to get pregnant. His idea to carry the letters. His idea to end things. It was Jonathan who wanted the child she carried. She had the proof. She had it all in writing.

The letters weren't where she'd placed them. She shifted through the bag again, more frantically this time. Removed camera bodies. The sonogram. Gellhorn.

"They're not there," Muhammad said as he pressed one finger on the barely visible creases in his forehead. "I took them. At the market."

"Give them back," Nadia said, her voice sliding an octave higher.

"That filth," Muhammad said. He looked like he wanted to wipe his tongue clean. "That has no place here."

Nadia sat, chastised and angry, the heavy vest pressed into her rib cage.

"You could've told me you knew someone." She felt like a child.

Muhammad laughed but the chuckle felt aggressive and taunting. "I didn't know Kadar would be here. That he could get you through," he said. "I just knew I couldn't use sex to help you pass."

Nadia's eyes bulged and pulsed, vibrating to avoid inevitable tears. That letter was the only proof she'd had that Jonathan wanted them. Now there was nothing.

Muhammad waited at the border. When they finally inched towards the front, Kadar was a few steps behind their car. People flanked him on all sides but he didn't blend. He was heads taller than the tallest man. He stretched a small Libyan flag over his head and Muhammad paused to chat with the guard, passed him a few scraps of paper: a ploy to make it seem like they had documentation. Their accomplice leaned heavily on his forearms and leered at Nadia. She felt clammy, unnerved. Her palms began to sweat. Then he allowed them through. Muhammad stomped on the gas pedal, sailing past the checkpoint as red dust kicked up behind them, and the girls and the tightly rolled red rugs, even Kadar, were visions from the past.

Nadia closed her eyes, unwilling to sleep next to Muhammad but needing distance the car couldn't provide. She knew he'd taken something from her that she shouldn't want, and the betrayal was an exposure she couldn't fixate on.

The hotel room in Benghazi was dirty with flittering flecks of dust and smudged glass. There were cockroaches whose exterior shells made loud crunching sounds, even under bare feet. Despite the ugliness and the dirt coating the pastel duvet, the lights in the room were bright fluorescents; bulbs hung so low she bumped her head. The bathtub was marked with a tan ring. The sink was so chipped it looked like cheap confetti, robbed of color.

Nadia opened the closet doors, and they made a loud groan. Each of her tunics rested in a single file line, revealing a sampling of dark hues—faded black, putrid green, charcoal. Propped in the corner, heavy and intrusive, was the navy body armor. It was the only pure and saturated color in the room. The Velcro straps hung open, an exposed hug. Nadia kicked it as she dressed. It rocked, teetered one way then another. It rested, still standing and unharmed. Nadia brushed her teeth and dressed quickly. She let her body armor remain in the corner as she pulled the green tunic over her head and hid her hair with a black scarf. In the lobby, a group of people talked about recent arrests, including a handful of American journalists. Muhammad sat, drank tea, and listened.

"We need to head to Shajara Square," Nadia said, without so much as a greeting. She fiddled with the cumbersome tunic, crumpled and contorted the fabric.

"Too dangerous."

"The revolution is nonviolent, Muhammad," Nadia said, trying not to scoff. "I have to move freely."

"Nonviolence doesn't mean no violence. The people seem nice but there have been grumblings." His voice was irritatingly calm. "Stop being naïve. Something bad could happen to you."

"If I want or need your advice, I'll ask for it," she said. "Get the car."

Muhammad sat his tea down disagreeably, slamming it onto the side table so hard that brown liquid sloshed over the rim. He jiggled the keys in his pocket and walked briskly to the rotating glass door.

The sound from Shajara Square hit Nadia first. Crowds chanted in a low cadence. The eeriness of their rhythm made Nadia shiver despite the heat. Then she saw the horde of protesters. She had been in Benghazi once before and remembered the square housed a wide round fountain, but now it was no longer visible. Instead, black hair and headscarves were sandwiched against one another, charging forward like a storm cloud. Around the fountain was a small city of white tents marred with dust. People held colorful signs, florescent poster board fastened to tree limbs. One had a black and white photo of Gaddafi. The paper was slashed where his throat would be.

Others held Libyan flags, waving them aggressively against the battering wind. The car couldn't navigate the street so they left it parked. People began to crawl on top, and the metal popped slightly under their weight. Someone bumped into Nadia, pushed her back into a sea of caramel-colored hands. She and Muhammad exchanged a look, their eyes drawn together and their mouths thin, mirrored lines.

"What're they saying?" Nadia asked.

"Corruption is the enemy of God."

The wind picked up and billowed her tunic, then switched directions so the fabric defined her bump. Her camera sat heavy over her stomach. The long lens pinged off people as she worked her way through the crowd. Most protesters were young. One woman had shiny black hair that peeked out from her hijab by six inches. A tiny boy wore brown pants that were too small, thick, and inappropriate for the weather. Nadia wanted to carry him from this tumultuous place. Another child had almond shape eyes that were soulful, sighs brimming from her to show how little she wanted to be there. They didn't speak to Nadia, too caught up in the aggression around them, but they stared.

Muhammad shifted cautiously, his eyes busy as he surveyed the crowd. "I don't feel good about this. If something happens to me, my mother will be crushed."

The crowd grew louder. Guards waited in the windows of the tall brick government buildings that outlined the square. Nadia's muscles felt like jelly as she raised the camera to her right eye. She took thirty pictures before the first gunshot echoed against the crowd. Muhammad tugged on her elbow, guiding her closer to the city's center. A signal to move on. She didn't stop though. Her pointer finger didn't leave the shutter as she pivoted, getting each angle.

Then the woman next to her lit a homemade bomb.

Nadia got a picture of the woman—her arm a slingshot, her hijab peeled back to reveal a toned bicep. Her hazel eyes flickering as they gazed beyond the flame. Her boy clung to the hem of her black hijab. He was probably nine. The flame seared Nadia's eyes. Smoke overwhelmed her, surrounded her like a cloak. The smell jabbed at her, making her retch. Then a ricocheting bullet sliced through the boy's shin. He clutched the wound, folding in half as he fell to the ground. The mother sheltered him with her body, desperation radiating from her. Muhammad squeezed Nadia's forearm as he bent to check on the injured child. The crowd pulsed closer, a living thing vibrating around them. Nadia tasted blood. She had broken the skin on her lower lip.

"We need to leave before things get worse," Muhammad hollered into the violent wind. His fingers left angry red indentions on Nadia's arm. Another bullet buried itself into a myrtle tree, somehow missing every protester despite the confined space.

"This is the story," Nadia yelled. She took pictures from every angle. She got signs. She raised her camera high and captured an image of the crowd. She used a wide-angle lens to get a picture of the machine guns on the roofs. "Closer," she said as she pulled Muhammad by his sleeve, pointing towards the fountain. He held his hands up, as if in defeat. She led him through the square.

Nadia climbed onto its beveled edge and pivoted to see where they had been. She snapped a picture of the men scaling their car. They looked about Muhammad's age. Each with beards. One had a vein that pulsed in his forehead. She zoomed in on his face, focused, captured the image. The army released tear gas. It scorched her eyes and burned the inside of her nostrils. She stayed low in an attempt to avoid it. The next bullet lodged itself in Nadia's shoulder blade before she heard it, as if some natural law had worked in reverse. It pushed her into the fountain. The warm water was dirty, more gray than clear. It smelled like used gym socks, likely a wash station for the protesters who'd camped there overnight. Nadia rubbed it into her eyes anyway, tried to grind away the heat of the mace. Blood ran in a quick, thin line to her waist and she felt for a hole in the front of her body, but there was no exit wound. Her body had accepted the bullet, protected it with surrounding muscles. Nadia felt lightheaded, her entire arm was numb and her fingers tingling.

She rubbed her stomach and wished the baby would move. He didn't. The crowd and the gas and the blood swallowed her. Soon though, a hand gripped the back of her tunic. Muhammad jerked her away from the water, shouting her name. He cradled his right hand and Nadia saw the perfectly round hole. Blood encrusted his wrist.

"This is hell. We have to get out of here." He supported Nadia as she crawled from the fountain. Nadia shivered. Her clothes clung to her body. Her face felt cold and sore, as if she'd been badly beaten. Her eyes wide, scanning. Her camera was slung behind her, like some useless cape. The leather strap that secured it around her neck was damp but it was otherwise unharmed. They limped to a doorway at the edge of the square. Someone is screaming, she thought before she realized it was her. Nadia slumped against the door, nodded in and out of restless consciousness. Muhammad lightly slapped her cheeks.

"Stay awake, Nadia," he said. Nadia groaned. He shouted her name. "Tell me about the baby. Tell me what you're going to name your baby."

"Leo," she said, but she knew her voice sounded garbled.

"What does it mean? Here names have meaning."

"It's my dad's name. It means bravery. Brave people."

Muhammad tore Nadia tunic. He created a few strips from the fabric and tied them around his hand. Then he started to wrap Nadia's shoulder.

"Stubborn," he said again and again, firmly. "Can't wear the armor. Can't leave. Can't take care of yourself."

"Stop," Nadia said. She wanted to stand, to walk away but couldn't find the strength. Muhammad leaned her against the doorframe.

"We need to get out of here. Can you walk?" He scratched his beard, dug at the flesh underneath. Then he pulled Nadia to her feet. He propped her against him. "Walk." He slapped her again. "You're in shock but you need to walk." Nadia shuffled her feet slowly. Muhammad lifted her a few inches from the ground, as if they were part of a dangerous three-legged race.

They walked that way for ten blocks. Nadia lost consciousness as they climbed into the back of an ambulance.

At Al Hawari, a hospital in the city's center, rows of people were placed on thin blue cots. Women were separated from men. The medics removed Nadia's makeshift bandages and re-packed the wounds in an attempt to save blood. Nadia gouged the fleshy heel of her hand with her fingernails as she wriggled with pain. She wore a bracelet, a sterling silver cuff that rattled up and down her arm. Inscribed on it was her blood type, AB Positive, and her allergies, blueberries and strawberries, in a thin, neat print. A Valentine's Day present from Jonathan. A romantic gesture for the travel savvy. Nadia pressed hard on her stomach. She wanted to feel Leo bump against her. Someone strapped a small ultrasound machine around her belly, and she saw his tiny erratic heartbeat. 156. 162. 158. With each beep, Nadia relaxed a little more.

"She needs blood, and the bullet should be removed," Nadia heard the medics say to a short nurse who looked like a fresh-faced teenager. Nadia's breath quickened and someone placed a plastic oxygen mask over her face.

"The wound is shallow," the girl said. "Numb her."

A bee sting. Her muscles loosened. Her body turned cold. Then, a scrapping tug against her shoulder. The girl used the needle to pry the football-shaped bullet from her muscle. When it was released, it pinged into a tin circular dish.

"Gauze and blood," the nurse shouted.

The nurse lightly pushed Nadia up, supporting her with her forearm as she rolled her over and wrapped the cotton in loops around her shoulder. Someone rubbed yellow iodine against the crook of her elbow and hung a bag of blood next to her. It gulped and gargled as it entered her veins. The needle itched as the clotted platelets went through her. Nadia wanted to doze but

Leo moved. A happy and safe flip-flop that Nadia wanted to relish.

When Nadia woke the needle, was still buried into a fold of skin. Her arms were yellow from the iodine and red from the blood. She was in a double room. Muhammad lay in a bed next to her, his hand bandaged, his wrist in a white cast. He was also connected to a bag of blood but he was using his free hand to pump it out. The blood was his own. He was donating.

"Hey," she said and her throat throbbed slightly from the effort. Her voice was hoarse from screaming and the drugs. Muhammad sat up straighter. He continued squeezing a small blue ball in his left hand.

"I asked them to put me in here. I hope you don't mind." He looked down at his paper gown and blushed. Nadia tried to sit up. "Your hand," she said.

"It's okay. My wrist is fractured. The bullet went in and out. Clear exit."

"I lost you out there for a minute." Nadia arched her back. She tried to stretch the sore muscles. The blood going in felt clumpy and intrusive. The point where the needle was inserted throbbed.

"I saw you in that water. Face down but your camera was high over your head. Protecting it."

"Work first," Nadia said, hating the truth in the words.

Muhammad smiled. "I'm sure your other arm cradled Leo."

She didn't recognize herself in that moment or in this one. She felt split, wanting to be a good mother and a journalist. Longing to know how to prioritize both.

"I'm sorry I didn't listen to you."

Muhammad sighed. "You remind me of my sister. The one I told you about before. Aya." Nadia tried to sit up in the bed, to rearrange and give him her undivided attention. Her shoulder and the blood transfusion prevented it, so she stared at the square-paneled ceiling. "She was determined to save everything. She taught me English."

"How old were you?"

"Eight." He paused. "She found this book in a second-hand bookstore near our house. *Charlie and the Chocolate Factory*." Nadia grinned. "She read it to me. She was going to America. She had spoken to a family there about babysitting. She was going to send money and help my sisters get visas."

"What about you?" Nadia asked. She imagined him sitting under the shade of a wide tree reading this book from her childhood. The cookies were different and the scenery was more quaint than the suburb where she was raised, but the words were the same. So was the feeling.

"Not too many men get to leave. We're needed for the labor force. Plus, their life here is so much worse than mine."

"So you just learned …"

"She got this look when she read. Her eyes would narrow and three tiny winkles separated her eyebrows. You get them too. When you look at a picture on your camera."

Nadia closed her eyes, a satisfied smirk staining her face.

"Now what?" Muhammad asked. "Where will you go?"

Nadia lightly scratched the needle incision. "Home. At least for a little while."

Nadia turned her head and watched as a dust storm shook the glass. Fat clumps of red sand spiraled through the air. Because of the wind, everything here tasted slightly of the earth. At first, Nadia thought just the vegetation at the local market tasted like dirt, bright fruit and beans and grains pulled from the ground. But then she realized she smelled dust everywhere. She smelled the dirt in the hospital and in the city square and in the hotel. The musk that rose from Muhammad's skin was mixed with the dust. *Ashes to ashes. Dust to dust,* Nadia recited in her head. Then she reminded herself that she was not dead. Muhammad was not dead. Leo was not dead. She took a long breath and counted to ten.

"To paint his room?" he asked.

"Yeah. Maybe I'll find bedding the color of the sand," Nadia said, looking outside.

"Will you come back?"

"I think so. I just need to stand still for a moment."

Nadia pressed the place where her camera normally rested. She held her hand just over Leo.

"I have to give you something. Let me call the nurse," Muhammad said.

"What is it?" Nadia left her hand on her belly. She felt Leo swim. His movements were like tiny bubbles popping against her stomach lining.

"Your letters. I kept them."

Nadia nodded. She understood why Muhammad couldn't use them. Why she still needed to. The nurse walked in.

"What do you need?" she asked. Nadia pointed to the brown case.

Muhammad's eyes grew wide, his hands flexing more steadily and quickly now so that the blood belched as it flowed into the bag. He didn't have time to protest.

Nadia pulled the camera from the bag and quickly centered Muhammad in the frame.

Angela Raper

THE CORNFIELD

The day Mama heard about the abandoned truck was a good day. She and Aunt Lula—who was actually my great-aunt—were out on the porch, relaxing in the wood rocking chairs, which were painted with a fresh coat of white every other May along with the front porch rails and steps. Mama had put puffy cushions with a bright floral pattern in the seats so she and Aunt Lula could sit comfortably. Overhead, a fan installed in the robin-egg-blue ceiling turned just enough to help the October breeze.

It was still warm enough that people were walking around in t-shirts and shorts even though we were coming up on Halloween. Mama had been sunning out in the yard that morning because she hated looking like she "just got out of the hospital," despite the fact she'd had several cancer spots removed already. It was late enough in the season that the fields around our house were empty, so she didn't have to worry about anyone coming along on their tractor and seeing her out there in her bathing suit. My granddaddy had once grown tobacco, cotton, peanuts, and corn in those fields, but ever since she inherited the property ten years ago, Mama had leased out the land. At thirty-five, I should

have been long gone, but I was her only child, her best friend—
her everything—and the weight of her need kept me pinned to
that spot.

I brought out lemonade on a yellow and orange plastic tray
Mama'd had since the seventies and poured three glasses, passing one to Mama and one to Aunt Lula before taking a seat with
the third. Aunt Lula smiled at me, her head wobbling on her
wattled neck. Her white hair was thinning, but she still got it
teased and stiffened to helmet-esque proportions every Friday.
Mama's hair was blonde, and every six weeks, she had an appointment to make sure it stayed that way.

"Did you see how tall my corn is getting this year?" Mama
looked expectantly at Aunt Lula. She had a garden out back every year, which meant I watered, weeded, and picked green
beans, collards, tomatoes, cucumbers, squash and corn from
May to November. Used to be that I just helped her, but her
back and knees couldn't handle the rigor anymore. She still
wanted the garden, though, because she liked handing out grocery bags stuffed full of vegetables to everyone she knew.

"I bet them ears are going to be nice and sweet," Aunt Lula
replied, and Mama preened at the compliment.

Mama was happy at the moment because she had company
to distract her. I could've gone inside and enjoyed some precious time alone, but I knew I'd better stay a few minutes, or I'd
hear about how rude and antisocial I'd acted to Aunt Lula, who
wasn't long for this world. To be fair, it was closer to the truth
for Aunt Lula than for most people Mama claimed were clinging
to life by fragile, cracked fingernails. She was eighty-seven, so
the odds of her funeral being the next one we attended were
pretty high. Still, there wasn't anything wrong with her other
than arthritis in her hands and knees and sometimes gout.

"Did you hear?" Aunt Lula asked as she leaned closer to
Mama, who was going deaf just like Granddaddy had but re-

fused to wear a hearing aid because she didn't want anyone to see she needed one. "They found an abandoned truck out on Highway 17. I heard it's been there at least a couple of days."

"Deer season opened up last week," Mama said. "It's probably just some hunter."

"Ain't no hunter goes off and leaves his truck for two days. 'Sides, it has Virginia plates."

Mama stopped rocking and faced Aunt Lula. "Maybe someone broke down and left it," she said, a hard edge in her voice.

I knew that tone. If Aunt Lula didn't stop ambling toward whatever point she was making, Mama was going to get irritated, and I'd be the one to hear all about it after Aunt Lula went home.

"Could be, but they didn't." A light of triumph flashed in Aunt Lula's brown eyes. She'd gotten a piece of news before Mama—a rare feat. "I heard the police were swarming all over it this morning. Seems there's a missing person report out on whoever owns that truck."

"Some hiker got lost in the swamp, then," Mama said with an air of finality.

The Dismal Swamp State Park was right off Highway 17, and people had gotten lost off the designated trails before, so Mama's theory was possible, but I wasn't so sure it was probable. It was strange that someone from Virginia had come down to the North Carolina side to hike or camp in the swamp when they had access to it up there.

"Then why park on the side of the road instead of the visitors' center?" I pointed out, earning a grateful smile from Aunt Lula and a scowl from Mama, who was always right, even when she wasn't. Disagreeing with her might rebound on me later, but I was caught up in the mystery of the abandoned truck now.

"Why don't you look it up?" Mama said. "Maybe they've

got something on the news."

I pulled my phone out of the back pocket of my jeans. Mama had a smart phone too, but about all she knew how to do on it was make calls, send text messages, and play her solitaire app. She relied on me when it came to looking up anything on the Internet. I opened WTKR's app, and sure enough, they had a little blurb about the missing person from Virginia.

"It's pretty vague," I said. "So far, there's not much more to it than what Aunt Lula said, except they started searching the swamp this morning. They're using the South Mills fire department as a home base."

Mama perked right up at that. "Why don't you go on over there and see what you can find out?"

I wish you to the cornfield, I thought. I did love my mama, but I'd been wishing her to the cornfield just about every day for the past few years. I got the idea from *The Twilight Zone*—the original series, not the movie or the remake. Every Thanksgiving, a channel I usually didn't get to watch ran an all-day marathon, and I caught a few episodes after the family left and Mama went to her bedroom for a nap. I had to turn the channel once she woke up because she didn't like action, science fiction, or horror. She claimed it tore up her nerves, so the TV stayed on *Lifetime*, *Hallmark Channel*, or *Fox News* when she was in the living room. One year, I caught the episode about the kid who could wish people who upset him to the "cornfield," someplace far away from which they never returned. I started trying it myself. True words have power, and I hoped maybe if I wished hard enough and often enough, it'd come true.

"Why don't you and Aunt Lula go?" I suggested.

"Because I don't want to bother anyone when they're trying to do their job."

But you'll send me to bother them. The true words pushed hard to get out of my mouth, but I knew better than to let them

loose. Most of the time, I asked myself, "Do I want to hear the
end of this one day?" before I said things that were likely to upset Mama. The answer was usually "yes, I do," so I kept quiet,
but sometimes things slipped out. As good as it felt in the moment to speak my true words, they weren't worth the cost of
revealing I wasn't a smiling, pliant Pollyanna-daughter.

When I got to the firehouse, the parking lot was full of cars
from the county sheriff's department and the highway patrol,
plus an ambulance and a couple of news channel vans. I parked
across the street and walked over. Dozens of people were milling around, and I scanned the crowd for someone I knew so I
could fish for information to take back to Mama. I spotted
Yancey Clemmons by the ambulance, loading some equipment
into the back.

Yancey and I went to school together. Actually, we went to
senior prom together. I was surprised when he asked because I
had no idea he liked me, but I said yes because no one else had
asked—or was likely to.

Mama had been thrilled when I told her I had a date for
prom. She took me to the big mall in Raleigh to find a dress, and
she made an appointment for me to get my hair done the day of
the dance. When he picked me up, she cooed over how handsome he looked in his tux and took dozens of pictures. But when
Yancey and I kept seeing each other after prom, her comments
changed:

"You're starting college next year, Lydia. You don't need
to get tied down."

"He's not even going to community college, Lydia. He's
going to be a farmer like his daddy. You can do better."

"I just don't see why you want to hang around that boy,
Lydia. He's not on your level."

Yancey and I lasted about three months before I broke up
with him, and Mama started smiling again.

These days, he was a full-time farmer—owner of more acres than any farmer in Camden County—and a volunteer EMT. He was married with two bright kids that I taught when they were in first grade, and we were all friendly when we saw each other. I waved to get his attention as I approached, and he stopped what he was doing to greet me with a one-armed hug.

"Hey, Lyds. Come to help out the search party?"

"No, I was just driving by, and I saw all the cars, so I stopped to see what's going on," I said, not wanting to admit I was on an intelligence gathering mission for my mother.

"We got ourselves a missing person," he said. "Some woman from Virginia drove down here and abandoned her vehicle. We think she's gone into the swamp."

"How do you know she's not hiking or camping or something?"

"'Cause her husband filed a missing person report day before yesterday." Yancey sat on the back of the ambulance and stretched his long legs in front of him. "You can tell your mama that's all I know," he said, winking at me.

"I will." I muttered a goodbye and forced myself to walk rather than run back to my car, pretending it was the sun scorching my face.

I got in and buckled up, but my phone chimed a text alert before I started the engine.

Aunt Lula's about to leave. Did you find out anything?

That was my cue to hurry back home. Instead, I closed the messaging app and opened the news app, scrolling through the weather forecast and the local headlines. I went back to the article on the missing woman and found it had been updated. Her name was Susan Hathaway, and she was from Suffolk. She'd left a note in the truck, saying goodbye to her family. They'd added a video clip too, and when I hit play, it showed the haggard face of a forty-something man.

"I don't know why she left," he said, looking at the reporter plaintively like he hoped she could give him some answers. "She seemed fine that morning. As far as I know, it was a normal day. I didn't know anything was wrong."

They could say the same thing about me, I thought.

I didn't feel any sympathy for the man's distress. I felt sorry for Susan and whatever happened to make her think walking into the swamp was a better option than remaining where she was a minute longer.

When I finally got back home, Aunt Lula was gone, and Mama was waiting in the kitchen, her lips pressed into a thin line. I appeased her with the new information, pretending I'd gotten it from Yancey.

After the debriefing, Mama lay down on the couch and picked up the newest *People*. I went to the computer to get some work done. I logged in to Moodle and checked the comma skills quiz first, giving zeroes to a couple of students who hadn't taken it. After that, I posted the reading and homework schedule for the next two weeks. Then I read through the emails sent to my school account, which were mostly from parents. The second I hit the reply button and began responding to the first one, Mama spoke up.

"Oh, listen to this! They've got a nice write up of that Kardashian girl's wedding."

I stilled my hands on the keyboard and stared at the computer screen, waiting it out until she finished reading the entire article to me.

"Doesn't that sound just lovely?"

"Mm-hm." I blinked to refocus my eyes on the email from Brittany Wooten's mother and resumed typing my response.

"Were you even listening?"

"Sure."

"Then what did I say?"

I rubbed my forehead with the pads of my fingers, fighting down the urge to tell her how little I cared about the Kardashians. "She had an expensive dress."

"You weren't listening. You never do. You're just like your daddy—selfish to the core. He always tuned me out, too."

"Mama, I'm trying to get work done," I said, using the gentlest tone I could muster so she wouldn't get wound up any further.

"Well, I'll just leave you alone!" she said as she threw the magazine on the coffee table.

Cornfield, I thought. My fingers were trembling, but I forced myself to keep working. I didn't dare stop now.

She turned the TV on and flipped back and forth between *Lifetime* and *Hallmark* until she decided to go with the movie about the abused housewife over the movie about the prince trying to get his tradition-minded parents to accept his plucky American fiancée. The noise didn't help soothe my jumbled thoughts, but I finally finished the email to Brittany's mom and opened the next one.

Mama picked up the remote and bumped up the volume a few notches. The abused wife was sobbing about how hard she worked to please her husband. I tried to ignore it, but Mama turned up the volume again. The commercials blared bouncy music, and I stared resolutely at the screen until the words blurred and ran together. The beat of the jingle pounded in my temples, and I could feel the true words rising in my throat, choking me, demanding to be set free.

"Mama, *please*! I can't get work done like this."

"Fine!" She turned off the TV and threw the remote hard enough that it bounced off the coffee table and landed in the middle of the floor. "I can't do anything in my own house."

Silence filled the room, buffeting against me as I abandoned the thought of getting anything accomplished, and I waited for the inevitable. A few sniffles were followed by a watery lament.

"You just don't understand how hard it is for me."

I spent the next hour in my cheap desk chair, trapped by well-worn tales of family history. Grandma's constant disapproval, Daddy's alcoholism that had ultimately killed him. Eventually, Mama got around to me as well.

"You were so warm and affectionate as a child. You wanted to do everything with me. I was your best friend. You told me everything. You've changed so much, but I still need you."

I imagined what it would feel like not to carry her around, her sharp teeth embedded in my stooped back. I pictured endless rows of tall, tasseled cornstalks swaying in a cool October breeze. I wished I had kept on dating Yancey. I wished I'd gone to college on the other side of the country instead of commuting to one nearby. I wished I'd made countless different decisions over the years until tears prickled my eyelids.

When I was younger, I cried out of guilt because I believed her when she said I wasn't a good daughter, and I twisted myself, pretzel-like, into the shape she wanted for as long as I could sustain it. I wanted to please. I wanted to be good. These days, I cried out of anger and frustrated longing for freedom. Mama didn't know the difference. She still thought my tears meant she had successfully broken me, and she lit up at the sight of them. She hurried over to embrace me, and I stood there with my arms dangling by my sides.

"You better hug me back!"

I lifted my arms and draped them around her, my mind still in the cornfield while she crooned that she forgave me and everything was going to be okay.

The next morning, I was sent back to the firehouse because Mama had convinced herself that Susan Hathaway was skulking around the county, waiting for a chance to break into remote farm houses like ours.

"I bet she'd just love to get her hands on my jewelry and our family silver. She could pawn it all and run off somewhere far away where nobody could catch her," Mama said.

Personally, I thought Susan was beyond skulking anywhere. I'd stayed up late, reading every scrap of news coverage I could find and staring at Susan's picture. I couldn't sleep anyway, and I wanted to spot some clue to why she'd entered the swamp. Had she meticulously planned an escape? Had she snapped and gone into the swamp on impulse? Did she and her husband have a big fight that pushed her past her limits, or was it some little thing that did it, like him leaving the toilet seat up for the six thousandth time since they got married?

I didn't bother pointing out to Mama that the police weren't calling it a search-and-rescue anymore, just a search. Instead, I headed off to the firehouse, because that was better than spending my whole Sunday cooped up with her. Tomorrow, I'd find a reason to stay late after work. I couldn't do that every day, though. Mama would praise my dedication to my students, but in the next breath fuss because I wasn't at the table when dinner was still hot.

The crowd at the firehouse was smaller, but Yancey said it was because the first round of search teams had already gone out, this time with cadaver dogs brought in by the state K9 Emergency Response Team.

"Think she's dead?" I asked.

Yancey sipped black coffee out of a Styrofoam cup and stared down the road. "I don't like to give up hope," he said at last. "But I think it's likely. She might've run into a black bear or a bobcat."

"Or taken care of it herself," I said. "Didn't she leave a note in the truck?"

"Yeah. I didn't see it, so I don't know if it was a suicide note or not."

I thought about Susan Hathaway walking into the swamp and leaving her unlocked truck behind. No matter why she did it, this decision was *hers*. Maybe her death was the first thing she'd had all to herself.

I thought about the three months I'd dated Yancey and how good it had felt to do something I wanted, despite Mama's objections. When we went to the movies, he always slid his arm around my shoulders, and I pushed up the arm rest between our seats so I could tuck myself against his side. Sometimes I lost track of what was happening in the movie because I wanted to savor the sense of normalcy I experienced there in the darkened theater. I forgot about Mama and became a typical teenage girl out with her boyfriend, if only for a couple of hours. Mama ground me back into submission eventually, but I still remembered how it felt to be young and hopeful. I wondered if Susan had remembered it too, and that memory had driven her into the swamp.

"Either way, she's free," I said.

Yancey frowned into the dregs of his coffee. "There are better ways of getting free." He glanced sidelong at me. "You know that, right?"

"Sure," I said. "Hey, is it okay if I stick around and help out today?"

I spent the next couple of hours handing out water bottles to returning search teams and playing gofer. I was twitchy at first because I'd shoved my phone under the driver's seat, and I kept having the urge to go check it in case Mama had called or texted. Usually the only time I was out of touch was when I was in the classroom, but I refused to let myself give in and get my phone this time. Instead, I crafted explanations for when I got home, ranging from the classic "My charge ran out" to "They needed an extra pair of hands, but we had to keep our phones off unless it was official business."

They brought Susan in around three o'clock that afternoon. Or rather, they brought in an olive-green body bag containing what was left of her. The team that found her gave their report in private, but it wasn't ten minutes before people were talking about self-inflicted gunshot wounds and partially eaten remains.

I caught a glimpse of the body bag, just enough to see the way it sagged under the uneven weight of her ravaged body. I followed the search team carrying it, hoping for a closer look. I wanted to unzip the bag. I wanted to see her face, if there was anything left of it. I wanted to know if she looked frightened or peaceful. I wanted to know if she'd gotten what she went out there for.

I loitered for as long as I could, but after they took Susan away, everyone started drifting on home, which meant I had to leave as well. When I got home, I found Mama in the kitchen with a bag of flour and canisters of sugar and cocoa on the counter.

"Did you have a good time at the firehouse?" Mama asked without looking at me. "I reckon you did since you stayed all day."

"They found her," I said. "Did you hear?"

"I haven't heard a thing, stuck up in this house by myself." Mama stood at the island, beating dark brown batter with hard, angry strokes.

"Well, they did." I pushed the knife block out of the way so I could hop up on the counter. She hated that. She claimed it was unsanitary, and maybe this time it was, given where I'd spent the day. "She's been dead all this time. She shot herself the first day."

"That's too bad." The wood spoon rang against the glass mixing bowl like it was keeping time. "I guess you couldn't call or send me a text."

"I was busy helping."

"Too busy to let me know you were okay?" The batter was smooth and glossy, but she kept beating it. "For all I knew, you got lost out in that swamp too, trying to find some stranger!"

"She's not a stranger," I murmured, running my forefinger along the smooth black handle of the butcher knife that poked out of the block. "Not to me."

"Out there worrying about some strange woman when I'm right here." Mama dropped her spoon in the bowl with a ringing clatter and turned to face me at last. "Did you eat?"

"Yes."

"Nothing but coffee and doughnuts, probably. I don't know why I'm making these brownies." She moved to stand at my knees and patted beneath my chin, where there was a small, soft lump of fat. "You don't need them. You're getting to that age where you can't lose weight as easy. I see your metabolism's slowing down already."

"My blood pressure and cholesterol are fine." My guts started churning, and I took shorter, shallower breaths. I didn't want to have this conversation. Not again. Not today. "My weight's fine, too."

Mama continued like I hadn't said anything. "But you've always had problems with your weight, haven't you? Not like me. It's from your daddy's side. You got everything bad he could offer. I should've turned you over to him when you were little."

She unleashed a litany of the myriad ways I disappointed her and failed as the good daughter she wanted. Every word was the zipper going up another notch, smothering me in a body bag of her making until I couldn't draw another breath. Bile rose up and coated my tongue.

"What do you have to say?" She stared at me, waiting for

my capitulation.

I closed my fingers around the handle of the butcher knife, and I heard the truest words of all come out of my bitter mouth. "It's time for you to go to the cornfield."

Blood speckled her cheeks beneath her shocked eyes, and the dull thump of her body hitting the linoleum floor filled the silent kitchen. I stared down at her with the knife still in my wet hand, and I no longer envied Susan, because this decision was *mine*.

I went to Home Depot and got supplies to make a sturdy scarecrow outfit. I used one of Daddy's plaid shirts, a pair of his overalls, and his gloves and work boots for the body because she never threw any of his clothes away after he died. I painted a smiling face on a burlap bag, and I lined the whole thing with plastic sheeting even thicker than Susan's body bag. I filled in the gaps with straw. Mama would have hated that the lumpy, uneven straw packed under Daddy's clothes made her look fat.

I listened to the soothing rustle of the corn stalks while I dug a hole for the post, letting the sound fill my ears and drown out all the roiling thoughts in my brain. I kept expecting her to sit up and start crying about how awful I was for abandoning her. The occasional sound of a car motor made my stomach clench, and I hunched down behind the swaying stalks, afraid Aunt Lula or some other bored, elderly relative might drop by for a visit. But no one ever turned off the paved road. Carrying her out to the cornfield gave me a new understanding of the term "dead weight," and I wondered if Susan's body had felt as limp and heavy.

Once the new scarecrow was in place, I heaped pumpkins around the base of the pole. Then I stepped back to survey my handiwork. Right now, the tableau appeared to be part of our autumn yard decorations, but I wondered how long the illusion of normalcy would last. We didn't get visitors every day, and

Mama didn't always return calls. How long would it take for someone—Aunt Lula? My principal?—to realize something was wrong? Would the thick plastic contain the smell or would some hapless visitor catch a whiff of rot on the October breeze? I knew she'd be found eventually. Even if the scent didn't give it away, the scarecrow would have to come down sometime.

I went back inside without another glance at the cornfield, and I filled a suitcase with jewelry, the family silver, and whatever else I could find that was small enough to fit. I didn't take any clothes. I left behind everything but what I could sell. I thought about leaving my car with a note in it somewhere near a bridge in South Carolina and buying a plane ticket with cash. Maybe they would interview Aunt Lula, and she'd be the one to say, "She seemed fine the last time I saw her. I didn't know anything was wrong."

Whatever happened, I didn't care. I couldn't feel Mama's teeth in my back anymore.

Michael Harris Cohen

EFFECTS VARY

"You are *unwell*," my old doctor had said, and though it sounded archaic, a 19th century novel's phrasing, he had the data of modern science to make me a believer. Like all who are dying, I believe in my sickness above everything.

That's why I came to this desert village; a place one reads only with a magnifier over the map. A name my tongue can't master, no matter how many times the locals or orderlies repeat it. I came for the cure.

My old doctor warned me against this trip.

"You're chasing legends," he'd said. "There's no proven efficacy. It's dangerous, probably fatal, considering your condition."

Of course if I did everything my old doctor advised, what sort of life would I have left? There would be endless surgeries and long recoveries, countless medications and treatments, often worse than the disease itself.

It would be a life he says, though this is just my thoughts that make him speak, just as my thoughts conjure him in this room where I mostly sleep.

His lab coat, like the sun here, is blinding in this daydream. He shakes his head at the squeaky cot on which I lie, clucks his tongue at the old fan above, as it whirs like a plane that can never land.

Such conditions. This place is rife with disease, he says.

And your condition. You will die here. You will die in a place you cannot pronounce.

I tell the new doctor about seeing the old doctor. I've told the new doctor practically everything: about my diagnosis, the procedures I've undergone. About my life before I got sick. I excavated the money-chasing and random fucks. I confessed the "*extras*," as my drug dealer called them. I elaborated the hole I've always felt inside. I quoted a line from TS Eliot's "The Hollow Men." I explained my dead wife. I even told him how the old doctor was against me coming here. Against him. His treatment.

I suppose I mentioned this last bit to gain his confidence. Perhaps thinking if I did, he'd reciprocate in some way to gain mine.

His slippered foot taps the cement as if he's bored or impatient. I ask about side effects again, but I don't tell him why or what I've been seeing since I started the treatment.

Tap. Tap. Tap.

"I say to you, effects vary," he says. "Pain for some, visions for others. Some witness the dead. For everyone, cure is different."

The new doctor does not wear a lab coat. He does not dress like a doctor or resemble one at all. His hands are rough and cracked. Hard-labor hands. Slippers like mine. His skin is dark against his sweat-stained shirt.

My own hands, slicked with sweat, somersault each other. I don't look at his face anymore. I can't.

"The trick is no fear. One wrestles demon, one becomes well. Always it is so."

I should be used to it, but I still wince at his platitude-laced speech. I avoid his face and focus on his peculiar accent. I try to imagine him speaking his native language, the one I hear outside my door when the orderlies shuffle past in pairs. It's a language of strangled sounds and whispers like wind over sand. A lexicon authored by serpents. My ears sift it for meaning and come up empty.

My eyes remain on the floor as the new doctor continues. My heart shimmies oddly. I follow the patterns in the faded carpet, fractured designs and overlapping shapes that dizzy me.

I do not tell the new doctor I am not afraid of the old doctor, that I know it is only a daydream. I do not tell the new doctor I am afraid only of him. Of what I have seen in his face. How it changes.

It could be the water or the heat. Or it is the treatment itself, the herbs and acrid tonics he prescribes, the mixtures that leave me nauseous or faint. It is one or all of these things that make me see it.

There's one other patient here who speaks English. I only see him at lunch as the rest of the time we're either in our rooms or with the doctor. Mostly we're in our rooms. We're allowed to leave our rooms, but it's discouraged. I've never done it or heard any footsteps in the hall, save for the orderlies.

At first I thought talking amongst the patients was also discouraged, perhaps even forbidden. The cavernous lunchroom rings with the clatter of silverware and the chomps of twenty-one mouths. Mouths that don't speak.

Lunchroom isn't right. It's more of an underground parking lot or bunker, damper and cooler than our rooms aboveground. A hazy ghost of oil lurks here, tainting our bland food.

One day the English speaking man leans toward me. He whispers in my neck. How odd and comforting, I think, to hear English. Crisp. Unaccented. English.

"What do you see?" he asks.

I don't want to explain; I want to listen. I want him to speak again, to feel his warm syllables of breath at my ear.

He asks again. "What do you see when you're with him?"

"What do you see?" I ask.

"I asked first." I smile at that, but he doesn't smile back.

"I see myself," I say. "I see me."

His eyes widen and then he shrugs and bends to his plate, rejoining the chorus of chewers and flatware.

First it was the new doctor's nose. His thick nose became thin. Then his eyes changed from amber to blue, the particular blue of my own.

Today it is his skin. I cannot help but look. Drained of color, his skin is pale and freckled like mine. There is a scar on his arm. I rub the same chevron of tough skin, a thumb's length above my wrist.

It is not stolen. *I am still me*, I think.

The new doctor's chair squeaks as he leans forward. My eyes fix on his scar. Our scar.

"What do you see? You are afraid, yes? What fears you?"

I am no stranger to fear. As a child, everyone else seemed privy to a secret, some sliver of wisdom no one shared with me. To move through the world pretending to be human, always out of step, this was fear. Dread in each stride, breath and word.

But I grew accustomed to dread. I even met a woman and married her. In her own way, she'd been equally ill equipped as a human being. She was awkward and shy, whereas I covered my fear with bluster and chattiness. Opposites. Yet we shared the same hole. Our flaws connected us. We'd spent five quiet years. Happy ones, I suppose, and when she died, I became unwell.

Fear drove me halfway around the world to this place; old bunker or tomb beneath the dunes, a metal shack above where we wait and sleep and wait for treatment. A place of inferno days and freezing nights. A place where only doubt replaces fear. How can this place make me well when it saps body and mind?

Nothing outside my window speaks of life. Nothing stirs. All that moves are stars and sand and my condition.

I envy the other patients here. I envy their burns and skin diseases. Their rotten stumps and sores. Their sickness is visible. Their sickness can be measured and perhaps only what can be measured can be healed.

The Englishman nods and slurps his soup next to me. He seems in perfect health. What is wrong with him? Does he have the same disease as I? The question seems it cannot be reached without laying the track of a dozen other questions first. But my mind is empty. Trackless. The silence of the room too large to breech. We are underground, but we may as well be underwater. *Do you believe in the treatment? Do you trust the doctor? What do you see?* I want to ask these things, but I say nothing and he does the same. We eat and return to our rooms. We sleep.

And sleep and sleep.

I become so weak, I can barely stand. I am too tired even to argue with the old doctor in my head. I am sure he is right, was right all along. I've made a mistake. I'll pay dearly for this desperate remedy.

I daydream the old doctor's sterile and ordered office. His endless tests that both terrified and comforted me, the humming sound he made as he reviewed my numbers or blood work, the methodical nature of his touch. I long for machines. Cool plastic and blinking lights. Electric beeps that signify life.

Instead I wake to the interminable fan and dryness in my nose.

Other deserts have smelled of creosote and sage. Of rain. Here it never rains. There is no smell in my room.

The new doctor now speaks in my voice. It is eerie, verging on absurd, to hear myself in broken English, as though I affect an accent and imitate this odd man. I try to distract myself from the sound of my voice with his smell. Cigarettes and curry. Gunpowder, or I imagine this. *My senses have become imaginative*, I think. My nose is hungry for smell.

"We go through it again," he says in my voice. "We go through it again until we understand. The cure is hard. Hardest thing. To die is easy, to cure is not."

He no longer taps his foot. He crosses his legs just as I do. His hands, my hands, press palms in his lap.

"The cure is in here," he says in my voice. "Right *here*." My gaze stuck to the floor, eyes wide on the rug's patterns, I cannot say if he touches head or heart or simply points to the room in which we sit, our folding chairs faced like chess pieces.

"Tell me what you fear," he repeats and repeats and repeats.

The Englishman breaks the silence. "Have you dreamed the snake?"

I don't tell him I don't dream, not here, not in sleep anyway.

"Snake?"

He squints at me and shakes his head. Drops of broth fall from his beard and splatter the table.

He grunts. "You're just in the beginning, mate. Barely there."

The man across from us taps a stump on the table. The Englishman picks up the salt and sprinkles the armless man's potatoes. After, he doesn't speak another word to me.

One day he doesn't show up for lunch. He's not there the next day or the next. Was the Englishman cured? Did he die? I'll never know what ailed him or what he saw. I never even learned his name or he mine.

The old doctor had recommended another place, a clinic in the French Alps.

"If you must go, go *here*. At least it's modern. At least they know what they're doing."

Their advertisements featured snowy mountains. A glass and chrome building arrived at by cable car. The rooms well lit with mountain range views. On sun-splashed balconies white-robed patients sit, ruddy and content, as though on holiday. The doctors all look like the old doctor: young, competent, concerned.

When I arrived here I thought, *snow or sand, makes no difference*. Now doubt whispers my nights. *The new doctor is a*

fraud. My condition does not improve but worsens. My
mind...my mind is not right.

The moon haunts me. Pale fire, it does not even shine with
its own light. I realize I am the same. My life is borrowed fire.
My illness, which will outlive me, is the shadow that smothers
it.

Now there is a smell in my room. The smell is not how I
imagined. It is not rot or infection or urine, the pongs that under-
line the lunchroom. It is not the smell of sweat on my unchanged
sheets or the burnt odor of sun on sand.

It is the smell of naught. Nix. An open door to a room
where no one ever lived, ever set foot, but it is your room just
the same. That is the smell of death.

I will tell the new doctor because I must. Charlatan or not, how
can he help me if I do not tell? How can I be cured?

I bunch my fists and move my gaze up his body. When I at
last reach his face, I see my face complete—my nose, my eyes,
my mouth, all construct my tight look of worry. He runs my
hand through my thinning blond hair.

In my voice he tells me, "You must wrestle what fears
you."

"Yes," I say, standing, no longer dizzy.

"You cannot run."

"I cannot run," I say and cross to me. A certainty I've not
felt since I arrived floods me, fills my limbs.

"Look inside," I say to me.

"I look inside."

"Good." I say as my fingers circle my neck. "Very good."

There is no fear in his eyes, in my eyes, as I squeeze. The
flesh of my windpipe crunches.

My eyes look up into my eyes and I smile. It is hard to speak, hard to understand my own voice, though I do not let up but only squeeze harder.

"Yes," I say, my voice hoarse as stone against stone. "This is good. Easy to die. Cure is hard."

I nod and squeeze. I am surprised at my strength, surprised at how fear slips away like a dropped garment. *I am almost there.* I think. *Almost cured.*

Until my neck crumbles in my grip and my face melts like torched plastic, muscle liquefies down to teeth and bone, bones, a skeleton. The frame of me in my clutch, and I force a laugh because it's absurd, macabre daydreams, bad-trip visions brought on by sour herbs and dismal nutrition.

Except it's not—the bones in my hand are solid as wood, dried flesh crunches, dead leaves beneath slippers, and a thing stirs in my gut. Uncoils. Flickering-tongued, scales scraping bones. I hear it. Feel it.

My mouth opens without willing it, words form, not my words, the new doctor's words, his thoughts in my head, not my head. His.

"Good," the new doctor says in my voice.

My voice…far off as the moon, I slither down a hole within, deeper, snake into darkness, a nothing of night deserts and what lies beneath—lost:

"Very good." The new doctor says. Now we begin."

Derek Des Anges

THE KRAKE HUNTER

The waters today are light and warm, a deep and brilliant turquoise descending from the roof of the world, perfect conditions for spotting the krake.

Yellow-spot is young and he is fast, and the prestige of his role is not lost on him—although, as a third-generation hunter of the venomous sea snakes for Squid Spears, he is perhaps a little complacent as to his suitability and skill at the task.

He allows himself to bask in the light, close to the surface, hanging with only the gentlest flickering of his tail fins to maintain his position, the fine-mesh ligament net loose and light in his agile, tender hands. Yellow-spot releases the bait from his belt pouch, and they flit anxiously away from him, flashing silver in this unfamiliar habit. They stick close together.

The krake hunter does not have long to wait; the black ribbon of sea snake silhouetted against the rays appears almost at once, ready to lunge for the silverfish as they scatter. It is banded—a potent venom, which will paralyse the vast, abyssal squid his bigger, older, battle-scarred shoalmates hunt. Or him, if he is slow or clumsy.

As a smaller, frailer male, Yellow-spot chases krake; the strong and daring females fight the kraken. It is the way things have always been. Without the venom of the sea snakes, the shoalwomen would suffer terrible losses, far worse than the usual; without squidflesh, the whole shoal starves. It is a great responsibility.

Thus it is also a matter of redoubled shame when, tensing to hurl the net in proximity to the banded krake, he fumbles his hold and releases it too early.

The net floats to the surface, blocking nothing but a little light, and the krake, startled, makes its squirming way away from Yellow-spot as swiftly as it can.

It is no *great* matter—krake are slower than the likes of Yellow-spot, and but for the unobserved embarrassment, it should be of no consequence that he must try twice. He gathers the net and flicks his tailfins in irritated pursuit.

The krake thrashes forward, squirming through the water beyond the surface of the waves. It is scared; there is no cover out here.

The net must be bunched against his stomach, so that it does not disturb his effective streamline. The krake is making good time, and the second throw will be harder; it is alert to his presence now and perfectly capable of taking evasive action.

Over the white, still sands far below, the banded krake whisks just below the choppy surface, ready for gasps of air to propel it on its way. Yellow-spot's tail does not quite break the waves, for from just beneath, he will have the best chance of trapping his prey.

And yet the krake remains out of his reach. Yellow-spot flattens his crests as low as they will go, empties his chest balloons, and exerts his tail fins, but somehow it continues to gain.

Familiar waters fall away from beneath him. And still the krake evades him.

A dark shape looms ahead of them, spreading across the surface like a shadow. Yellow-spot hopes to the Lord and Lady of the Many Currents and their children of the High Waves that this isn't a kelp forest, for he will have his work cut out following the krake through such a maze, and it will have the advantage. An ambush strike could easily paralyse him, and without his shoalmates to move his gills by hand until the poison passes, he will suffocate.

As he, and the krake, draw closer, he can see none of the fronds waving in the current that might indicate the forest, nor the tell-tale movement of the usual denizens of a kelp forest. Which means no bloody sea lions, a small mercy. This is an unfamiliar place. Yellow-spot hopes it is unfamiliar to the krake too, and he readies his net.

He is stymied.

A silhouette of something floating above reaches the krake before the shadow and bumps into the exhausted reptile. Desperate, his quarry squirms atop it.

If the krake thinks this will save it, it is mistaken. They have tried this trick enough in the eons of hunting that the People of the Deep have learnt their own rejoinder; Yellow-spot opens his chest balloons, closes his gills, and breaks through the surface.

Squinting his large, round eyes against the burning light and dry air, Yellow-spot sees the island that has saved the krake temporarily is furred, like the wretched sea lions are furred.

The krake reposes in the sun; Yellow-spot is less composed, for the sun is stinging his flesh.

The thing which is furred is not a sea lion, for it is the wrong shape, and it is unequivocally also dead. Yellow-spot does not recall the sun stinging like this before, but he also very rarely has cause to break the surface, for he is usually an adept hunter. He reaches for the krake, which twists and squirms and bares teeth in an open-mouthed retort to his hand. It coils, and thrashes, as if in agony.

Yellow-spot tries to ignore the pain in his own eyes, hands, his skin and scales—

The krake opens its mouth and strikes a defiant pose against the sky; Yellow-spot's face begins to burn as if he has thrust it into a jellyfish.

Perturbed, he drops back beneath the surface, the better to breathe in a way which is familiar, easy, and comfortable. He tries to re-open his gills and finds them weak and painful.

He has no further concern for the krake, though he thinks he knows now exactly how the snake feels.

Farther down he swims, away from the light, towards the cooler, deeper blue beneath, trying to chase away the suffering the way his People always have: retreat to the Depths.

The burning, stinging sensation subsides and settles to a steady stubborn itch almost as bad as the burning was. Frustrated, Yellow-spot scrapes at his flesh with his hands, then his teeth, bringing his forearm up to his mouth to scratch his hide with his needle fangs. He is careful, even in his ecstasy of irritation, to refrain from shedding blood; it is delicious to his predators. A shoal may easily deter even the big and hungry Mako, but a lone Person of the Deep is easy prey for the bigger sharks, even before a frenzy, and he is far from home.

How far, Yellow-spot cannot be sure. He would have cause to curse his own persistence, but instead, he can only curse the itching and stinging which will not leave him, like Man-o-war tentacles wrapped about his body. He knows the old stories too—those who remain in the light too long blister and burn— but they spoke of days, not moments above.

Yellow-spot hangs still in the water, light from above blocked by the unfurling darkness that floats, translucent and strange, upon the surface. He sees now his scales, his skin, both peeling, both dull and ugly. Befouled.

A scale slowly detaches from his belly and drifts away, caught in the current.

Yellow-spot's gills flutter anxiously in that same current. He understands now. This is some form of toxin, but like the nudibranch which sickens with a touch and not a krake, which must bite to deliver its venom. Perhaps it came from the dead thing. Perhaps it killed the dead thing. Perhaps it has already killed the krake. He does not wish to risk a look.

He releases the net to its own fate and gives closer examination to his hands. He does not remember touching the dead thing, but his hands are swollen and discoloured, dark and mottled as in a plague. He cannot tell if his face, if his eyes, are too. He fears they must be.

One thing is certain: if he returns to his own territory—if he can *find* his own territory—he will bring this with him. He will touch and be touched by his shoalmates, as is customary, and they will, too, be harmed—maybe killed—by this thing which disfigures and itches him.

It is wrong to bring back a toxin to the shoal. Diseases spread; poisons fester. He has known this since he has known anything. Parasites must not be spread. Tender isolation is the way of healing, or death if this is impossible.

Yellow-spot would very much rather die with them than alone. He does not want to be the shoalboy who vanished while hunting krake. He does not want to be a story.

But there is little choice. His net is gone. He has no krake. He may carry a toxin on his scales. And besides, he is lost.

Yellow-spot begins to feel very sorry for himself.

The People of the Deep are long livers and a People who have experienced many of the hardships that the ocean has to offer. Yellow-spot tries to recall in his mounting distress and self-pity what, exactly, his ancestors and shoalmates would do in a situation like this, but he can only remember telling his great friend Pale-eyes that only a fool gets lost. He remembers this with humiliating clarity, until it is almost all he can remember, as his skin begins to ooze.

He *can* just about recall that Pale-eyes, now she is on his mind, once blundered into a large patch of anemones and then rolled on a nudibranch in her confusion, when she was very young. They had thought she was going to die, but she was kept from infecting the shoal as her body oozed and passed some of the poison from her in the slime, and she was able to recover. She was never as strong after as she should have been, and that was why she befriended the weak little males, instead of taking to the Depths.

He tries to remain calm and let the ooze do its work of cleansing him, but his eyes are very sore and he cannot see. In the dim light that makes it through the film and the pain, he spies something large moving with lazy tail flicks towards him, feels the water disturbed by its passage, and the faint electric pulse of a living thing which is bigger than he is.

Yellow-spot knows the shape and he knows the swimming gait, but his mind is so clouded by despair that he cannot determine what it is.

All the lessons of his life teach him to be still and alert.

The thing is closer, and he thinks of Pale-eyes, weak and helpless after her mistake. She had told him, with a bizarre pride, how her gills had hardly fluttered at all. He feels panic rise in his stomach and makes the warning sign with his arm crests. He expels bubbles from his balloons to scare whatever the thing is away from him—

He must replenish them, and in his anxiety, forgets that they cannot be refilled below the surface. Balloons in the body must contain air, not water. But he gasps with his balloons open, and they fill with water.

His gills agitate, but they are weakened by the toxin; foolish as a newborn, foolish as the kind of idiot who gets lost hunting krake, Yellow-spot thrashes for the surface, making a target of himself to what he is sure must, *must* only be a shark, and though he hopes it is a whale-shark, he knows it must be a white, for the kind of luck he has only comes in threes—

The large animal in the water moves towards him.

As the light goes black within his mind, Yellow-spot feels close by the loud thump of an air-breather's heart, and the shrill echo of song.

The sun has made a sheepish return to the sky after the passage of a cloud that threatened but couldn't quite deliver on torrential rain. But while the wind that unveiled the stubborn sun also made off with the sweaty closeness the cloud brought, something still feels uncomfortable to Emmanuel Olawale.

It is his rest day, and obscurely he resents that his decision to use the time to rest— instead of fill out returned paperwork for reimbursing his flights which had come back a fifth time, or to restock the kitchen in his assigned housing, or even to join the other various aid agency workers in some form of drinking contest—has been punished by a sense of ambient disquiet.

He will give it another hour, maybe walk along the beach, and if he still feels this way, he will abandon the notion of rest and present himself back at the nurse's station and swap with someone else, assist in inoculations instead of nodding his way through a jittering video call to his auntie.

She does not like the screen, anyway. She would rather phone, but she knows it is impossible.

By the water, the wind has picked up and the tops of the trees are whispering a loud song of rustling fronds. The birds, of course, make no fuss about the conditions. They dive and roll in the sky, like the dolphins did about the boat on the last leg of his journey here; Emmanuel makes the decision to blame his disquiet on the location. To go from a landlocked city and a landlocked childhood to an island stranded in the centre of a sea he is not confident he can swim in is a shock like cold water to the face.

The storm has evidently broken somewhere farther over the sea, for the tide has brought up detritus. There are great, stinking fronds of seaweed, covered in flies and froth. The froth he recognises as polluted, and not with the detergent usually used to break up oil spills; in his training videos, they spent a half hour on identifying chemical spills. The seaweed, indeed, is discoloured in places, almost pink.

Among the weed—Emmanuel resists the urge to poke at it with ungloved hands—there are dead fish, and fish gasping their lasts. With his feet in sandals, it may be foolish to try to prod them back into the water, but he searches the sand for drier driftwood, until he can flip one or two of the lighter ones into the surf. Whether it will help, he cannot be sure, but it has never been in his nature to do nothing.

That is, after all, why he is here. It is why he trained. It is why he travels.

He walks on, tapping the stick against his shin, until he sees the seaweed banked over something. It looks a little like the hull of a discarded canoe, and he hopes with a sinking feeling that it is not a wrecked vessel. If anyone is lying beneath it, they are almost certainly dead by now, and while it would explain his foreboding, it brings no joy to anyone to find a death they could have averted.

Emmanuel skirts the rest of the froth-corrupted sea plants and hurries over the white sand to the bump.

Now that he is closer, he sees it is too uneven for a boat. Perhaps it is one of the dolphins. That is still sad, but less so than the potential for a funeral. It is still a bad omen; the islanders here believe the dolphins, among many other things, are their ancestors. Emmanuel sees no reason why they should not be; it is much the same, between and beneath the book-having faiths, in his own home city.

He lifts a frond of the seaweed from the bump and takes a step backward.

At this, he almost collides with a person behind him; startled, he jumps and drops the stick. The woman behind him jumps as he bumps her, and as he turns, he sees her speak.

"What?" Emmanuel collects himself enough to watch her face. It is Clare Wing Zen, an American. She is not with the aid workers, but a scientific survey. Some of the other aid workers have tried to convince the survey to socialise with them, or at least to relax their inexplicable coldness towards the islanders, but the majority will not.

"Sorry," she says, when he can see her mouth. "I forgot— called to you. What *is* that?"

"I think," says, Emmanuel, remembering to enunciate, because Americans like neither his accent nor his deafness, "it's a person."

She looks at him oddly and picks up the driftwood. Clare reaches past him with it and uses the driftwood to half point at the end of the lump closest the water. "It has a tail," she says, turning around.

"I don't see it?" Emmanuel holds his hand out for the stick. She passes it to him, and he lifts the weed; his arms are longer, and he is more able to bend than she; her brace prevents it. There is, beneath the dark weed, a mottled blue-black tail not dissimilar to that of a large tuna, though more sinuous. Upon one fin is a large yellow splodge.

He lowers the stick.

"I saw a hand," he insists.

When he looks at Clare, she has her hand over her mouth. He wants to tell her this is not helpful, but she collects herself and removes it. "I see it," she says.

Her face is drained of colour.

"What should we do?" Emmanuel asks. "It must be an unlucky islander. We must find someone to identify it."

"We should get it off the beach first," says Clare. She touches him on the shoulder. "Can you carry him?"

Emmanuel nods. He asks her if she has gloves; Clare says, with an uncomfortable expression, that she never goes anywhere without them. "In case I find something interesting."

He draws the latex gloves on over his hands, and with Clare's help, armed with the stick, pulls away the rest of the seaweed.

After a moment of staring, he becomes aware that Clare must be speaking. She is animated. She drops the stick. Emmanuel turns reluctantly away from the thing he has uncovered, and asks her to repeat herself, but she does not. He cannot follow what she is saying, only that she is agitated. Words and phrases like, "What the fuck," and "why is my phone always out of battery when I need it?" he recognises, because people use them so often.

Emmanuel taps her with his elbow, unwilling to touch her with dirty gloves. "Step back, Clare, please."

He squats to put his hands under the impossible animal, the strange chimera which looks like living Photoshop, and as he is about to slip his arms underneath it, the fins along what he cannot help but think of as its arms stand up, flicking water over him.

Cautiously, Emmanuel reaches out again. It may just be a reflex not yet killed by the draining of life from the animal's body. He has seen dead bodies roll their eyes and had nightmares for weeks afterward.

The creature stirs, curling away from him, its back hunched. He turns to Clare, who shrugs.

"Should I push it back in the sea?" he asks, watching her face. She is, after all, a scientist, not a conservationist. She may wish to catalogue it more than to save it. It would be a choice that disappoints him, but he acknowledges that the world must be understood in order to protect it. He also recalls that Clare Wing Zen is not a marine biologist, and her interest in the animal will be for her colleagues' sake, not her own.

She hesitates.

The beast opens its mouth, beneath dull, disc-like eyes, revealing needle teeth in an absurdly human face, beneath tangled fronds of what look like limp, dying anemone tentacles at the place he would expect to find a full head of human hair. It inhales, choking on sand.

"Maybe it breathes air—" Clare is saying, helplessly, when he looks back at her. "Just get it *off* the beach."

Emmanuel takes this as his cue. He braces himself and slides his arms beneath the creature. He lifts it, rising to his feet as he has been taught when lifting a frail, elderly person in times when no stretchers are available, or emergency dictates.

The animal is heavy, taut with swimming muscles, like a fish. It is hard to keep a grip on, slime soaking into Emmanuel's shirt immediately; it breathes the air, shallowly and with difficulty. Its fingers twitch like the limbs of a dreaming cat.

It rolls in his grip until it is face down, for which Emmanuel is grateful. Its face makes him uncomfortable above all things.

Water dribbles from the thing's open mouth, and the breathing becomes less laboured.

Clare steps up beside Emmanuel and takes his arm gently, to guide him. He can no longer see his own feet on the uneven sand, and she pushes him with her hip when she means for him to be careful.

Very slowly, Emmanuel allows her to guide him back towards the field laboratory.

The field laboratory is distinguished by better air conditioning than the nurse's station, which has been making do with a series of electric fans and a solar generator, and Emmanuel finds the time to be resentful of this, too, even amid his bewilderment and the ache in his arms. The creature is struggling weakly by the time Clare begins to fish young sea turtles out of a shallow blue tank, into a smaller box. She shares the space with several disciplines, he recalls.

As Emmanuel stoops, his back suffering, to lay the creature in the tank, the film on one of its disproportionately large eyes rolls back, like a translucent eyelid, and the depthless black of its pupil dilates almost instantly and contracts just as quickly, like the focusing of some huge camera.

"Ack!" Emmanuel drops the fish thing into the tank in surprise, and it bumps the far side, rushing away from him.

Clare touches his shoulder, and when he looks at her, she looks almost as amused as she is intrigued. "It's alive, then."

He glances back into the tank. The beast is displaying angrily, its crests bright red: forearms and throat and waist, eyes wide, mouth open in the gape of fear shared by so many animals. Like some angry ape, the animal—clearly a male—has even displayed its penis as a gesture of aggression. Emmanuel looks the thing in the eye, and wonders if the emphatic "hand" gestures it is making really *do* resemble the ASL for "fuck off" or if he is imagining it in the flurry of distress the creature is emitting.

Giving in to his delusion, Emmanuel asks Clare.

"I don't know," she tells him. "What does that look like? It seems like it would be a useful thing to know."

Emmanuel shows her, his back deliberately to the thing in the tank. He doesn't mention that the first thing anyone wants to learn, in either ASL, NSL, English, or Yoruba, is always "fuck off." He's sure by now that he knows "fuck off" in thirty languages. It was the first phrase he learnt on this island.

Clare watches the fish creature as the air conditioning turns Emmanuel's sweat to ice. "It does look almost exactly the same."

He turns back to the creature. Whatever it—he, Emmanuel supposes, on the evidence of what it has so prominently displayed—is, it needs to stop thrashing about. Already the efforts at escape are weakening it, and something has torn on the back of its—*his*—arm, leaking dark blue into the tank water.

Calm down, he tells the startled fish. *Calm down, calm down. Be calm. Don't hurt yourself.*

For a moment, as it fails to react, Emmanuel is sure the supposed ASL was his imagination getting the better of him, that it was simply coincidence. Then the fish closes his gape abruptly, as if affronted, and his pupils, contracted under the bright lights, blow up again. The red crests begin to fold back down, disappearing eventually into seamless black smears against his body.

Don't kill me.

Emmanuel breathes out, slow and heavy, and realises that Clare is talking. He does not trouble to find out what she is saying; he has an instinct that it is in line with his thoughts, which are composed of *oh shit*, and some undertones of more coherent stunned jubilation that a true form of communication between man and not-man has somehow been established, some fleeting suspicion that somehow a prank is being played, and monstrous and total shock.

Emmanuel, however, is sure that as Clare has not understood what the fish is saying, she does not have the immediate thought he does.

We won't hurt you. We're trying to help.

"He is afraid we want to kill him," he tells Clare, to ease her frustration at being left out of the conversation.

She taps him urgently on the shoulder.

"I have to tell my boss," she says, when he turns to look at her. "Dr Xennakis is going to *fully shit* over this. He is going to shit his *entire brain.*"

"Not yet," Emmanuel says. He realises he should have phrased this as a question, but it is too late now.

"*What happened? What happened to you?* He asks the fish.

Clare goes across the room. Out of the corner of his eye he sees her pick something up off a table and lay it down again in frustration—presumably it is her phone. She starts digging through the lockers.

The fish raises its hands again, signs, *Something burned me.*

There is no mistaking it this time. Emmanuel has almost no experience in treating sealife. In some places he has been sent, people brought their livestock in a hope that the aid charity had brought along a vet as well. Valuable animals only; but with animals there was often little that could be done by the medics that couldn't be done by the locals themselves, or hadn't already been attempted. The worst placement he'd been on—supply lines in chaos and hospitals collapsing—the antibiotics were rationed: for human use only. An infected horse was a dead horse. They'd used a respirator on a dog once, *once*, because the shell-shocked girl accompanying him had no one else left; they'd argued it was a psychological necessity.

The dog lived. The girl lived. Dr Tregowan got a permanent warning.

All the same, he can see that there are patches upon the skin of this stranger, which look irritated and inflamed, some where the skin has broken entirely.

A chemical spill, Emmanuel tells him, after a moment to recall the correct signs. He wonders if this stranger from the sea knows what a chemical spill is. "A chemical spill," he says, for Clare's benefit.

I broke the surface to chase a krake and then everything burned. The krake was burning, too. There was a dead thing in the water. A furred thing. And the water was dark and shining on the top. The sea-stranger concludes his urgent report with a flare of his crests, but they settle down again. To Emmanuel's relief, the penis has been tucked away back inside. *And now I am lost and imprisoned, and you are going to kill me if I am not already dead.*

He realises then how beyond-alien the field laboratory must seem for someone who has spent their whole life far enough out at sea that no human has ever seen them before. *You're not dead, and we're not going to kill you. We want to help.*

"An extensive chemical spill," he tells Clare.

It must have been a whale, the stranger from the sea explains, but Emmanuel doesn't understand, and only looks for Clare.

She comes across the room, elbows him out of the way. In one hand she has someone's phone. In the other a handful of litmus strips, clasped against a plastic jug of milk.

"It's for the tea," she says. "The Scots? Kimberley and Kevin? Fucking obsessed with it. I don't know what to use if it's an alkaloid. I thought we had vinegar somewhere but it's gone."

Emmanuel takes one of the strips and shows it to the sea-stranger. *We are going to find out what has poisoned you, with this. I will touch you with it. Do not be afraid.*

"We should take blood," Clare is saying, when he looks to her. "Right? At the very least. A small sample."

"Are you mad?" he asks, as he reaches forward for the sea-stranger's arm. "He is terrified. I do not want to stick a needle into him and confirm that he is under attack. We could kill him with the stress of it."

He successfully catches the soft, slimed arm with one gloved hand. The sea-stranger smells of nothing more than fresh fish, nothing exotic or strange, nothing pungent or unpleasant. Only fresh fish, straight from the water. It is a pleasant smell. Emmanuel thinks that if he smells so well, he cannot be so sick as all that, even though he knows this to be nonsense.

The litmus strip, pressed gently against the broken skin, slowly turns pink.

"An acid," he says.

It occurs to him that perhaps the acid is the natural state of the sea-stranger's skin, but he cannot very well expect a coherent answer if he asks, and he cannot think of any vertebrate for which this might be true. There is not much that can be done for the open wounds themselves without suturing, and he is sure that a needle will only cause alarm.

Clare hands him the milk. He has the impression that she is in a bad mood, but he cannot ask her about what it is she thinks he *ought* to be doing.

He shows the milk to the sea-stranger and places it on the end of the tank, where it can still be seen while he signs. *We will try to help you with that. It is milk. We will put it on your skin to help stop the burning.*

The sea stranger stares at the plastic container. *What is milk?*

Emmanuel recalls the mention of the whale. He at least remembers the sign for that. *It is what whales feed their young.*
Should I drink it?

Emmanuel thinks that, even in the alien lines of the sea-
stranger's face, his needle teeth and his disc-like eyes, his mottled and blueish hue, he can see an expression of disgust.

No—rub it on your skin. Where it burns. Tip it onto your
burns.

He picks up the jug again and makes a tipping gesture, raising his eyebrows, inviting the sea stranger to come closer with a
gentle beckoning of his finger. It takes effort not to speak to this
person from the water like a small child from a war zone; he has
the same wide-eyed caution, the same blank, desperate aggression peppered with expressions of heart-rending, youthful
curiosity. But as far as Emmanuel can guess, this might be an
adult. There is no call to be insulting.

The stranger snatches the jug out of his hand so fast that
Emmanuel flinches, and it sinks back on the far side of the tank.
If Emmanuel stretched, he could reach—it is not a large tank,
and most of it is taken up with this large aquatic guest—but he
does not stretch. Slopped with sea water, he only watches patiently as the stranger carefully tends to each of his own hurts
with the milk jug.

Emmanuel turns his head in time to see the door flap open
and closed, as Clare departs.

When the burning has at last subsided, Yellow-spot accepts that
while he is probably dead and in a place much stranger than any
legend has prepared him for ending up in after his death, the
thing which looked like a tiny-eyed, flat-toothed, very small female or female-coloured Person of the Depths from at least the

belly upward—wrapped in some kind of bags—was not deceiv-
ing him. The whale food has helped.

He tries to ask the helpful, no-tail female pygmy person
thing with the whale food where he is or what is happening or
why it can speak with him at all, but it isn't watching him. It
flies out of the room like a gull taking off from the surface of the
waters, with huge long heavy gull legs, a bird from the belly
down.

Yellow-spot recalls some talk of legs in the Time Words
Came to the People, but the stories never made sense: the fire
from the sky, the white cloud spreading tangible over the sur-
face. It became only colours and weights: heavy, ugly, sinking.
Green. Pink. Blood, and drowning. Words, pictures. Treasures.
And death. Always death.

It occurs to Yellow-spot that if he is able to get home—it
seems less hopeless now he is not in pain—they will tell very
different stories about him than they will if he stays and dies.

He braces his hand on the rim of the trapped water, the little
cave pool barely big enough for his body that they have him in,
and lifts himself up, pressing his tail against the bottom. The
shallows are no place for people like him, past infancy.

The edge of the trapped water is narrow, like the wall of a
shell. It takes more effort than Yellow-spot could have predicted
to heave himself up—the air is unsupportive, and he supposes
this is why birds must always be flapping and flying fish cannot
stay aloft, although there is no time to marvel at the cruelty of
air now—but he has miscalculated, and inside this bright cavern,
Yellow-spot flops painfully against his belly, spins, and finds
the wind knocked out of him as he falls. A bright light is above
his head, as if he is floating on his back. But his back is on a
floor as unforgiving as any boulder of the abyss and much less
easy to push off from.

He slaps his tail against it, but all that happens is pain.

The tiny female with legs and its shoalmate that can't speak return. They are dismayed—they throw up their hands and make faces. Yellow-spot tries to raise himself, but the cave floor is unforgiving and the air is weak.

The unspeaking pale shoalmate departs again, flying on its legs, across the floor.

The little dark female touches Yellow-spot on his shoulder. Her touch is gentle. Her hand is dry and very warm, like an air-breather, like a whale calf or a sea lion pup. She tells Yellow-spot with small gestures that he must lie still so that she can return him to the sea—she looks over her shoulder at the direction the pale one left in, flying on its legs.

The tiny female folds her legs. This one must be a female; it is the same colour as the females of the deep; the other has gone, and no longer matters. Suddenly she is beside Yellow-spot, very close. She is warm. Her hands and arms slip under him, and then—up. He is flying in her arms; although the little female is even smaller than Pale-eyes, who is nearly as small as a male of the Depths, she is very strong and carries Yellow-spot out of the cave.

Outside, it is so bright that Yellow-spot covers his face with his hands and can see nothing. The only thing he can feel is the heavy pulse of the flying-female, and the heat of the sun. He works his throat to calm a sudden burst of fear—he will cook to death—it is too hot—it is too hot and too bright—

The flying-female halts.

Yellow-spot opens his eyes, peers between his fingers. There is a sheer wall, like a cliff with an overhang, but out of the water instead of under it. It is green with limp weed and algae the nearer it gets to the water on its thin poles. Beneath him, he can see the shallow shore water. Barnacles on the poles.

The flying-female drops him: he forms himself like the dolphin falling back into the waves after a leap, and slips into the blessed cool and salt without a pause or a splash. His skin tingles, but it does not itch and burn.

Yellow-spot breaches the surface, meaning to thank the strange female, but he is overcome. The service she has done him in saving him is more than simple words could ever express, and he knows then that he must take her to the Elder Mother, to tell his story, and to have this kind stranger gratified properly for her generosity.

Yellow-spot seizes her by the hand and pulls.

She falls off the overhang, the slimed overhang with its fronds of something not-quite-kelp, and hits the surface badly, flailing. He cannot decipher her words—she seems startled—and so, as is always the way, Yellow-spot takes her by the arm and pulls her down, as close to the Depths as there are in these bad shallow waters—to calm her, as a newborn must be calmed.

It does not work—if anything, the stranger thrashes more, and harder. Yellow-spot is concerned—the panicked dance will call down a shark, and he is not capable of fending off any but the smaller sorts alone.

He speeds up, towing his new friend eagerly towards the open water. Perhaps the Elder Mother will welcome her into the shoal. Perhaps they will tell stories about her, too.

After a while, his friend calms. Her struggles cease.

After a little longer, she is entirely unresisting, and Yellow-spot begins to feel an uncomfortable sensation in his belly, like sinking too fast through the thermoclimes. He stops. He is almost in familiar territory, and if he tells her this, perhaps her worries will fade. He will let her rest, though it seems now he has exerted most of the effort.

As his reinvigorated gills flutter in the following current, Yellow-spot turns to look at his new friend. Her bags float—hanging loose in the water. Her eyes are fixed open. There is a silver bubble caught in her nose.

Horror-stricken, the rock in his stomach solidifying fast, Yellow-spot releases her arm as if it has stung him. He touches his own face; she floats meanwhile, hanging face-down beneath the surface of the water.

He does not know if he should return home, or tow her with him, or stay, or—

Yellow-spot calms himself and smooths down his agitated crests. He must still return home. Even if they do not believe him, he must return home.

As he turns to begin swimming afresh, heavy of spirit and dull of hope, no longer caring for whatever story they will tell when he has been reabsorbed into the shoal, a loan banded sea krake passes along the surface of the stranger's arm, moving like the last fragments of a fading dream.

Christine Eskilson

WEDDING BELLE BLUES

The last thing I wanted to do eight weeks after giving birth was read a poem at Lainey's wedding. I had picked out a crystal vase from the Bloomingdale's registry and sent polite regrets, but Lainey, being Lainey, wouldn't take no for an answer. She called me right away.

"Of course you have to come, Maggie," she insisted. "How can I possibly get married without my freshman roommate? You were the first person I ever shared a room with!"

I definitely deserved an award for that, I thought, rolling my eyes at Charlotte. My new daughter stared back at me solemnly from the folds of her blanket. Lainey at nineteen had been selfish, careless, thoughtless—and those were her good qualities. We had been roommates for one year at Mount Holyoke by fate, and I never would have described us as close friends. Still, Lainey had held a certain allure for a limp-haired scholarship case from suburban Cleveland, and over the years, our paths occasionally continued to cross.

"Besides, Dan will be devastated," Lainey continued. "You remember Dan, don't you? He was the good-looking one I brought to our fifteenth. I know he thought very highly of you, with the magazine and all."

All of Lainey's boyfriends over the years could have walked straight out of a Ralph Lauren ad, but I vaguely remembered a tall, dark-haired doctor with perfect teeth hovering over her at our college reunion last summer. I don't think we had exchanged more than a perfunctory greeting at the bar.

"I'm not going back to the magazine for a while," I reminded Lainey. "For the next six months, I'm going to be home hanging out with a munchkin."

Propping my cell between one shoulder and ear, I put said munchkin on my other shoulder and gently rubbed her back.

That's why this is so perfect," Lainey pressed. "It's a weekend away at the Cape, and you can bring Charlotte. You'll get plenty of help. Phoebe's been dying for a grandchild—she'd almost given up on me—but she'll have to wait at least nine months. She'd love to practice now."

I reconsidered as Charlotte drooled on my shoulder. It so happened that my husband Jim was going to a software convention in Las Vegas the weekend of Lainey's wedding, and his mother had already announced she'd happily come to Boston so I wouldn't be alone. I looked around our cramped one bedroom, envisioning a yowling baby and a very opinionated mother-in-law. The Cape sounded better the more I thought about it.

"But what about the poem?" I asked. I was not one to leap at public speaking opportunities, particularly when I'd probably still be dressed in something resembling a tent.

The response was vintage Lainey. "The poem? Did I ask you to read a poem? Forget about that. Just get yourself and your little girl down here. Did you get the outfit I sent? Wasn't it darling with the matching hat and all?"

On a brilliant, sunny day in mid-September, Charlotte and I were tucked in a corner of a wide wraparound porch. The porch belonged to a sprawling hotel overlooking Cape Cod Bay where Lainey had spent many childhood summers. Except for Jim's absence, the moment was perfect. Charlotte had been a peach at the rehearsal dinner the night before and was much admired by all. Lainey seemed very much besotted with Dan, and I was beginning to think marriage might be a good influence on her. She had arranged for assorted baby paraphernalia at the resort so I didn't have to lug everything from stroller to crib down from Boston.

She had given her four bridesmaids lovely bracelets of twisted silver that Phoebe, her mother, told me Lainey had designed herself based on a family heirloom. And, as we all spooned crème brûlée at the end of the rehearsal dinner, Lainey told a sweet story about the way she and Dan had met at a New York sushi takeout joint. She even poked fun at herself for following him home with extra wasabi for his spicy California roll.

I slowly rocked Charlotte as she nursed. We had a few hours of solitude before we had to get ready for the five o'clock church service. Lainey had organized a horseback ride at the resort stables for the wedding guests, and apparently, it was a command performance. I was grateful for the exemption provided by my daughter's presence. Charlotte's eyes were closed in contentment, and the sun and the motion of the chair nearly lulled me to sleep as well.

But I wasn't the only non-rider in the bunch. I was jolted back to reality by harsh voices from the patio below.

"Goddamnit, you have to listen to me!" A man's voice raised in anger.

A woman answered, the words soft and indistinct.

The man spoke again. "No, it's not too late. You just have to give me more time. I'm going to be able to work it out with her. You'll see."

This time I almost jumped out of the rocker, and Charlotte mewed in protest. I adjusted her again on my breast and tried to listen hard. From where I sat, I couldn't see either of the two speakers, but I recognized the man's voice. It was Dan. I was sure of it. Who was he talking to? Were he and Lainey having a prenuptial squabble? Or was it someone else?

If the woman replied, I couldn't hear her, but Dan continued, his voice confident now. "We're going through with it tonight. We have no choice—everyone's here. But you have to trust me. I'll talk to her. Everything's going to turn out fine."

Fine for whom? And what did he mean about going through with "it" tonight? Was he talking about the wedding?

I finally could make out some of the woman's words, but I still couldn't tell who she was.

"You'd better get…You're not going to make a fool out of…Nobody makes a fool…and gets away with…Remember…one more chance…the last…"

The woman must have started throwing things at Dan because I heard a shower of glass smashing on the patio and then metal dancing across the flagstones. The last sound was her heels clicking furiously down the stone steps to the lawn below.

I stood and moved to the porch railing, hoping to catch sight of the woman when she reached the lawn, but I was too late. Charlotte was still latched onto me, and she was by no means convinced about me standing and her feeding at the same time. She abruptly stopped nursing. I cradled her in my arms and leaned over the railing in time to see Dan bend and brush away pieces of broken glass. He picked something up on the flagstones. I half-expected to glimpse Lainey's rock of an engagement ring, but as the sunlight glinted on the silver, I could see it was a bracelet. It looked like one of the bracelets Lainey had given to her bridesmaids the night before.

Charlotte and I had met all four women at the rehearsal dinner, and I tried now to remember their voices. Even if they hadn't all been wearing little black cocktail dresses, it would have been hard to distinguish between them. They were all slim blondes like Lainey, and they'd all grown up with her in a horsey suburb north of Boston. I thought the one in spaghetti straps was named Darcy, but it could have been Marcy, and I didn't even want to get started on the sleeveless one called Perry, who could have been Carrie. I had no idea which one of them could have been arguing with Dan about what sounded like a secret romance.

Below me, Dan stuffed the bracelet into his pocket and looked up at the porch. I felt like an idiot, staring down at him and clutching Charlotte with my shirt unbuttoned. I tried to think of some light-hearted joke to camouflage my obvious eavesdropping, but my mind was mush.

"Uh, hi, Dan," I said and was relieved when Charlotte started crying so I could swing into mother mode. "She needs a burp," I announced to him and an elderly couple who had just come out onto the patio.

I needn't have worried. Dan seemed stunned by my sudden appearance from above and didn't say a word. He just grunted and bolted down the same stairs as the woman had.

The couple on the patio stared up at me as I patted Charlotte's back. I was rewarded with the burp and a healthy dribble of spit-up milk on my shoulder. That decided my immediate course of action. After making sure I was respectable, I nodded to the couple and headed back into the lobby and up to our room to change.

Charlotte had fallen asleep in my arms by the time we got there and, holding my breath, I laid her down carefully in Lainey's rented crib. I had not yet mastered the transition from babe in arms to babe in bed, but today, I seemed to be successful. As I threw on a t-shirt, replaying the patio scene in my head and trying to figure out what to do, I heard a knock at the door.

"Please don't wake up Charlotte," I muttered in every mother's voice as I rushed to answer. "Please, please, please."

To my surprise, it was the bride to be. Raising my finger to my lips, I let her in.

"What's up?" I asked in a whisper.

"I saw you come in from the porch with the baby," Lainey replied, keeping her voice as low as mine. "I just stopped by for good luck. You and Jim seemed so happy at the reunion last year—I hope Dan and I end up the same way."

Her eyes were glittering with excitement, but if there was ever a time to warn Lainey about the bracelet throwing brides-maid, this was it. I tried to start in gently.

"You probably know already that the most important things in marriage are trust and communication," I said, feeling like a feeble excuse for Ask Amy. "I hope that you and Dan can tell each other everything about—"

"Damn," Lainey interrupted, her eyes on the clock next to my bed. This time she didn't lower her voice, and I heard Charlotte stir.

"I've got Jackie in from Boston to do my makeup, and she must be here by now." Lainey gave me a quick peck on the cheek. "Thanks for the words of wisdom, Maggie. You've always had your head on straight. Listen, I've got something else for little Charlotte—a family thing—but I can't seem to find it. I'll send it when we get back from Bali."

Before I could say anything else, she was gone, slamming the door behind her. After the door smacked into the frame, my darling offspring was off and screaming.

"I tried," I told Charlotte as I picked her up. "She wouldn't have listened to me anyway."

Lainey had always been able to take care of herself. One secretly heartbroken bridesmaid wouldn't faze her, even if the heart had been broken by the groom. Still, Dan's promise to the mystery woman that everything would turn out fine nagged at me.

The church ceremony went smoothly. Lainey was beautiful in a sleek, white, lace dress with billowing bell-shaped sleeves, and the bridesmaids wore pale espresso, floor-length gowns. I couldn't help but study them closely, trying to see which one was missing the twisted silver bracelet. No such luck. Darcy/Marcy, Perry/Carrie and the other two were all wearing them.

Maybe I had been hallucinating out there on the porch, I told myself, and I even shed a few tears when Dan's sister did an a cappella version of Irving Berlin's "Always." Weddings brought out the sap in me, and I wished Jim were here to poke me so I'd stop crying. I felt better when I noticed a few other tears—Phoebe, of course, and a couple of the bridesmaids. I bent my head over Charlotte and pretended to fuss with her bonnet.

The reception was held on the first floor of the hotel. Cocktails and serving stations were set up in various rooms off the lobby. I secured Charlotte in her sling and aimed for the grilled tuna in the library where the jazz trio was playing an instrumental version of "Somewhere Over the Rainbow." I had already exhausted my tolerance for small talk at the rehearsal dinner. Tending to a baby was a great excuse not to circulate with people you hardly knew, didn't really want to know and were unlikely to ever see again. I figured I'd done my face time for Lainey and had gotten a nice weekend to boot. A quick meal and then I'd disappear upstairs.

I collected my tuna with marinated vegetables and dilled baby potatoes and looked around for a secluded spot for Charlotte and me to sit down. There appeared to be a private room off the far corner of the library, its door just slightly ajar. Holding my plate and a glass of sparkling water, I pushed at the door with my sandal.

We would not be alone. Dan was sitting on the couch with one of the bridesmaids—the one named Perry or Carrie. Even though she was wearing the bracelet, she had to be the one from the afternoon. This time, I was close enough to hear her every word.

"How could you do this to me?" I heard her hiss as the door swung open. "After all we've been through. This can't be happening. I can't let this happen." She took a deep breath and her voice steeled. "I won't let this happen."

Dan was holding her and stroking her hair. "Perry, honey, I'm so sorry," he said.

It must have been Perry on the patio with Dan this afternoon, but this really was none of my business, nor did I want it to be. As I retreated, one of them had the sense to leap up and close the door behind me. It didn't get any better. When I turned around, I saw Lainey standing next to the library fireplace. She was staring right at the door of the room I had just left. I didn't think she'd seen Dan and Perry, though; a radiant smile appeared on her face as she headed toward me and Charlotte.

"Have you seen my husband?" she asked. "I can't seem to find him anywhere."

I shook my head, certain I was turning as bright red as Charlotte did when she wasn't getting what she wanted, and I mumbled something about having to nurse the baby. In truth, all I wanted to do was flee to the relative sanity of my hotel room.

"Don't go upstairs yet, Maggie. You haven't even eaten yet." Lainey took my plate, and I followed her to a table closer to the band.

"Sit down here," she ordered, putting the plate down. "You can eat and Charlotte can listen to the music. I think she likes Duke Ellington." Lainey reached out and absently stroked Charlotte's tufts of dark hair.

I dutifully sat down with Charlotte in my lap, feeling like I'd been programmed from our freshman year to obey Lainey.

"Phoebe wants to give a little speech soon—it's just an excuse to drink more champagne—and then we'll have the cake. After that, you can go upstairs. Now if you'll excuse me, I've got to find Dan."

Lainey was right. Charlotte did seem to like the music, or at least she wasn't crying about being kept up at the reception. She was fascinated by the lights in the lantern centerpieces on the table. I definitely enjoyed the grilled tuna, and even though I still had a good ten pounds to lose, I took a second helping.

After a waiter whisked away my plate, all the guests were directed to the lobby for a wedding toast. Figuring one glass couldn't hurt, I accepted a champagne flute and grabbed a spot with Charlotte on the central staircase. Lainey and Dan appeared, surrounded by their bridal party, and Phoebe welcomed Dan into the family. Standing in front of the table that held the three-tier wedding cake, Lainey looked triumphant. Dan just looked distracted. I tried to check out Perry, but her face was tilted away from me. I did notice she was holding two crystal glasses, and when Phoebe finished, Perry handed them to Lainey and Dan.

"That was lovely, Mother," Lainey said, blowing a kiss to Phoebe. She looked at Dan. "Why don't you say something, darling?"

Lainey turned around to place her glass next to the wedding cake as Dan cleared his throat. I admired the plunging back of her dress. Stammering slightly, Dan mumbled assorted thank yous to Lainey's family and his parents and to their friends from far and wide.

"I'll never forget this day," Lainey announced when he was done. Laughing, she brushed back her sleeve to pick up her glass and link her arm with Dan's.

"To us," Lainey said, raising her glass to his lips.

Dan hesitated for a moment, then raised his glass to her mouth. They both drank deeply.

The guests applauded, and I savored the rest of my champagne. Sitting on the staircase watching Lainey and Dan cut the cake made me think of my own wedding. The reception in my parents' backyard was much simpler than this lavish resort, but there were no jealous bridesmaids or grooms with divided loyalties (at least none that I knew of).

I had just decided to go upstairs when Dan suddenly dropped the silver cake knife and crumpled to the floor, his body seeming to twitch uncontrollably. The convulsions continued as Dan's back arched upward and his arms clenched at his sides so that only his heels and the back of his head were on the floor. A woman shrieked. I thought it was Lainey, but it turned out to be Perry. Lainey sank to the floor, her wedding gown spread around her. Guests rushed forward to help, and I was afraid Charlotte and I would get trampled. I escaped upstairs with her and called Jim. I had never been so glad to hear his voice.

As it turned out, Dan didn't stand a chance. The champagne in his glass had been laced with strychnine, a poison that paralyzes your muscles, including the ones that control breathing. Dan suffocated before he made it to the hospital, and it was an agonizing way to die. Apparently, they used strychnine in the resort stables to control the rats.

The police questioned me, along with all the other wedding guests, and I told them about the fight Perry and Dan had on the patio and their conversation at the reception. Perry was arrested for Dan's murder within the week—they'd been having an on and off again affair. The police believed she'd tried to poison Lainey's champagne, but when Lainey switched the glasses, everything went haywire.

Perry pled not guilty and went on trial the following year— at just about the same time as what would have been Lainey and Dan's first wedding anniversary. Unfortunately, because of what I'd overheard, I ended up being one of the lead witnesses against her. Lainey, strangely enough, stood staunchly by her friend's side, even testifying as a character witness on her behalf about Perry's volunteer work at the equestrian center where they'd ridden as kids. The prosecution pointed to it as an opportunity to learn about rat poison, but Perry's lawyer tried to milk it for what altruism he could.

Sick ponies didn't sway the jury, however, and Perry got life. I heard from Phoebe a few Christmas cards ago that she had died in a prison fire. Lainey dropped out of sight as far as I was concerned. I read in our alumni magazine that she had remarried and was running a bed and breakfast on Crete.

There's one more piece to this story. Yesterday was Charlotte's fifth birthday, and when I got home from work, an overseas package was sitting beside our front door. *I promised this to Charlotte a long time ago*, read the note inside, *but things got in the way. It's been in my family for ages. Take better care of it than I have.*

I recognized the distinctive scrawl and sat down on the steps, my heart pounding. The package contained a bracelet wrapped in a piece of white lace. An antique bracelet made of twisted sterling silver. The same bracelet Dan rescued from the hotel patio after his killer had flung it at his head.

Lainey.

Lawrence Salani

THE EUPHORIANT

Horror and the unknown are usually associated with desolate or secluded areas, but the city, with all its development and teaming masses, holds other forms of daemons that writhe and wallow in the darkness of deserted alleys and dimly lit back roads. Labyrinthine streets spiral web-like amongst the towering agglomeration of buildings. Lost souls wearing filthy rags, begging for coins, sleeping in dirty alleys or under store fronts, frequently appear among the crowds of strange, foreign faces who are too busy to care as they hurry to their respective destinations.

Deformed trees along the roadside are a sad parody of their former majesty as their severed limbs reach for the eternal, cold, blue sky. Handmade leaflets, plastered to light poles along the roadways, advertise accommodation while weathered and faded photos on poster-splattered hoardings or shop doorways proclaim mysteriously lost relatives or friends. Amongst this kaleidoscope of modern life, I found horror that would forever haunt my existence.

The man stood outside a grimy train station entrance distributing pamphlets, and what made him contrast with the masses swarming around him was his abnormal look. Middle aged, he wore an old, frayed, brown suit, which looked as though it had not been cleaned for years. His pants—held up by a worn, leather belt—were too short and exposed the white socks and scuffed, black shoes he wore. A length of rope slung around his neck held up an old, wooden box containing the pamphlets he distributed to the passing crowd.

Long black hair cropped at an unusual angle surrounded a puffed face, and the thick-framed glasses he wore made his dark brown eyes appear twice the size. His pear-shaped body stood like an unmoving boulder in a stream of madness, hoping that someone—anyone—would take a pamphlet, but nobody did. More out of pity than any real interest, I accepted a colored leaflet. Probably some sort of religion, I thought while unconsciously stuffing the paper into my coat pocket.

Shops provided a constant source of entertainment as I wandered amongst the crowds before stopping at a small cafe for lunch. The table I chose fronted a window that looked onto the street, allowing me to see the motley crowd walking by. Seldom having visited Sydney, I had decided to spend some recreational time there. The lure of bright lights was a temptation, for the ennui of suburbia had made a break from my everyday routine necessary. Gradually, the grayness of evening descended over the thinning crowd outside, and as cold shadows of sunset lengthened over the roadway, I returned to my rented room.

Exhausted after the long day, my only thought was for an early night's sleep, but upon entering the apartment and placing my hand in my coat pocket, to my surprise, the crumpled pamphlet I had taken from the man at the station earlier that day was still there. My immediate reaction was to throw it away; however, the bold black heading drew my attention. I examined the wrinkled sheet after smoothing it out on the bedside table. It was an invitation for anyone needing salvation, and at the bottom of the page there was a date, time, and address for the next gathering of the Order. The hall was within walking distance. A strange sense of curiosity overwhelmed me while reading the leaflet. Consciously I wanted to attend, but sub-consciously my mind was questioning. Ambivalent, I left it on the lone bedside table and allowed the soothing embrace of slumber and the new day to decide.

As the morning sun crept through the jumbled maze of towering buildings, a shaft of light shone through a gap in the curtains of the small window in my room awakening me from a deep sleep. After showering and making plans for the new day, I noticed the pamphlet lying on the bedside table. The yellow paper seemed to beckon strangely in the somber grey tones of the room. Picking it up and re-reading the pamphlet, I realized the meeting was scheduled for that evening. After much deliberation I decided to attend.

The endless stream of traffic, crowds of people, and vast array of shops during the day completely erased any thought of the meeting. New sights were a constant source of wonder until evening shadow and cold, dimly lit darkness replaced the daytime warmth. The crowds of shoppers had thinned; deserted, alley entrances gaped ominously between somber, concrete towers as I strolled back to my apartment.

Having decided to relax after showering and a meal, I suddenly remembered the meeting planned for that evening. There was still time before it was scheduled to commence, but the chill night breeze made me hesitate. My curiosity, however, was overwhelming, so, after putting on warmer apparel, I again traversed the tree-canopied road lit only by dull, murky streetlights.

Upon entering George Street, noise and colored light illuminated the darkness. Flickering neon lighting from the various entertainment establishments beckoned, as I hurried through trying to avoid people spilling onto the footpath from the crowded cinema precinct.

I became somewhat apprehensive, however, after leaving the main road and the streets became darker and less populated. Only a few straggling people remained along the deserted footpath, and bright lights gradually grew dimmer along the ominous back streets leading to the address advertised on the leaflet in my pocket. As the illuminated signs of the few remaining cafes began disappearing, the hall finally came into view.

The building was remarkably larger than expected. Morose, darkened towers loomed on either side of the squat dilapidated structure. A murky, orange tinge cast by a row of dull fluorescent lights beneath the awnings lit the entrance. A lone figure stood in the dimly lit doorway, which, on closer observation, proved to be the peculiar man who had been distributing the pamphlets at the station entrance.

"Welcome," he cordially greeted before ushering me into a capacious room filled with chairs arranged in a semi-circular pattern around a small stage. Approximately one hundred and fifty people filled the hall, and, while walking to a seat near the stage, I noticed a mixture of people among the congregation— not only the homeless but the better dressed working class. A faint murmur arose from the crowd awaiting the arrival of the last of the gathering.

A hushed silence heralded movement from one side of the room. Heads in the crowd turned towards the direction of the sound as two plainly dressed men entered with a long trolley carrying something tall beneath a white sheet. They approached the small stage in the centre of the hall then awaited the arrival of a third man who entered wearing an elaborately decorated robe and stood on a slightly raised platform adjacent the other two men.

"Greetings to the faithful," his glassy stare scanned the gathered crowd. "Blessings and eternal happiness be with you. May you be guided to the gates of perpetual freedom and ecstasy."

An ominous silence fell over the hall, as anticipation surged amongst the gathering when the man in the decorated robe motioned his assistants to unveil the trolley. The domed shape stood at least two meters high and in diameter slightly larger than one meter. As the two men slowly uncovered the dome, only the sound of muffled movement could be heard drifting through the hall. The noise gradually subsided when the cloth fell to the ground and the dumbfounding sight was exposed for all to see.

Beneath the white sheet was a glass dome, which contained the most beautiful flower I ever beheld. Although its petals were larger and thicker, it resembled an oriental lily. Effulgent, white petals were tinged blood red, and in the middle of the five enormous petals a dark hollow extended towards the stem. From the base of the flower grew a mass of large, five pointed, emerald leaves, each point tapering into a long thorn. The coarse, succulent texture of the leaves created an uncontrollable urge to reach out and touch them. Tiny, green strands of hair-like fibers, which seemed to move or breathe, covered the leaves, and through the middle of each leaf there ran a large, pulsating vein-like structure that attached to the main stem of the plant.

Beneath the mass of iridescent, green foliage, the flower bore a cluster of round fruit approximately twenty-five millimeters in diameter; each piece appeared perfectly spherical and was of the most incredible iridescent red hue. The great talon tipped leaves were protecting the precious fruit and moved gently beneath flood lights illuminating the stage.

At this point, murmuring among the assembled spectators recommenced, but this was only a distant drone because the incredible sight held me transfixed. A flower bearing fruit was amazing, but the magnificent color, beauty, and strange movement held me in incredulous wonder.

"The Flower of Dreams!" exclaimed the man wearing the robe, his arms outstretched to show fully the bizarre decorations adorning the brightly colored cloth. Again, he motioned to his assistants who began lifting the glass dome from the flower. A hush blanketed the crowd. We sat in silence watching the spectacle as a delightfully, addictive scent crept through the room; a scent that bought back memories long forgotten; an aroma as only the flowers of the lost Garden of Eden could emanate; a perfume not found on this earth. While inhaling the scented air of the great hall, my eyes were fixed upon the flower when, to my horror, the flower's five thick petals began to move! And as I watched them unfold my horror increased a hundred fold, *for from inside the hollowed centre, a great globular eye appeared and began watching the unbelieving spectators before it.*

Silence filled the hall, for now the visions began.

Incredible images inundated my mind; one could describe it as a dream, but the verisimilitude was astonishing. Crystal clear, blue sky, the air filled with the sweet scent of springtime. An eternity of happiness was mine, for there was no death, no sickness, no pain, for this was nirvana. Unbelievable cities unfolded before my eyes, teeming with happy life. Time had been conquered, and all were young and healthy. The delights of life were again ripe for picking. Everlasting towers, made of an unknown metal gleamed in a sunless sky. A soft caressing light, not the harsh, burning light of the sun, radiated perpetually from a clear, azure sky. Gleaming streams of sparkling clear water flowed through majestic valleys of bright yellow and green; everything was vibrant and alive, and nature lived in harmony with mankind.

Walking through the marble paved streets and opulent courtyards, an ethereal, ecstatic feeling surrounded my body. I could but look in amazement at the towering, intricately carved structures that loomed around me and wonder of their creators. There was no night, for this was eternity. The universe had cascaded into one moment of joy, and, as the truth to existence began to dawn upon me, I could feel the presence of others around me and knew we were one; happiness filled my being. Looking across the beauty and wonder of the majestic landscape, I felt that this was where I belonged.

But the scene slowly faded and the feeling of completeness and contentment evaporated. When I awoke in the shabby, badly lit hall surrounded by the others, the smell of sweet perfume was gone; only the rank, musty smell of the old building filled the air. The flower was covered by the glass dome again, and we were all staring at its incredible beauty and listening to the words of the robed man before us; the gold and silver designs of his dark robe shimmering under the bright lights like a galaxy of stars in the night sky.

"Only a small sampling of the flower's scent can bring visions of wonder. The fruit of the flower will bring joy which cannot compare to anything of this earth...," he cried, raising his arms towards the ceiling and exposing the coruscating, intricate patterns contained within the robe. "But," he continued more softly, "the price is death."

Speechless, I turned toward the person seated next to me. The spectacle unfolding before us held him in awe, but upon noticing my bewildered expression, he turned and looked at me, and the first thing I noticed were his remarkable blue eyes. Framed by long, wild hair, his gaunt, wrinkled face showed signs of intemperance and years of abuse, whilst his clothes, although relatively new, smelt unclean.

"The Flower of Dreams!" he exclaimed, as he motioned towards the stage; his bright, blue eyes were wild with excitement. "Eating the fruit will bring an incredible sensation filled with unimaginable dreams never experienced in this world. Some say it is well worth the price."

Anticipation surged amongst the gathering as the ceremony slowly came to an end. "Are there any that wish to partake of the fruit?" the man in the robe asked the crowd. Murmuring within the congregation quickly diminished, and only a thick silence filled the shadowed hall.

The speaker waited several minutes before turning to his assistants who began draping the white cloth over the dome. A brief ceremony ensued after which the speaker left. I checked my watch while the crowd dispersed. Only an hour had passed, yet an uncanny feeling that much more time had passed filled me. The man who had been seated beside me watched the two assistants take the covered flower through a small door at the far end of the hall. When they disappeared into the gloom, he rose and began shuffling through the crowd towards the exit. I decided to follow him and gather more information regarding the events that had transpired.

My new acquaintance proved more loquacious than I had expected. Our shadows cast abnormal shapes on the graffiti-splattered walls and worn concrete path as we walked along unfamiliar, badly lit, back streets leading, hopefully, to the better lit George Street from where I had come.

"I've been attending these meetings for more than a year, and the visions have become stronger. The flower's perfume is delightfully addictive. The euphoric sensation it produces cannot be explained in words." His eyes glimmered in the dim streetlight as he looked up at the towering apartment buildings to see if there was any movement in the darkened windows. "It's the Flower of Dreams, you know? They say it fell to earth from another world, another galaxy, and was found in a desert. Eating the fruit it bears opens the doors of paradise. The feeling you experienced tonight is but a minute fragment of the ultimate sensation."

As we sauntered along blackened back streets, there was a tremor of excitement in his voice as he spoke, and his wild, blue, eyes flickered with an insane gleam. His erudite manner and speech made me wonder how he had degenerated into the miserable state in which he now existed. We continued talking as the lighting from the still open cafes slowly came into view beneath the shop awnings, and the darkness was gradually replaced by the gaiety of the city nightlife.

"The flower has changed my life," he said putting his smooth, slim hands into his coat's pockets. "And it can change yours, if you allow it to."

I looked at him but could not imagine what he meant.

"Come to the meeting again next week," he pleaded. "Unimaginable vistas will open up. You will experience happiness beyond anything you can possibly imagine in this miserable existence. The pseudo-happiness these fools around you think is enjoyment is but a sham when compared with the pleasures of the flower. Come, smell the perfume again; paradise beyond your dreams awaits you." He turned and was engulfed by the gloom of a small alley. His silhouette moved down the lonely, darkened lane before gradually disappearing among the shadows of the graffiti splattered walls and back entrance doorways.

The whole night seemed unreal. I stared into the thick blackness of the alley. "This isn't possible," I whispered to myself while walking under the brightly lit shop awnings, the crowds slowly thickening as I made my way back to the cinema precinct and the main entertainment area around George and Pitt Street.

Still unbelieving, I trudged back to my lodgings. The movement of traffic and laughing people around me was a blur as I passed through the crowds in a bewildered daze. They faded into the distance; their laughter, shallow and unreal, drifted into the silent shadows of the cold, badly lit road leading to my apartment. I put my hands into my coat pockets seeking warmth and could feel the yellow pamphlet that still lay there.

The oblivion of sleep completely erased the occurrences of the former night; only a faded impression of what seemed an unbelievable dream remained. But as the morning progressed, the poignant visions of the former night began to fall into place, and my mind was again filled with my new companion's words when he had departed.

The flower, it had moved! In my mind, I could still see its unblinking eye when it had stared at me, and the memory of its sweet, irresistible scent as it unfolded its thick, luscious petals still filled my body with yearning. The visions remained until I was consciously longing to inhale the flower's perfume again and anxiously awaiting the passing of the week so that I could visit the hall and see the flower.

My week passed uneventfully. Roaming the city streets among the multitude of faces, my thoughts were constantly on the night I had experienced the delights of the flower. As the days passed and the night of the next meeting drew nearer, I found myself again walking towards the meeting hall.

The tangled jumble of towers along Pitt Street obliterated the night sky; the myriad of darkened and half lit windows resembled an incomplete jig-saw puzzle above the brightly lit street below. Passing again through George Street, I made my way towards the outskirts of the city. The countless stars resembled tiny painted dots in the clear night sky, and while walking along the gloomy, badly lit road leading to the meeting hall, a tingle of anticipation surged through my body as memories of the past meeting cascaded through my mind.

In the distance, the strange man who had been distributing pamphlets at the station entrance was once again standing in the doorway, greeting people as they arrived. When I reached the entrance, he gave me a knowing look before ushering me to the main hall where I found a vacant seat as close to the front as possible and then waited for the hall to slowly fill with people.

Approximately two hundred people were assembled in the hall when the flower, under the covered glass dome, was bought out by the two assistants. The robed man again recited the ceremony before the flower was uncovered. This time, as the perfume drifted throughout the hall, the scent seemed stronger and sweeter; the visions were more vivid, and the feeling more euphoric.

If I could but put into words the experience of the night, the wonders unfolded, and the fantastic visions of landscapes and cities not of this world nor of any world imagined by man. But most incredible was the feeling of complete freedom and ecstasy, as if the thing that was my body, which had only been a burden in the past, was now a discarded, empty receptacle; a feeling of overwhelming joy filled my being. I roamed this paradise for what seemed days, but upon awakening realized only an hour had passed.

When the flower was covered by the dome, the robed man raised his arms towards the ceiling and asked the gathering if there were any that would taste the fruit. An ominous hush fell over the crowd, for all knew the implications of acceptance. An unnatural silence filled the hall, for few had the temerity to speak, until from the midst of the assembly there ushered a loud cry, "I will!" The gathering turned towards the direction of the shrill voice as it reverberated through the old hall. To my astonishment, standing amidst the seated assembly was the man I had spoken with at the previous meeting.

Shuffling excitedly through the crowd, he made his way towards the domed flower. The speaker again outstretched his arms, revealing the silver and gold decorations of his dark green robe glittering under the floodlights shining from the ceiling. He stood before the gathering while the dome was again raised slightly. The now familiar scent of the flower drifted through the room as one of the attendants reached for a bright red globe. Great spikes on the ends of the leaves menacingly rose toward the offending hand, but the attendant quickly removed the fruit and the dome was lowered before the plant could strike. Luscious petals opened to reveal a great bulbous eye maliciously staring at the attendant and the appropriated fruit. The bright, red sphere was given to my acquaintance who devoured it without the slightest hesitation before the cover was again draped over the glass dome.

The congregation looked on in wonder, as the assistants wheeled out the trolley carrying the flower, leaving the robed man and my friend before the crowd.

"Conrad," he said, "has tasted the fruit of the flower."

This was the first time I had heard his name, for I had not formally introduced myself after the previous meeting.

May the delights of the flower be many and long. The fruit will transport him to realms that will never be known or imagined by humanity. May he be gently guided to eternal ecstasy by the hand of Hypnos."

The two assistants appeared from the shadows at the rear of the hall and stood on either side of Conrad whose eyes had begun to glaze strangely. Again, the robed man addressed the crowd, "The fruit is available to any who wish to try it, but the ultimate decision rests with you." The bewildered crowd watched silently as the man then turned and followed Conrad and the two assistants from the stage and into the deep shadows at the back of the room.

The crowd slowly began leaving. Bemused and frightened, I waited as the hall emptied before inconspicuously blending in with the last of the crowd and finally walking back onto the darkened street. The strange man who had given me the pamphlet was standing at the doorway as the last of the fluorescent lights beneath the awnings were extinguished. A strange look appeared in his eyes as he stared at me, and his rotund body and puffed, puppet-like face glowing in the sickly light of the few remaining fluorescent tubes sent a tingle of fear through my body; his comical appearance now appeared more like something aberrant and unwholesome; a pernicious disease.

Winter's claw had stripped the truncated trees of their foliage. The skeletal forms swayed gently in the yellow street light, casting lunatic shadows on the grimy path. Walking along the dark, deserted streets, my thoughts were on the recent occurrences, and my feelings for Conrad were a mixture of sadness and incredulity. My mind constantly wandered back to the night I had spoken to him, for if I had known he had been contemplating eating the fruit, I would have helped him to reconsider. With a sense of relief, I left the back road, and lights gradually came into view in the distance. My apartment seemed an eternity away as I trudged along the brightly lit streets, but the crowds of unaware merrymakers provided a feeling of relief and comfort after the unfolding of the night's events.

My rest was troubled that night. I drifted in and out of sleep until the morning sunrise when I lay in bed contemplating what could have become of Conrad. Throughout the day, although I tried to forget, my mind constantly wandered back to the occurrences of the previous evening. The crowds of shoppers seemed unreal. Their masses were a source of comfort, but, as the days drifted quickly by, the compulsion to return to the hall and find out what had happened to my companion grew too strong. Hopefully, during the daylight hours there would be no people to disturb my inquiries.

Turbid grey covered the morning sky. A chill in the air heralded a storm which drifted threateningly over the horizon. Hoping to finish my investigation before the impending rain, I quickly walked along busy Pitt and George Streets, then down the less populated side streets leading towards the small back roads of the city. Darkened front windows of vacant tenements desolately revealed their tattered, black interiors. Trees canopied the roadways with bare skeletal branches as decaying shop fronts began to replace the newer towers. The hall eventually appeared in the distance, so I quickened my pace. The exterior of the building was as dilapidated as the surrounding neighborhood, for darkness had hidden all the defects easily discernible during the day.

All the main entrances appeared locked, so I searched for a side or back doorway whereby I could gain entrance.

A small, deserted alley provided a gate to the back of the building. However, the gate being securely locked left me no option but to climb over the rusting tin fence using a solid, wooden box, which was lying among the piles of debris that lined the small roadway. Once over the other side, my next problem was finding an entrance to the hall. Fire exits and the back doorway were securely locked, but one of the grimy windows had been broken and boarded up. The boards crumbled effortlessly when I pulled on the rotting timber; the window, however, proved a little more difficult than expected, for the latch had rusted. But, after removing some of the broken shards of glass from the frame, I easily crawled through.

Diffused light from the dirty windows shone eerily throughout the capacious building. Carefully, I crept through the shadows towards the main hall. An unearthly quiescence made the slightest sound echo terrifyingly through the semi-darkness, causing me to tread warily over the rubble strewn floor.

My story to this point seems clear, for the surreal atmosphere had intensified my senses, but when I walked through the main hall to the door where the attendants had taken Conrad and looked inside, I could now no longer be certain. It may have been the rumble of thunder when the storm began or the maddening sound of the heavy rain hammering on the corrugated iron roof that made my heart jump and cause me to lose my nerve; but, after opening the door and the accursed lightning flash illuminated the room, I cannot readily accept the bedlam of images that cascaded through my mind.

Inside the dimly lit room, lying on a long, stout, wooden table was the figure of a man, and judging by the hair and clothes, it must have been Conrad. Standing in the doorway, I felt the blood drain from my body and fear hold me paralyzed. From the face of what was now a corpse grew a flower. The features were no longer recognizable, for the roots of the flower had burrowed deeply into the head. Light from high windows inside the room shone dimly over the thick, violet, finger-like roots pulsating and sucking nourishment from the rotting, bluish flesh. The strange blossom had grown, in such a small amount of time, to approximately one meter in height, and leaves with talon-like spikes were forming around its base.

While I stood in the doorway and looked inside that charnel room, it was as if the legions of darkness had gathered in some wild, blasphemous orgy. As the storm outside thundered out its anger, lightning washed the badly lit room in waves of light, and the flower moved its thick, succulent, lily-like petals slowly toward me. The cacophony of rain pounding on the roof, compounded by the sight before me, filled me with terror, but the uttermost horror came when a fateful flash of lightning illuminated the room; the shock that stunned me to wakefulness as the first hint of that exquisite scent filled the air and threatened to send me into a euphoric dream world and then to oblivion.

Lightning lit the room for only a few seconds, allowing me to see the flower more clearly. Within those few seconds, the flower had turned towards me and unfolded its succulent, red-streaked petals. I could feel the daemons of hell squeeze my heart and death caress my spine with its icy touch, *for amongst the open petals was a bright, blue eye, and in that blue orb I could see the sad, knowing look of my lost acquaintance, Conrad.*

My maddened scream was drowned out by a roar of thunder.

Blindly, I stumbled through the semi-darkened hall, almost falling in my haste. Lightning continued to illuminate the deep shadows that had been formerly only silent, brooding blackness. Human shapes began to appear within the darkened corners as each successive flash outlined their contours more clearly. They stood—unmoving—watching with a sorrowful look on their pale, bloodless faces. Fear of what may be waiting ahead caused me to stop and think rationally. I could feel their presence as I tentatively walked through the hall, guided only by the wan light shining through the grimy windows.

A sudden flash of lightning engulfed the room!

How can I describe my emotions when I saw clearly what lurked within the shadows?

The face was of the man who had given me the pamphlet at the station entrance and had welcomed me on the night I had attended the meeting. Only he was without glasses or hair. A jagged cut along the middle of his head, extending downwards towards his back, had been sewn closed by rough cord, making the figure resemble an overstuffed rag doll that had been stitched wrongly. His obese, shapeless body appeared boneless as he glared murderously beneath the light cast by another flash of lightning.

Other figures were hiding within the shadows of the room, but my recollections are only of the deep sadness embedded within their eyes. Their sorrow was beyond any misery that can be contemplated in life, beyond the very pain of eternal damnation. Fleeing from the insanity that filled the accursed hall was my only thought, as I ran wildly through the darkened rooms.

Finally reaching the window from which I had entered, I crawled through and blindly collapsed onto the muddy ground outside, insensible to the cuts from the glass still within the broken frame. After scaling the fence, I ran through the torrential rain, covered in mud, oblivious of the bewildered people that watched or the storm raging around me, for the insane legions of the black abyss surely followed close behind.

I continued running until safely inside my rented apartment, bedraggled and blood splattered from the cuts inflicted while climbing through the broken window.

I left the city soon after.

Memory of the nightmare will never be obliterated, and life has suddenly acquired a different meaning. Ecstatic dreams have been replaced by nights of torment, for my mind is tortured with visions of the radiant beauty of the flower, but with its beauty there lies the memory of Conrad as I saw him on that fateful day. Horror swarms through my mind like a black pestilence, and a shudder surges through my body when I think that the same fate would have befallen me had I not the temerity to investigate what had happened to my companion.

The city, its teeming masses, maze of streets, and shadowed back alleys now hold little attraction, but I often wonder where the flower originated and who the strange, decadent people that looked after it were. My questions will hopefully remain unanswered, but, although I have seen the fate of those who inhale the perfume of the Flower of Dreams, the sweet scent is difficult to forget.

Cary G. Osborne

LIKE THE SPIDER IN THE MIDDLE OF HER WEB

O h, Papa. It's so exciting."
Espee jumped up from the writing desk and ran to her father the moment he came through the doorway. She put her arms around him and hugged him tightly, her cheek against his. He returned the embrace slightly less enthusiastically.

"Are you sure? Is this what you want."

"Of course. It's a famous and powerful family. And look." She ran back to the desk and picked up the miniature portrait to show him again. "He's so handsome. And not like the others who have been so much older."

"But the rumors. And that strange questionnaire."

"Clearly, they must be careful whom they invite to the castle to marry the heir of Belle Isle. Any girl would be flattered to meet Prince Arnof."

She fiddled with the pearl pendant on a chain around her neck that had come with the portrait. It was of a good size, milky white, matching the color of the skin it lay against. She was so fair and so young, and at sixteen, of marriageable age. But she knew her father considered her too young and ignorant of the ways of the world. But she knew her heart, and this marriage was what she wanted, what she had been schooled for.

Lord Brune returned his daughter's smile. "Let me know when you've finished the questionnaire."

She said she would and, laughing, returned to the writing desk. He retreated to the hall, closing the door behind him.

As she picked up the quill, she couldn't help thinking about her life in Castle Brune, held by her father and his father before him. It was the only home she had known, having never ventured farther than her mother's home in Lurey to the east. Her father spoiled her, giving her everything he could, but she knew nothing of privilege or the lack thereof, having nothing with which to compare.

Her happiness had increased when the messenger came from Belle Isle, where resided Prince Bernard, to whom her father owed fealty. There had been messages before, of course, the prince asking for men to defend a border or perform work on some project. None of those had been of much consequence, really. Her father had never gone himself, letting one of his many lieutenants take the lead.

For two days, Espee worked on the questionnaire. Some of the questions were strange, such as "Are you afraid of spiders or other insects?" Others were very personal questions, as in "Did your mother come from a large family?" The meaning of that last one was clear: would she be likely to bear many children? It worried her as her mother, Lenore, and father had only two living children, Espee and her younger brother, Edmund. She died trying to give life to a third child who also succumbed. Brune chose not to remarry right away, and the years turned into more than a decade.

On the third day, the messenger was sent back with the responses to the myriad questions, four pages of them, along with a miniature portrait of Espee. That night as they supped, Brune questioned her desire to marry Arnof, Prince Bernard's son.

"The thought of losing you pains me," he said.

His eyes shone with unshed tears, and Espee realized his hair had grown very grey, and there were laugh lines around his mouth and eyes. He squinted when trying to read. She always saw him as the young, robust father of her childhood. Even now, his hands were steady, and his head did not shake as Jerrold's did, he who had been her grandfather's steward and still faithfully served the lord of the castle.

"You've always known that I would marry and leave one day. You wouldn't want your only daughter to remain a maiden and live out her life alone."

He shook his head, but without much conviction.

"The only other choice might be to marry a second son, who would, of course, come here to live. But that wouldn't do, would it? Plus, if I do marry the heir to Belle Isle, that will also raise the family's station."

Frowning now, he leaned back in his chair, contemplating the food he had barely touched. When he raised his head, the worry on his face alarmed her. He could refuse to give her to Prince Arnof in marriage, which could be bad for all of them. If he proposed, she reminded herself.

"You know nothing of the Prince and his family. There are rumors, stories…"

"All of them are only that," she said.

"Not all."

"What do you mean?"

"I told you that I once joined Bernard and his father when the western border was threatened." She nodded, hoping not to hear the same old stories again. "I know I've told you many times," he said, guessing from her expression what she was thinking. "But there is much I haven't told anyone."

"Please, Father. I don't need to hear it all again."

"Yes, you do."

She sighed. He took a swallow of wine, then began.

In his youth he had also received an invitation from Belle Isle, from Prince Maurice, Bernard's father. The estate there was very much larger than Castle Brune, perched on a cliff looking down on the river Doge, its turrets sometimes lost in the clouds when they sank toward the earth.

A war was brewing between Belle Isle and a neighboring kingdom, and various lords were called on to serve. Owing allegiance to Maurice, Lord Brune, Espee's grandfather, had answered the call by sending his eldest son and a hundred soldiers. It was a journey of three days for a group of young men eager to prove themselves, and when they marched through the gates, Brune the Younger had immediately felt uneasy. Darkness shadowed his vision a moment. Then it cleared as he received the welcome of Prince Bernard. They were near the same age and eager to prove themselves in battle.

He and Bernard practiced together; they were competitors, yet they became fast friends. They went wenching together in the town, the young women flattered to have the attention of a prince and the son of a distant lord. They ate and drank together, telling stories of what they would do, rather than of past triumphs.

Preparations lasted a week. When all was ready for the army to march out, the two were inseparable. They thought alike, spoke alike, agreed on the tactics Maurice would use when they faced the enemy, who wished to take control of the source of the River Doge. Prince Maurice and his ancestors had controlled the river for generations as a part of Belle Isle.

In the encampment on the night before the battle, Brune had been out checking the pickets and the horses. It was very quiet, as if the world listened for some sign of what was to come. Being his first battle, he was nervous, his heart beat a bit faster, and his palms were sweaty. Most nights on the march, he and Bernard had spent together in their tent talking of old battle stories they had heard. They bragged about the bravery they would exhibit, laughing, and hoping they sounded like seasoned soldiers.

But this last night, Brune wanted to be alone with his own thoughts. Bragging did not appeal to him, nor did drinking or laughing. He was not frightened of the morrow. All of his life he had accepted the possibility of dying in battle—a better end he could not imagine.

He rose from the rock he had been sitting on and wiped at the moisture on the seat of his pants from the accumulated humidity. Purposefully, he walked toward his and Bernard's tent. As he reached for the flap, he heard a strange mumbling inside. He listened a moment, then pulled the flap aside.

Bernard was on his knees, chanting as he swayed side to side. Candles burned in a half circle on the small camp table. His right hand rested palm up on the table with the candles around it. In his palm a small figure moved. It was difficult to see what it was, but it appeared that it was some sort of insect, a rather large one.

Carefully, Brune pushed past the flap and walked slowly toward his friend who concentrated on his hand and whatever moved there. Brune felt a prickling in his scalp and the back of his neck.

He had gotten within four feet of his friend, realizing with a start what Bernard held. It was a large spider, a deadly one. Its two front legs raised as it swayed side to side in rhythm with the chanting.

Ever so slowly Brune stepped backwards, retreating toward the outside, away from the strange scene. He knocked over a bucket with a soft thud. Both the man and the spider turned to look at him. Bernard looked angry, but when he saw his friend, a smile came to his lips. The spider, front legs still raised, stayed perfectly still.

"Ah, Brune," Bernard said. "We are nearly done. Come back in a few minutes."

Brune raised his gaze from the spider to his friend's face. The smile was on his lips but not in his eyes.

"Of course," he said. "A few minutes."

The cool air chilled his face, covered with sweat. He took a deep breath, pulling the cold down his throat, into his lungs. He shivered, thought of moving to the nearest fire, but three soldiers already sat on stools at its edge. He wanted no company.

He stood where he was pondering what he'd seen. Was it some sort of witchcraft? A game? More than likely it was a trick of some kind, something to show off to friends in a tavern.

"Brune, come back in. It's cold out there."

He looked around at the sound of his friend's voice, screwing up the courage to return to the company of this man about whom he knew so little.

You know him, he thought. *You've trained together, drunk together, and slept with the same women. He's your friend.*

Once inside, Bernard handed him a cup of mead. He took it, but at the same time, his eyes searched for any sign of the spider. They toasted the day to follow, welcoming the opportunity to prove their courage, and Bernard led the conversation to speculation on the battle.

"Of course, there are many ways to win a battle," he said.

They discussed the ways, but Brune had a vague feeling that there might be more than he could imagine. A couple of times, Brune looked up from his cup to find Bernard watching him.

Just after midnight, Bernard and Brune made ready for bed. Brune lifted the blankets on his cot to make sure there was no sign of a spider within its folds.

Brune lay awake for a long time, unable to wipe away that scene. Was it really a spider in Bernard's hand? What could he have possibly been doing with a spider? If he let his imagination loose, he would guess that he had witnessed some sort of ceremony. That would make Bernard a... what? A wizard? Superstitious was more like it. Just a silly superstition, nothing more.

He turned over, pulling the blankets closer around him. Bernard was a friend. A warrior. And the son of Prince Maurice. Nothing more nor less.

Towards dawn he fell deeply asleep, only to be awakened by Bernard shaking his shoulder.

"Wake up, my brother. It is time for battle."

"I'm awake." Brune threw the blankets back and sat up. He shivered, and his breath was visible in the cold air. Bernard handed him a cup of hot buttered rum.

"To warm you from the inside."

He was almost fully dressed and Brune hurried to catch up. The groom stood just outside the entrance with their horses. Some men were mounted. The camp was a confusion of activity as others mounted and those already horsed spun their steeds, both to show off and to exercise the animals.

"Form up!" the command came.

Metal jingled on horse and men as they formed their lines. Maurice was at their head with his son and his friend in the first row, among the warriors who would draw first blood. It was considered a place of honor in battle, but it was also the line of men who most often died early.

Brune's heartbeat pounded in his ears and as they rode forward; his vision was blurred. His first battle. And he suddenly realized that he was afraid. Was the worst thing running away or being killed? Last night he knew the answer to that. In the darkness before dawn, he was no longer certain.

They rode in formation to the rise above the field where the battle would take place. It was still too dark to see if the other army was in place across the way. As the horizon lightened to the right east, no enemy army stood opposite.

Prince Maurice motioned for the army to move forward. There was mumbling among the soldiers, but they followed. The wet grass soaked their boots in short order. Across the field they went and up the opposite rise. Sounds began to reach their ears, but not of soldiers and horses marching.

Sunlight touched the land before them. At a distance, the tents of the enemy were bright spots, glowing in the light. Pennants waved in the breeze above them. Maurice led them on. Brune felt a chill, not from the damp morning air.

Movement beyond the tents caught his attention. As he watched, chaos resolved itself into soldiers in various stages of undress running away. Some were on horseback and several riderless horses fled to the north. He glanced sideways at his friend who sat with perfect calm, even satisfaction.

The order was given for the foot soldiers to surround the camp while the mounted warriors rode in. Everything was quiet except for those few soldiers escaping on the opposite side. Stacks of armor, placed among the tents, were still in place. Brune dismounted to get a closer look.

The swords were covered with some sort of white mesh. But as he came closer, he saw the truth. Each weapon stack was covered with spider webs, so thick that the metal could scarcely be seen.

Maurice turned and looked at Bernard. "Good work, son."

Bernard smiled with pride.

What sort of warfare was this? Had Bernard's little ceremony the night before caused this? Brune turned, looking over the stacks and stacks of weapons seemingly frozen in place. He went into the nearest tent. There were four cots. Three were empty. A man's body lay on the fourth one, his face covered in a spider web, exactly like the ones covering the weapons.

Up close, it was possible to see one eye, open, staring upward, seeing nothing. Brune imagined the face contorted in an expression of horror. He reached down, thinking to pull the delicate lacework away. Two spiders raced toward the place he intended to touch. Both raised up, waving their front legs. He jerked back. They were near the size of the one Bernard had communed with the night before.

Someone entered the tent behind him.

"Don't harm them or interfere with their work," a familiar voice said.

"By the gods, what is this?"

"Your gods have no place in this. In fact, no gods at all."

Brune turned. "It's magic then?"

"Some might call it that."

"What do you call it?"

"My legacy."

"What do you mean?" Brune asked.

"It isn't exactly a power. It's more of an ability. My family, anyone with our blood running in their veins, can do it with practice."

"It?"

"We ask, and they obey."

"And what do they gain from their obedience?"

"Our gratitude. And our protection."

He pushed past his friend whom he realized he didn't know at all. Within the week, Brune led his troops home. As he rode out of the courtyard, he turned and looked up at the parapet. Bernard stood there, watching. He returned his friend's salute, turned and rode away.

He told Espee of this and of other odd memories which flashed through his mind.

"I never saw or spoke to Bernard again. When the letter came, I was reminded of those events. They haunted me, my dreams. As the years passed, I thought about it less and less. Until now."

Espee held out the framed miniature portrait of Arnof. "Is this the face of a man who would practice the black arts? No. Your memories are false ones, Father. They must be."

"He looks very much like his father."

"That doesn't mean he is like his father in every way."

The return message came in nine days, this time delivering an invitation to Belle Isle. Espee was beside herself with joy. There had been dark moments, instances when she had wondered about her father's story. It was just bizarre enough to be true, and she had always trusted her father to protect her. But with the invitation, all doubts fled.

Preparations took little time as she had kept the staff standing ready for just such a moment. They rode leisurely as it was Espee's first visit to her father's and mother's homes, and the journey to Bernard's castle took five days. All the while, Brune tried to discourage Espee from seeing it through, and she wondered if it wasn't just the length of their train and making it easy for her that delayed them. She was determined to make a good marriage, and in that vein, she should at least meet the young prince, so she chafed at the delays.

Brune reminded her of the memories of his youth and the mystery of the spiders. She decided he remembered things incorrectly after more than twenty years.

Espee knew that, as his youngest child, she was the love of his life. He treasured her for herself and for the reminder of his late wife. Now, with his only son receiving training in another castle, the thought of losing Espee was unbearable.

Less than a day's ride from the castle, a herald was sent ahead to let Bernard know they were near. Just past noon, a group of riders was spotted heading their way. As they grew closer, they could see the pennons bearing the prince's coat of arms. In the lead was Arnof.

They stopped and waited. As the five men reached them, greetings were exchanged.

"I couldn't wait with you so near," Arnof said. "My eagerness got the better of me."

The guards had surrounded Espee at the approach of unknown riders. Brune signaled them to let her through. Espee came forward slowly, trying not to show unseemly eagerness. She knew she was at her best with the gown in light lilac trimmed with gold thread. Her long brown hair was bound with gold threads woven into a narrow band. Arnof bowed.

"You are even more beautiful than your picture."

"Thank you, milord."

She bowed in return while her heart beat so hard she could feel it against her breast. Her ears were filled with the sound of it, and she could scarcely breathe.

"So, your father allowed you to learn much," Arnof said. It was a statement rather than a question, as she had just reminded him of her responses to the questionnaire.

"Of course. He would not allow either of his children to be raised in ignorance."

"But many say that an educated woman will be a willful wife. Can a prince let himself marry such a woman?"

"If he loves her, I imagine he can."

"Love conquers all?"

"Yes."

Arnof laughed and she was immediately irritated, feeling that he was making fun of her. Before she could rebuke him, he made apologies.

"I may have to test that theory," he added.

Espee felt herself blushing as he took her hand and kissed the back of it. He turned the conversation to the history of the gardens, which his mother had loved very much. He led the way to her favorite bower where she would read.

"Yes," he said, "she could read. But she preferred needlework. The large tapestry in the dining hall is her work."

"It's lovely."

That evening, after they had dined, she found herself alone with her father beside the fire in the great hall. Standing before the great tapestry, she studied the figures, mostly from mythology. Here and there, however, small spiders had been added. Dozens of them. Brune asked how things stood between her and Arnof.

"Very well," she said. She smiled in remembrance, dismissing the tapestry. "We talk of many things. Sometimes he seems very strange, then he will make me laugh with a joke or funny story."

"Good."

"How are you and Prince Bernard getting along?"

He found the company of his erstwhile friend very pleasant, he told her, with none of the mysterious overtones he had half expected. After eight days, he had been put so at ease that he had ceased wondering about his memories of the earlier time.

For the next several days, she saw the two men, prince and duke, ride out of the castle. They were getting re-acquainted and it pleased Espee every time she saw them together.

They had been in the castle four-and-a-half weeks when Espee rushed into her father's chambers. With a cry, she threw herself into his arms.

"Daughter, what is the matter?" he asked as he tried to soothe her.

"Nothing, Father. Absolutely nothing." She leaned away from him so that she could look up into his face. "Everything is wonderful."

"Ah, I see."

"Oh, Father. He asked me to marry him."

"I suppose it's about time."

She laughed. "We were sitting in the arbor. Suddenly, he slipped to the ground on one knee and took my hand in his. He…"

"Please, please, don't tell me the rest," Brune teased. "It is all too sweet and lovely."

"Yes, it is."

She twirled away from him, in utter bliss.

"So you do love him?"

"Oh, yes, Father. I do."

"And when do you two plan the wedding to be?"

"In two months."

"My goodness, that's very soon. As I recall, there are hundreds of dresses to be made. Food to be planned. Guests to invite."

"Our Jerrold and their Phillipe will work on the arrangements. But we must return home in order to have all of those hundreds of dresses made."

The next week was busy with planning and messaging and sudden fits of glee. Several messengers were dispatched to Brune Castle to advise the staff there on what was needed and how it was to be done. Jerrold took the whole occasion in hand. His messages indicated that all went well. But the day came when Brune and Espee had to return for dress fittings and other details.

She had written up several long lists for Phillipe. One list of guests from her side. Another of food to be served not only at the wedding banquet but also for a few days before and after. A third was for flowers to adorn the great hall for the ceremony.

The bridal party reached home and proceeded to work at a fast pace to get everything ready. A month, two months, passed. Two shipments were sent by mule train to Bernard. Brune was surprised to learn that the groom's family would provide the bride's wedding dress. It was a traditional gown, worn by Arnof's mother, and which Espee had not yet seen.

Espee began to notice that her father had become pale and nervous, eating less, and often found pacing, hands behind his back, in the great hall.

Surely he hasn't started worrying about the old tale, she told herself.

The day of departure came too soon. Yet, it was inevitable; pledges had been made and most of the work was done.

"I understand how you feel," Bernard said. "It's tradition. The bride is put into isolation for four days before the ceremony. I know it's a long time, but it is necessary. She will be taught the ways of our women. Her duties as wife to the prince. The physicians will examine her to verify her maidenhood. The wedding dress must be fitted. There are a hundred and one things to be done, and she must be free of distractions."

Brune looked over at his daughter on the other side of the table. They were in the small dining room. He had lost his appetite the moment Bernard started talking about the days of isolation.

"Will I be able to see her at all?"

Bernard shook his head. Espee looked from face to face, feeling more and more frustrated. She was not part of this conversation, even though it pertained to her more than anyone.

"No. Only servants will be allowed in."

"How will I know that she's safe?"

"You must trust me, old friend."

"Arnof?" Espee said, turning to her bridegroom. There were a hundred questions in the one word. Would he protect her? Was this what he wanted her to do?

"Yes, my love," the young man said. "This is our custom. No harm will come to you. I promise."

She looked over at her father and nodded. She appeared calmer now that she had received assurances from Arnof. But Brune was worried, and she knew it.

Four days before the wedding, Arnof himself wakened her early in her chamber. "What is it?" She pulled the covers up modestly.

"It's time," he said. "The four days of confinement."

"Oh."

Her maid came into the room and began laying out a dress for her. Arnof sent her from the room.

"Your new clothes are in the other chamber. You will dress there."

He handed her the robe from the chair beside the bed and turned his back. She left the bed, shivering in the pre-dawn darkness and slipped into the robe and slippers.

"All right."

He offered his arm. Then he led her up one floor and down a long, dark hall, until they stood before the door to another chamber. Without a word or look in her direction, he opened the door and motioned her inside.

She stepped over the threshold and put a hand to her mouth. She would have screamed but the scene before her was too bizarre, too frightening to be real.

The room was fully furnished with chairs, a large wardrobe, a tester bed, drapes at the windows. But little could be seen of these except for their shapes. Everything but the floor was covered and draped with spider webs. Their makers, small and large, scampered about, in and on them. She took a step backward. As Arnof reached for her, she moved to her left, and stepped back into the hall. Arnof grabbed her from behind, trying to guide her toward the bed. Espee struggled. Her husband-to-be wrapped her in his arms. She kicked and screamed.

"No one can hear you, my love," Arnof whispered in her ear.

He shoved her toward the chair beside the bed.

"No," she cried. "Let me…"

A woman servant came rushing up, helped him hold her still. Espee kicked and hollered for help. A flash of regret. Why hadn't she listened to her father?

"Ah, she's here," a second servant said as Arnof continued to hold his bride-to-be in front of the chair.

"Yes," Arnof said. "And she's as ready as she'll ever be."

"Good."

Espee twisted her shoulders, but Arnof held on. Shifting his grip as necessary, he continued to hold her as the two women stripped her down to her shift. The chair was on a raised platform and free of both webs and spiders. He lifted her and placed her on the chair. She froze as a very large spider ran up to the arm of the chair. It raised its front two legs as if to see her better.

The man she loved held her in the chair from behind while the servant placed her arm within reach of the spider. She tried to pull away, but the hold on her arm was too strong.

Her skin crawled as the spider ran up her arm to the shoulder, across to her neck. "It won't kill you," he whispered in her ear. The bite stung like a needle piercing the skin. "See?"

She tried to respond, but already the poison was working its way through her system. She could not open her mouth or utter a sound. She tried to raise her arm, but it lay limply on the chair arm. Within seconds, her whole body refused to move. Even her breathing became shallower, and she feared it would stop altogether. She closed her eyes, wishing with all her might that her father would miss her and come looking. She realized then that her eyes worked just fine. She could look from side to side—although without turning her head—and up and down. Closing and opening her eyes was also possible.

She could still hear everything going on. In fact, her hearing seemed to be more acute. Even the whispers of the conspirators were clear.

Her hair was brushed and arranged on top of her head. All the while, the movement of spiders over her torso and body continued. The humans left, and after what she judged to be half a day, a web was spun over each of her arms. She could see only the lower part, and the lace they spun was the most delicate and beautiful she had ever seen. Yet, every moment, she wanted to scream and leap from the chair, to go bolting from the room.

Just before dark, the spider bit her again. That must mean that the poison could wear off and she would eventually regain control. Was there hope in that?

The servant returned toward evening and gave her a strange brew to drink. It seemed to strengthen her.

The work continued through the night, the lace growing over her breasts, down to her stomach. The next morning, she was raised from the chair to stand so that the work could continue, completing the bodice and beginning the skirt. Hours passed and she continued to stand without a break. She felt weary, but incapable of collapsing. Mugs of the brew were brought, alternating with bites from a spider.

The end of the second day saw the skirt half finished. The bodice and sleeves clung to her skin, soft and warm. As beautiful as it was, she would have torn it away from her if she could.

Tears filled her eyes and spilled down her cheeks. Several spiders rushed to her face and in a moment the moisture was gone.

The third day brought faintness, and once she swayed as if she would drop to the floor. In minutes, the door opened and the servant brought in a mug of the brew, holding it to her lips to drink.

"Mustn't have you moving about and tearing your lovely dress. No, that wouldn't do at all."

The woman stepped back and looked at the work.

"Very nearly done, my lady. Once they've completed the skirt, they will start on the veil. Don't let it frighten you. Just think of how beautiful you will be when you marry."

As promised, work on the veil began the next day. Espee could feel a web being woven closely around her hair. They worked over her head, front and back. Strands dropped before her eyes. Three of them wove the delicate lace, so closely that she could see the hairs on their legs and sometimes light reflected from their eyes. Most of the time she kept her eyes closed, opening them only when someone came in, or some change came in the way the weaving felt. All the while, she tried to flex fingers or toes.

The veil grew longer. Once it hung below her chin, breathing became more difficult. More mugs of the brew were brought. How could the servant press it to her lips through the veil? The problem was solved with a straw of hay.

The morning of the fourth day, the servant awakened Espee from a drowsy state she had fallen into. "Oh, yes. Magnificent." The woman walked all the way around. "They did well."

Espee realized that spiders no longer moved across her body or down the veil. The front of the veil reached to her waist, but she couldn't tell how long it was in back. The skirt was full and stiff enough to stand away from her body. The bodice caressed her like a second skin.

For the hundredth time, she tried to move some small part of her body. It had been longer than usual since the last bite from the spider, and she hoped that the effects might wear off soon. With the dress completed, there would be fewer bites to keep her immobile. Perhaps there would be none. She would be taken out to her wedding at any time, and she struggled to move even one finger, concentrating with all her might. The thought of marrying Arnof now terrified her.

"I know!"

The door opened to the voice of the young prince. He was clearly angry.

"We had no idea he was on his way. He never sent word."

He moved into her field of vision.

"Absolutely beautiful," he said.

"We can't wait much longer," the voice of the servant said just out of her field of vision.

"They're getting everything finished now. Her brother certainly has made a cock up of everything."

Espee blinked. Edmund was here?

"Yes, beloved. Your brother just arrived. And now we have to wait for him to be ready. It's all very inconvenient. But not to worry, my love. We will be wed by the noon hour."

Another hour or so and she would at least be free of this room. If only she could make some sign, say one word, to free her of this marriage. She strained to lick her lips, but every part of her body felt as rigid as before. How was she to walk down the hall, much less down the stairs? They couldn't carry her since any movement might tear the webs.

When the time came, it became clear that the lace had set in place and was no longer as apt to tear. Still, two servants held her hands as six burly men raised the platform she had been standing on. Pressure from the back indicated that someone else was on the platform, balancing her. Very carefully, they made their way to the stairs, then down. Outside of the great room, whose doors were closed, they lowered the platform.

Why isn't my father here? He should be walking me down the aisle.

Bernard appeared at her side, praising her beauty and the work of the spiders.

"I will be escorting you down the aisle, my dear," he said.

How? I can't move!

He took hold of both of her hands and gently urged her to step forward. She found she was able to shuffle her feet forward, although she felt as if they were disconnected from the rest of her.

Is it because the bites were made on my neck? Is my lower torso losing the effects of the venom faster than my body above the waist?

They stood before the massive doors as trumpets sounded in the great hall. The door opened revealing a crowd of people, most of whom were strangers. The wedding of the heir to Belle Isle was a lavish affair, indeed, worthy of his position. To be married to a man with such authority should be the dream of a young woman's lifetime. But she could only believe it would remain a nightmare.

Her toes! She could wiggle them. Such a small thing, but it gave her hope.

At Bernard's continued pressure on her arm and his whispered words, they moved forward slowly, over the threshold and into the room. Arnof stood at the other end of the chamber, smiling toward her. People smiled at her from either side, and she wanted to shout to them for help. Then she spotted her brother's face in the crowd. His expression was quizzical, concerned.

If only I could get him to come to me, she thought. *If only...*

If only she could trip over something, even over her own feet. But Bernard held her steady, moving her along. And everyone still smiled, believing that their slow pace was as it should be for a bride's walk to the altar of marriage.

As her right foot moved forward, her leg twitched, and she stumbled. She had felt it as her leg gave way. The venom was wearing off more and more.

As much as she could, she pushed her foot farther to the right. The lower skirt of the dress flared out, hitting Bernard's left leg. In his panic to move clear of the dress, he pulled Espee slightly off-balance. It was enough. She fell forward, face down. The sleeves gave way as she tried to break her fall. Voices rose in shocked surprise. The dress began to crack and crumble beneath her.

All around people shouted for others to help. Someone grabbed her right arm and gently turned her over. She looked into the face of her beloved brother.

"Leave her alone," Bernard shouted. "We will take care of this."

"*This* happens to be my sister," Edmund said. "I will take care of her."

Hands lifted her and began carrying her away. She was surrounded, jostled, but she felt safe as they practically ran toward the main door.

"Where are you going?" Bernard shouted after them.

They continued to run without answering. In moments, she wore only her shift.

Horses waited, saddled and excited by the hubbub that followed in the wake of the escapees. Espee was transferred to other arms, then lifted onto a horse. Edmund whispered in her ear to hold on, but she could not grip anything as yet. The horse leapt away. She moaned in relief. In a moment the shouts and curses receded into the distance. Flooded with relief, she fainted.

It was a very nervous party that raced toward Brune Castle. They covered the distance in a day and a half, not stopping more than an hour at a time. Feeling gradually returned to her body and limbs, but it was days after they arrived home before she could walk without help. As they settled in to await the outcome of what Belle Isle would most likely see as their treason, she first told them of what transpired in what she called the spider room. Then she learned what had been going on while she was confined.

"After they took you away, I begged them to let me see you," Brune said. "There were more and more spiders. They appeared to have a purpose, rushing through rooms, totally ignoring anything and anyone in their paths. After what you've told us, I suspect that they were supplying the silk for your dress."

She shivered at the memory of the lovely horror of that dress.

"As you know, Edmund was still in training at Hillsboro, and he was meant to come home later. That first day they took you away, I knew I had to do something. I sent a messenger off to him to come immediately. He left his horses saddled in the courtyard with the excuse of not delaying the wedding."

"Thank goodness he did, " Espee said, her words still slurred. "It was the delay caused by his late arrival that gave me the time I needed. My legs and feet were gaining feeling and tripping myself…" She sighed, unable to continue.

When it came time to retire to her sleeping chamber every night, two maids accompanied her. Her fears would take longer to disappear than the paralysis.

For weeks they all slept with one eye open, awaiting the retaliation they expected any day. Guards were set to watch for anything unusual at the edge of the forest that surrounded the castle. Especially for large numbers of spiders looking for the path to the castle.

Sharon Frame Gay

MUSE AT THE CEMETERY

I am always so taken with the soft breeze, ruffling petals on the flowers while the rest of the graveyard lies still. The air is an interloper, stirring up dust above ground while those beneath slumber in silence. The wind is boasting, "See what I do? I dance, riding the fresh breath of earth, while you are dead."

Two Sarus Cranes fly overhead in tandem. In my country, they are symbols of marital fidelity. The male and female do not differ in plumage. One flies no higher than the other as they bank and glide along the tree line.

I think of the small finch once kept in a wicker cage in my garden. Despite the loss of freedom, she bravely sang her sweetest song each morning. How many times did I walk past her and not seek to understand the beating heart within?

Does the caged bird always love its captors as it walks its perch like a sailor on a plank? Or does it look to stab at their hands with its beak and dart through the cage door when next it opens?

Our culture allowed my captivity. I was just a woman, after all, and you the Magistrate's son. I had little value the moment I drew breath, held briefly by my father while he examined my genitals, then set me in Mother's arms with a look of disgust on his face.

"Another girl," he grimaced, then strode out of the hut, shaking his head as though he could not believe the stupidity of Allah.

Ah, but I was the pretty one. The one who had flesh soft as velvet, deep tan skin that lay silken upon my bones, eyes large and wide, hair shimmering down my back in waterfalls of blue-black strands.

It was no surprise to my mother when you noticed me one day in the market while we were peddling curry powder. I perched alongside Mother obediently though my eyes were anything but submissive.

Oh, how you loved my lively countenance then. You rejoiced in my spirit and lusted after the long limbs that peered from under my dusty skirt, fluttering in the breeze. You had to have me, the way a child has to have a favorite doll. Admiring my beauty from afar was not enough for one like you.

All you had to do was snap your fingers, and Mother rose like a servant, bowing before you, expectation and eagerness on her face. She was hoping you wanted a packet of curry, but was over-joyed to learn that your interests were far more fortuitous than that. When you asked my name, and she introduced us, I felt her quivering beneath her garments, as she pushed me forward, her offering.

That night, in our one room dwelling, I was the center of attention. My importance rose with every word, until the smaller children were gawking with wide eyes, and even Father smiled at me with respect and deference. I was no longer to attend market, Father said, but stay home in my finest clothing and wait for you to come courting. So I sat, freshly dressed, the aroma of blossoms rinsed through my hair, hands folded in my lap on the small stool outside the hut, breathing in the sounds and smells of those passing on the well-worn path to town. You did not come. Days went by, and still there was no sign of you, just the grunting of the cattle as they were prodded and stumbled along, the sound of children play-ing, voices behind garden gates, the dusty wind kissing my face.

When you finally arrived, it was with great fanfare. I saw the entourage coming far down the trail, voices raised like a clarion call, dust in great clouds as you sat upon a fine horse, his ears cocked forward, prancing, chaffing at the bit, just as you were.

You dismounted and stood before me, a shadow darkening the sun. When I looked up, there was at first a slight frown, then a smile that broke through the clouds.

"Ah, Alika, you are as lovely as I remember," you said, and with great arrogance, reached out and touched my face as though picking me out of a basket of fruit.

When my father stepped out of our hut, I thought he might slap your impudent hand away, but instead, he bowed low and smiled, his broken teeth gleaming in the sunlight.

"Welcome," he said, then gestured behind him. "Please come in, have something to drink, and we shall talk."

I waited in breathless limbo for hours and wondered about the future. It seemed like an eternity until you emerged, tipped your head at me, and headed back down the road, a cloud of men following behind.

Father came to me, jubilant, and announced that we were to marry in two weeks' time. Until then, I was to prepare for my new life.

Is it wrong to admit that I was excited about this news? Knowing what I know now, it was stupid and careless to build my hopes on a man I had seen for only a few minutes in my entire life. Yet I had built our future in my imagination for days on end. When I learned the joyful news, I shed tears of happiness, and believed that my life was golden, touched by fate in such a way that I was going to dance the rest of my life.

My meager trunk filled with threadbare clothing followed my family and me up the hill to your home, a house of walls, gates and many rooms. As we stepped over the threshold, the servants bowed in supplication, not daring to look up into my face as they led the

way to the great hall where you and your father sat in chairs, waiting our arrival. I shivered slightly as you walked over and gently
took my hand, placing it under your arm. My mother and father
bowed low, turned on their heels, and herded my sisters back out
the door, startling me.

"They are not attending the ceremony?" I asked, bewildered.

"No, my Alika," you explained. "It is not fitting."

I realized then that there was no place at your table for the
lower caste family that raised me.

Your father walked around me in slow circles as though ap-
praising a bowl of jewels.

"I see why she is special to you," he grunted in acknowledgement. "But I warn you that things won't be easy with this one. She
does not know the finer ways at all."

"I will teach her," you said, holding my hand tighter.

The Magistrate flicked his fat fingers and said "So be it; marry
her now, and let us be done with it before society talks."

A holy man stepped from the shadows, and before I drew
breath, he pronounced us married. I was led away by a servant
through hallways, past countless rooms, to a small outdoor garden,
where I was bathed and brushed, rubbed with oil, then the finest
cloth draped over my body, my hair wound into a soft braid.

That night you were tender with me. Our lovemaking was
tense at first, then I yielded to you like a lotus, my heart filled with
a happiness I could not express. I slept curled about you like a kitten, and for many nights afterward, purring my contentment into
your back, my hands rubbing your chest until we both fell asleep
under the billowing netting.

Days were spent with scholars and wise women, learning the
ways of my new life, fitted for clothing I only dreamt of as a child.
Hours were spent drifting through the gardens, waiting impatiently
until nightfall when you came to me again.

However, the gentle breezes halted soon enough, replaced by dark clouds and the sharp intake of winter. You found fault in the little things I did, small things at first. I scrambled to correct them, eager to please. The demands grew larger and longer until, one day, I burst into tears. That was the first time you slapped me with your hand of many rings. I went down like a cloudburst, hitting the floor, ears filled with the sound of buzzing bees. There must be a mistake, I thought, but you stood over me and recited all the worthless things about me and the ways I had disappointed you. My heart shred, an open maw of sadness that yearned to be fed with love.

Would the world want to know how long I endured this abuse? I think not. It seemed like a lifetime for me, a barren lifetime because I could not give you children. My sorrow was all the worse for your impatience and brutal rapes, pulling my hair in your anger, expecting me to swallow your manhood and your hatred, and from that produce another human being. My tortured womb refused to allow this, even if I could not, and each month when my menses began, I felt a small flicker of victory. You could not control my body, nor direct my soul.

You tired of me. Soon I was banished to a room down the hall, then a guest bed far on the other side of the great house. Finally, I was left to sleep with the servants, except the few nights you tried to make an heir. Afterward, before the sweat even dried on your chest, I was sent straggling back to the servants' quarters, humiliated and heartsick.

I did not mind living with the servants. They welcomed me and were protective. Mira, my ladies' maid, taught me how to weave the finest silk into cloth that glimmered in the candlelight in iridescent shades of blues and greens like scales on a fish. We made bedding from the cloth, and although I was living as a pauper in your great house, my legs slid along the silk all night in my solitary bed.

In the evenings, when the chores were finished, we gathered in an old stone courtyard and spoke of our lives, hopes and dreams. Mira was my age and had given up having a family of her own. The old cook had been here as long as anybody could remember. She often told tales of you, husband, when you were a little boy. Bit by bit I saw a pattern emerge, a pattern of indulgence and tantrums, privilege and status. It is no wonder why you wanted me, then did not, as though you had grown tired of a kitten or puppy.

Month after month, I was escorted down the hall to your room, beaten and raped, then pushed out the door to stumble back to my pallet by the fireplace at dawn.

Finally, my body gave in far sooner than my spirit had. I knew one day I was with child. Dutifully, I told you, trembling at the thought of your reaction. Your delight was infectious as you whirled me about the great hall and called out to your father with such happiness that, for a moment, I believed things might change.

I sat once again in the dining room with you and the Magistrate, my gowns shimmering about my growing belly, tilting my head side to side to converse and laugh, though even then my smiles seemed strained and my laughter tinny. I took smaller amounts of food on my plate, sending the finest pieces back down the halls to the servants' quarters, so I could share my largesse with them. Baskets of food and fabrics were transported down the hill to my family, as your generosity knew no bounds. You moved me into the room next to your own, furnished with silks and finest linens, incense and oils fit for a queen.

At first I could do no wrong. We strolled along the promenade in town, bowing to society, your arm tucking me against you with a sweet possessiveness. Dare I say, I warmed to you again as brandy to a candle, convincing myself that the punishment was over and that now we would truly be husband and wife.

But within a few weeks, your temper flared. I knocked over my cup at dinner because I was uneducated, you said. The puffiness about my ankles was because I could not turn away from the sweet meats in the basket on the table. I said the wrong things, did the wrong things. You told me again how worthless I was. It was a mistake to set eyes on me in the market, much less marry me, you sneered. I was a waif with no future and you a soft-hearted soul who rescued me from disease and disaster. You prayed that our child would take after you, not the hopeless low-class oaf that was bearing him. The Magistrate prayed to Allah that I would spare you both the insult of producing a girl child as useless as I was. I was warned that should a girl be born, it was my fault, and I would be severely punished.

One day I was walking past your room, and you stepped out into the hall at the same time.

"Alika, come in," you beckoned, "I want to show you the new mare I bought."

I obliged as you led me to the window. Outside was a beautiful, gray, Arabian mare, her tiny, cupped muzzle gently nudging the groom.

"Oh, she's lovely," I said, turning shining eyes to you.

With no warning, your hand reached out and slapped me full across the face.

"I can get a new wife as easily as this mare," you hissed, grabbing my arm and twisting it.

"Remember this, Alika, for I am tired of you and your low caste ways."

I drew back in shock and pain, and for the first time felt a rage that replaced the sadness within my heart.

"I am carrying your child," I said with dignity, straightening the gown over my growing belly. "Do not touch me like that again."

I turned to walk out of the room when you grabbed me—do you remember this, Husband?—and threw me to the ground. With a mighty force, you kicked me in the belly.

I curled around my womb in disbelief, crying "Our child!" You hesitated, foot poised to strike. Then you stepped over my prone body, stalking out of the house in a rage.

Mira found me on the floor crying. She and two servants carried me to their quarters where they soaked rags in tea and patted my forehead. Mira rocked me in her arms, hands warm and gentle on my belly, as I cried into the blue silk sheets until there was nothing left but hiccups and sighs.

That night, Mira ran frantically to your room.

"Come quick," she said, pounding on the door. "Alika is bleeding!"

You came rushing to my pallet and witnessed the blood that poured from between my legs.

"The child is gone," I wailed. I retched and moaned, thrashing from side to side, my legs slick with wetness and sorrow.

Turning in disgust, you went back up to the sleeping rooms, knocking on your father's door. The two of you made haste to the great hall. With Mira's help, I stole along the walkway, hiding in the shadows. I cradled my belly with each painful step, scattering droplets of blood like tears on the floor. We crept to the door, listening, my life at stake because of your cruelty.

We heard the Magistrate first.

"You must get rid of this wretched woman, Son. She cannot give you children, and our house will forever be cloaked in darkness."

There was not even a moment's hesitation as you answered, "Yes Father, but how?"

Mira and I held our breath. It was as though the walls themselves strained to hear.

"Poison," he said. "Put it in a drink for her. Do it quickly, so everyone will think she died with the child."

"Yes, Father."

That was all I heard, as Mira dragged me back to my room and placed me upon the blood soaked sheets.

It was not long before you entered, my husband, with a chalice in your hand.

"Poor Alika; how you must hurt. Please drink this. It will calm you," you said, bowing before me with a look of concern across your features.

I closed my eyes in fear and great sadness and thought about how much I had once trusted you. How I would have obediently drunk this potion while you stood by and stared into my eyes as I took my final breath.

"I cannot keep it down," I groaned, retching in great heaves while Mira held my head over a bowl.

"You must!" you roared, stepping forward menacingly.

"I will have Alika drink it as soon as she stops vomiting," Mira promised, stepping between us, taking the chalice with shaking hands. "Go back to bed, my lord. I will take care of it." A tiny droplet spilled on Mira's hand, and she winced.

As I lay tossing and moaning, you decided that this might be a good thing. Mira would give me the poison later and be punished when I die. You would be free and rid of me forever.

"Make sure she drinks this before morning. You must promise. It will help her pain."

Mira nodded, head down, trembling. You turned on your heel and left the room. Mira's hand was already blistering, the foul smell of burning flesh permeating the room. She set the chalice down on a table and poured cool water over her hand, shaking in terror.

Mira turned frightened eyes to me. "Alika, you are in grave danger. All of us who serve you, too."

"We know what we are to do, my Mira," I replied simply.

Later that night, it was astonishing how fast and furiously the house burned, embers catching in the night wind, the eager flames sending souls straight up into the stars, darkening the night with hearts that knew no dawn. It is amazing how none of the servants heard your screams until it was far too late to rescue you and your father.

I was found safe and cool in the courtyard. The servants brought me gently back to my pallet by the fireplace, telling the constable that I had been there all night.

Even more remarkable is how the blood of a dove can resemble that of a woman's, poured upon silk sheets and rubbed between my thighs.

We had a son, you and I. He is beautiful and strong. I did not name him after you.

I taught him to be kind to the servants, to respect and honor women, good to all people. When the day comes that he brings a wife home, I will welcome her with open arms, and we shall start anew. These wretched, blackened walls will from that day forward bear the sounds of joy and love. This will be a new family, one not tainted and poisoned with old beliefs.

Every year on this day, I mount the beautiful Arabian mare and ride through the village to the graveyard where your ashes and fragments of bone lie beneath the hard-packed earth. I sit upon the ground near the mound that houses you and watch the flower petals ruffle in the breeze. Then slowly, I remove my satin shoes, dig my toes into your grave, and with the help of the wind, begin to dance.

Diane Arrelle

MAGGOTY JO

lorida couldn't believe her eyes. Maggots—thousands, maybe hundreds of thousands of them—covering the trash, the sides, and the inside lid of her garbage can. She had walked out to dump her daily bag of cat litter and gasped when she saw the horde of death eaters.

"Holy shit!" she yelped and slammed the lid down, then backed away from the vile creatures escaping the can by dropping from the edge of the lid like an oozing flood of dripping, slimy, white lava.

She ran to the garage and, after digging through all the piles of stuff jammed onto shelves and in boxes scattered over the cement floor, she found what she needed: a household spray bottle of insecticide, and just in case, a gallon of super-strength, super-toxic, pest remover, which had probably been labeled too dangerous to the environment at least 10 years ago. "Thank goodness Ralph left this behind when he split. Maybe he wasn't so good for nothing after all," she muttered and then yelled, "No, kitties, don't go outside until I'm done here. I certainly don't want you to get poisoned."

She closed the garage doors, then closed the warped wooden backdoor to the house to stop the dozen or so milling cats from getting out through the torn and rusted screen door.

She took out the spray can first and saturated the disgusting white carnivores feasting on her refuse. "Die, vile scum!" she screamed, not caring if her neighbors heard. She did a victory dance around the canister as the maggots writhed, and with the weight of their tiny bodies pushing the lid ajar, poured over the lip and plummeted to the ground. The dancing stopped abruptly as they wriggled to get out of the sunlight. None of them seemed to die and actually seemed to wriggle as a unit toward the shade under the broken webbed chairs on her driveway.

"Huh?" she said in a puzzled tone. "Why aren't you suckers dying? I used the whole can on you."

The maggots seemed intent on ignoring her as they sped across the blacktop.

"Well, bastards, I'll get you yet!" She bellowed, anger making her voice harsh.

She opened the container of toxic insecticide and dumped half on the maggots fleeing the sunlight and, opening the trash can lid all the way, dumped the rest of the incredibly potent smelling liquid into the can. She slammed the cover back down and watched the escapees writhe some more, but they just wouldn't expire.

With the summer sun beating down on her, she felt sweat forming on her forehead and upper lip. She decided to finish the whole ordeal and went inside. Stepping over the lounging cats, and gently pushing the wandering cats out of her way, she filled the teakettle and put it on a lit burner.

A few minutes later she filled a mug with the boiling water, dropped in a dried, used teabag and then took the almost full pot outside and dumped it on the maggots, who all seemed to be unfazed by the chemicals she had just used on them.

At last she felt satisfaction. With the scalding water pouring over them, most stopped moving and died. The few that appeared to be immune to every torture continued to flee the light. She ignored them and slammed the trashcan lid closed to make the insecticides do their job. She grunted at the carnage and went inside. She looked at her cup of hot, almost clear water she'd made before going outside and decided she deserved a new teabag as a reward for vanquishing the filthy, germ carrying, carrion eaters.

A few hours later, the dead maggots crisping in the sun, Florida finally opened the wooden backdoor and let the cats wander in and out through the rusted, torn screen on the flimsy aluminum storm door. All was right in her world except that Jo, her ten-year-old calico had disappeared a few days ago. Florida knew that older cats tended to wander off to die, and she feared that Jo had been sick. The poor cat had lost a lot of weight, and her fur always looked matted and dull. Florida had raised enough cats over the last 30 years to know the signs of a cat that was dying, and even though ten years wasn't an old cat, it was old for a sickly cat.

She walked outside, glanced down at the multitude of tiny white carcasses and grinned. "Chalk up one for the human," she said licking her pointer finger and making an imaginary line in the air. Then she got down to business. She walked up and down several blocks calling, "Jo, Jo, come home, Jo. Jo, I'm sorry you're sick. Please come home and let me make you comfortable."

But Jo remained at large.

The next morning, Florida opened the door and was greeted by what seemed to be dozens of flies. Bigger than the average housefly, they were buzzing louder too, like an incredibly discordant horn section of an orchestra. "Good lord," she shouted and got the rest of the bug spray that she hadn't completely used up. She sprayed the screen, but the flies ignored the poisonous liquid. Florida squinted and was sure she could see them drinking it up.

"Now that's impossible," she harrumphed and opened the door to shoo them away. As they took off, she saw dozens more on the trashcan. Running over with a broom, she shooed them away as well and then opened the lid.

A black swarm poured out and upward, many of them settling on her arms and hair. She screamed, dropped the lid and, slapping at her head, ran into the house, slamming the wooden door behind her.

She sat at the table, looking at the cats eating from the unwashed dishes all around the kitchen. If one got near her, she'd pet it for a moment. The day was hot, but she kept the unscreened windows shut as well as the door and wished she still had a working fan. She watched the flies gather on the outside of the glass and wondered how she could get rid of them. Nothing came to mind.

Sweating and dizzy from the oppressive heat, she tried to remember what she knew about flies. She'd had maggot infestations before over the years. They were born in trash, lived on trash and eventually, in a few weeks, turned into flies that she took great pleasure in swatting. But this was all wrong; these maggots wouldn't die like they were supposed to, and how had they gone from the middle little-white-wormy stage to huge annoying flies overnight? And how come the insecticide didn't kill them or at least chase them away?

She decided to take a cold bath and soak in the water for the rest of the day. She removed the three litter pans and the wet sour towels from the tub and ran the water. Finally, she settled down in the bath, felt cool relief and drifted off to sleep.

Hungry meows woke her, and she looked out the bathroom window to see the setting sun through the veil of flies. "Okay,

306 · PICK YOUR POISON

babies, I'll feed you. Shhh. I know it's late, but mommy loves
you," she called, standing up. Naked, water-logged and dripping
wet, she went and fed her cats, then refilled the tub and spent the
night in the bathroom.

The next morning, the flies were gone. Florida tentatively
cracked open the door and found a cool, morning breeze keeping
the heat at bay for a few hours. She relaxed, not realizing how
she had hunched her shoulders in anticipation of an attack. She
swung the door open, stepped outside, and gasped. "Jo?"

The cat lying on the driveway said, "Merow?"

Florida stepped toward the calico stretched out, catching
some rays. She shook her head in amazement. This cat was the
spitting image of Jo, same markings, same meow, but she could
tell immediately that this was a different cat. This cat was fat,
not sickly like Jo. As she approached this new kitty, she saw the
flies hovering around it and landing on it. She stepped back, but
the flies ignored her. The other cats wandered around, happy to
be outside after being locked in a stifling house for twenty-four
hours. They rubbed against her legs and purred loudly, sounding
like small toy motorboats. They looked at the new cat in the
yard, and the purring ceased. They backed away, backs arched,
legs stiff and went toward the front of the house, turning the
corner and going out of sight. Florida shrugged, looked at her
new kitty and said, "Cats. Whatcha gonna do?"

The new cat meowed in answer, and Florida laughed.

She grabbed a newspaper laying on the ground and waved
the flies away. "Shoo," she yelled and the insects backed off,
buzzing around the now empty garbage can. She bent down to
pick up the cat and saw it was injured. Its back haunch was cut,
and suddenly she was fighting nausea and revulsion when she
saw maggots feasting on the wound. "Oh, you poor baby!" she
whispered, so as not to scare the cat. "Here, let me clean it."

She ran inside, grabbed some mismatched gardening gloves, and soaked a rag in alcohol. Going back out, she gently brushed the vile larva off the wound, then hugging the injured feline to her, she covered the cut with the rag. To her shocked surprise, the cat settled into her arms and purred instead of screaming and trying to get away.

"What a good baby," she cooed. "What a good kitty." She looked at the pile of wiggling maggots on the ground and stomped on them until she didn't see anything move.

"There now, let's get you inside and keep your leg clean, and you'll get all better." She cuddled her new baby, and carried him into the bedroom. She put him gently on the unmade bed and cleaned the wound again. "You look so much like Jo, so very much, so I'm gonna call you Jo; Maggoty Jo. You and me, we'll just keep on killing those maggots and then all the flies. We'll show 'em who's boss! Right Kitty?"

She sat with her new cat all day. When the others finally came in for dinner, they kept their distance. They ate their dinners and stayed on the opposite side of the room from Maggoty Jo. "What a bunch of poor sports you all are," Florida scolded. "She's your new friend."

She frowned, annoyed at her cats for not welcoming her new Jo. "Well, that's just fine; all of you can sleep out here tonight. Jo and I are going to bed together." Florida grabbed her new cat and marched off to the bedroom, placed Jo on Ralph's old pillow, and went to sleep with her newest cat purring away.

Sometime in the small hours of the morning, she woke to the sound of the purring changing in tone to buzzing. The room was filled with flies, huge flies as big as fingers, stinging flies. Florida screamed, slapping at the insects that seemed to be everywhere. She managed to smash several of them with the book she had been reading. They squished out yellow guts that smeared across the book's cover. She jumped from the bed and ran from the room slamming the door behind her.

How'd they get in, she wondered. Then, as she looked at all the cats staring at her with their unblinking eyes, she remembered. "Maggoty Jo!" she yelped and started for the door only to stop. Those flies were in there, and they were relentless. She looked at the bites, and they *were* bites, with blood running down her arms and legs, and as she touched her sore cheek, she realized even her face.

"Oh, kitties, what can I do?" she wailed. "I can let them kill him!" She stood at the door and waited for her hands to stop shaking and then opened it a few inches, ready to slam it if needed. To her relief, a paw grabbed the door corner and pulled it open a bit more. Then the calico squeezed out of the room. Florida waited, but no flies followed.

She walked away from the slightly opened door, hugging the cat, and sat on the sofa. None of the others joined them. Suddenly, they were back, the flies. They swarmed around her, biting and tearing at her head, her arms and her legs. She slapped them away, but they kept coming back until the pain grew too much. Florida passed out, recognizing the faint smell of the insecticide.

She woke to a sea of pain. Everything burned, and as she tried to move, the flies that had been covering her flew off, leaving blood spatters over the floor and walls. She didn't know what was happening. The pain was bordering on unbearable. As she weakly brushed at a deep gouge on her arm, her fingers came away bloody, and she screamed as she saw the tiny eggs on her fingertips. *How...what...why...*the questions tried to come together, but the pain stopped her from thinking clearly.

An involuntary shudder ran through her. Eggs! The flies were using her for a nest like some dead or injured animal. She smelled a strong pungent odor, a chemical odor, and shuddered.

Able to think a little better despite the acid-like agony eating away at her, she realized the eggs smelled of the aerosol insecticide. The flies hadn't died from the poison she'd use. No, she realized, they became stronger; the stuff must have actually accelerated their growth.

She knew she had to find the strength to get up and wash off every bite before the eggs hatched. She had to get up. Slowly, she sat and watched Jo come toward her. But as she looked at the cat, she realized that it was coming at her with an unnatural gait, stiff legged, staggering. As it reached her feet, it suddenly shuddered, and she saw movement under its skin. She forgot about herself for a short moment, the searing pain dulled as the cat opened its mouth and vomited thousands of quivering maggots.

The smell was overpowering as the air became foul with the toxic stench of the bottled death she'd dumped on the maggots just two days ago. Gagging, she managed to whimper as the cat folded up and collapsed into a flattened pile of fur and skin as it emptied.

The chemically tainted maggots converged on her, settling into the wounds, all the openings on her they could find. She screamed until they filled her mouth and wriggled down her throat toward her lungs, and then she wished she could scream some more as she waited to see what would kill her first, the maggots or the poison they carried.

Leslie Entsminger

HOW DOES YOUR GARDEN GROW?

Charlotte cleans and oils her shovel with quick precise strokes as she sits, content, on an old stump beside her shed—the remnant of an oak her grandfather planted. A couple of butterflies flit a do-si-do above her shoulder and she slows, glances, doesn't stop. It's been a good morning; her muscles ache with a satisfying pain. The earth in her two largest garden beds has been turned where the annuals are to be planted; the perennials fertilized for the coming summer. The garden seemed to laugh while she worked; Charlotte imagines it felt like a marvelous back rub.

As she labors now, her mind turns a word over—polishing, examining, attempting to dissect why it is that she finds the word so attractive, so pleasurable. Is it the onset consonant cluster of the "spl" beginning? The short second syllable that tap dances on her tongue?

Splen-
did.
Splen-
did.

Or is it the fact that the word surprised her when Dr. Weston used it? In fact, upon hearing the word, it was the first time Charlotte felt any affinity at all for the withered Chair of her department. Charlotte disregarded the following adjective that Dr.

Weston had used to describe her: disgrace. That word didn't matter—and it certainly didn't apply.

Humming, she hangs the shovel in its place on the wall of the shed then checks on the latest concoction brewing on the small table. Brown liquid not quite as dark as it should be, so she adds a sprinkle of dried herbs from a glass bowl and dusts her hands on her jeans.

Today, as always, she sweeps the floor before leaving, casually grinding a stray spider beneath her shoe then sweeping its twitching carcass out with other dust from the day. She pulls the rattling door down and locks it, putting the extra padlock in place, as she isn't planning on returning until tomorrow.

Sweeping the path to the shed, Charlotte hears the phone ring through an open window in the house. She puts the broom away in a closet in the mudroom and closes the door, leaning her forehead against it briefly. She presses the playback button on the answering machine while putting the kettle on for a cup of tea.

"It's Doris." Charlotte waits patiently as Dr. Weston's admin continues, "your appeal's been heard; can you get over here before five? You know she leaves promptly."

Of course Dr. Weston will be leaving at five as usual. What if *my* earliest convenience is after five? Then I'd be out of luck—as usual. Splendid.

As Charlotte walks briskly to campus, she ruminates on the fact that her academic panel met fairly quickly after they refused her dissertation—light speed in the academic world. This is unusual, but whether it's good or bad is still to be seen. She hadn't pressured them and had made most of the agreed changes to her dissertation.

She thinks about walking across campus the day they'd been introduced, when Dr. Weston had politely, awkwardly, invited Charlotte to lunch. As they climbed the steps to the Student Union, Dr. Weston said, "I read your Master's thesis on Seventeenth Century Herbal Decoctions twice. Exciting that you plan to investigate even further back into the Fourteenth Century. It's plain the University will be a good fit for your doctorate, Charlotte. We can talk about the addition of tincture and some of the lesser-known mixtures you're interested in when you've gotten a good start."

Dr. Weston's face, dominated by large sunglasses, was strangely animated. She didn't take them off when they reached the cafeteria, only removing them while she ducked down to the water fountain. Charlotte remembers the spectacular black eye. When the older woman stood, fitting the glasses once more to the bridge of her nose, she noticed Charlotte's glance. "Oh," she said, lifting a veined hand to wave at her face. "I'm so clumsy. I ran into the doorframe."

Charlotte smiles when she remembers her surprise that Dr. Weston lied so easily—and was so bad at it.

Doris, the admin, nods at Charlotte as she knocks lightly on Dr. Weston's closed door.

A muffled call and Charlotte enters; she's prepared for the reek, but when her nervous stomach combines with the sharp, bitter odor of stale coffee, it makes her nauseated. She takes a seat in the one hard chair and looks over scattered, dirty, half-full cups, (was that mold in one?) into Dr. Weston's thin face. Charlotte thinks she looks tired; her wattles appear longer— giving her nose a more pronounced, beak-like look. They exchange superficial pleasantries, and Dr. Weston starts in, opening with, "Based on your dissertation, once more, the committee *does not* recommend you be awarded your doctorate."

Charlotte tries not to show any emotion, remaining still, not flinching, even though her face is burning and her heart is flipping out of her chest. Such a blow; she had made all the changes. She worked so hard.

Dr. Weston continues on in her prim manner, "I can only remind you that you ignored our suggestions to change the course of your research."

"I did change it, Dr. Weston. I changed it completely." This was all so wrong.

"Please, Charlotte. I know this has to be difficult for you, but let me finish. You changed what you wanted to change, but

you made no attempt at a revision based on the committee's recommendations. As we discussed before, your technical
proficiency is obviously excellent, but how can we possibly
judge it when we are *History professors* and this is once more
written for chemists? All of the equations, those odd recipes,
which we asked you to remove, are still included. Granted, you
provided more explanatory material, but how can we question
your defense when we don't understand what you are trying to
prove? The literature you've linked these concoctions to is based
on the flimsiest evidence—"

"Dr. Weston, please. The formulas are important. You cannot remove Biochemistry from History. They revolve around
one another—"

"Do not interrupt me again, Charlotte." Dr. Weston's face
grows pink. "If you wish to continue with this line of research, I
suggest you propose it to the Chemistry Department. No doubt
they will be as uncomfortable with the subject matter as we were
when we advised you previously. It would be irresponsible of us
to let you publish a manual on distilling fourteenth century poisons and psychotropic compounds."

And fifteenth century. "As you are well aware, this subject
matter is already on the Internet and has been for some time."

"Not in as great a detail as it would be if you ever manage
to get this published."

"But the manuscript would be restricted to access within
university settings. It would be almost impossible for it to fall
into the wrong hands."

Dr. Weston picks up papers from her desk and smacks them
smartly to align the pages. "I'm sorry, Charlotte, but the committee has reached a final decision."

Charlotte wants to retch. She leans forward over the desk
doing her best to appear gracious. "I'm deeply disappointed in
the results of the appeal, but I have no choice but to accept the
committee's decision at this point. I will, of course, speak to the
Provost."

"You can try, but I assure you, the Provost will not be able
to change our minds. It would take a major revision—taking *all*

of our recommendations under consideration—for us to even have another look at your dissertation."

"I understand," says Charlotte. She rises, *be dignified* she tells herself, and moves toward Dr. Weston's door.

The next morning, Charlotte has retreated to the shed, checking on her concoctions, wiping a few tools, when her sister, Anne, finds her. Anne stands at the entrance to the shed swatting at mosquitoes, looking around. "I haven't been out here in years. It's always so damp, so *buggy*; how can you stand it?"

Charlotte doesn't look up. "Doris called you." It's a statement.

Anne leans against the frame. "Well. I guess this was expected, huh? I mean, they told you they didn't like your paper or whatever it's called. What do you want to do?"

"I don't know. I guess I need to think about packing up my office at some point."

"I meant today."

"Oh." Charlotte aimlessly moves a few things around, shuffles her feet, picks up a small bulging package in brown paper, moves it behind a bowl full of dried leaves.

"What's that?"

Charlotte says, "Nothing," a bit defensively.

"Really?" Anne moves into the shed. "Looked like a bag of coffee beans to me. What are you brewing in here? It smells awful, like something died and rotted." She moves forward, invading, advancing. Charlotte skitters away. Anne picks up the bowl of leaves, sniffs at it, then picks up the bag. "I was right; it's coffee." She drops the bag on the table with a thump. "I've always been curious about what you do back here, thinking you're some sort of herbal genius, and here you just brew coffee. Weird coffee—" she gestures at the bowl "—but coffee."

Charlotte is expressionless.

Anne puts her hands on her hips. "It's a joke, Charlotte— bad timing, though. Let's go get some lunch."

"I'm not hungry."

"Well, if you're not hungry, then you can drink. It might do you good to get drunk. "C'mon, sis." Anne reaches out, wrapping an arm around Charlotte's neck, the slightest bit too tight. "It'll do you good. I'll buy."

Charlotte agrees. It will be a distraction, whether good or bad is still to be seen.

A half hour later, Charlotte's sister crosses her legs and takes her time lighting another cigarette, even though the hostess stands behind her with the menus, waiting. She finally leans back, and the frowning woman hands them the wooden and cork boards, stalking away.

A drop of sweat runs behind Charlotte's ear as she studies the trendy menu. Anne insisted they eat outside under the umbrellas, though the cooler screened-in patio had empty tables, and made Charlotte take a seat in the sun, telling her she was too pale. Spring and Anne already wears the deep tan and bleached hair of late summer. She looks partially roasted, not quite done but almost there. Next to her, Charlotte thinks, I *am* pale, chicken raw, served up on a plate of frizzy hair. When people see them together, they always peg Charlotte as the older one, though she's younger by two and a half years.

"Isn't this nice?" Anne says, gesturing at the tables. "It's much nicer than that old bar you suggested, and—" she raises plucked eyebrows "—it's better if you aren't too near the University anyway." She just can't help starting in right away. "So, what are you going to order?"

Charlotte tries to focus on the menu. "I don't know. I'll probably try one of my usual standbys, either tuna or chicken salad. I said I wasn't hungry."

"God, so boring. When are you going to branch out and try something different?" Drawing the ashtray closer, she tilts her head. "I'm sorry, Charlotte. I know you've had quite a blow, but maybe it will do you good to step outside your comfort zone. Why don't you try the polenta fritters?"

"I don't want the polenta fritters. I'll have either the tuna or chicken salad." Charlotte lays the menu down.

"Be that way then," Anne snaps as if she's been disappointed in some way. "I'm thinking of ordering the marinated Octopus over arugula because *I'm* not the one who's afraid of my own shadow."

A memory arises in Charlotte of the two of them as young girls on the boardwalk with their grandparents. The sun glints off the ocean so bright and hard they shade their eyes, beg for ice cream, then take their dripping cones onto the sand to walk among the seagulls. Charlotte can't resist chasing a gull, laughs as it shrieks, but her ice cream falls.

Go ask Grandma and Grandpa for another cone, Anne says. *No*, Charlotte says, *I'm afraid. They'll be mad*. Anne pushes her, again and again, *Go ask. Go ask.* Finally, Charlotte walks back and explains. They look at each other and say, *No*. Anne makes a show of eating the rest of her cone.

Charlotte's reverie is interrupted by the arrival of the server to take drink orders. Anne looks at her pointedly, and Charlotte orders a beer. Anne frowns while ordering a martini, says, "I thought you were going to drink."

"This *is* me drinking."

Anne laughs. "Pathetic."

Anne talks while Charlotte sips at the beer. She and Hayden are going to the Caribbean in a few weeks; he's loving his new job; he thinks he can make partner in less than two years; some fashion line excites her. The words wash up against Charlotte, pound against her, and she adds a nod here or there. It all seems to add up to a rich and full life, and Charlotte feels something; is it anger? She squashes it. Emotions are not useful; they just cloud the mind. Besides, she needs to figure out what to do, how to proceed now that her academic plans are dust.

"Are you listening?" Anne sits back against her chair, waving at a fly buzzing near her large white sunglasses. "You weren't, were you? You were moping over your school stuff. I don't understand the fascination with plunging your hands into worms and dead sticks. Look at your hands—they look awful; you have dirt under your fingernails, and you might try some polish sometime."

Charlotte holds her hands out and considers her nails.

Anne extends her own manicured hand to squash the burning end of the cigarette in the ashtray; then drops the butt onto
the concrete under the table.

Charlotte shifts in her seat, gazes at the butt. Anne is talking
now about the garden—Charlotte's garden—but the remnant of
the cigarette smokes feebly under the table. It makes Charlotte
uncomfortable. Years ago, Anne told her, "Someone will sweep
it up. I don't want to look at them while I eat." By the end of
lunch, the area under her chair will be littered with the dead ends
of little white cylinders. Dry husks stained red on one end. Charlotte could ignore that for a while, but there's was no way she
could continue ignoring what Anne just said.

"What?" Did Charlotte hear correctly? "A bully? I don't
understand why you would call my garden a bully."

"I didn't mean to call just *your* garden a bully." Anne
stretches, arms above her head. Something about the movement
makes Charlotte ill at ease. "I basically meant to say that all gardens—" Anne draws out the plural "—are bullies. It seems to
me that you've spent too much time on it already when you have
other things to do now. Gardens need so much attention, they're
like children, always needing watering or weeds pulled or something like that. You're not even growing anything you could eat,
only random flowers and the leftovers of whatever Mother and
Father had growing in there."

"They're not random flowers. They're specific medicinal
herbs, and you know they're important to my research."

To which Anne replies, "Right. *Were* important."

This jolts Charlotte, irritating her with her new reality. It's a
grain of sand in her shell, destined not to be a pearl.

Anne twists around. "We've been waiting forever. You'd
think that server would have come to take our order by now.
Anyway, I think you're avoiding what you need to do."

"And what is it you think I need to do?"

"Deciding whether or not to clean out your office should be
your number one priority. You're not teaching any classes this
semester, are you? You can get it done right away. Be done with
this. Move on."

"I'll do it in a few days." Charlotte turns away from her sister to the few other diners on the patio, only women, all in sundresses and sandaled feet. What is it about lunch that attracts women in bright clothes and unlined faces? Their polished toenails provide a welcome distraction. Colored toenails always fascinated her. What if people were born that way? What if you could make a bouquet of toes, each strung on an individual wire, so when you gathered all the wires together into a bunch the colored nails waved and rippled in the wind. Would they look like flowers?

"Really? Well, then…that's that." Anne moves her hands together in the classic wiping 'done-with-that' movement.

Charlotte plays with a drop of water on the glass table, smearing it and watching it reform. Easy for Anne to brush away years of her life as if it were so much wasted time. She'd never seen the value in pursuing a doctorate. Not that Anne had ever inquired into Charlotte's studies—distilling herbal concoctions referenced in fourteenth and fifteenth century histories wasn't 'her thing.'

Anne leans forward until Charlotte's beer looms like a huge alien object reflected in the lenses of her sunglasses. "So what are you going to do after all this? Drown your sorrows in your sandbox?"

Charlotte takes a deep breath. She hates it when Anne calls the garden names. "The garden makes me feel better." What Charlotte means, what she won't say to her sister is, I need the garden and it needs me—it's so peaceful there. It tells me I'm not a failure.

"That's so dreary, Charlotte. It's only a bunch of plants. You need to get over this. So the committee denied your appeal, where's your gumption? Go talk to Dr. Weston about your appeal. Ask her for a meeting and figure out what you need to do to move forward."

"You just said I should be done with all this."

"I wanted to see what you'd say. I didn't think you would give up so easily."

Two months later, Charlotte comes out to the garden to walk along the orderly paths. Her hair is longer now, and she's taken care with her clothes, wearing a skirt that could almost be fashionable, a hint of color on her cheeks. There's a bit of grass growing at the base of the Datura, so she pulls it out while admiring the hanging flowers. Upside-down, fluted trumpets casting intricate shadows that bounce, joining and separating with air currents.

She holds the bit of grass as she continues on, checking on poppies frilled by crepe-paper petals. The gentle breeze pulls at her hair as she deposits the grass in the compost bin and takes a pharmacy vial out of her pocket to harvest more Morning Glory seeds. The Oleanders are beginning to fade, and she stops to see if aphids have attacked them again. Pink and white flowers litter the path, and she notes that she'll need to sweep soon. It brings her such peace, this walk. All is as it should be with no sound other than wind and bird. She can breathe here.

Charlotte is sixteen again. Flying down the road on her bicycle. Every day she rides. The only sounds are the wind by her ears, the birds, and the skreek, scrunk rhythm of the bicycle as the pedals turn. She is at peace but hears Hayden pull up in his convertible behind her, and her heart thumps. Inside sit Anne and Trish. Her only consolation is that Anne is not riding in the front seat.

Hey, says Hayden.

It's the first time he's spoken to her. *Hey*, she says back.

He says *Want a ride?* with a grin that makes him look golden, radiant.

Charlotte looks to Anne, who smiles and Trish says, *Come on.*

What about my bike?

Trish says, *Leave it by the side of the road; no one will bother it.*

Charlotte lays it down gently and walks to the car as Hayden reverses. He drives over her bicycle as she watches.

Oops, he says, and they drive away. Charlotte realizes Anne hasn't said a word.

Later, when their parents tell Charlotte they are not buying her another bike, she asks why Anne isn't being punished. *There was nothing she could have done*, they say.

Two weeks after the bike is destroyed, Charlotte idly turns the pages of a magazine. She has sequestered herself in her room every night. At first, she cried fiery tears that burned and stung as much as her self-imposed exile. She wants them to miss her, but it's apparent they do not. A knock at her door surprises her; her mother strides in and crosses her arms at the foot of the bed.

"You are taking over the garden tomorrow," she says.

"I don't want to, and besides, why me? Why not Anne?"

She holds an index finger out to Charlotte. "All you do is waste time up here mooning over those useless magazines. At least Anne is out with friends. Where are your friends? Oh, I remember. You don't have any. You *are* going to do this; you'll help the family by weeding."

Charlotte hurls the copy of *Scientific American* down on the bed. "How is Anne helping?" But she knows the answer, and anger makes her go too far. "Is she helping by letting Hayden put his hand up her blouse? Isn't that a little like selling her, mother?"

Charlotte's mother lifts her hand as if to strike her. "How dare you? You think money grows on trees? Anne is helping your father with business." She draws the "s" out snake-like, and Charlotte can't help imagining her mother with a forked tongue.

Charlotte gets it—it's simple enough. Hayden's father owns the Cadillac dealership, and Father needs a job.

The next morning, Charlotte is marched out to the garden early with brief instructions on what to pull out of the ground and what to leave. She stands for a while, alone, then savagely pulls everything. When her mother returns, she has cleared the whole garden bed of all plants.

That evening, her father removes her from her locked room. Holding her upper arm in a grip so tight her hand goes numb, he pulls her to the room in the house he and Mother call The Library. The room is spoken of with hushed veneration and kept locked. They profess to respect knowledge, but Charlotte has guessed the truth. It terrifies them in a knock-kneed, cringe on the floor sort of way. Knowledge is out of their control, and it is dangerous.

Charlotte does not want to enter the room. She despises it. Libraries should be living places; this one is long dead, smelling of must, mildew and rotting leather. None of the titles were published past the Thirties. It is a monument to past wealth, preserved like something disgusting in formaldehyde.

Father shoves her into a chair and removes several tomes from the shelves. Silverfish fall out as he drops the books on her lap.

"Here," he says. "These are about plants. Learn what to pull. I will be quizzing you." He gestures to the books and leaves, locking the door behind him.

Charlotte throws the books on the floor, wanting to tear them apart but afraid of the additional punishment. She imagines pulling every book off every shelf, but she will be the one to put them back. She moves to the floor and lies on the carpet, staring up at the water-stained ceiling until her back hurts. It is futile to cry, even more so to scream. She pulls a book over and creates a breeze by shuffling the pages. The odor makes her stop, and she decides to read one page at random. The book falls open to "Nerium Oleander." A boring black etching of the bush is underlined by the word, "Toxic."

When Charlotte's father finally unlocks the door, she has turned down the page corner on every plant described by that word.

Later, she disguises her budding enjoyment of the garden by pretending to pout when her mother sends her out. No, she complains, send Anne. She knows her mother won't, but suspicions might grow if she is too compliant. She recognizes that Anne's success is important to the family. Charlotte's bookishness is not attractive—she will bring the family neither accolades nor reflected triumph nor a job for her father. It tires her to think about it, the shining star and the ugly duckling; she is trapped in a cliché.

But she is content to let the disappointment and hurt dissolve into the various solutions she starts fabricating in the tool shed. It feels like a wonderful lightness every time she adds leaves or seeds to a battered pot filled with water and lets it stew in the sunshine. She keeps the garden with just enough weeds to be seen as a typical teenager and hides her experiments from all but the rats that come to investigate. Poor rats. Charlotte supposes when she dies she will have to face the countless rodents who paid the price for her knowledge. She does bury them. Will they thank her for that?

After a year, her parents suffer from a variety of ailments. Some come and go, some stay with serious consequences. Charlotte keeps meticulous notes. Poor parents. She does not mourn them.

Charlotte shakes the memories off and continues her walk, ending up back at the tool shed. Her laboratory now, she has moved all the old tools into the basement. A spotless white Formica table holds her processing instruments, and she sets the vial down. She checks on a distillation process and is satisfied that all's well. She closes and locks the door, dusts her hands and heads to her house. Anne is picking her up for lunch and Charlotte is light as a feather, happy. She has finally given up that most terrible of emotions, relentless hope. The hope that one day the sister of her imagination, the nice one, would show up. Charlotte knows now it's not going to happen; there is no changing someone's nature. There is only the garden and its loving whispers.

They return to the same restaurant and sit on the patio as before. It's sweltering when they're seated, and they quickly order two iced teas. As cigarette butts begin to pile up, Anne says, "You look better than you have in a long time, Charlotte. Like you've turned a corner."

Charlotte smiles. "Yes, I feel better. I've been thinking of sending out applications. Hopefully, something will come of one of them."

"Well, I can't imagine where you'd apply? You've no aptitude for anything other than your weird history project and that garden—perhaps Hayden can see about getting you a job doing something with files at the firm? At least then you would be out in the real world."

"Perhaps."

They sit silently until the drinks are set down, both of them squeezing their lemons and Charlotte stirring her tea with her index finger. It is a habit she knows Anne abhors. Anne watches, shakes her head, sets her spoon down with a sharp clack.

Later, Anne takes a long drag off a now short cigarette, little more than a filter. She's been nattering about Hayden and her life while Charlotte pretends an avid interest and daydreams about the cigarette burning her. Charlotte wants the burn to run from Anne's fingertips all over her body—turning into a glowing red shape and then blowing away. Charlotte sees her rising on the wind—a cloud of embers.

"…and what ever did you do to your little finger? That blue nail looks disgusting. You might try some polish over it."

Charlotte returns from her daydream and laughs, delighted. She holds her hand out for Anne to see. "It is nail polish. I'm so glad you noticed. It's a new pet project of mine, an organic nail polish. I'm trying it out, plus it dissolves in water."

"Interesting," Anne says in a way that indicates she could not care less. "Try a different color next time. That color makes your hand look like it belongs on a corpse."

The server comes back with their meals, and they eat their chicken salad in silence. Anne pulls out her phone and gets busy tapping, occasionally laughing. The server returns with the iced tea pitcher, puts their glasses together and makes a show of refilling, pouring from a height of more than a foot, splashing tea onto the table. Anne grimaces but goes back to her phone. Charlotte squeezes their lemons and stirs the teas. Anne looks up briefly when Charlotte moves her tea across the table.

"Thanks," Anne says, distracted and engaged by whatever is on her phone. She lifts the glass, takes a sip and then wrinkles her nose. "Tastes funny."

"Oh, sorry," Charlotte says dreamily. "I must have squeezed in too much lemon."

They pay and when Anne leans in for a goodbye hug, Charlotte backs away. Anne's eyebrows lower, and she puts on her sunglasses, and takes Charlotte's hand, squeezes it. "It will all work out, Charlotte. When one door closes another one opens."

"Yes."

"Oh, look." Anne holds Charlotte's hand up and points to her pink-nailed little finger. "It does dissolve in water."

Charlotte strides by Doris on a Tuesday afternoon and is amused by her startled expression. She knocks on Dr. Weston's door before Doris can stop her and hears the familiar, "Come in." Charlotte enters, shutting the door, and watches as Dr. Weston sits up straight in her chair.

"This is a surprise, Charlotte. What can I do for you?" she creaks.

Charlotte smiles, making sure it shows in her eyes. "I've had time to think, and I don't want any hard feelings between us. You and the committee did what you thought was correct. While I may disagree, I have decided that truly moving forward would be in everyone's best interest. I thought I'd ask for a recommendation, as I've decided to apply to several pharmaceutical companies. I think I can count on you to write one?"

Dr. Weston relaxes back into her chair. "I don't think I can do that, Charlotte, for the exact reasons you were denied your dissertation. It doesn't make sense. Again, I would urge you to take your observations to a different department. Good day."

Charlotte walks to the door and turns around. "Dr. Weston?"

"Yes, Charlotte?" This is uttered with an aura of benighted resignation.

"Your husband. I never told you how sorry I was." Dr. Weston blinks her pale blue eyes. "Cyanotic for a while, wasn't he? Blue lips? Blue fingernails?" A pink spot appears on one drooping cheek. "I heard they thought it was something pulmonary...such a shame they never did figure out the cause. Perhaps you weren't uncomfortable with my distillations after all."

Dr. Weston and Charlotte face each other for a series of moments until Charlotte opens the door wide. Dr. Weston pulls a pad of paper across her desk. "Of course, Charlotte. I'd be more than happy to write you a very good recommendation based on your work. You understand I am not a chemist, as I have expressed previously, but I will be happy to see what I can do."

"I felt sure you would be able to help me, Dr. Weston. I will forward the names and addresses of the personnel departments this afternoon. Please do your best to get them done by the end of the week. I'm sure you don't need to see me again."

Dr. Weston's eyes are bright. "Of course."

Charlotte turns to go, stops. "Oh, yes, I almost forgot." She reaches into her purse to pull out a fragrant wrapped package. The rich scent of ground coffee fills the room. "I brought you a pound of your favorite coffee. Consider it a parting gift." Charlotte sets it on the desk where Dr. Weston regards it with lowered brows.

"Thank you, Charlotte," she says, taking the coffee and perching the bag on her desk next to the waste bin. "Perhaps this next step is for the best."

Charlotte leaves her office, smiling broadly at Doris standing near Dr. Weston's door. Charlotte's positive Doris has heard everything. Charlotte almost skips when she hears the unmistakable thump of the bag as Dr. Weston pushes it off her desk.

Charlotte spends the rest of the week dismantling her small lab in the tool shed, carefully cross referencing recipes and diagramming set ups for refining and purifying liquids and powders. All goes into a small black notebook. Such wonderful knowledge; she knew she would find a group that appreciated her research. She releases a handful of garden spiders inside the shed and when she finishes, it looks like it had been abandoned years ago, down to rat droppings, spider webs, dust and rusty tools. Anyone peeking in would decide it hasn't been used for anything but the most mundane daily gardening chores.

On Monday Charlotte receives an e-mail from Doris addressed to everyone in the department. Dr. Weston's body has been discovered in her bedroom—she apparently died over the weekend after complaining to a friend of a headache. Charlotte immediately sends her condolences and cleans the house, expecting a visit from the police. No one comes. With Doris' help, they must have drawn the conclusion that the relationship ended on friendly terms.

Particulate dispersion can be such a tricky thing. With this particulate, the one Charlotte had soaked the coffee beans in, a person walking in and out of the office might notice the slightest of headaches after three or four days, but a person sitting *in* the office, their unemptied wastebasket next to their desk and given four days of exposure, why by the fifth day, *they* would start spitting blood. When the blood appeared, the concentration in the bloodstream would already be quite lethal, so lethal, that at that point, it's mere minutes before unconsciousness. Too short to write a note or make a phone call, and the absolute best news was that they cleaned the offices and emptied each wastebasket, every Friday night.

Now, early fall, Charlotte thinks of leaves twisting and curling. No longer bright with youth, the garden prepares for dormancy. She will miss the garden. Her friend. Her bully, according to Anne. Never. Charlotte knows what bullying is, and her garden was never that. She loves this time of year equally as well as the period brimming with life. The smell of leaves crunching underfoot and dried shells of flowers once so bright.

The breath that escapes her chest is filled with sadness as she imagines the garden coming back to life next spring without her hand to guide and protect it.

She sits in the grimy basement café of the psychiatric hospital sipping a cup of weak tea, gazing out the barred windows. Hayden enters through the double doors and walks to her table. She gestures to the cup of hot water across from her and he sits. With unsteady hands, he opens the tea bag, drops it in.

Charlotte asks, "Need sugar?" He nods and she hands him several packets she'd stowed in her pockets from the station near the cashier.

"Thanks," he mutters.

He appears exhausted, deep bags under his eyes, frown lines etching their way deep into his forehead. He seems weak, diminished. He holds his tea with both hands a moment, then covers her hand with one of his. She can feel the warmth of the hot tea on his skin.

"I'm sorry," he starts, then hesitates, looking away at a wall painted a drab color of institutional green.

Charlotte doesn't move and, after a minute, he starts again.

"Anne and I used to think you were kind of crazy." He pauses again. "We could never figure out if you were an earth mother or just bat-shit crazy. We were wrong. You've been such a rock in all this, and I appreciate it." He lifts his cup and blows on his tea, still leaving his hand on Charlotte's. "The doctor says it might be a much longer hospitalization this time. This time is so much worse—she tried to chop her own hand off." He starts to cry. "She was screaming that she was bleeding spiders." Shoulders trembling, he drops his head. "I can't believe we used to make your life so miserable. You're teaching me so much about forgiveness…"

"Oh, Hayden." Charlotte pats his shoulder with her other hand. "Water under the bridge. We're all adults now, and that was a long time ago." Her chest feels warm, a nice sensation.

He coughs and rubs the back of his other hand across his nose, wipes his eyes. "When are you moving? Not soon, I hope."

"A few more months. Long enough for me to finish helping and see Anne safely settled in this caring institution. I know they'll be able to help her."

He shivers and stirs his tea. "What did that company hire you for again?"

"Well, it turns out I'm a genius at herbal distillations and dispersions. Who knew?" Charlotte smiles, turns her hand to squeeze his. "You'll take care of the old house and garden for me, won't you? I found out that old tool shed was infested with rats, so I'm having it demolished tomorrow. You won't ever have to worry about it."

Hayden squeezes her hand back, harder. As if it is a lifeline he's clinging to. "I'm so glad you're not moving for your new job yet."

"Me too." She covers his hand with her other.

Jason Rubis

THE TOXICIST'S DAUGHTER

The shop of Vennis the apothecary was cramped and dusty, not unlike the man himself. Unlike its provincial-minded owner, the shop was multitudinous, filled to the last corner with exotica and bottled nightmares. Aranda had often been brought here as a child and allowed to wander the aisles while her father spoke at length with the old druggist, trading anecdotes and theories related to their mutual passion.

The walls were lined with chests of small drawers that reached to the ceiling; many of the drawers had not been opened for decades, and little Aranda had made a game of imagining them filled with horrible surprises: eyeballs still wet and wobbling like jellies, or living salamanders ready to pounce out and scorch a girl's curious fingers. A stuffed crocodile hung from the ceiling, its glass eyes seeming to trade glares with her. It was there still, and as Vennis laid out his bottles and jars for her consideration, Aranda smiled at it. It was a temptation to cross her eyes at the crocodile as she had in the old days. But today was not a day for joking.

"The venom of the spider known as the Bloody Mystic," Vennis croaked, holding a tiny phial up to the scanty sunlight infiltrating the shop. The phial glowed amber in his gnarled, nicotine-stained fingers. "Very highly regarded by poisoners in the tropic climes to which it is native. Highly esteemed for the immediacy of its effects. It is virtually undetectable except for a single tear of blood shed by the victim upon his demise. A nice touch; very dramatic, I always thought.

"And here," the apothecary went on, reaching for a crumbling wafer of a greyish-blue substance, "is a concoction derived from the droppings of the catoblepas of the Eastern Plains. So pestilential is this beast's nature that its very gaze is said to be fatal. It passes that fatal nature on to its innards, and all that pass through them. Naturally the stuff is inedible, but when allowed to soak in water and secreted in your victim's bedchamber, it conducts its essence through the very air itself. The victim expires in great agony, but the fewmets themselves dissolve away to nothing. A great favorite of Zindam Taroi in his heyday; you've read his *Memoirs?*"

Aranda nodded politely, carefully refraining from comment.

The old man heaved a heartfelt sigh. "You'll pardon me for my boldness, miss, but your father would have been proud of the way you've carried on his interests. He and I would talk for hours on the various venoms and toxins. It may sound odd my saying so, miss, but had he been born in old Taroi's days, he would have made a first-class poisoner himself. But there, he's not the first gentleman born out of his time. One must be practical, after all."

Yes, Aranda thought bitterly. *Even if that practicality means marrying off your only daughter to the worst of your debtors, a fat old man with nasty tastes.*

"Have you given any thought to finishing his book?"

The question made Aranda start a little. "I...well, not really. Perhaps. I've read through it, of course." Mountains of paper filled the cabinets in her father's old study, covered with his henscratchings, the product of a life of amateur scholarship. But in the year since his death, she had grown desperate for the information they might provide her.

"In a way, Mister Vennis, that's what brought me to you today. My father had made rather copious notes on a substance called *Xisia Solun*. Have you heard of it?"

"Ahh, *Xisia Solun*," Vennis sighed, as though inhaling a rare perfume. "The name means 'Water of Remorse,' you know. Yes, I can well believe your father would have written at length on it, even if only speculations. It was one of his obsessions. A great many toxicists refuse to believe it actually exists; they believe it's a folktale. Even the master poisoners of the very highest rank never laid hands on it, if the stories are true. When I was at school, the journeymen would talk about it endlessly. The arguments!"

"I understand the debate extends as far as the water's actual effects."

"Yes," Vennis said, nodding his head vigorously. "Some call it the peerless necrotic, causing the victim to all but melt away, no ingestion required. Then there those who claim it freezes the victim like a plunge into polar waters, so that the merest tap with a hammer shatters them into dust. Others believe it simply stops the heart with one sip, bringing an instant, though far from painless death."

"My father's notes," Aranda said carefully, "hinted that you possessed a sample."

Vennis' response was not what she had hoped for; instead of tittering and preening, the old man went silent and gave her a frank, even cold stare. His eyes darted to the shelf behind him, examining the rows of neatly labeled bottles and flasks.

"He said that, did he?"

"Yes…but only as a sample, obtained as a collector's item."

"His book said *I* possessed this sample? Corlat Vennis. He mentioned me *by name*?"

Aranda shook her head. "No, of course not. He only mentioned you as 'V' and called you a 'colleague.'" This was nothing but the truth, and it had been difficult enough as it was to make sense of the passage in question. But the identity of the "colleague" could be none other than Mister C. Vennis. She had come here hoping against hope that he hadn't sold the stuff, that he had retained it as the jewel of his private collection, as a miser would hold onto a particularly fine gem.

"My father never came close to publishing his notes, as you know. If he had, I'm sure he would have deleted mention of your name."

"I see." Vennis' face relaxed and gradually resumed its smile. "I'm sorry, Miss Aranda, please forgive a foolish old man. You must remember, owning or selling *Xisia Solun* carries terrible risks. Really, I'm by no means certain that the substance in my possession *is Xisia Solun*; it might easily be ordinary spring water. I acquired it…well, I won it, is the truth, from an acquaintance of mine, a rather odd fellow known also to your father. It was my friend who advised me to keep quiet about it, otherwise every toxicist from the Wastes to the Isles would be kicking my door in."

"Yes, of course. Really, Mister Vennis, I'm very sorry I caused you distress by mentioning it." The groveling note in her own voice disgusted her. "I only wanted…well, I was going to ask if I might see the substance. Out of curiosity. My father had been so fascinated by it, you see. But I can see it's a sensitive matter for you…I wouldn't dream of causing offense."

It was a risk, but it paid off. Vennis beamed and chortled, making a show of indulgence toward his old friend's daughter, then turned—as Aranda had prayed he would—to the shelf at his back, taking out a stepstool so he could reach for a specific bottle. Naturally he would keep the stuff in plain sight but almost out of reach.

"There you are, my dear," Vennis said a moment later, setting the bottle on the counter with a decisive *click.* "One bottle of alleged *Xisia Solun.*"

"Thank you *so* much, Mister Vennis," Aranda murmured, reaching for the tawny, red-streaked lily that adorned her lapel. "You have just guaranteed my future happiness."

She stroked the lily's fleshy petals, as one might stroke a lapdog's ear; the bloom stiffened briefly under her fingers and made a snapping noise. Vennis fell to the floor, gasping and fumbling at his wattly neck in a futile effort to dislodge the tiny thorn that had pierced him there. Eventually, he lay still, a bit of foam bubbling from his slack lips. Aranda snatched up the bottle and, thrusting it into her handbag, exited the shop as quickly as she was able.

Aranda had bought the deathsnap lily that morning from a botanical not a few steps away from Vennis' apothecary. The man who sold it to her had no idea it might be used—in fact, *had* been used in remote western regions—as a sort of living pistol. Such knowledge was limited to those, like her father, who had made a specialized study of such things. Likely the cultivation of the deathsnap would have been illegal otherwise.

At least the thorn's poison worked relatively quickly— which was precisely why it didn't suit her real purpose today. For that, only the agony caused by *Xisia Solun* would do. And the shop was in an isolated neighborhood, rarely patronized. It might be days before Vennis' body was discovered. *It's a sin what I've done*, she thought. *But I'll pray later for forgiveness. Not for one death, but two.*

When Aranda made it home, she found the new maid, Liris, bawling in the kitchen.

"Liris, whatever's wrong?" she asked, though she knew exactly what was wrong. The ceiling overhead creaked alarmingly; Odrun was in their bedroom, pacing from one end to the other, as he did when he was agitated. Every other moment something dropped on the floor and there was muffled cursing. The house her father left them was small and not particularly well made; sounds from one room echoed throughout the entire structure.

Liris turned her face away, not merely ashamed, Aranda saw, but afraid as well. Why shouldn't she be? At any moment the bell might start ringing, and she would be required to go serve the master. It was something she had learned to fear herself.

Aranda pursed her lips. *No more of this. As soon as I can manage it, it ends.* "Alright, then," she told Liris. "Make yourself some tea. I'll be down later." She slipped her gloves off and climbed the stairs, hugging her bag tightly to her.

Odrun was waiting for her, glaring as he balanced his weight on his stick. There was still something of the man he had been in his face, a hint of good looks, but years of overindulgence and lassitude had all but buried it. Ultimately it wasn't the fat that disgusted Aranda, but the gleam of cunning cruelty in his eyes when he saw her. Maids were good sport, but they couldn't compare with the young wife who had bought her father's freedom with her own.

"You've been gone long enough," Odrun said, backing into a chair.

"I had business in town." Aranda said, placing her things on a table. "I wanted to talk with that man at the *Standard* about writing some pieces for him. It'll bring in some more money."

Odrun grunted, only somewhat mollified. More money was always desirable. He hadn't held a position since before their

marriage. "I want my tea," he said abruptly. "Have the girl send
it up." His eyes glimmered again. "I like her," he told his wife.
"Nice slender ankle on that one." His grin widened. "I wager
she'd squeak if she were pinched."

Aranda caught her breath and held it. She had planned to
put her plan in motion the following morning, when Odrun was
muzzy with sleep and thundering for his breakfast. Was this a
chance to finish things earlier?

"I'll make it for you," she said, making for the door.

Odrun was out of his chair much more quickly than she
would have thought possible. "No," he said with ominous patience. His paw was clenched around Aranda's wrist, and he
squeezed it. "I want the *girl* to make it. Make it and bring it up
here to me."

Aranda waited a moment, letting the pounding of her heart
slow. "Alright, Odrun," she said finally. "Then that's the way
it'll be." She was released and moved the few steps to the doorway, where she called down to Liris.

"I'm feeling good tonight," Odrun said, watching her narrowly. "I could do with a bit of fun."

"Yes," Aranda said dully. She sat down and began undoing
the buttons of her boots.

"Aren't you glad? Glad I'm feeling good?" The leer in his
voice made her feel sick.

"I am, Odrun. Of course."

By the time Liris brought the tea, Odrun had already had a
bit of fun—not much, just enough to ensure Aranda's thighs
would be bruised the next morning.

When his cup was poured, he took it, watching the trembling girl. "You wouldn't try anything clever, would you?"

"Clever, sir?" The girl's face paled visibly.

Odrun glowered. "You wouldn't put something in my tea,
f'rinstance? As a sort of joke?"

It was a favorite game of his, inspired by the poisons Aranda's father had been so fascinated by. He had put Aranda through it often enough. Anger coursed through her as she watched him.

The fat pig. I'll pour it over his head tonight while he's in his bath and watch the lard melt off his bones.

"But no. You wouldn't. Because you're not clever enough. Not like *her*," Odrun said, nodding his heavy head at his wife. "She's the little schoolmistress, aren't you, dear? The little scholar, swatting away over Daddy's books."

"Yes, Odrun." She was shaking now. *I'll force it down his throat like feeding a goose. It'll sizzle away his guts. His eyeballs will boil in their sockets.*

"You know what I think might be nice?" Odrun lifted the cup to his lips and slurped at his tea. "I might have the both of you. I've been thinking about it for a while now. In bed at once. What do you think of that?"

What happened next shocked Aranda, but she couldn't help herself. She watched her hands snatch up her handbag and pull out the bottle. She heard the shriek of long-suppressed outrage as she tore out the cork and, turning, dashed the bottle's contents into her husband's face.

"You stupid bitch!" Odrun stood, his gown dripping, his cup and saucer shattering on the floor. "What the hell's taken you? I should cane the skin off you."

Aranda stared at him open-mouthed. Nothing. No billowing clouds of steam rising off his flesh, no sudden darkening of the extremities, no foul odor as Odrun was corrupted and liquefied from within. None of the reputed effects of *Xisia Solun*. Her husband was only very wet, and very angry.

It was spring water after all, she thought dully. *Oh, poor Mr. Vennis, what have I done?*

"Come here!" Odrun said, not so much speaking as grunting. He caught her wrist easily and pulled her close. Anger and arousal in Odrun were much the same. She could smell both on him, and the first was rapidly giving way to the second. Seeing him in this state, she saw the rest of her life. He would murder her as she had Vennis, but very, very slowly.

The cry he made next startled her. It was shrill and altogether un-Odrun-like. For a brief moment, Aranda had the ridiculous notion that Odrun had a little bird hidden in his mouth, and it had just chirped. She felt an urge to giggle, like a lunatic. But then his eyes bulged and his mouth yawned open, and there was no bird, though his teeth had tongue had turned an alarming shade of dark blue. He staggered about clutching his stomach.

"Hurts," he whispered. "Hurt...what...what'd you do? What the hell'd you do to me?" It wasn't Aranda he was speaking to, but Liris. Aranda was startled to note that the maid was standing upright, breathing heavily, but watching her master with a certain detachment, as well as a cold underlying fury.

"I expect someone put something in your tea," she whispered. "As a sort of joke."

Odrun collapsed, without even reaching out to break his fall—it was as though all his insides had turned suddenly to porridge. He didn't move once he hit the ground, but groaned, and whimpered, and after a time lay still.

"Taska wort," Liris said in a more brisk tone than Aranda had ever heard from her before. "Grows wild almost everywhere. It has a lovely scent when dried; the country folk use it for decorations. It also makes a very nice tea...unfortunately, it's a fatal cup. I had some in my bag; my sister gave it to me last I saw her so I could scent my pillow. I must have confused it with the honest sasweed in your kitchen. A terrible accident."

"Taska wort," Aranda said dully, still unable to tear her eyes away from her dead husband. "Yes, of course. A *terrible* accident."

"Miss, please come away with me to the kitchen," Liris urged, taking Aranda by the arm. "You've had a terrible shock. I'll make you a proper cup. The coal man can deal with the master when he gets here. A very understanding fellow."

As they made their way downstairs, Aranda asked, "Liris? Have you ever thought of making a serious study of toxins?" "Oh, miss," the girl smiled, steering her like an invalid. "Now who on earth would be my teacher?"

Cara Fox

THREE FRENCH HENS

Johnny gritted his teeth and clenched the stem of the wine glass so hard that it snapped clean in half. With a muttered curse, he hid it behind his back and sidled out of the room, planning to conceal the jagged fragments of crystal in the trash before his wife noticed. Her high-pitched, sneering voice floated out of the room as he walked towards the basement to hide the evidence of his latest misdemeanour.

"Johnny, darling, don't forget to iron the tablecloth before you lay it out!" Georgette called after him. Her words were slurred, betraying the generous measures of brandy that had already slipped between her rouged lips despite the early hour. "You know that Mamma hates to see a creased cloth on the table, especially at Christmas."

Johnny stomped along the perfectly polished floorboards with a tight grimace that contorted his heavily lined face. "Of course, Georgette," he said, feigning a calm that he didn't truly feel. "Anything else?"

She didn't hear the sarcasm in his voice—either that or she simply chose to glibly ignore it—just as she must have done over the long years together, whilst his slow-burning anger steadily built up into a raging furnace, each cutting word stoking it further out of control.

"Oh, Johnny, must I always repeat myself? I've tacked the list to the notice-board in the kitchen; you *know* what it is that you must do before Mamma and Francine arrive."

He breathed in deeply and counted to ten in his head to cut off the biting retort before it could fly unbidden from his lips. Georgette's voice was still coloured with the faintest of French accents despite the many years she had been living in America as Johnny's wife. He mentally added that stubborn accent to the ever-growing list of things he detested about her.

Johnny hadn't always hated his wife, of course. Once, many years ago, he had been madly in love with her—or so he believed at the time. When the first flush of heady, consuming lust faded away, he recognised that what he mistook for love so long ago was, in fact, nothing more permanent or meaningful than a simple chemical reaction.

Unfortunately, by the time he reached that revelation, he had already eagerly signed up to a marriage to Georgette and all her associated baggage, chief amongst which were the overbearing mother and sister who had haunted his every move since.

He reached the heavy wooden door that blocked off the basement and wrenched it open, finally exhaling as he hastened down the cold stone steps. He yanked on the cord as he passed and reached the bottom just as the flickering, dim light sparked into life to pierce through the gloom of the damp basement.

For the first time all day, Johnny relaxed. Georgette's voice couldn't penetrate down here, despite its persistently high-pitched and screeching qualities. For a few stolen moments, perhaps he could immerse himself in the bliss of pretending that she didn't even exist.

He ran his hands lovingly along the dusty shelves and revelled in the dirt that was found nowhere else in the prim and proper house. It was his sanctum, the one place that he could be alone. Georgette wouldn't venture down here, so it was all his. He deliberately made sure it remained unkempt and disorganised as his one small act of daring rebellion against his wife.

The jars and tins that lined the shelves were a collection gathered over many decades, and most of them were untouched since their arrival. The antique labels were yellowed and peeling away from the containers, rendering many of them unreadable. Johnny's eyes, though, settled upon one that was still clearly legible—one that bore the sign of toxicity, the grimly unmistakable skull and crossbones.

He set the broken pieces of crystal down when his hands reached out, as if compelled to pluck the bottle of cyanide from the shelf. A cloud of dust puffed gently into the air, and he coughed and spluttered, gripping the bottle tightly as he lifted it towards the light.

The seed of a terrible, glorious idea steadily took root in his mind and extended its reaching tendrils, fast taking hold of him as his eyes widened and his heart picked up its pace. It horrified him, but he couldn't deny, not even in the privacy of his own mind, that it was a wicked temptation to follow through upon its promise. The thought of living the rest of his life with his wife stung more sharply with each passing day, but he knew it was the fate that he condemned himself to. His devoutly Catholic family would be devastated were he and Georgette ever to divorce, and he couldn't bring himself to do that to them.

Divorce, though, wouldn't be a necessity were he only to follow through upon the scheme in his head. The tantalising voice danced through his mind, and before he realised what he was doing, he moved the tiny glass bottle closer to his eyes. It was cold against his hand, cooled by the chill of the winter air that penetrated the poorly ventilated basement. It demanded his attention, and he was powerless to defy.

His eyes darted rapidly across the words that screamed out a warning, emblazoned in once glaring black ink along the bottom of the label. "POTASSIUM CYANIDE!" it proclaimed in bold capital letters. "Highly toxic—ingestion of substance will cause cardiac arrest."

Johnny had forgotten until now that this bottle was even here still. It was one of those he salvaged from his father's garage upon the old man's death. His magpie-like tendency to hoard was just another of the many things that so aggravated his wife.

He ran his thumb over the cork stopper. The white crystals seemed to glitter, playing in the reflection of the harsh electric light that still flickered overhead. His tongue darted across dry lips as the enormity of what he was contemplating sank in, and a heavy, leaden weight settled upon his chest.

No. He couldn't do it. As much as he wished he could find the strength to dole out the greatest of punishments to Georgette for the way she had treated him over the years, Johnny simply couldn't do it. He didn't have the strength. His hands shook wildly as he set the bottle back on the shelf and turned away from it.

With a heavy sigh of resignation, he trudged back up the stone steps to resume his task of polishing Georgette's treasured wine glasses before her mother and sister arrived for their customary festive dinner.

No sooner had he reached the top of the steps, though, than the shrill tones of the doorbell rang out in the hallway to strike ice-cold terror throughout the length and breadth of his body. He froze, heart thumping, for he knew it must be Georgette's mother, Agathe, and her sister, Francine, come to invade his home and torment him once more with their undisguised disdain.

Georgette rushed past him in a flurry of silken skirts and cloying floral perfume, her lips curved back into a sneer as she spared him only the briefest of dismissive glares. Johnny shuffled along the side of the wall and tried to fade into obscurity as his wife threw open the door, allowing the biting chill of midwinter air to flood into the hall.

"Mamma!" she exclaimed, all graciousness and smiles once more. "Francine, *ma chère soeur*! Come in, come in. Johnny is dreadfully behind with preparing dinner, I am afraid, but I shall entertain you whilst he finishes his tasks."

"It does not surprise me, Georgette," Agathe said, clutching her brash fur coat closed around her throat. "He has always been an abject failure, after all. I have no idea why you married him, my darling girl!"

Georgette and Francine's mocking laughter filled the hall as Johnny clenched his fists. He knew perfectly well why Georgette married him. The way she had frittered away his once substantial fortune over the years made that very plain, and Agathe and Francine had done equally well out of him. They coldly milked him through Georgette to fund their love of extravagance in every way, from fashion and holidays, to the finest wines and foods, always taking everything to the excess.

Breathing heavily, he forced himself not to react to the taunt, and finally the sound of the cruel laughter faded away, to his intense relief.

"Why don't you go through to the parlour, Mamma? Johnny has much to do, and I am sure he does not want us under his feet in the kitchen." Georgette said brightly. She was never more vivacious than when in the presence of her mother and sister. When Johnny and Georgette were alone, she rarely even offered him as much as a smile these days.

Johnny had a sudden vision of his wife the way she was when they first met. It stole his breath away, and he slumped against the wall. She was so very beautiful. He'd adored her from the first moment he caught sight of her at the dance, and he had been so astounded that she'd bestowed her brilliant smile upon him that he did everything she asked of him, obeying her every wish like the most eager of puppies.

It shamed him now to think back upon how subservient he had been to her. She loved it, of course; her dominant personality seized upon Johnny's willingness to please, and she took every possible advantage of it. He had installed her in the beautiful home she'd begged him for, and he didn't press her when she point blank refused to even consider having a child for fear of losing her figure, even though it was his dearest wish to fill their large house with sons and daughters to love and cherish.

Her refusal, though, had been to no avail, for she was nothing more than a shadow of her former glory, Johnny thought savagely. The bitter thought startled him as Georgette darted around her mother and sister to help them out of their coats. Though she'd drained his bank accounts over the years to fund her battle against aging, even the most skilled of cosmetic surgeons could no longer conceal the marked, wrinkled skin on her face, and despite the fact she had splashed his cash on numerous sessions of liposuction, the pounds stubbornly crept back on every time. It was hardly a surprise when she saw fit to stuff her face with French pastries and fine wines, showing no restraint whenever she unleashed her passion and love for those edible delights.

If Georgette had shown him any love, then none of that would have mattered to Johnny. He wanted nothing more than to love his wife, but she made that impossible with her cruel behaviour.

A deep-seated and consuming rage began to build in his chest. The resentment of a wasted lifetime finally broke through the barriers he built against it as he stared at the woman he now realised he detested with as much passion as he had once lusted after her. She came towards him and he smiled, a tight, false smile that masked the turmoil and rage that now consumed him.

"Johnny, can't you smell that?" Georgette hissed out of the corner of her mouth as she thrusted the coats at him. "The base for the frangipane tart is burning! Stupid man—you know the tart is Mamma's favourite."

Her viciously sharp nails dug into his arm to rake a line of fire across his skin before she turned on her heel and stalked off to follow Agathe and Francine into the parlour.

Years too late, Johnny saw the truth with a painful clarity that sent shards of ice through his heart, as tangible as those creeping across and crystallising the window from outside.

He was, it seemed, the very definition of a hen-pecked husband.

He would stand for it no longer.

The smell of the burning pastry floated towards him as his tumultuous emotions ferociously jumbled together, and they combined with his fury to spark off the most incredible idea.

The frangipane Agathe so enjoyed was made with almonds and, as always, it was solely Johnny's responsibility to create it. None of the three women would be able to distinguish the cyanide from the almond flavour until it was too late. Even the smallest amount of potassium cyanide could be fatal. Just a few, precious little fragments would do it.

Yes.

Unnoticed by the women, he softly pushed the door to the basement open once more and hastened down, breathing heavily as he retrieved the brown glass bottle from where he'd left it. His resolve didn't flicker for even a moment, not now he had reached his decision. Finally, he knew his own mind again, and the liberation was intoxicating.

No longer resenting all the jobs that Georgette left for him to do, for the completion of each would only bring him closer to victory, Johnny whistled cheerfully as he returned to the kitchen. The precious cyanide was safely concealed in his pocket, but for all the attention Georgette paid him when she bustled in and out of the kitchen for more wine, he might as well have been dancing naked with the bottle clenched between his butt cheeks.

Finally, a fresh base for the tart was ready, and it was time to assemble the frangipane filling. With a practiced and unfailingly steady hand, he creamed together the butter and sugar before whisking in the eggs. Next came the ground almonds and flour—and with them, Johnny's Yuletide gift for his wife and in-laws.

He held his breath as he removed the stopper from the bottle, holding the cork carefully between his thumb and forefinger whilst he sprinkled a generous helping of the white crystals into the mix. Shoving the cork back into the neck of the bottle, he pocketed it again and lovingly poured the frangipane mix over the halved pears before carefully placing the lethal concoction into the oven to cook.

Normally, a meal with Georgette's family would have Johnny's nerves jangling, every snide remark that shot his way stinging painfully and his body tensed as he awaited the next thinly-veiled barb. This time, though, the smouldering awareness of what awaited his wife and guests was enough to soothe away all pain, much to Georgette's irritation.

She caught hold of his arm as he stood to clear their main course away. "Johnny, darling, you are in a good mood," she said through gritted teeth. "Have you been helping yourself to the wine whilst you've been cooking?"

Georgette's burst of tinkling laughter did little to hide the venom in her pale eyes, but it couldn't affect him as it previously would have.

"Can a man not simply enjoy the company of his wife and her family at Christmas?" he said with a smile, chuckling to himself as her eyes narrowed and she let go of his arm as if burned. Stacking the plates with a skill born of decades of doing so, he hurried to the kitchen to deposit them in the dishwasher before turning to the fridge to reverently retrieve his creation.

The tart had been cooling whilst they ate, and now it was the very vision of perfection. Johnny warily sniffed the air and, to his horror, he was certain he could detect the faintest whiff of acerbic bitterness amongst the distinctive almond.

His eyes darted frantically from side to side until, to his desperate relief, they settled upon a large carton of double cream. Agathe was always heavy-handed with the cream on her desserts—he could claim he had simply pre-empted her in his eagerness to please.

Johnny cut three slices of the luxuriant tart and arranged them on plates before applying a liberal dollop of cream to each and balancing all three plates on his arm. He felt more alive than he had at any point since he married Georgette, and there was a long-forgotten spring in his step when he delivered the plates to the three women.

"Ah, good boy!" Agathe said, grinning toothily up at him as her jowls wobbled. "Plenty of the cream—perhaps you have finally trained him successfully, Georgette!"

"Tuck in ladies, please."

Johnny leaned back against the wall and rubbed his hands together as he waited for the show to begin.

"Are you not joining us, Johnny?" Georgette said.

"Ladies first, please."

He had to fight to conceal a faint grimace. He had no intention of eating the tart. He could taste Death in the air, but there was no way he would die tonight now he was so close to finally getting his freedom back. If Georgette insisted on waiting for him, all would be ruined.

His wife's hunger, though, proved to be the death of her.

349 · PICK YOUR POISON

In unison, the three French women shovelled a forkful of poisoned tart into their mouths.

The effect was instantaneous.

The forks fell with a clatter to the floor as the women clutched at their chests whilst shallow, rattling breaths escaped their painted lips. Johnny clapped his hands in shocked delight as first Agathe, then the two younger women, slipped sideways from their chairs.

"J-Johnny!" Georgette's nails flexed out like talons as she tried to drag herself across the plush carpet towards him. "Call an ambulance!"

"And why would I do that?"

Her eyes widened with fury as the cold truth sank in, and she began to hiss and spit like a cornered animal whilst her mother and sister sobbed and whined, arching their backs off the floor as the poison spread through the vast expanse of their bodies.

Johnny shook his head as he reflected dispassionately on how foolish it was to ever marry for beauty alone. No woman's beauty would last forever. When they submitted to the grasping throes of death, beauty was the last thing to be weighed up when taking account of their lives.

The three women writhed and convulsed on the floor in front of him, thrashing desperately as he stared down at them. Their whining pleas were beginning to frustrate him. The perfect solution struck his mind, and Johnny's lips drew back into a grim smile.

His fingers blocked his ears as he wandered down the hall and kicked open the door to his precious basement before returning to the grand dining room. Its ostentatious decor was no longer an irritation, for now it was simply a backdrop to the death of his wife and her family. It was the sweetest of all scenes.

Seizing hold of Agathe and Francine's collars, he dragged them along the hallway and tossed them into the basement like the trash they were before he returned for his wife.

Georgette was barely conscious. As he lifted her into his arms to deliver her to the basement, her heavily made-up eyes rolled back in her head. He stared down at her, feeling no remorse even as her breathing slowed then ceased entirely.

The ghost of her last spew of bitter vitriol was still etched upon her face, but his wife was finally silent and unmoving. For the first time in thirty years, Johnny was free to sit down and enjoy a drink in peace.

AUTHOR BIOS

DIANE ARRELLE, pen name of Dina Leacock, has sold over 250 short stories and two books including *Just A Drop In The Cup*, a collection of short-short stories. She recently retired as director of a municipal senior citizen center and resides with her husband and cat on the edge of the Pine Barrens (home of the Jersey Devil).

GEORGE BREWINGTON is a respiratory therapist as well as a writer of dark fantasy. This is his second short story published by Owl Hollow Press, having appeared in their last anthology, *Dark Magic: Witches, Hackers & Robots*. His debut novel for young readers will be published by Godwin Books (Macmillan) in 2019. He lives with his wife and daughter in Folly Beach, South Carolina.

NICHOLE CELAURO has a cat possessed by the spirit of an author more talented than her. Philadelphia based, she majored in Writing for Film & Television at the University of the Arts, and minored in Petty Hexes. Nichole was one of eight finalists in the 2013 PhillyPitch! screenplay pitch competition. The seven finalists ahead of her all went bald by Christmas. Tragic.

MICHAEL HARRIS COHEN has work published or forthcoming in various places including *Fiction International, The Gigantic*

Book of Tiny Crimes, The Dark Magazine
and *Conjunctions* (web). He's a recipient of a Fulbright grant
and fellowships from the Atlantic Center for the Arts, The
Djerassi Foundation and OMI International Arts Center. His first
book, *The Eyes*, was published in 2013. He lives and teaches in
Bulgaria.

DEREK DES ANGES has been writing almost continuously since
1996. His arms are very tired. He lives in London, and so the
topic of poison or pollution is close to his heart, or at least to his
lungs.

LESLIE ENTSMINGER graduated in May of 2016 from Old Do-
minion University's MFA program in Creative Writing/Fiction.
Her recent work can be found in *The Cincinnati Review,* the
Barely South Review, and *Shark Reef Journal.* She received an
Honorable Mention for the 2015 ODU Ruhi Dayanim Poetry
Prize and was nominated for a Pushcart by *The Cincinnati Re-
view* in 2016.

CHRISTINE ESKILSON received honorable mentions in the 2012
Al Blanchard Short Crime Fiction Contest and the 2012 WNBA
Annual Writing Contest, and third place in the 2017 WNBA
Annual Writing Contest. Her stories have appeared in a number
of mystery anthologies and magazines.

CARA FOX is an English author, editor and journalist trying to
write her way out of the dark. Inspired by authors such as Mary
Shelley, Daphne du Maurier, Bram Stoker and Jules Verne, she
favours steampunk, horror and Gothic romance, but you can find
her anywhere that the stories sink their claws into you and the
wine is flowing freely.

SHARON FRAME GAY grew up a child of the highway, playing
by the side of the road. She has been published in several anthologies, as well as *BioStories*, *Gravel Magazine*, *Fiction on
the Web*, *Literally Stories*, *Halcyon Days*, *Fabula Argentea*,
Persimmon Tree, *Write City*, *Literally Orphans*, *Indiana Voice
Journal*, *Luna Luna* and others. She is a Pushcart Prize nominee.

TOM HOWARD is a science fiction and fantasy short story writer in Little Rock, Arkansas. He thanks his family and friends for their inspiration and the Central Arkansas Speculative Fiction Writers' Group for their perspiration.

CHARLIE HUGHES lives in South London with his wife and two young children. He began writing suspense, horror and dark psychological short stories three years ago. He's since been published in various magazines and anthologies. His story 'The Box' took the first prize in the 2016 Ruth Rendell Short Story Competition. 'Together' appeared in Ellery Queen Mystery Magazine in March 2017.

AARON MAX JENSEN is an emerging author who lives in Westminster, Colorado with his wife and children. A Colorado transplant, his fiction explores the landscapes of his blue collar Southern upbringing. He has a bachelor's in Creative Writing and English, and is a student in Converse College's low-residency MFA program.

KEVIN LANKES studies creative writing in the MFA program at Sarah Lawrence College and pens content for clients primarily in the science, tech, and healthcare industries. He grew up in a small town in the Allegheny Mountains and now splits his time between central Pennsylvania and New York City. In his lifetime, he has toured the U.S., lived on couches, and survived cancer.

FRANK ORETO is a writer and editor of weird fiction whose work has appeared in numerous publications including *Pseudopod*, *Fantasy Scroll Magazine*, and *Triangulation: Lost Voices*. You can check up on what he's working on by following him on twitter or staring raptly at his Facebook author page.

CARY G. OSBORNE is the author of nine published novels in science fiction, fantasy, and mystery, and more than 20 short stories in all of those genres, as well as horror. She is or has been a member of Science Fiction Writers of America, Science fiction & Fantasy Writers, and Oklahoma Writers Federation, Inc.

COLLEEN QUINN has short fiction appearing in various magazines and anthologies. She currently resides in Brooklyn, New York, in an apartment that is hardly haunted at all.

ANGELA RAPER holds an MA in literature and an MFA in fiction writing. She has taught literature and composition at the university level for over twenty years. She writes primarily Southern contemporary and historical fiction, often with a feminist slant.

JASON RUBIS lives in the Washington, DC area with his wife, daughter and dog. His fiction has been published in WEIRD-BOOK, ABERRATIONS and anthologies from Circlet Press, Northern Frights and Drollerie Press.

LAWRENCE SALANI lives near Sydney, Australia with his wife and child. He has been interested in horror since childhood, and he draws inspiration from pulp horror writers of the past. His interests also extend to fine arts, drawing and painting. His stories appear in *Danse Macabre*, Edge Publishing; *Darkness Ad Infinitum*, Villipede Press; *Gothic Blue Book 4*, Burial Day Press and *Dark Magic*, Owl Hollow Press.

KATIE SHERMAN is a freelance journalist who covers fine food and parenting in Charlotte, NC. As an undergraduate, she was mentored by Pulitzer Prize nominee George Esper at WVU. Katie is currently pursuing an MFA degree at Converse College. She has an affinity for Southern Gothic literature, cider beer, Chicago, and morning snuggles with her family—Ben, Ella and Addie.

REBECCA SNOW is a Virginia writer who lives in a house bordering on two cemeteries. Her fiction can be found in several small press anthologies. She's working on a collection of her own stories between breaths. Her cats keep her laughing.

LEIGH STATHAM has lots of kids and lots of pets and lots of bad habits. She writes YA and MG books, terrible poetry, and ranty articles about special education. Her newest novel, *Daughter4254*, is coming soon. Follow her on Twitter, Facebook, and Wattpad.

BENJAMIN THOMAS writes from New England and loves traveling, hiking, and quoting seemingly random movies. He earned an MFA in creative writing from Albertus Magnus College while working as an emergency room technician. He is the author of *Jack Be Quick*, and his short stories have appeared in publications such as *Flash Fiction Online*, *Winter Tales: A Fox Spirit Anthology*, and *One Night in Salem*.

CLAIR WATSON is a PNW author living in the state of Washington. She attended The Evergreen State College, located in Olympia, WA, and just received her MFA from Converse College, in Spartanburg, South Carolina. She is constantly writing in the company of her cat, Houdini, who is a shrewd critic.

DEVON WIDMER is grumpy graduate student by day. Scribbling daydreamer by night. Sleep deprived parent fulltime. Currently, she is meandering down a long, winding road toward a PhD in physical chemistry. Her talents include drinking copious amounts of coffee, forgetting where she set her glasses, and laughing at her own jokes.

More information about the authors and links to their social media profiles can be found online at owlhollowpress.com.

EDITOR BIOS

EMMA NELSON has an MA in American Literature, with an emphasis in folklore and cultural studies. She writes and edits in a broad range of genres and topics, but her most recent writing can be found in *Channeling Wonder: Fairy Tales on Television* and *The Routledge Companion to Fairy-Tale Cultures and Media.* Her mom's chemotherapy treatments were the inspiration for the theme of this collection. Despite the alleged helpfulness of that poison, she passed away a few weeks before the anthology released.

HANNAH STILES SMITH is an educator, has a BA in History, and has worked for years as an editor, helping bring fabulous books to their full potential. She spends her spare time escaping between the pages of a book, and a foray into publishing seemed like the best way to channel that energy. She lives in rural Virginia with her husband and four rambunctious children.

For more information and to discover other books by
Owl Hollow Press, find us here:

Website: owlhollowpress.com
Twitter: @owlhollowpress
Facebook: Owl Hollow Press
Instagram: owlhollowpress

OWL HOLLOW PRESS

WORLD-ALTERING STORIES, REAL AND IMAGINED

Made in the USA
Middletown, DE
26 October 2017